AFTER MIDNIGHT

Susan Sallis

BANTAM PRESS

LONDON · TORONTO · SYDNEY · AUCKLAND · JOHANNESBURG

TRANSWORLD PUBLISHERS
61–63 Uxbridge Road, London W5 5SA
a division of The Random House Group Ltd

RANDOM HOUSE AUSTRALIA (PTY) LTD
20 Alfred Street, Milsons Point, Sydney,
New South Wales 2061, Australia

RANDOM HOUSE NEW ZEALAND LTD
18 Poland Road, Glenfield, Auckland 10, New Zealand

RANDOM HOUSE SOUTH AFRICA (PTY) LTD
Endulini, 5a Jubilee Road, Parktown 2193, South Africa

Published 2005 by Bantam Press
a division of Transworld Publishers

A catalogue record for this book is available from the British Library.
ISBN 0593 05395 8

Typeset in 12/14pt New Baskerville by
Falcon Oast Graphic Art Ltd.

Printed and bound in Great Britain by
CPI Mackays, Chatham ME5 8TD

3 5 7 9 10 8 6 4 2

Papers used by Transworld Publishers are natural, recyclable products made from wood
grown in sustainable forests. The manufacturing processes conform to the
environmental regulations of the country of origin.

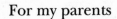
For my parents

With grateful thanks to Harvey and Jackson Copeland, Donald and Margaret Smith, John White of the Forest of Dean Railway and all my railway friends and colleagues.

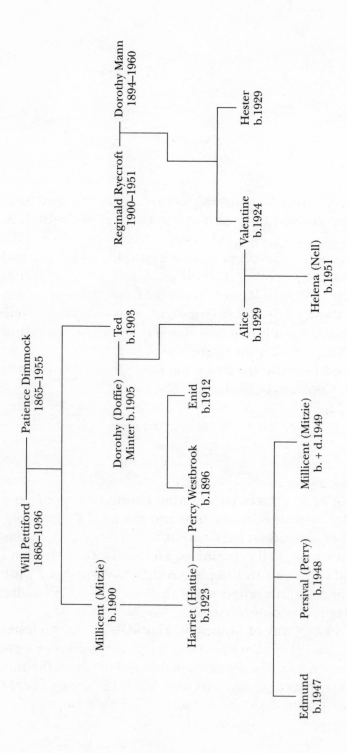

The Pettiford/Ryecroft Clan

One

Nell Ryecroft, sprawling untidily across one of the armchairs
in the new conservatory at Lypiatt Bottom, thought how
ridiculous her aunts sounded as they bickered over her. Like
two fat cats patting a ball of wool and suddenly snarling and
lashing out at each other. Even their names sounded funny.
Aunt Hattie and Aunt Hester. And Hattie was really some sort
of cousin though she was twenty-eight years older than Nell.
Nell promised herself that one day she would work out how
that had happened. Aunt Hattie was so crazy that she might
have slipped into the family by the back door. Nell grinned
to herself. Cupboards. Skeletons. She loved them.

Aunt Hester poured more tea and crossed her long,
elegant legs as she sat back in her armchair. She was Dad's
sister, so she was definitely a proper aunt. No skeletons there,
or . . . You never quite knew with Aunt Hester. She was not a
fat cat physically; just materialistically. Money and possessions
meant a lot to her. It was darling Aunt Hattie whose generous
body spilled over waistbands, bras and the tops of tights. She
too took her tea and sat back with it balanced on her bosom.

'I'm not saying Nell is brainless, Hester. That is not what I
meant and you know it. I'm just saying why should she push
herself unnecessarily when she can float through teaching
and have time to enjoy herself?'

'Float. A good way of putting it, Hattie dear.' Aunt Hester
smoothed her linen skirt, her long fingers so rigid they were
bent almost backwards. 'I've always thought of you as floating
through life, grabbing at spars and life rafts—' She caught
the flash of pain that crossed Hattie's face then and stopped

abruptly. It was over twenty years since Hattie had lost her baby daughter and for a time she and Uncle Percy had clung quite desperately to various life rafts. Never the same raft at the same time, however.

'I didn't mean ... then,' Hester went on, only half apologetically. 'You had to float as best you could then. You were marvellous, Hattie. I always said you were marvellous. But I meant before ... and since too. You float happily about, quite inconsequentially ...'

'You mean I am superficial.' Hattie grinned, composure regained. 'That means shallow, Nell. You see, your poor old aunt has a vocabulary after all!'

Nell grinned back. 'I think I'm dropping the aunts.' They both looked at her, shocked. 'Not dropping *you* – of course not! But you shall be just Hattie and Hessie in future. It makes it less disrespectful when I tell the pair of you to shut up!'

Hattie bubbled with laughter; Hester tried to look fierce as she explained that a great many aunts would not care tuppence about their nieces, especially when one of them was a hoyden with no dress sense, in fact not much sense at all, who seemed to think that teaching was a part-time job with very long holidays when in fact it wasn't a job at all: it was a calling.

Nell said, 'It is for you, Hessie. I recognize that. I'm proud of you. You love your subject and you give it your all. But I haven't got a favourite subject. And I want a bit of life for myself. Is that so dreadful?'

'University would have given you that too, Nell.' Hester looked almost pleadingly at her niece. 'And it would have enabled you to find that favourite subject instead of this all-round thing. You are an English scholar, Nell, and you don't even realize it!'

'Maybe.' Nell did not want to talk about it. Her course at the teacher-training college had not inspired her, she admitted to herself. It had not inspired many of the students. But the others had compensated by 'finding themselves'. It was, after all, the start of the seventies; the sixties had produced free love, what would be next? Nell had a nasty feeling that she would find the answer to that only at the beginning of the eighties.

Hester was rabbiting on about the *spaciousness* of university life. 'You're given time, darling. Time not only to read, go to theatres, talk, but to think. To sit for long hours, thinking.'

To silence her once and for all, Nell swung her legs down from the arm of the chair with a decisive clunk.

'And to have sex, of course,' she said. 'I think it happened for you at the end of your first year, didn't it? I have to admit a deficiency there. Though that's something to do with me personally, I'm afraid. Most of the girls in my education group have managed it. And with the lecturers too – it was your lecturer, wasn't it, Hessie?'

'Helena Ryecroft! How could you?' It was Hattie who spoke. 'Your aunt Hester is a private person and – and –' she tried frantically to give Hester time to recover from the knowledge that Nell knew, actually knew, about her past. 'Now if your remarks had been addressed to me,' Hattie went on, 'it would have been quite different!'

She laughed a little crazily. Nell, remorseful now, turned her gaze from Hester's set face to Hattie's over-made-up one.

'Darling Hattie. I have to admit I feel a failure. Especially in this family – d'you know, Mum was only nineteen when she married Dad! Four years younger than I am now! And I'm still a bloody virgin!' She mimicked Hattie's crazy laugh and added, 'Will it be all right if I seduce Perry this summer?'

Perry was the younger of Hattie and Percy's boys. He was three years older than Nell but she always treated him as if he were still twelve.

Hattie threw her head back on a roar of laughter. 'You're very welcome, darling! Perry would probably think it was an early Christmas!' She composed herself, dabbing at her lipsticked mouth, wiping her eyes. They all pulled themselves together and the aunts began to make preparations to leave. Hester accepted that Nell was sorry for her outspokenness;

both aunts accepted that they must not give unwanted advice to their niece but knew they would do it again; after all, Nell was the only girl in the immediate family. Nell decided that Hattie and Hessie were anachronisms anyway. Everyone was amiable again as they negotiated Nell's old doll's pram, which was filled with spring flowers from the woods behind the house, on their way to the front door.

Hattie said ridiculously, 'You'll be all right here on your own till your mother gets back?' And Hester replied for Nell, 'Of course she will! She's over twenty-one now, Hattie dear. You were a fully fledged entertainer at that age.'

That was a sop indeed. During the war Hattie had toured every dance hall and camp in the south of England, singing and dancing her way through air raids, buzz bombs and the dreaded V1s; but hardly a fully fledged entertainer.

Almost embarrassed, she pecked Nell's cheek and said, 'D'you know, I would have thought you would have wanted to seduce Edmund rather than Perry.'

Nell felt her face flame. The thought of seducing Hattie's eldest made the tops of her legs tremble.

She hugged Hester and then said seriously, 'Hessie darling . . . I might not be wrapped up in one subject but I just adore kids. And I noticed, when I was on teaching practice, that they quite liked me.'

She watched as the two of them got into Hester's car, reversed on the gravel drive and chugged off down the lane. Hester rarely took her car out of third gear so it appeared to chug everywhere.

Nell closed the door and went back down the hall to where the long mirror appeared to double the length of the short space and throw more light into the dark corners. She stood and surveyed herself. Hessie was right, she did look hoydenish. Her long legs were scarred by the brambles in the woods – she had picked the pramful of flowers that morning. She wore tennis shoes, no socks, a very old cotton frock from her pre-college days, and her white hair was scooped into a pony tail with a rubber band. It *was* white too, though Mum always described her as a platinum blonde. She was practically albino, what with the pale blue eyes and spiky fair lashes and brows. No wonder Edmund treated her like a pet rabbit. Slowly she pulled out the rubber band and looked again. No better. He was so damned clever he knew the truth about her; that she was not clever, not interesting, certainly not beautiful. Whereas Perry – short for Persival, could you believe it, and not madly clever but much nicer than his brother – had said to her only last Christmas that she knocked Marilyn Monroe into a cocked hat. He came out with old-fashioned phrases like that sometimes. She smiled widely into the mirror and wondered whether it might be fun to try it on with Perry.

Hester Ryecroft dropped Hattie Westbrook off at Leckhampton House but would not stop long enough to say hello to old Granny Westbrook, who was stubbornly clinging to life until she received her telegram from the Queen.

'The boys have been out – last game of the season,' said Hattie, 'and Percy has taken Enid to that outdoor concert in the Winter Gardens. Granny will be bored to tears and longing to see a different face.'

'Hattie, I'm sorry. I'm in a hurry. And you know how she hangs on to people.'

Hattie made a face; she knew only too well. 'Is Dickie Tibbolt coming down for the weekend?' she asked, struggling to get her bulk out of the front seat.

'I don't know,' Hester came back, repressively.

Hattie paused, one leg on the gravel drive, the other still in the car. 'I can see you're still upset about Nell's teasing. Surely you don't imagine that Dickie is a secret? My God, Hessie, he comes and goes to the flat most weekends. I should think everyone knows he's your lover.'

Even Hattie realized what an awkward term that was; she looked over her shoulder and laughed apologetically. 'I can't call him a boyfriend, can I? He's too old for that.'

'He's a friend, Hattie. A respectable friend from my

university days who still lectures, who still has a family. I know his children and I know what handfuls they are. We talk about them. We talk about the latest Booker winner. We've got a lot in common.'

'Of course.' Hattie could see that Hester's face was crimson. 'So why get upset about Nell's reference?'

'Because she obviously knew when it started. I was just a child. He seduced me, Hattie. She probably knows that too. Ted and Dorrie must have talked about it in front of her. Irresponsible, especially as they're Nell's grandparents! Such a pair of – of – blabbermouths.'

'Oh, for goodness' sake, Hessie. As if Nell would listen to her grandparents! I expect Val told her, in his sensible way. Probably she is wildly jealous. She expected something like that to happen while she was at college, and it didn't. It's as simple as that.'

'Well, you would say that. You used to pop into bed with anyone who knocked on the door.'

'Don't start on me again! Let me tell *you* something now, Hester Ryecroft. I thought at one time you and Val might have something going. Your own brother! How does that sound?'

'Bloody disgusting if you want to know!' Hester could hear herself descending to the level of Hattie. Hattie was a Pettiford and the Ryecrofts and Pettifords had always had a love-hate relationship. Hester had liked to think that she was above all that pettiness. And that she had never felt anything for her brother except a perfectly natural sisterly devotion.

She said brusquely, 'Don't bother to phone me with an apology for that very unpleasant remark, Hattie. Now, as I'm in a hurry, perhaps you would get out of the car and let me be on my way!'

Hattie did so, then leaned back in to hug Hester impulsively.

'Darling, I don't know why I said that! For goodness' sake, in spite of our differences, we're still good friends. And we both love Nell. Forgive me?'

14

Hester said impatiently, 'Of course. As usual. I would just say, Hattie dear, that if incest interests you, take a look at your husband and his sister. Percy has been consoling Enid for twenty-five years now. Quite a long time.'

Hattie stood up, surprised, and watched the car chug back down the drive. She had felt quite smug about that apology. Now she wished she had not made it.

Alice Ryecroft pedalled her bicycle between the pump and the lychgate of the church and turned up the lane towards the little row of pre-war houses that backed on to the bluebell woods. This had been her home, off and on, since she was six years old. She had been Alice Pettiford then, living from day to day, in a close relationship with God, scoffed at by her best friend, Hester Ryecroft, adored by her parents and grandmother ... and now adored by her husband as well. She smiled as she dismounted and shoved the bike under the porch. She had been so lucky, so very lucky. And the best of it was, all that love had regenerated inside her and could now be poured out on almost everyone she knew. Especially Nell of course.

She opened the kitchen door and cooeed to Nell. There was no reply but a savoury smell coming from the brand-new cooker proclaimed her presence somewhere.

Alice went into the hall and flung her jacket over the banisters.

'Helena Ryecroft! Come forth wherever you are!'

Nell's muffled voice came from the bathroom. 'Washing my hair – won't be long.'

Alice smiled again and went back to the kitchen to look in the oven – a casserole of the beef skirt she had bought yesterday – and to put a match to the fire in the living room. It might be spring but there was very little warmth in the watery sunshine. She admired the doll's pram full of daffodils, cuckoo flowers and half a dozen brazen dandelions – trust Nell! – found a hanger for her discarded jacket and then went to make tea.

Nell called from the top of the stairs. 'Hattie and Hessie were here earlier.'

'Hope you got the decent china out!'

'I did. Honour of the family and all that.'

Alice poured tea into two mugs. 'How was Hattie?'

'Overdone. Too much of everything.' There was a pause, then, 'Will Dad be home soon?'

'You know when he gets in. He's got the car at Cheltenham so . . . about seven, I expect.'

'I made a casserole with that beef. It'll be ready too soon.'

Alice carried the two mugs of tea into the living room. Nell appeared to be sitting at the top of the stairs.

'What are you doing? I've poured some tea and the fire is burning up well. You can dry your hair by it.'

Nell stood up and descended the stairs slowly. When she reached the hall she paused again.

'Listen. I don't want you getting in a strop. It'll wash out gradually, it's not a permanent thing. I just thought . . . you know . . . I've promised Hattie I'm going to make certain Perry falls for me this summer and how can I do that if I've got white hair?'

'What on earth are you talking about?' Alice put the mugs in the hearth and collapsed into Valentine's chair. It held her comfortably, just as Val himself held her. Her smile widened as Nell came round the door. And then she gasped. Nell no longer had the same kind of hair as her father. It was bright red.

Two

Valentine Ryecroft had changed very little since he had dropped out of university thirty years ago and joined the Great Western Railway. His tall lankiness had solidified into a leanness that emphasized a kind of whipcord strength; his face was longer too and he was lantern-jawed; but his hair was still the colour of bleached straw and his pale blue eyes always seemed to be looking at something other people could not see. His daughter said to him once, very fondly, 'You're too clever for your own good, Daddy.' She had been taken aback by his sudden look of pain and had added quickly, 'I simply meant that there are no challenges left for you, dear old Popsy! You've sorted out British Rail. You've worked out a co-ordinated road and rail scheme to solve the transport problems. You've even advocated reopening the canals.'

He was laughing at her, shaking his head as if in despair. 'Don't you realize, oh perfect daughter, that none of my wonderful schemes have ever been implemented? Oh, I get all the praise I can take – too much, when I know full well that none of my oh-so-clever plans will ever come to fruition. The branch lines continue to be closed down. Stations become derelict. People stop using them because there are no connections, so the lines are redundant . . . You know all about that too, I'm sure.'

'Well, that's everyone else's loss, Daddy. Not your fault.' She was indignant for a moment then saw that she would not be taken seriously so she changed tactic. 'I completely forgot to mention that you have also won for yourself a perfect wife, who then produced a perfect daughter. You've got a halfway decent sister—' He rolled up his newspaper menacingly and she retreated before him. 'I was going to mention your in-laws, the Perfect Pettifords, but I can see you're not really in the mood for all this praise—' The conversation had ended when Alice brought in a cottage pie, the dish swathed in a towel, steam emerging as if from a volcano. Nell had dodged back, spluttering giggles. 'Sorry, Mum. It was Dad. He was attacking me.'

Val had simply grinned. Since the day of her birth she had been the apple of his eye. Sometimes, as she was growing up, he thought he had the best of so many worlds. Alice as she was now and Nell as Alice must have been before he really knew her; when she was just his sister's best friend; the daughter of Doffie and Ted Pettiford; the granddaughter of Patience and Will Pettiford, one of the most respected railway families in the Forest of Dean.

Val took his daughter's sudden change of hair colour better than Alice had. He arrived home that spring evening while Alice was still clasping her hands and wailing, 'What have you done – oh my God, what have you done, Nell?'

He took one look at the brazen figure reflected in the long mirror at the end of the hallway and said calmly, 'Hello, you two. I say, Nell, I like the hair. Is it henna? Indian women use it a lot, you know. Makes you look very interesting.'

Nell, shrinking inside herself, hating the hair, said, 'You need not be kind. Say what you really think.'

He pressed Alice to him warningly. 'I'm not being kind, darling. Anyway, what's for supper? I could eat a horse.'

Alice swallowed and said, 'I'm not sure that's on the menu tonight. How would Nell's casserole of beef suit you?'

'Down to the socks.'

They all trailed into the living room. Nell said, 'I just want to be noticed. I'm like a ghost wandering around. No colour anywhere. And I'm determined to make an impression on Perry before I get a job. And I mean an *impression*! I don't stand a chance if he can't even see me!'

Val stirred up the fire and squatted by it easily. 'Take it from me, Perry notices you.'

'Well, Edmund doesn't. He's so bloody lofty and almost as clever as you, Daddy. It gets on my nerves. He deserves to fall for someone who will lead him up the garden path and drop him like a hot brick.'

Val became very still. Alice said, 'That's not a bit nice, Nell. It doesn't sound like you at all. You're all scratchy tonight.'

Nell gave her mother a look and said something about scratchy is as scratchy was. Alice laughed. 'Take no notice of my initial reaction to the hair, sweetie. I shall like it by next week. Just a case of getting used to it.'

'Same for me,' Nell admitted, looking sheepish. 'Seemed such a good idea at the time. The really awful thing is, I stole the stuff. From Hattie this afternoon.' She waved her hands at her mother's appalled expression. 'Hessie and Hattie were going on and on – you know how they do – and there was Hattie's bag with the stuff sticking out of the top – two bottles, so I'm not depriving her or anything.'

'She would have given it to you – you know that!'

'Quite. No fun being given stuff. I wanted to steal it. Shock you all. One way or another.'

Val stood up at last. 'Well, you've done that. Was Hattie all right?'

'Of course. Isn't she always?'

'No.' Val spoke decisively. 'What about Hester?'

'Fine.' Nell made a moue at her father. 'So were you when you came in. Now you're not.'

'Yes, I am. A lot on my mind.' He smiled sideways at Alice, who was looking suddenly anxious. 'It's all right, Allie. I'll tell you later when this strange redhead has departed.'

'Where am I departing to?' Nell asked, wide-eyed.

Val leaned forward and kissed the tip of his daughter's exquisite nose.

'Your godmother invited you to the theatre to celebrate the end of your course. Had you forgotten? She will be

19

collecting you at seven pip emma and driving you to Cheltenham. Afterwards I gather there will be supper at the Queen's.'

Nell did not look thrilled. 'Will Uncle Edward be there?' she asked.

Edward Maybury had been superintendent of the Gloucester Division of the Great Western Railway when there had been such a thing. Both her parents had great respect for him.

'Of course. As will another guest.'

Nell said glumly, 'Someone else Aunt Helena has taken under her wing, like that girl from the flower shop. And like me too, I suppose.' She went to the stairs. 'I'd better not have any of the beef, Mum. And when I think how I slaved over that hot stove . . .' She gave a yelp as her father began to roll up the newspaper, and leaped up the stairs two at a time.

Alice flapped the cloth over the table and made for the kitchen. She spoke through the open hatch. 'I know what Nell means, Val. It's because Helena had no children. She is always adopting some stray or other. And she spoils Nell to bits.'

'Everyone does.' Val straightened the cloth absently and fetched the cruet from the sideboard. 'How did work go today? Have you broken up?'

Alice was one of the many secretaries at the new college on the outskirts of town.

'The students have gone down, of course, but we're supposed to keep going in for the next two or three weeks. Get all the records straight.' She strained a saucepan of potatoes and glanced through the hatch. 'What about you?'

'Frustrated. As usual.' He grinned at her reassuringly and placed knives and forks with precision. 'I popped in to see Ted tonight. I'd asked him to do something for me and I went to hear the result.'

'You're being very mysterious. What's it all about?'

He took the plates that appeared at the hatch; they were hot and he huffed and puffed as he set them on their cork mats. Alice came through the door with the casserole. He went behind her and closed the door to the living room, came back and closed the hatch. Her eyes followed him, widening all the time.

'What on earth—'

'Read this while the food cools slightly.' He waited till she had settled herself in her chair then spread a letter in front of her. It was from a firm of solicitors in Cheltenham. Alice glanced at him apprehensively; solicitors usually meant trouble. 'Go on. It's interesting,' he said.

She read the letter quickly, gasped, looked up at him, then went back to the beginning and started again. She was a long time at it. She turned it over, looking for more information, checked the date, peered at the heading on the paper.

Then at last she said slowly, 'These are the solicitors Joe went to when he heard that he had inherited the railway coach from his mother. Back in – in . . .'

'Nineteen forty-nine,' Val supplied.

'Yes. So really, behind these solicitors, Joe is writing to you.'

'That is how I see it,' he agreed. 'Joe has instructed them to sell the railway coach and its site and I – we, of course – are being given the first option.'

'The only ones likely to be interested.' She dropped her gaze to the letter again. 'After all this time . . . all this time.'

'Not quite the only ones. Hester would be interested. She and Dickie Tibbolt go there still, you know.'

She put her hand palm down on the thick paper and stared at the steam coming from the vent of the casserole. She murmured, almost to herself, 'It was all he had of his mother. And now it's going.'

Val took the lid off the earthenware dish and placed it carefully on one of the mats. He began to serve Alice. She watched him though he knew that she did not see him.

She said at last, 'Why did they write to you? It's addressed to you. And you took it to show Dad. And you said nothing to me until now.'

'Are you angry?' He spoke with a kind of objective curiosity.

21

'I'm not sure. I think I should be. Perhaps I feel . . . piqued. Perhaps I think that if anyone should have been told about this sale, it was me. Not you.'

'Yes. I thought that. But before you went there with Joe, I took you. And, actually, Allie, I was the one who found it. So I saw it before you did – before Joe himself saw it.'

He looked across at her. She was moving her hand slightly on the single sheet of paper; as if . . . as if it could put her in touch with Joe. He blinked, telling himself that all that – all that had happened – was twenty-five years ago now.

She gave a small smile and said quietly, 'And later . . . when we wanted Nell so much . . . we went again. It was our magic place.'

He was holding the ladle, full of gravy and carrots and swede, poised above his plate, ready to tip. And there it stayed because their eyes met and held. They could not look away.

It had not happened for some time. She had used to call it a merging of their spirits; Val had always teased her and called it 'soul sex'. However much they tried to explain it, it remained indefinable, unexpected and totally precious. This time, with the letter reminding them of so much in the past, perhaps it was even more precious. They sat there, almost falling into a void together, the ladle still poised, the steam rising, sounds of banging from Nell's room above, the fire suddenly falling in, sparks flying up the chimney . . . Then she reached for his hand, her eyes full of tears, and he put down the ladle quickly and carried the hand to his face and she went to him and held his head against her.

They had almost finished their meal when Edward and Helena Maybury arrived to pick up Nell. The letter and its contents had been temporarily shelved and they were both smiling as they tried to reconstruct the moment when their daughter, newly qualified and full of ideologies, had decided to steal hair dye from her aunt.

They opened the door together.

22

Helena in her mid-fifties was elegant and fine-boned, her thick brown hair in what she called a ballerina bun, her clothes from Jaeger in Cheltenham's still chic Promenade. She entered in a flurry of perfume.

'Don't you love the lighter nights – summer is definitely on the way . . . oh Alice, my dear, did you pick these flowers? . . . Nell? She's got your eye – and in a doll's pram too! Edward, don't you just love this hall? Hasn't Val done wonders with it? That mirror is just right, Val.'

Edward said, 'You're having your meal. I do apologize, Val. No, in any case we can't stop. We're meeting one of Helena's misfits outside the theatre and he doesn't know Cheltenham at all, so . . . Alice my dear. You are looking well.'

Edward Maybury had retired five years ago, leaving his beloved railway work without regrets. 'I've had the best of it. Time for someone else to try their hand.' Already he seemed to be from another age, his manners courteous in the extreme – he unobtrusively walked on the outside of the pavement, doffed his hat when he greeted someone, opened doors for his companions, shook hands but never hugged in public. He told Alice that he did not mind the constant swearing but there was one word he could not stomach: modernization.

Nell came downstairs in what appeared to be a black satin petticoat covered by a grey angora cardigan she had knitted herself. Helena, in an obvious quandary about whether to mention the outfit or the hair colour, suddenly found the right words. 'You are like a burst of sunshine, Nell! Oh, we're really going to enjoy this evening! I rather like these variety concerts, don't you?'

Nell grinned, pecked her godmother on the cheek and said, 'Well . . . I suppose if one turn is dreadful, there's always the hope that the next will be worse!'

Edward guffawed. Helena said, 'Stop being blasé, it doesn't suit you.' Alice said, 'Honestly, Nell!' And even Val remonstrated. 'A little appreciation wouldn't come amiss.'

And then they were gone, Edward's French car taking the

rutted lane smoothly past Mrs Mearment's house and disappearing towards the Cheltenham road.

Val closed the door and followed Alice back into the living room; she sat down and picked up her knife and fork then said, 'Well, obviously Joe must *mean* it. Otherwise he wouldn't have done it so officially through a solicitor. And anyway, it sounds as if he is unloading it rather than giving it away.'

Val smiled; the awful nostalgia had gone. 'What are we going to do?' he asked.

She lifted her shoulders. 'We don't want it, surely? If you seriously think that Hester would like it . . . I mean, I'd hate it to be broken up, the lease cancelled . . . Obviously it means nothing to Joe now. But I think of his mother.' She turned down her mouth. 'It was hers, Val. And she had such a rotten time.'

He finished his meal and sat back. 'If Hester has it and uses it as a love nest . . . which was why it was put there in the first place, remember . . . would that be all right, d'you think?'

'I think so. Wouldn't it? I mean . . . it wasn't just a love nest, Val. It had magical properties. And – and . . .' She looked slightly embarrassed. 'My grandfather was often there.' They rarely spoke of Alice's ability to contact her dead grandfather.

Val did not even smile. 'He was in the cathedral too, wasn't he? In fact he and Gran are never that far away.'

She smiled at him ruefully and for a while they were silent, remembering their first years in this family house when they had looked after Gran and let their marriage build into something strong and indestructible.

Val said, 'The thing is, if Hessie has it, it will continue to moulder away. It's been there sixty years now. It might go on another sixty years – though I doubt it – but the point I'm making is that it's going downhill all the time.'

She opened the hatch doors and put their plates through.

'You're leading me somewhere, Val. Just tell me what you've got in mind, for goodness' sake!'

'It – it's something rather big. Enormous. I don't want you to be shocked into instant rejection.'

24

She looked at him. 'You want to buy it and resell to some development firm. You've already heard of someone. A builder. A new village, accessible to Gloucester, Bristol – oh Val!'

'No. Anyway, can you see the Freeminers allowing that to happen? They still own the lease, you know. It will be sticky getting them to agree to anything. But there's a chance . . .' He looked at her. 'Your father thinks it might work. He has said he would come with me to talk to the old miners.'

'So Dad knows all about your plans?'

'I have to admit he is cautious. But he would give it a try.'

'Val, just tell me. Please.'

'Well . . .' He bit his bottom lip, then smiled at her. 'We're railway people, Allie. And the railways are driving me mad. And you're not exactly thrilled with your job at the college. How would you like to rebuild a light railway? Own it, Allie. Get it running again like it did back in the eighteen-hundreds. Find an old steam loco somewhere and get it working. Open a network of lines in the forest and take people on rides. They've done it in Sussex. They're working on it down in Somerset. D'you think the Pumpkin Coach would extend its magic and help us to do it in the forest?'

Alice stared at him. She had not seen this enthusiasm for a long time. She smiled slightly.

He said, 'It won't be easy, my love. We shall have to borrow money and maybe sell this house and live in the coach for a while . . . I don't know whether it can be done and whether we should do it.' Her smile widened. He said warningly, 'You're simply seeing the romantic side of it, Allie. And it won't be romantic in the middle of winter when we're having to sweep the lines clear of snow and – and—'

Her smile nearly split her face in half. She said, 'It sounds romantic all the same. An adventure, Val. A real adventure. After all, we're quite good at adventures.'

He started to laugh, got up and took her in his arms.

Three

The precinct of Gloucester Cathedral was very quiet that early Friday evening in April. Crocuses flew their small orange and blue flags here and there on the sward and starlings congregated in the ivy that clothed Hester Ryecroft's house. She lay supine on her bed listening to them. She thought they made the sexiest sound she had ever heard. She reached to her left, found Professor Tibbolt's hand and placed it on her breast. He chuckled deeply.

'What?' she asked.

'You. You are insatiable.'

She was almost offended and riposted with, 'Now you're in your fifties, sweetheart, I feel I have to give you a helping hand now and then!'

He rolled on to one elbow to look down at her. She had undone her long rope of dark hair and it lay luxuriantly over her right shoulder. He moved his hand so that he could run his fingers through it. His former wife's breasts had been firmer than Hester's but she had never had – no one he had ever known had had – such hair.

He said softly, 'Hessie. Why won't you marry me?'

She tried to shrug. 'I see no need.'

'Don't my needs enter into it? I need to be married to you.'

'Why?' She was genuinely surprised.

'So that we can live together all the time. Not just go to bed together.'

'But, Tibbolt, we do other things. We go to the theatre. Art galleries. We have meals together, walks in the country. We go to the Pumpkin Coach.' She reached up and traced his eyebrows; they were still thick but no longer dark. He had gone prematurely grey twenty years before. 'Darling, would you like to go to the Pumpkin Coach? We could pick armfuls of daffodils and fill it. Lie on them. Swim in the pool afterwards.'

'It will be freezing!'

'Yes.' She shivered with delight. 'We shall have to think of something to get us warm afterwards.'

He sighed. 'Do we have to go to the coach ever again? Sorry, darling, I know it has magic properties for you but it's damp and cold and usually dark. And the pool is supposed to be bottomless and filled with dead babies.'

'Tibbolt!'

'All right, that's probably legend. But I can never understand why all your family feel the need to swim in it at the drop of a hat.'

'You have to *immerse* yourself in the whole ambience of magic! It has – it has – *properties*. Surely you can see that?'

'For someone who learned everything by rote in order to get her honours degree, you are exhibiting the strangest symptoms of – of—'

'Of what?'

'Of sentience, I suppose. All this business about magical properties, Hessie. It's not you. I can understand Alice – my God, she actually talks to dead people. And Val – well, he would go along with anything Alice thought, did, said. Even the ghastly Hattie, practical in nearly everything, waxes fey at times. But you? Don't tell me that my wonderful, commonsensical, sexy mistress – well, that's what you are, for God's sake – yes, you are – simply because you won't marry me.' He held her down without much difficulty and stopped her vocal protests with his mouth. When she became still he lifted his head and whispered, 'If you want to go to the bloody Pumpkin Coach, then we'll go. But will you do something for me in return?'

'I thought I did.'

'Oh dear Lord. Of course you do. All the time. But this is something else.'

27

She thought she knew what it was; he was going to make a bargain. The Pumpkin Coach for her marriage vows. She closed her eyes, smiling blissfully. After all, why not? They had been together for years now, though sometimes there were breaks when he discovered another student who needed his expertise. But he always came back to her.

She murmured, 'Oh, very well then. Anything to have another weekend at the coach.'

He lifted his body slightly to look at her. 'Would you talk to the twins?'

Evadne and Tobias – Eve and Toby – were his children, legally taken from him by his wife, Hermione, when she decided that 'all men were the same' and made a permanent home in Provence with another woman artist. Eve and Toby had grown up 'naturally' and become wild children of the sixties.

'Your kids?' Hester was shocked out of her blissful state and arched her neck like an angry swan. 'What can I say to them, for God's sake? They're both over twenty-one. If they choose to live like tramps and smoke pot all day—'

He stopped her again with a kiss. Then said, 'Sweetheart, they listen to you. You know they do. Because you are this strange two-sided person, living with a foot in two worlds . . .'

She struggled to sit up. 'What the hell are you talking about, Tibbolt? I am head of the English department at Whitsom Hall School. That's all they know!'

He caressed her for a moment and she subsided.

'All right, they know about you and me. They probably think we're rather unconventional not to get married and set up house. Even so—'

Richard Tibbolt rolled on top of her so that she could not move.

'Darling, darling girl. Think about it. Think about the past.'

For a moment she was puzzled. 'Is this something to do with my father? Surely I cannot be more approachable because my father died in a hospital for the insane?'

28

He sighed. 'Eve and Toby are living together. They are *living* together, Hessie.'

She was still, looking into his clear grey eyes so close to hers. His eyes had always made her melt . . . That first time in Provence when she had been an eighteen-year-old student and her professor had taught her the meaning of life . . . a life that was not dominated by her sadistic father.

He had rescued her and she had repaid him with a kind of half-relationship; no commitments from either of them. It had seemed fair but she knew it was not. She tried to speak, to justify her caution which had been far more than simply caution. She had enjoyed being in charge, dominating him. Rather as her father had enjoyed dominating her mother. She swallowed the lump in her throat and he kissed her, little butterfly kisses all over her face. She must not cry and let him taste her tears.

He lifted his head and spoke quietly. 'You had a brother – I never had a sister. You understand how it could be . . . might be.'

He was right, of course. She would have gone mad if it hadn't been for Val.

'Let me get up, Tibbolt. I can't think with your weight on me – get off!'

'No. There's a chance you'll agree to help me if I can pin you down! Come on, Hessie. Commit yourself to this at least. Just try . . .'

She tried to laugh. 'Hattie said something . . .' She could not quite remember what Hattie had said earlier but it had made her angry at the time.

'Ah.' He smiled slightly. 'I thought you were more defensive than usual! What did she say?'

She tried to shake her head. 'Nothing. You're right, I have got a brother and when we were children we were close. I depended on him a great deal. He was the only thing that made life worthwhile when Father was going mad and torturing Mother and our house was full of fear! No wonder I was glad to get to university! No wonder I fell into your arms that first summer! My God, you must have seen me coming a mile away. Clutching Virginia Woolf to my chest and gazing into the middle distance.'

He started kissing her again. 'All right, all right. I was a lecherous hound and should have known better. But admit that you have now got me exactly where you want me and you're afraid things might change if you married me!'

It was horribly true; she saw that now.

'I've known for a long time,' he said. 'It makes me love you more, not less.' The kissing was incessant; she could not stop the tears. 'Don't cry, darling. It's good. It's excellent.' He began to caress her and she sobbed.

'Oh Tibb . . . I do love you. Honestly. I do.'

'I know, Hessie. I know.'

He made love to her tenderly while the starlings chattered outside. Then he got up and made tea and dried her tears and told her how beautiful she was.

Ted Pettiford gazed out of the oriel window of the enormous first-floor flat in Northgate Street. He and Doffie had moved out of the house in the little village of Lypiatt Bottom with few regrets. Ted had cycled back and forth to the office for quite long enough; they both had to go into Gloucester for work and it was four miles away. And anyway, they had started married life in the dirty old city and were more than happy to return there. It had been a joy to see Alice's face when they handed over the house to her; she and Val had moved there to look after Gran and had settled in immediately.

Doffie had half an eye on the television, where there were the usual arguments going on about the Common Market. The other half was following a knitting pattern from *Woman's Weekly*. Yet she still said, 'Ted, come away from that window. You've been brooding there for almost half an hour!'

There was no reply and he said nothing and continued to gaze sightlessly at the deserted evening street. Doffie sighed and concentrated on her knitting. There was a time when his silence would have infuriated her and she might have provoked a row to break through it. But now she had to accept that it did not always mean he was displeased about something; sometimes it simply meant his mind was elsewhere. She murmured to herself, 'After all, he's seventy-one now. And I'm not much younger.'

Though her voice was barely audible above the commentator on the television, Ted picked it up this time and said sharply, 'What's that?'

'Nothing.'

'I heard you say my age. I'm not seventy-one till next month. And even then I'm not exactly senile!'

'Possibly a little deaf,' Doffie said sweetly. 'At least when you want to be. Selective hearing, I think they call it.' She knitted into the slipped stitch, then put her wool aside. 'Come on, Ted. Sit down, for goodness' sake. There's nothing out there to see.'

'More than on that thing.' Ted jerked his head at the television. 'I was thinking of the times that Alice must have stood just here. This was the office where she worked – you remember! – and the box files were kept on the oriel window ledge. She must have looked out so many times and thought of Joe Adair.'

'Yes.' Doffie got up, switched off the television and joined Ted at the window. It had been a promising spring day but now the light was going and somehow it was bleak. She shivered slightly. She remembered Joe Adair during the short time she had known him: the quintessential English schoolboy, snub-nosed, with honest brown eyes. And Alice had been forced into marrying Valentine Ryecroft.

Ted put an arm round her shoulders. 'You never really cared for Val, did you, Doff?'

Surprised, she said, 'Maybe not at first . . . I hoped it didn't show.'

'He couldn't help being the son of his father, you know.'

'Of course not.'

'I sometimes think you have never really got over the shock of what happened that day.'

'When Reggie Ryecroft attacked me, d'you mean? Honestly, Ted, I hardly think of it. And strangely enough I never think of Val as being Reggie's son. He might look like Reggie but his ways are his mother's ways. I loved Dorothy Ryecroft, she was like an older sister.'

'He's certainly got her brains.' Ted glanced down at his wife's head. He hardly saw the grey; for him she would always be strawberry blond.

'Nell's got some of them too.' She smiled down at the street, where a sudden outflow of people from the Catholic church hall meant that Friday night's bingo session was finished. 'Imagine, little Nell a teacher. She's only a child herself.'

'She's going on twenty-four, Doffie.'

'I know.' She leaned hard against him. 'Sometimes it frightens me.'

She felt him shiver but he said nothing and she knew he was thinking of his parents and his wayward sister and life in the small country station house at Leadon Markham and his long career working for the old Great Western Railway.

She said very gently, 'We must never let the past become a weight we have to drag around, Ted.'

There was another pause; that typical Pettiford silence.

She said, 'Wear it proudly, my dear. Like a – like a—'

He grinned suddenly. 'A mink coat?' he suggested.

'You know what I mean!' She turned and punched him gently.

'Actually I was thinking of Valentine's latest scheme. D'you think it might come off? Or shall we all end up in the workhouse?'

'You sound like your mother! She would never believe that workhouses had gone for ever.' Doffie released herself and made for the kitchen. 'I'm going to phone Alice. Then we'll have a cup of tea.'

'Alice might not know about it yet, Doff,' he warned. 'Val was planning to tell her tonight.'

'I'll sound her out. We can't do anything until she knows about it.'

'Why? It might be better to wait until Val has sounded out a few other people.'

Doffie shook her head decisively. 'Alice is the important one.' She gave her husband one of her very straight looks. 'And you know why, so don't pretend you don't!'

'I don't. Doffie, I seriously do not. Val need not worry Alice for some time yet—'

'He is going to tell her as soon as he thinks it's halfway viable.' Doffie paused by the heavy door and gave him another look. 'You know very well that Alice is the only one who can talk to your father.'

His voice became a bleat. 'For God's sake, Doffie, Dad died when Alice was six years old!'

She went into the hall. It was time for her to be silent. She knew that Ted would never admit that at least three times in her life Alice had been in touch with old Will Pettiford. And if anyone knew a thing about the railways of Dean Forest, it was Will Pettiford. He would have something to say about this scheme of Val's. Ted might not admit it, but he knew it.

Nell had felt strange all evening. It was probably the hair; or the fact that Helena and Edward kept referring to her 'achievement' at successfully completing four very boring years of teacher-training. It could well have been that the variety show was completely awful, or that she very much regretted not wearing a bra because the black satin petticoat hid nothing, absolutely nothing. But she knew it was none of those things. It was Helena's latest misfit. He was like a thorn in her side, a stone in her shoe, a hangnail, a pimple on her face, a . . . a . . . and of course he was male! Helena had not produced a male misfit before; they had always been women who were down on their luck. Well, this one certainly seemed to be down on his luck. He had that in common with Helena's usual cull.

Nell shook his hand but kept her distance. He wore

jumble-sale clothes, which Nell had affected often while at college – all the girls did. But hers had always been washed if not pressed. The double-knit pullover and serge trousers worn by Mo Checkers still had the aura of their last owners blended with the dust from the church hall where the jumble sale had been held. And Mo Checkers? What sort of a name was that?

'Mo is from the east,' Helena said as they took their places in the dress circle.

That explained a lot. He was shorter than Nell and his hair was exceedingly black, his brown eyes very brown and almond-shaped.

Helena went on serenely as if it were the most natural thing in the world. 'We found him sleeping in the old station buildings on the Honeybourne branch . . . well, Edward found him. Not quite four-star accommodation but adequate.'

Nell tried to smile but it was difficult. There was something about this Chinese boy that she did not trust. Which was terrible as China was going through such a frightful time. He'd probably got on a sampan or something and rowed to Hong Kong. Or did she mean Singapore? He did not say a word so probably did not know any English at all. How on earth had Helena and Edward communicated with him?

Nell smiled again and with much more warmth. 'Poor thing,' she said to Helena. 'He looks half-starved.'

Helena pursed her lips to check a grin. 'He ate fairly heartily at lunchtime, darling. And with a knife and fork.'

'Oh . . . good.' Nell released his hand and sat down. He pushed past her and sat on the other side of Edward. Which was a great relief, what with the language and the smelly clothing. But . . . but did it mean he did not like her? She hoped she wasn't like Hattie, who needed to be liked by absolutely everyone. Even so, most half-starved, young male refugees would have chosen to sit by her rather than by Edward, who, though a darling man, was definitely old hat. That was when she looked down and saw her nipples clearly

34

outlined in black satin. She hugged her cardigan round her.

The show was nearly all appalling. At the end of the first half they struggled to the bar for drinks and it became apparent that Mo Checkers spoke English.

Edward said, 'What is your tipple, young man?' and he replied, 'Rum and ginger, please, sir.'

Mortified, Nell tried to remember what she had said to Helena. And then she was cross. They had all been playing a joke on her. They often did it and it could be endearing. But not now.

She said, 'I'll have a gin and tonic, please, Edward.'

He looked surprised, then nodded. 'And coffee for you, darling? As usual?'

'Lovely.' Helena beamed at Nell. 'I'll go and help Edward while you two have a chat.' She leaned into Nell. 'Sorry, darling. But I rather think there's more to him than meets the eye.'

She was gone. And there was this undersized Chinese refugee who could say rum and ginger without a trace of an oriental accent – whoever heard of an Oriental ordering rum and ginger anyway? – and there she was, obviously much too tall, in an unsuitable dress and with newly dyed hair, doubtless looking like a prostitute if you came from a country where women wore uniforms.

The simply awful thing was, he said not a word. And she really did not know what to say. So they stood there while people jostled around them and waited for Helena and Edward to return. And when they did, irony of ironies, Helena said happily, 'I'm glad you're getting on. Mo is going to stay with us while he looks round Gloucestershire, so you can teach him to play tennis, Nell. The court is never used these days but it won't take you long to mow it and set up the net.' She raised her coffee cup. 'Here's to you, Nell. Our very special goddaughter. Congratulations on getting your Bachelor of Education . . .' Edward was hear-hearing and the ghastly Mo Checkers was looking at the front of her dress and she wished she was home.

But the really strange part was yet to come. The last turn of the second half featured a comedian as a country bumpkin going through a routine that relied heavily on loud and grating 'Aaaars' at the end of each joke – 'to remind us to laugh', Nell whispered to Helena. But after fifteen excruciating minutes, he suddenly whipped off his hay-rick wig, stood humbly before the mike and began to sing. He sang two very sentimental songs, probably from the First World War. One was 'Roses of Picardy' and the other was 'April Showers'. Unexpectedly, staring down at the small man standing in the spotlight, so ridiculously dressed, singing his heart out, Nell found her eyes filling with tears. She had gone often with her parents to hear music at the cathedral; she had seen the effect it had on them, apprehended their emotional involvement without understanding it. Suddenly, somewhere during these two stupid songs, she understood. It was so ridiculous. She leaned back in her seat, feeling for her handkerchief, furious with herself. A movement caught her eye and she glanced to her left. Mo Checkers was leaning back too. He turned and looked at her. Just for a moment their eyes locked in. And then she pulled away.

After that, the after-theatre supper could not really be more embarrassing. Both Helena and Edward had picked up on the atmosphere and rather than force the two 'young people' together they tried to find a topic of conversation that would interest everyone. Obviously, being Edward and Helena, that was the state of the railways.

'I was talking to your grandfather just the other day, my dear. We can remember only too well when the whole of Gloucestershire was serviced by a network of lines. There was not a village that did not have its station. Its station house. Its station master. Its gardens. Its—'

'When your mother and I were working in the general office, Nell, we could pick up the phone and talk on the old bus line to half a dozen different railway stations at once. It was such a good way of collecting and collating information—'

'D'you mean listening to the latest gossip?' Edward asked quizzically.

'That too, darling. It's important, you know. We were able to welcome in new babies, grieve when old railwaymen passed away.' They went into a spate of reminiscences that Nell had heard before. She glanced at Mo Checkers, met his almond eyes, looked quickly away and began to button her cardigan.

'Ready to go, Nell? I suppose you've been racketing round all day visiting your college friends, congratulating each other on the results.'

'There are no actual results, Edward. We have simply completed the course.'

'Your mother told me that your thesis was well received, Nell.'

'So modest.' Edward beamed. 'I'll fetch the car round to the front. We'll have you home before midnight, Cinders!'

She wanted to explain that the outside examiners had not even seen her thesis yet and it was simply her personal tutor who had 'received it well'.

Helena was saying confidentially, 'Isn't it amazing, Nell, that your grandparents are actually living in our old office? Of course Edward just loves it. It means whenever he visits Ted he can wander through the building and see what is happening. I wish you could have seen it then, darling.' She turned to include the boy. 'The toilet facilities were atrocious, Mo. One small triangular basin and one closet for all of us. Men as well as women. Can you imagine that now?'

Mo Checkers looked mystified. As well he might, Nell thought. Helena must be losing her marbles completely

He – he being Mo Checkers, of course – scrambled into the back seat next to Nell. She kept a space between them but the space itself burned with a life of its own and she knew if she turned and looked at him she would not be able to look away.

*

Her parents had waited up, needless to say. They were drinking cocoa and looking ... different. Either cross or excited; difficult to say which.

Her mother raised her brows and her father waited.

Nell said, 'OK. So it was a boy. Chinese. He did not speak a solitary word to me – and before you jump to the wrong conclusions he could speak English and probably understand it too. The show was terrible. Amateurish. Just terrible. Some man singing "April Showers"—'

'Al Jolson,' her mother murmured.

'I suppose. It was just so boring and awful. I hope I never see him again.'

'Helena will make sure of that, don't worry. She is so tactful—'

'She has arranged for me to go up there next week, mow the bloody tennis court, fix up the bloody net and play bloody tennis with him.'

'Oh dear.'

Her father stood up. 'Let's go to bed and sleep on it. All of it.'

'Why? Has something happened here? I thought you looked funny. Hattie left Percy at long last?'

Her mother frowned. 'Stop talking like this, Nell. You sound like a student. D'you want some cocoa?'

'No, thanks. I had a gin and tonic during the interval and another one during supper. Probably that's why I'm so – so – bloody ... *unhappy*.' She looked at them both, shocked by her own self-revelation. Then she put her hands to her newly red hair and burst into tears.

Four

Alice took an afternoon off and met Val at Cheltenham. He had been to Swindon, where the long-term plans for closing the railway engineering works were already being discussed, though nothing had been put on paper as yet. Alice went the long way through the lanes, remembering the number of times she had cycled this way, first to school, then to work in the superintendent's office in the old Bishop Hooper buildings where her parents now had their spacious flat. She smiled and thought sentimentally how life came round in a circle if you waited long enough. Was it really going to loop the loop now and return to the old railway coach almost buried in the foliage of Dean Forest? How could it? She and Val rarely visited the coach now and Hester, who went there more often, reported that it was in an advanced state of decay.

Alice turned right on to the Tewkesbury road and got behind an open-topped Triumph. The driver was a girl not unlike Nell, blond hair streaming behind her. Alice's smile became rueful; poor Nell, after four years at college her immediate future must seem rather an anticlimax. And that awful visit to the theatre the other night . . . Alice intended to have a word with Helena. She really must not foist her down-and-outs on poor Nell. It was so inconsiderate.

The little Triumph continued towards Tewkesbury when Alice turned right again for Cheltenham. She almost gave it a farewell wave as she slowed right down and made the wide turn by a sign that told her she was entering the Garden Town.

She wound down her window; it was warm for the

beginning of May and she wondered whether they would have a decent summer this year, and then why on earth Joe Adair was trying to saddle her with the undoubted burden of the Pumpkin Coach. And then she thought of Joe . . .

Hester Ryecroft enjoyed Fridays. She had a free period at the end of the day, which meant she could tutor the university entrants, mark the Upper Fifth's Hardy essays or go home. That particular Friday she went home.

It was a glorious day, absolutely right for the Pumpkin Coach. Of all the people who had been captivated by the secret history of the old railway coach, Hester was the most unlikely. She was the best teacher of Eng. Lit. Whitsom Hall School for Girls had ever had; her photographic memory never forgot the name of a character, the plot of a book, the connections with other books. Probably she would have made a brilliant scientist, but Alice Pettiford had adored English when they were at school together and what Alice did Hester had usually done as well. And better.

That was why the Pumpkin Coach had intrigued her in the first place. If Alice could find true love there – twice over apparently, because hadn't she gone there with Joe Adair as well as with Val? – then so could Hester.

She went through the small house in the cathedral precinct like a dose of salts, tidying, folding, laying out her books for Monday across the dining-room table, twitching the slippery bedspread into position. All this domesticity was no indictment of the aptly named Mrs Marvel, who had 'done' the little house from top to bottom that morning. It was as if Hester had to reclaim it for herself. And once that was done she took her weekend bag from the wardrobe and began to pack a few things. Just for one night. Nobody actually slept overnight in the ancient sleeping coach. That was why they called it the Pumpkin Coach. As with Cinderella's coach, slippers, dress, the magic disappeared at midnight.

But Hester had been adamant when she telephoned

Richard Tibbolt. This was her way of showing him that he was wrong about her and her brother. That was one thing she did not want to share with Alice and she had to prove it. She was not in love with Val. Somehow the Pumpkin Coach would convince her of that, and once she knew it, surely Tibbolt would know it too.

Val was thinking of Joe Adair while he sped towards Cheltenham on the London train. He watched the familiar Chalford valley drift like a summer dream past the windows and remembered Joe Adair and that terrible day over twenty years ago when Joe and Alice had said goodbye. At the Pumpkin Coach.

Val closed his eyes tightly, then opened them wide as if forcing himself to face the truth. Surely the truth – as dear old Gran Pettiford would have said – was in the proof of the pudding. And the pudding was their marriage. The tenderness and the caring and the intimacy of their exchanged glances. Soul sex. He recalled his own words and smiled.

Chalford platform whipped by; the station canopy was already hung with baskets of flowers. That's what the economists forgot: the personal commitment of the railway staff. Someone, the station master, a porter, a signalman, had resurrected the old wire baskets from the lamp store, cleaned them up, lined them with moss and planted them. It was a way of life that was disappearing fast. Val shivered; he knew he could not stop it from disappearing. His acclaimed schemes for a national transport system would end up, like so many schemes, with the waste paper. Unless . . . unless this strange request from Joe Adair could be used in some way . . . There would be a kind of cosmic justice about it. The Pumpkin Coach, planted there so long ago as a love nest, would come into its own.

The train was approaching Cheltenham and Val stood up abruptly as if to escape the particular memory. That day . . . that terrible day when his father had finally fallen into the abyss of madness and attacked Alice's mother . . . when poor

Hattie had lost her baby girl . . . when Joe and Alice had gone to the Pumpkin Coach and said goodbye . . . that day, if Alice had not already been married to him, and if Joe had not had a wife waiting for him in Newcastle – what would have happened then?

The Mayburys' gardener had mowed the tennis court but the net still sagged on to the grass and the wire was almost rusted through. Aunt Helena had given them lunch in the kitchen but she and Edward hadn't eaten anything because they were going to some function at Cheltenham Town Hall.

Helena was wearing a serviceable pinafore over her flowered summer dress; she poured ice-cold milk from the fridge into tall glasses and added straws as if they were still children. Helena had always wanted children; a big family. And she had to make do with other people's.

Nell said, 'This reminds me of when I was about ten and you thought I was lacking calcium.' She tried to make it sound humorous but everything was so difficult with the awful Mo Checkers around.

'You make me sound like a dragon godmother!' Helena smiled. The daughter of a signalman, she had been a typist in the Great Western Railway's divisional office in Gloucester and had married the superintendent. Yet she had always looked like an aristocrat. In her garden-party dress and linen summer hat she could have been a duchess. 'As a matter of fact you always adored cold milk – nothing to do with calcium!' She hugged Nell from behind and kissed the top of the hated red hair. 'Listen. I have to go. Have a lovely time whatever you do. Mo dear, is there no way I can persuade you to stay here for a while? You are probably trespassing in that old signal box.'

'I have bed and breakfast now, Mrs Maybury.' Mo smiled up and under the hat and for a moment Nell thought he looked almost nice. 'But thank you. You are so kind to me.'

He returned to his glass of milk and Helena exchanged glances with Nell. Bed and breakfast did not sound like a hippie down-and-out at all. Nell tried to put some kind of accusation into her glance; a what-are-you-trying-to-get-me-into-now sort of look. But Helena was already turning away.

'I have to go. I can hear Edward revving up. I wish he wouldn't do that in the garage. The fumes come through into the hall.' She was at the door, picking up bag and gloves en route. 'If that net has gone past the point of no return, don't bother. Just find some deckchairs and sit and relax.' And she was gone.

It was more than awkward, it was intensely embarrassing. Nell started off determined not to speak first, but Mo Checkers seemed to find no need to fill the ghastly vacuum that followed. When she got to the last of her milk and the straw sucked horribly, she felt bound to titter ridiculously and say, 'Sorry.'

He looked up and gave her the smile he had given to Helena. She stood up quickly and gathered the glasses. There was a hint of that premonition she had had in the theatre. He was somehow outside her ken. The badinage she enjoyed with her two cousins, Edmund and Perry, simply did not exist here. Just what did he want from her?

Eventually, after a lot of clattering washing-up, they went outside and began to struggle with the net. He held the wire up while she flopped the rotting webbing down as best she could, then they both went to the winder. The ancient handle that would wind the wire taut simply would not turn. She struggled, unwilling to admit failure; the thought of the deckchairs and the non-conversation was too dreadful; she would not give up. He waited patiently by her side and eventually put a hand on hers.

'Stop. I will try.'

She sprang away from his restraining hand as if it were red-hot but he did not appear to notice. However, he could not budge the old mechanism and the silent deckchairs loomed closer. Then, suddenly and – obviously – without explanation, he walked away, through the wire gate and off the court, and Nell stood there feeling more of an idiot than before, if that were humanly possible.

After a while she picked up her racquet and the net of tennis balls, then her cardigan from where she had flung it as she had grown hotter and hotter and, deciding that this was the best possible thing that could have happened because now she could fetch her bike from the side of the house and just go, she too turned to the wire gate. And there he was, running from the garage, actually running, across the lawn and jumping the rose beds, which unfortunately had been pruned right down so that he didn't rip his trousers to shreds and land in an undignified heap at her feet. He paused in front of her, waving an oil can triumphantly. Not only that, but then he spoke!

'The genie of the lamp!' he said.

He passed her, whipped through the gate on to the tennis court and applied oil to the recalcitrant handle as if his life depended on it. Needless to say, within less than a minute he had worked in the oil and the thing turned and the net came up beautifully. There was, after all, no escape.

He played like a demon. She might have guessed it, with his compact body and those strangely intent eyes; physically and mentally he was equipped for all kinds of athletics. Nell enjoyed a game of tennis with either of her cousins or her mother; Hattie and Percy had a hard court at Leckhampton House and enjoyed giving tennis parties. Perry always called it pat-ball and let her win every other game; Edmund was a complete rabbit and she allowed him a set now and then. But her mother played a good game and they were well matched. Tennis had always involved a great deal of laughter. There was no laughter on the Maybury court that afternoon. Just once the score reached deuce; otherwise Nell had to call 'love' each time. What a word to use for that particular game. And why did *she* feel bound to call it? Why didn't he say one solitary word?

After he had beaten her thoroughly he came to the net and held out his hand. She let hers brush it and laughed.

'Congratulations. Wish I could have given you a better game.'

He said, 'I'll get the chairs out and fetch some water. We must be dehydrated.'

'Oh, sorry, I really have to go. My parents will be back by now.'

She crossed the lawn and made for the side of the house where she had left her bicycle. Her aertex shirt was sticking to her. She must be a rotten loser because suddenly she wanted to cry. He was right behind her but peeled off and went into the garage with the wretched oil can. She desperately wanted to be rid of him, but the fact that he had not protested and was not coming to say goodbye to her was almost the finishing touch. He was completely boorish.

She stuffed her cardigan into her bicycle basket and took hold of the handlebars. The next instant he was behind her, pulling her hands, twisting her away from the bike, slamming her against the wall of the house. He might be shorter than she was but he was amazingly strong.

He held her there and looked straight into her eyes. So he couldn't be that much shorter after all. Maybe it had been her shoes the other evening. Or something. But he was still so strange. Those dark eyes . . .

He was panting and he had not been panting before. He said, 'Why did you let me win? Are you sorry for me?'

For some reason she was panting too, though she made no attempt to free herself. She said furiously, 'Don't be an absolute idiot! I didn't let you win! I wouldn't have done that!'

He said nothing and there was a stillness settling around them that had the threat of something much, much more.

She added quickly, 'And why would I be sorry for you? You're not a down-and-out at all. Don't imagine you can fool me like you've fooled Helena and Edward!'

He slackened his grip slightly but she did not move.

'I haven't fooled them. How can I? Everyone can see I'm a half-caste!'

She was astounded. The term half-caste had not been acceptable at college, where several students had been of mixed race. She blinked and looked at him anew. Those eyes. They were almond-shaped and the body was economical, compact and neat.

She whispered, 'Your father was . . .'

'My father was English. My mother was Chinese.' He spoke hoarsely.

'I didn't think. And it would have made no difference. Except that it might explain your name.'

'I gave it to myself. Mo from Mao Tse-tung. Checkers from Chiang Kai-shek.'

'I see. You wanted to establish your Chinese . . . identity. With all parties.' The whisper was more of a gasp now. She was finding it hard to breathe. And she could not look away from those tea-brown eyes.

He said no more. After another few seconds of total awareness he leaned his head towards her and very deliberately fitted his mouth over hers.

She jerked back, an involuntary movement that he totally ignored. And then she was still, very, very still. She had been kissed before; last year there had been a mature student from Loughborough who had called her his 'wild child'; before that, long before that, yet unforgettably, Edmund had kissed her. She had been ten and had imagined for a long time that they were engaged to be married. Neither time had been like this. She gave herself up to this kiss, recalling her father telling her mother that they must stop indulging in 'soul sex'. She had thought he was being funny; now she knew he was not. This curious boy-man had taken her to a new dimension and as his mouth moved over hers she knew exactly what her father had meant.

And then the hand that had held her against the wall slid down to the hem of her aertex shirt, went under it, slid up again on her bare skin and cupped her breast. Suddenly they were no longer on a higher plane; suddenly she was being groped against the Mayburys' wall.

Disappointment curdled into anger and she shoved him away ungently.

'What the hell are you playing at?' she gasped. 'Get away –
get away from me, you nasty little – little—'

He was startled at first, then appalled, then quite calm. 'Go
on. Say it.'

'You are just another grubby little layabout on the make!'

'Layabout? Don't you mean half-breed?'

She was already stumbling to her bicycle, forcing herself
not to sob, not to show how upset she was.

'Oh shut up!' She wheeled the bike away and then sat on
the saddle and prepared to push along the drive. 'Half-caste
a minute ago, now half-breed! You probably think that
sounds more glamorous! You probably think every girl in this
country will want you if you call yourself—'

He shouted, 'Shut up yourself! Spoiled! Arrogant!
Ignorant! Just go!'

So she did.

It took her an hour to cycle home and by the time she had
pedalled laboriously past the church and the pump and
down the lane to the house she felt really ill. She put her bike
in the shed and noted that her parents were not yet home,
then she went inside and leaned against the kitchen sink and
wailed aloud. Then she splashed water on her face and said
fiercely, 'It was what you wanted, you fool! You wanted to lose
your virginity. What would have been so awful about losing it
to a – a – *half-breed*?'

Mrs Mearment from the house back down the lane tapped
on the window.

'I heard a funny noise, love. Are you all right?'

'Perfectly, thank you, Mrs M.' Nell opened the door, wanting to kill their neighbour, who was the same age as Granny
Doffie but looked about a hundred. 'Come on in and we'll
have a cup of tea. I haven't seen you for ages. Lots to tell you.
Sit down. Feet up. What do you think of the hair?'

The reply was not 100 per cent in favour but Nell was
already at the tap filling the kettle and did not hear. Besides,
all she could think about was Mo Checkers. Mao-Chiang.
Good Lord, who did he think he was anyway?

Five

Alice and Valentine sat on one side of an enormous mahogany table; young Mr Venables sat on the other. Young Mr Venables must have been all of ten years old when the Bracewell family had decided that the derelict railway coach in the Forest of Dean could be offloaded – legally and generously in the rather uncomfortable circumstances – on to their unknown, unwanted and definitely illegitimate descendant, Joseph Adair.

And now, here sat young Mr Venables, papers spread before him, explaining that there was still some time to run on the lease for the land, that the Freeminers had agreed to transfer it to Mr and Mrs Ryecroft, and that Joseph Adair would be happy to let them have the coach for the nominal sum of five hundred pounds.

'Mr Adair's representative has set this figure based on the cost of second-hand caravans. It is completely open to negotiation.'

Val looked from Mr Venables's prematurely bald head to the papers on the desk. 'Representative? May we meet this representative to conduct negotiations?'

'No. Mr Adair is adamant that there should be no personal contact. Written communication will be through my firm.'

Alice flushed slightly. Obviously Joe would not want to meet either of them again but surely a letter would have been . . . acceptable.

Valentine glanced at her quickly. 'Is Mr Adair still living in Newcastle?'

Mr Venables looked up at him and smiled. 'I am not at

liberty to tell you anything about my client. Any queries you have . . . any more details you may need to know . . . I will pass them on.'

Valentine sat back in his chair. 'You will understand our . . . curiosity, of course. Mr Adair was a colleague of my wife's. They worked together in the same office. In fact the divisional headquarters of the Gloucester district railway.' He paused as Alice moved convulsively but when she did not speak he added quietly, 'It was a long time ago.'

Mr Venables glanced at Alice. 'I know there is an acquaintanceship from the past.' He looked back at Valentine. 'That is all I know, Mr Ryecroft.' He shuffled some papers. 'I have been instructed to deal with the transaction – if there is to be a transaction. To that end I have already consulted with the Freeminers. And now I am consulting with you.'

Valentine pressed his spine against the chair back, wondering why he had seen Joe's strange offer as a gift from the gods. He remembered talking to his father-in-law about it, and Ted – the head of the old GWR Pettiford family no less – had looked at him with a kind of hope and said, 'Could you make it work, Val? The lines must be there still. Somewhere underneath the forest.'

Val himself had seen it as an exciting opportunity. More than that, a quest, an adventure, a challenge. His clear-thinking mind had already worked out a strategy, already compiled a list of people he would need to see . . . persuade . . .

Now, sitting here in this heavy, old-fashioned office, where Joe himself must have sat when he found out that the Pumpkin Coach and its land belonged to him, he was less sure. Joe had been cut out of their lives for a quarter of a century. So far as any of them knew, he had never visited the Pumpkin Coach since the day he had said goodbye to Alice – and if he had, he had done so secretly. Was this a final separation? Or was it some labyrinthine method of re-connecting with his old life?

Val said, 'I rather think that if we turn down this offer, Mr

Adair will be forced to remove the old sleeping coach, since it is disintegrating?'

A slight hesitation from Mr Venables confirmed Valentine's guess, so he did not wait for a reply.

'I think an offer of two hundred and fifty pounds is fair in the circumstances. Perhaps you would consult Mr Adair and let us know if this is acceptable.'

Mr Venables looked steadily across the mahogany divide.

'I am authorized to accept any reasonable offer.'

Just for a moment Val was lost for words. He told himself it was absurd to feel hustled. Yet wasn't that exactly what was happening?

The silence stretched invisibly between the two men; then suddenly Alice sat forward in her chair.

'That seems more than fair, Mr Venables. Thank you very much.' She reached across and took Val's hand. 'Perhaps . . . we'll never know, of course, but perhaps Joe needs the money. Or less responsibility. Or . . . something.'

Unexpectedly, Val had a sudden flash of his recent journey from Paddington. The little stations between Swindon and Cheltenham, some of them hung with flowers, cared for by families like the Pettifords. Railway families.

He turned and smiled right at her and had they been any-where else it could have been one of their special moments. But then he turned back to Mr Venables and said simply, 'Where do I sign?'

Not for the first time Hester Ryecroft was grateful that school terms were longer than universities'. Since her weekend with Richard Tibbolt in the old coach in Dean Forest, she had thrown herself into the summer term at Whitsom's with a kind of abandon. She had never had much to do with the end-of-year entertainment before, but this year when Sally Gold – a brash girl in the Lower Sixth, unfortunately in line to be next year's head girl – had said, 'How would you like to front our little show this year, Miss Ryecroft?' she had said briskly, 'Very much, Sally. From what I have seen of your rehearsals, it needs a certain gravitas or else it will all fly out of the window!'

Sally had chuckled appreciatively and warned, 'We've stepped up rehearsals, actually. And you need to see the order of play – well, the state of play really.'

'I do understand the duties of a commère, Sally. Will it mean every lunch hour?'

' 'Fraid so. And the dress rehearsal is going to be most of that last Saturday. Can you bear it?'

'Of course.' She hesitated. Sally Gold was pretty and made everything sound like a joke, but if she was asking the head of English to step in at the last minute she must be floundering. She said, 'Is it excruciating, Sally?'

The girl grinned conspiratorially. 'Well, yes. The younger girls want to mime along to the Osmonds or the Stones. But they all auditioned for the music department so at least . . . Anyway, you can send them up and make the whole thing a sort of *Saturday Night Live* event.'

Hester knew better than to ask what *Saturday Night Live* was; she could sort that out with Hattie or the boys. Edmund and Perry were always only too glad to 'put her in the picture' or 'bring Hessie up to scratch'.

Sally sensed her doubts and said reassuringly, 'You'll be the star of the show, Miss Ryecroft. You know the whole school thinks you're wonderful.'

Hester watched the girl walk off towards the Sixth Form sitting room, as it was now called. A more appropriate name these days, Hester considered, when the older girls did a lot of sitting and very little studying. She knew she was seen throughout the school as a bit of a dragon but Sally Gold's heavy-handed sarcasm was absolutely uncalled-for. Hester made a mental note to watch her like a hawk; for one thing, her skirt was much too short.

Meanwhile Hester needed something completely different from the usual timetable. She had always been able to summon Tibbolt for what she called her scatty moments. But since the weekend in the Pumpkin Coach she had not felt able to summon him for a scatty moment, or for any other moment either. She dared not face the fact, but there was a distinct possibility that she and Tibbolt were . . . well, finished. And that meant that in the times when she could not busy herself at school or at home, she had to face other facts that were always waiting in the wings, ready to pounce. Her father had died in a hospital for the insane; he had abused her mother (and she had known it and refused to face it – she realized she was good at not facing things); he had beaten her brother, raped Hattie's sister-in-law, tried to rape Doffie Pettiford . . . The list was probably much longer and more dreadful but thankfully she did not know it. And anyway, Reginald Ryecroft was dead and buried and dear Mother had said at his funeral, 'Now we must try to understand him.'

Hester frowned, remembering those wonderful compassionate words. But why? Why must they understand him? Why couldn't they just let him go? She knew the answer, of course. They must understand their father so that they could understand themselves. She and Val. Tainted children of a man who was criminally insane.

She went home that night and tried to force herself to compose suitable introductions for the end-of-year concert. 'And now here is a group from the junior school with a case of mistaken identity. Ladies, I give you the Spiders! Oh . . . I beg your pardon, I think that should read, the Beatles!' Would that be too much for them to bear? Well, they could always roll their eyes and moan about Tough Piecrust. She knew they called her Piecrust; strangely enough, she rather enjoyed the name.

Prebendary Nicholls was crossing the close as she emerged from the tunnel of Elizabethan houses. He waved perfunctorily and disappeared into the deep porch of the west door. He was a widower and Hattie had suggested that he would be a very suitable match for Hester. Hester had laughed but Hattie had been serious. She thought the preb could make her happy and she wanted everyone to be happy.

Dear old Hattie. Too much make-up, too much gossip, too much intense mother-love and – probably even now – too much sex.

Hester unlocked her door and went into the tiny hall. Mrs Marvel had left a note. 'Fish pie and rice pud in oven'. Hester imagined herself lifting the dishes on to the kitchen table with the oven gloves made for her years ago by Nell. She visualized herself sitting and eating the food. A lonely old maid. No, not an old maid at all but most definitely a spinster.

She sighed sharply and went about settling herself in: gloves and bag on the hall table, briefcase beneath it; upstairs to change her clothes and swill face and hands. She forced herself to think of Hattie again and how she had overflowed with . . . everything. She recalled Hattie Pettiford as a girl during the war, full of life, oozing excitement, already prone to putting on weight in spite of the rationing. And then, the first time Hester had gone to Leckhampton House after Hattie's unlikely marriage to Percy Westbrook, the way they had all danced attendance on Hattie – even old Mrs Westbrook, certainly Percy and his sister Enid. It seemed to Hester that Hattie had always been pregnant then; the atmosphere of fecundity in the house had appalled and repelled Hester in those days. Yet she saw now only too well that Hattie had used her sexuality to take command of everything and everyone. How had she done that? How had she *done* it?

Hester went through the motions she had already visualized: place mats, cutlery, wine glass, wine, oven gloves, fish pie . . . Mrs Marvel could cook as well as clean. She really was a marvel. Hester found herself scraping the bits from the edge of the rice pudding basin; she felt better.

She stayed at the kitchen table to read the Lower Sixth's work on modern children's literature. Sally Gold had chosen to compare *Catcher in the Rye* with *The Owl Service*. She had done it well . . . she had done it excellently. Hester reluctantly made notes to that effect and awarded her an A plus. Then, without pausing, though subconsciously she must have planned this all the time, she picked up the phone and dialled Hattie's number.

Hattie said, 'Nell will be here on Saturday but she comes to see the boys, not me. And darling Percy is taking Enid to an afternoon concert. I was invited but I'd so much rather talk to you, Hessie dear. Come to lunch, why don't you? We ought to talk privately about this hare-brained scheme of Val's.'

'Scheme of Val's? I know nothing at all about it.'

'Well, you will. He's after money and moral support. And you and I can offer both.' Hattie laughed. 'He knows you'd give him anything. Come to that, so would I.'

Hester said out of the blue, 'Hattie, have you ever slept with Val?'

There was the tiniest pause. Hattie said, 'Have you been talking to Doffie? I absolutely adore darling Doffie, but on the subject of Val she is slightly off-key. Never really approved of him and Alice, you know.'

'That's because Val is the son of a madman,' Hester said calmly. She hardly heard Hattie's frantic protests. She knew now that Val and Hattie had been lovers at some point. She managed to quell a moment of intense jealousy and said laughingly, 'Only joking, Hattie. I'll see you on Saturday for lunch. I'll bring flowers for Grannie. Chocolates for Enid. What would Percy like?'

'A chaste kiss, I imagine. He's in such awe of you, Hessie. He would just love it if you let him in a little.'

Hester felt her eyes widen with surprise. She replaced the receiver. She would unload her heartbreak – if that was what it was – on dear old Hattie on Saturday. But already the peculiar Pettiford magic was at work because now Hester had something else to think about. Val and Hattie. When? Where? But most particularly, when?

Hattie replaced the receiver, reaching across Percy to do so. They were in bed although it was only six thirty and the June evening was still full of sunshine. Hattie enjoyed making love at unusual times and now that Percy was retired and home all day there were lots of opportunities. Besides, it let the boys know that their parents were still 'capable', as Perry put it in a disgusted voice. And it reminded old Granny Westbrook and Enid – especially Enid – that Percy still wanted her. That was important.

She lay on her side facing Percy. 'That was Hester,' she said.

'Yes. What was all that about kissing me? Letting me in? What are you up to?'

'Darling, she's not happy. That soppy professor isn't her type. She wants someone dynamic.'

'Are you suggesting . . .'

'Not exactly.' She kissed him lingeringly, smiling, contented. 'I'm much too possessive to lend you to anyone, darling. But if you could accept the kiss . . . respond just a little . . . it would make her realize that there are other fish in the sea and that she is still desirable.'

'She's more than desirable.' He withdrew slightly. 'She's very beautiful, Hattie. What if I fell in love with her?'

'You couldn't because you're in love with me. Besides, her father was as mad as a hatter.'

'He was Val's father too. And I just heard you tell Hester that you would give Val anything.'

'I know Val looks like Reggie Ryecroft but actually he is very like his mother. Whereas Hester looks like her mother but—'

'Would you give him anything, Hat? Would you? Would you?' He was heaving himself on top of her, tickling her, making her helpless with laughter and the windows were open and the boys doubtless sitting outside . . . Sometimes she wondered how much Percy knew about the affair with Val. If that was what it had been. She wasn't sure now; it was so long ago. If only he hadn't married darling Alice, she would be tempted to do it all again. After all, the fifties were not considered old any more . . . Look at darling Percy, he was on the way to eighty and he was not past it. Definitely not. She held Percy's head into her neck and let out a long moan. She hoped it would reach Enid's ears, wherever Enid was.

When Enid opened the door to Hester at twelve o'clock precisely on Saturday morning, Hattie did not press Percy forward with the welcoming committee. Edmund was his usual enigmatic self, pecking Hester's cheek politely and making way for boisterous Perry to hug her and tell her that her perfume was smashing; Enid hung back nervously as usual and that left Hattie herself to surge up, drying her hands on a tea towel, then throwing towel and hands round Hester's elegant fur collar and kissing her full on the mouth.

'Oh Hattie!' Hester drew back immediately, though she knew that Hattie greeted everyone in this uninhibited way. 'You'll have smudged my lipstick!'

Perry laughed and Edmund said he would see about some drinks; both boys disappeared into the dining room. It was then that Percy appeared from his mother's room.

'Thought I heard a commotion!' He smiled at his wife. 'Should be used to it by now.' He moved the smile to Hester. 'And my dear cousin-in-law – is that our relationship?'

Hester raised her brows. Percy was not known as a conversationalist and banter was completely foreign to him.

She said, 'I'm not certain. My brother is married to Hattie's cousin so . . .'

Percy put his hands on her shoulders. 'Ah. But our relationship is more complicated than that, isn't it? We are all intertwined like the roots of a tree.'

Both Hattie and Hester had heard this before from Alice, who at one time had been determined to bring their families together. They exchanged glances over Percy's shoulder just as Percy drew Hester very close indeed and kissed her.

Hattie smiled to herself, well pleased. And then stopped smiling. The kiss went on rather. At first Hester was rigid; she had seen Percy kiss his mother, his sister and his wife, no one else at all. But then, almost imperceptibly, she relaxed into the kiss. Hattie could not see their mouths but she was certain that Hester parted her lips. It was absolutely and totally disgusting!

She forced herself to laugh loudly, then touched Percy's arm.

'All right, darling. I know I told you to kiss Hessie but you don't have to frighten the poor girl away for ever!'

Hester moved back as if stung and Percy, deprived of her support, stumbled a little, then straightened and smiled at both women.

'Sorry, old girl,' he said easily. 'I told Hat that I think you are very beautiful, Hester. So you two have only got yourselves to blame if I get carried away.'

'You'll get carried away all right,' Hattie scolded, flipping him towards the dining room with the tea towel. 'Go and make sure the boys have given Hessie and me a really large sherry while I take Hessie's stole.' She drew Hester towards the cloakroom. 'Darling, I'm sorry about that. Percy is so highly sexed, I simply cannot keep up with him.'

Hester was so flummoxed she did not reply and Hattie swept on. 'Let's just call in at the kitchen and check on what Enid is doing about lunch. Then Percy can fetch Grandmamma and we'll all sit down together. Isn't this nice? It's ages since you were here. And I'm intrigued about what you have to tell me. I won't pester – you know I'm not like that – but just tell me, is it about Nell? She's always here lately – it's delightful, of course, but she doesn't come to see me. I'm not sure whether she's after Edmund or Perry!'

Hester did not reply to this either. She forced a smile in Enid's direction – the poor woman was terrified of her simply because her father was Reggie Ryecroft – then they were in the dining room and Perry was asking her what the latest crop of sixth-formers was like and Edmund was handing her a sherry and saying he had finished the reading list she had given him and could he have another. Percy was nowhere to be seen, which was just as well. He was an old man, for goodness' sake, and her body was tingling from his touch. It was

57

absolutely and totally disgusting. Nevertheless when Enid came in with the enormous leg of lamb still sizzling from the oven, followed by Percy with the vegetables, she could not bring herself to look at him.

She was determined not to confide in Hattie after what had happened, but by the time Nell arrived with someone called Mo – really, names were getting more unlikely with every generation – she was only too glad to be taken upstairs to watch the four youngsters playing doubles on the newly dragged court.

'Darling, you're all upset.' Hattie was genuinely concerned. 'Is it Percy? You mustn't take any notice of him. I told him to be a bit more welcoming than usual and he did it to annoy me. We play these silly games – they mean nothing.'

Hester said, 'They mean everything, Hattie. They – they're the coinage of your marriage!' It was a ridiculous, flowery sort of statement and she felt her eyes fill and overflow. What on earth was the matter with her?

Hattie's eyes widened; she looked almost frightened.

'Hessie! You're not – you're not *crying*, are you?'

Hester put her hands to her face. 'Of course not! How could I possibly cry because bloody Tibbolt has finished with me? What do the young people call it? He's dumped me! Hattie, Tibbolt has *dumped* me!' Her voice became a wail and Hattie pushed herself out of her chair – no mean feat these days – and crouched beside her.

'Darling . . . come here. That's right. Let it out . . . let it all out . . .' Hattie held Hester's aristocratic head against her shoulder, then on an impulse pulled out the pins from her hair and let its luxuriant length fall about Hester's immaculate navy-blue linen dress. 'Sweetheart, no man is worth this. And in any case, there must be some misunderstanding. He's been dotty about you since you were eighteen, Hester! You've had him at your beck and call like a puppy-dog—' The wail became louder and Hattie glanced down at the tennis court, hoping, this time, that no one could hear.

'That's what he said! Almost the same words! I used him

58

like a trained pet! That's what he said after I'd made him go swimming in Bracewell's Pool with me! I just laughed – I thought he liked me pulling him in – I didn't know he hadn't brought a change of clothes – he knew we were staying overnight – oh God – he said I never kept a bargain – he would not share that awful moth-eaten bed with me and he must have been frozen because the other blankets just fell to bits when he tried to wrap himself up in them!'

'What on earth did he mean about you never keeping a bargain? You're the most straightforward person I've ever known—'

'Apparently he thought I'd said I would talk to his wretched children! They're living in some horrible, sordid squat in Bristol and they won't even see their father. He reckons I could talk to them because – because – oh, he's got some silly reason for thinking I understand these sort of people.'

'Drug addicts, do you mean? They are drug addicts, aren't they?'

'One of them certainly. Yes. And I did not actually say . . . Oh Hattie, I am missing him so much! I think I must love him!'

'Well, of *course* you love him.' Hattie managed a little laugh. 'And if all you have to do to get him back is to go and see his twins, then do it! All right, you won't get anywhere with them – why on earth he thinks you will I do not know. But you will have tried.'

Exhausted, Hester rolled away from Hattie's shoulder and leaned her head back against the chair. Her hair fanned round her like a shawl. She spoke wearily now, her voice catching occasionally on a sob, but the tears already drying on her face.

'There's more to it than that, Hattie. He wants us to be married, settled. A "conventional couple", as he puts it. And I don't want that. I'm my own mistress. I can't subjugate myself to a man. Especially a man who has as many faults as Tibbolt. He's not his own master, never has been. There are still students who hang on his every word—'

'Well, of course there are because he's a damned good teacher! That doesn't mean he is seducing every one of them!'

'He seduced me.'

'And then he fell in love with you and that was your chance! You've been punishing him ever since, Hessie. Welcoming him into your bed when you feel like it, keeping him at arm's length the rest of the time.'

'Is that how you see it?'

'That's how it is, darling.'

'Is it? Oh God, Hattie! Is it really?'

'Hester, stop beating yourself like this. What is the problem? Tibbolt wants to get married. You didn't. Now I think you probably do. Isn't it that simple?'

'I don't know!' The wail was back. Hester closed her eyes and dropped her chin on to the bodice of her linen dress. 'It was a kind of trial run. We've never actually slept together. I mean—'

'I know, darling. Gone to bed, gone to sleep, woken up.'

'Yes. And the weekend in the forest was a trial run. And we didn't. We didn't.' She lifted her head and looked at Hattie wildly. 'We *didn't*, Hattie!'

'I know, darling. You didn't.'

'You're humouring me. You're remembering that my father was—'

'Shut up, Hessie. I think it's marvellous that you've got these depths to you, darling. I mean, I've known you all this time as Alice's friend. And since all that awful business with your father and Enid, we've somehow grown very close. Yet I haven't known this side of you. This is what Tibbolt knows and loves. No wonder he wants to – to have a claim on you. That's all it is, Hessie. He wants to be with you all the time. Openly. And you think that you only enjoy the relationship because it's clandestine. And because that keeps him . . . well, in his place.'

'I sound horrible! I hate myself!'

'What rubbish you do talk at times, Hester! You might be a clever teacher but you are the most idiotic woman I have ever met.'

'Thank you very much!'

'That's more like it! Now listen. The mistake you made was in staying – actually staying – overnight in the Pumpkin Coach. You know very well that after midnight it loses its magic completely. Alice knew that right from the beginning.' Suddenly Hattie's face changed; she looked her age. 'My mother discovered it back in the twenties – she was so young when I was born, Hessie.'

Hester blinked and refocused. 'Poor Mitzie.' She looked at Hattie, recalling that Hattie had called her dead baby Mitzie after her doomed mother. She felt the treacherous tears welling up again. 'Oh Hattie . . .'

'I know. I know, darling. But we cannot linger too long in the past otherwise it swallows us up. And you should be planning a wedding.'

'He hasn't phoned once . . . I've gone too far, Hattie. I know it in here,' she said, tapping her tear-stained bodice. Then she laughed. 'Listen to me! I sound like Alice and Doffie rolled into one. You Pettifords are all so dramatic!'

Hattie ignored that and frowned thoughtfully. 'First of all, you have to contact the dreadful Tibbolt twins! Where do they live – Bristol? Right. We'll go there, darling. Tomorrow? Are you free tomorrow? What do you mean, you're always free? Now don't start crying again, I meant that you could be in the middle of tutoring the university entrants or anything . . . Hessie, stop it!'

'It's just that you're so sweet, Hattie! And I haven't told you the whole thing about the twins and I hardly know how to after what I said to you not long ago.'

'Hester, you are becoming completely incoherent. Now, just be calm for a moment. You've let go beautifully – something to do with your hair being free. Let me brush it out.' She got up and fetched her hairbrush from the set on the dressing table. She began to brush expertly, with long, slow, regular strokes. Hester let her head fall on to the back of the chair; her eyes closed.

Hattie said, 'Gramps gave me this brush when I was ten years old. It's never had to be re-bristled or re-backed. The enamel is as good as new.' She waited, looking down at the upturned face and recognizing that Percy had been right: Hester Ryecroft was classically beautiful. A tear formed on the long lashes and rolled down the creamy skin. Hattie said quietly, 'I am unshockable, Hester. Just tell me what is really so dreadful.'

Hester whispered obediently, 'Tibbolt says they're incestuous. The twins. And he wants me to talk to them. As if I'm some kind of expert!'

Hattie smiled through the window, noticing the 'children' for the first time in an hour. They were whacking tennis balls as if their lives depended on it; no laughter, no crazy accusations. Quite uncharacteristic.

She said, 'He meant because you're close to your brother.' She aimed a kiss at the top of Hester's head. 'I know what I said. Forgive me.'

'But he – Tibbolt – must think . . . something. And I do feel a kind of sympathy for them. Eve and Toby. They were awful when they were younger. They've come together because no one else understands them.'

'Ah . . .' Hattie paused, brush mid-air. 'Poor little things.'

'They must be almost thirty years old, Hattie!'

'Now don't start again, Hester! Just relax. I can see what Tibbolt means. Because of the business with your father, it might – it just *might* have happened for you and Val—'

'No! Val would not have allowed that! He never felt anything for me at all!'

'But your feelings do make it possible for you to sympathize a little with Toby and Eve. Tibbolt was right there.' Hattie went slowly to the dressing table and replaced the brush, then sat down next to Hester. 'And I think you were right when you made that very snide remark the other week about Percy and Enid. Enid needs the security of her brother and he needs to be the protector. They don't sleep together – I'm not saying that at all. You didn't sleep with Val. But you understand to a certain extent how it could happen. And I think Percy also understands.'

Hester stammered, 'I didn't think Percy was . . . so outgoing. I've never really thought about Percy. I'm so sorry, Hattie.'

'Nobody knows Percy. Everyone thought I could have done better. Didn't they? Be honest. They thought I married him for his money – this house – the gardens – the tennis court—'

'Hattie! I'm sorry – so sorry—' Hester stared at her. 'You had the boys so quickly, Hattie.'

'And Mitzie. I loved being pregnant, Hester. If Mitzie had lived we would have gone on and had a really big family. But Mitzie didn't live.'

Hester frowned slightly. 'So Percy was wrong. He could father children?'

Hattie forced a grin. 'Obviously.' It was true, after all. Percy had fathered both Perry and Mitzie. She changed the subject quickly. 'Listen. Ask him. Ask Percy about his feelings for Enid. Tell him why. Confide in him, Hester. He will appreciate it and he might tell you something that would help.'

'I couldn't possibly . . .' Hester was suddenly unbearably hot. She unbuttoned her bodice and fanned herself quickly. And at that precise moment the door opened and Percy came into the bedroom.

He saw his redoubtable relation with her glorious hair all over the place, her face streaked and filthy, her dress undone . . . She looked totally wanton.

He smiled. 'Am I interrupting anything?'

Hattie stood up. 'Well, yes. But you've come at a very opportune moment, darling. As you so often do.' She went to him and kissed him, holding his arms tightly and warningly. 'Hester needs to ask you something. It's difficult for her so give her time.' She went to the door. 'I'll organize tea and see if the children are all right. There's a feeling of tension coming from the tennis court . . .'

She was gone. Slowly Percy crossed the room and sat in his wife's chair. He looked at Hester.

'I think if I were thirty years younger I would be on the verge of falling in love with you, Hester. You used to scare me. Not any more.'

Hester began to cry again.

Six

Nell was in the house alone when the telephone rang. She eyed it warily, wondering whether to answer it, then, knowing she had no choice because it might be important, she picked it up and held it to her ear. When nobody spoke she knew it was Mo. Just as she had done three times previously, she replaced the receiver.

It was ten thirty and she was due to play tennis with Perry after lunch. She had intended to cycle to Leckhampton House but it was hot and she felt slightly sick. She picked up the phone again and dialled the Westbrooks' number. Edmund answered.

'Edmund, it's me. Nell.'

'Yes.'

'I was wondering . . . as it's so hot, would you mind asking Perry whether he could come over in his car?'

'Certainly.'

There was the sound of the receiver being placed carefully on the hall table, then silence. Edmund was certainly a man of few words; in the past Nell had found it one of his many attractions. But this was ridiculous. He could have offered to come himself; perhaps she should have asked him outright. Perhaps he thought she wanted to see Perry particularly. And actually she had done because she could have continued with the seduction more easily in the car than on the tennis court. Oh God. She felt like a boiling cauldron of jam, very hot, seething . . . If Perry did not at least kiss her this afternoon she might go mad.

Edmund was ages. She walked the length of the telephone

cable and pressed her nose against the bottle glass of the front-door window. If only Perry weren't Hattie's son she could have talked it all over with Hattie. She did not want to make a fool of herself as she had done with Edmund all those years ago . . . of course she had been a child then . . . She stopped breathing and concentrated on looking through the glass. A wavy image was coming up the garden path from the direction of Mrs Mearment's house. It couldn't be. He'd been on the telephone two minutes ago. But there was a telephone box next to the church gate. She started to breathe again; she was shaking.

Perry's voice said in her ear, 'That's fine, old girl. About two-ish be all right?'

She gripped the receiver hard. 'Listen, Perry. Could you come now?'

'Not really. Hester's coming to lunch and Mum's making a bit of a fuss about it. We've got to do the host thing.'

'Oh.' The watery image was almost in focus now. It was the detested Mo Checkers.

'Nell? Are you all right?'

'Yes. Fine. Make it as soon as you can.' She almost ran back to replace the receiver. Then, like an absolute idiot, she started to climb into the cupboard under the stairs. The doorbell rang. She stayed very still, half in and half out of the cupboard. It rang again. She knew what would happen next. He would push open the letter box and peer through and there she would be in plain view, or at any rate her bottom, protruding beyond the triangular door of the cupboard. Gingerly she began to push her way through the hanging coats, the hockey sticks, the winter shoes; then she stepped very carefully indeed over the vacuum cleaner. The next thing she knew, the ironing board had fallen on her, opening as it came, trapping her flailing arm in its supports. She yelped.

'Nell? Is that you? Oh my God, what has happened?'

He sounded genuinely anxious. She made reassuring

noises and the legs of the ironing board clamped hard on her arm so that she yelped again, only louder.

'Hang on,' he shouted. 'I'll come round the back. Don't try to move!'

He released the letter box with a bang and gravel scattered as he ran round the house. The back door was open anyway and he was with her in two seconds flat. He leaned over her and opened the ironing board and she stood up. Dad's old raincoat fell on top of the vacuum, she caught her foot in the hose, he was struggling to prop up the ironing board: it was like a rugby scrum.

She extracted her foot and went into the living room, leaving him to deal with the mayhem in the cupboard. She heard him doing so very efficiently but, as usual, in total silence. She went to the mirror over the mantelpiece, looked at her dishevelled reflection and mouthed, 'Damn, damn, damn!'

He came in and said, 'You were hiding from me.'

'Don't be ridiculous! Why on earth would I—'

'I have telephoned you several times since our last unfortunate meeting. You always replace the receiver when I identify myself. Today you replaced it without waiting to find out—'

'Only you would make a call and say nothing!'

'You find my lack of conversational skills off-putting.'

'And your way of making statements rather than asking questions.' She turned, trying to look as cool as a cucumber. 'Assuming that was a question – yes, I do find your lack of conversational skills –' she mimicked his voice childishly – 'very off-putting. Not to say rude. Not to say bloody rude!'

'Anything else? And that was a question.'

She went to the window and looked down the garden. Two pigeons sat on the bird table, their heads nodding in synchronized pecking. Normally that would have made her smile; today she felt unexpected tears behind her eyes.

'You know what,' she said in a low voice.

'I made a pass at you. I shouldn't have done it. You called me names that were . . . unacceptable to me . . . and I reacted badly. I wanted to apologize. You would not answer the phone—'

'I did not call you names! I did *not*!'

'Perhaps you did not actually speak them. Perhaps I am oversensitive where you are concerned. Whatever, I do apologize, Nell. I cannot help fancying you like mad. But I should have controlled—'

'You *groped* me!'

'Nell, I am so sorry. I didn't mean it to be like that. I wanted so much to hold you. Your whole body—'

'Shut up! Stop talking like this!'

'In the theatre. When we first met. Did you not feel something special then? Some connection?'

'No!' But she was lying and he knew it.

'I have bought an old seventy-eight of Al Jolson singing "April Showers". I play it again and again.'

She was silent, trying to control her shaking. He was right behind her; she thought she could feel the heat of his body through her cotton dress.

She said, 'You really must stop talking like this. We cannot – cannot – conduct our lives on – on – things like that. Whimsical things. I don't understand you, you're not like people I know. And you won't allow me to get to know you, perhaps become friends. I mean, I cannot imagine at this moment that we could ever be friends—'

'We could be friends after. We could leave that aside. Become lovers first and then—'

'Mo! I said, stop it! No wonder you don't say much, because when you do you are completely – completely outrageous!' She turned angrily, then realized he was much too close and sidestepped. 'Can't you see what you are doing? If you'd lived all your life in the East it would make some kind of sense. But you haven't! Which . . .' She escaped back into the hall and into the kitchen. The door was still wide open and she went out into the open air and breathed deeply, closing her eyes. Of course he had followed her. She held out a hand as if to ward him off. 'Which – I'm sorry – makes you thick! We've met twice. Twice. And you talk about being lovers.' She opened her eyes. He was at least six feet away. She dropped her hand to her side. 'Listen. Perry is coming to pick me up. He's my cousin. We're going to play tennis. I'm not making up excuses. You must go. And I want you to go now.'

He said nothing, staring at her with his dark eyes, willing her to return the look and risk the consequences.

'Now,' she reiterated.

He said quietly, 'Let me stay until he comes. Please. I promise we will do everything your way. We will talk and know each other and become friends.'

'No. I don't think that is a good idea.' She risked looking at him. 'I mean it. I shall be going for an interview next week. A school some way from here. It's not worth it.' She swallowed to clear a constriction in her throat. 'Perry won't be here till two o'clock. It's a long time. We would have to make conversation. Proper conversation.'

'I can do it.' He glanced at his watch. 'It's past eleven already. That's less than three hours.' He looked up. 'Please, Nell.'

She stared, shocked. He was going to cry.

'All right. But the moment I say it's finished, it's finished.'

'Of course. But you must help me. If I start to say the wrong thing—'

She was already marching to the back door. Now she stopped, incredulous all over again. 'Do you mean you honestly don't know when you put your foot in it?'

'Honestly.'

'So that's why you hardly ever say a word?'

'Yes.'

She rolled her eyes humorously. 'Oh my God.' She went inside and made for the fridge. 'We'll give it a try but frankly I don't think you stand a chance. So let's have an early lunch.'

His smile nearly split his face in half.

*

It was a difficult tennis match. Perry and Edmund played Mo and Nell with their usual careless bonhomie. Edmund was a man of few words but he seemed garrulous compared with Mo, who assumed that his efforts at conversation could be forgotten on the tennis court. Perry joked his way through several double faults but when it was Mo's serve and they proved unreturnable the jokes gradually died. Even Edmund, who was used to being beaten, was less than amiable. Nell, playing alongside Mo, was embarrassed. They won three straight sets. The balls came over the net predictably enough and were sent back at lightning speed and very unpredictably. In the silence, Hattie and Hester could be heard through the open upstairs window. When Hester began to cry, Nell bit her lip, totally bewildered. She had never seen – or heard – her aunt in tears before and wondered whether she should walk away from the game and go upstairs to her.

Edmund held up his racquet in surrender.

'No more! It's too hot and I'm too weak!' He smiled over the net at Nell and she smiled back gratefully. It was so typical of him to take a solution upon himself. He was completely different from Perry, who appeared so frank and open and yet was not truly honest. Edmund appeared to be a closed book but when he opened a page he was completely truthful. She smiled again, fleetingly, at both of them and resolved to think about them really analytically when she had time. She had set her sights on 'seducing' Perry because she had thought he was the easier target and more fun. But at the back of her mind Edmund always lingered, in spite of the humiliating, long-ago memory of asking him so insouciantly when they were going to get married.

Perry swaggered up to the net alongside his brother. 'We could have whacked the pair of you into the ground!' he asserted, tossing his racquet into the air and catching it as if it were a gun in a Wild West show. Mo just smiled. Nell, who would normally have pretended to swipe at him, said nothing. It was all so embarrassing, Perry finding Mo ensconced at the kitchen sink in Lypiatt Bottom as if he lived there, her own sudden invitation to Mo to join them for the afternoon, the ghastly cut-throat game in the full heat of the June day and then the sound of Hester's sobs coming from the upstairs window . . . What would happen next?

'I'll go and rustle up some lemonade or something,' Edmund said. 'Can you give me a hand, Mo?' He waited until Mo had stacked his racquet against the wire then added, 'And you two – get the chairs out and for God's sake put them under the tree.' Somehow that relegated Nell and Perry to infant status and he and Mo were the adults.

Nell trailed after Perry into the summer house. Indignation was in every line of Perry's back. He waited until they were inside and then rounded on her.

'There's only a year between us – less – and he treats me like that! And in front of that – that –' She waited for him to call Mo something awful and wondered how on earth she would respond. 'That jumped-up twat of a research student – who the hell does he think he is? And as for you, madam!'

He had never spoken to her like that before; she had always been mistress of any situation between them. He took her by the shoulders and shook her, and though he was not as tall as Edmund he was broader and stronger like his father and there was no escape.

Her own anger met his.

'How dare you, Perry! It's been a horrid afternoon, I agree, but none of it is my fault—'

'Who invited the little stinker? And why? To make me jealous? You've been after me since you came home in the spring, my girl – don't think I haven't seen through you! And now this!' He held her rigidly, her feet almost off the ground. 'All right, if you want it so much, here it is!' And he kissed her.

It started roughly but, given time, it might have softened into something else. It might even have saved the awful afternoon from complete chaos. But it was not given time; Mo had made some excuse and run across the garden after them. He was a smaller, more compact version of Perry but he was just as strong and far quicker. His fist caught Perry on the shoulder and Nell found herself released so suddenly that she fell back among the garden chairs and cushions. Perry cursed loudly and turned, holding his shoulder. Mo's next blow caught him on the chin. He staggered back against a pile of paint pots. The noise was deafening. It seemed to bring Mo to his senses; he began to stammer apologies and held out a hand.

Perry cradled his shoulder with one hand, his jaw with the other.

'I was only *kissing* her,' he said plaintively. 'I wasn't about to rape her or anything!'

'No. Of course. I did not mean . . .' Mo left Perry and went to extricate Nell. She slapped him away furiously. He said to her, 'We have an agreement. Everyone is friends. Friends only.'

'Perry is my *cousin*, for God's sake!'

'But we agreed——'

'You and me! We hardly know each other. I've known Perry ever since I was born!'

'That makes it worse.'

'Rubbish!'

'It is not rubbish. You are closely related. And anyway, he was forcing you.'

Perry was up and dusting himself down.

'Like heck,' he said.

Nell turned on him. 'Well, actually, you were. You had me by the shoulders, my feet off the ground——'

Edmund's voice came from outside, low but urgent. 'Ma is right behind me.' He pitched his voice higher. 'What on earth's going on here? Oh, you've knocked over all the paint pots!' He turned and smiled over his shoulder. 'Only the paint pots, Ma, nothing to worry about. Sounded like a bomb attack.'

Hattie arrived at a panting trot and took in the situation at a glance. She almost smiled.

'Darling Perry. Just look at the state of you – off to the bathroom like a good boy and tidy up. And Nell, you'd better come too. You look so hot and dusty. We'll have our drinks in the sitting room with the French doors open. It really is most awfully hot, isn't it? Darling Hester has been talking to me about her mother. Do you remember Dorothy Ryecroft, Nell dear? No, you wouldn't. Such a sweet woman. It upset Hester a little but probably did her good too.' Hattie went on talking in this vein all the way up the lawn, through the kitchen and into the wide hall. Perry grumbled about being treated like a kid; Nell was silent. Behind them, Edmund put a hand on Mo's arm to restrain him from following Nell up the broad staircase. Nell looked down from the landing; Mo was looking up at her as if she were about to disappear for ever. Which, as far as he was concerned, she was. He must realize that this put the absolute kibosh on their so-called friendship.

Perry paused at the bathroom door and said sarcastically, 'I hope you won't mind if I hog the bathroom for the next three hours. I am completely exhausted after apparently raping you!'

He caught her eye and the next moment they were both holding their sides against wild laughter. Then she shoved him into the bathroom and was about to slam the door on him when she had second thoughts. She went through into the small space, pinned him against the washbasin and kissed him. It was meant to be what he would have called a smackerooner, but after giving a surprised grunt he wrapped his arms round her, grunting again at a painful twinge in his shoulder, and kissed her properly and with great affection.

'I didn't mean it, Nellie-belly,' he said. 'I fully intended succumbing to your charms at the next opportunity – which was to be today! That's why I've been in such a mood with Mike whatever his name is. Sorry, love. I'll come over to-morrow and take you into the bluebell woods and do the job properly!'

She spluttered and pushed him off. 'You will do no such thing! We're cousins, remember. It would be incest!'

He spluttered too then held his jaw. 'Oh God. I can't kiss anyone now! That little so-and-so—'

She smiled and turned to go. 'My knight in shining,' she told him over one shoulder. 'And why did you call him Mike?'

'Well . . .' He worked his jaw experimentally. 'I assume that daft name is a shortened version of Michael. His mum doted on him and said –' he spoke in falsetto – '*my little Mikey-kins . . . my little Mo . . .*'

She shut the door on him with some force, then, still smiling, went on to Hattie's bathroom. Sounds came from the bedroom. So Hester was still there. Nell pushed the door and looked through.

Hester looked like Nell had never seen her look before: with her dress in disarray, her beautiful hair all over the place, thankfully hiding her bare breasts, and, worst of all, Uncle Percy, clinging to her like a barnacle to a wreck, kissing her wherever he could.

It was the most horrific sight Nell had ever seen. She moved back sharply and went into Hattie's bathroom. Please God they hadn't seen her.

Seven

Alice walked slowly down the nave of the cathedral towards the stone figure of Edward II. She had insisted on coming alone; Valentine had wanted to come with her and sit at the back of the nave or even in the Lady chapel but she knew she had to be alone and standing close to the murdered king.

It was a glorious day, and after the heat of the dusty old city the shadows of the lofty nave struck cold on Alice's bare arms. She chose a pillar coloured by the light from the stained-glass windows and leaned into the purple and red reflected on the stone. It crimsoned the back of her hand; she looked down and thought that if she had worn a cardigan it would have looked like blood trickling from beneath her sleeve. She smiled, imagining what Nell would have to say about such whimsy. Nell called Alice's little peculiarities 'whimsies'. It was the only way she could accept them. Only Doffie and Valentine knew without any doubt that there were occasions – rare ones – when Alice could talk to Gramps and Gran. Even Hattie thought it could be explained by using words such as 'projections'. Once, long ago, when Hattie had lost her baby girl and the world became a dark and cruel place, she had burst out almost resentfully, 'They brought me up, Alice! D'you think if they're drifting around as ghosts they wouldn't talk to me and offer me some comfort?'

Alice could offer no comfort herself, no explanations. As a child she had spoken often to God, begging him to spare her loved ones from Hitler's bombs, and then, out of the blue, when God had seemed to desert her, Gramps had spoken to her in her head. He had been sympathetic, but cross with her too. He gave her no advice; he pointed out that free will and intervention were opposite poles; she had the one so she must forfeit the other. He could not even reassure her about the future because that was completely in her own hands. Yet . . . he had helped. His presence had helped. And she had continued to seek him out, though not always successfully. She remembered the wonderful time when she had been conscious that Gran was with him. They were together. With all their imperfections mixed up together like a good strong tasty nourishing heavenly stew . . . even better than the stews Gran used to cook up from such unlikely ingredients as sheep's heads, pigs' trotters or lambs' tails.

Alice smiled and lifted her hand so that the reflected colours crept up her arm to the inside of her elbow. That morning, another Saturday, they had gone to see young Mr Venables, the solicitor, who had received a letter from Joe that was in effect a reply to their letter making clear their plans for the Pumpkin Coach and its land. Although they had written to him directly, beginning their letter with 'Dear Joe' and ending with 'Kindest regards from us both', he had chosen to write back to Mr Venables. It was a rebuff; no doubt about that. Val had tried to pass it off, saying, 'He'll want our signatures in blood at this rate!' And here she was with what looked like a bloodstained arm, standing by an effigy of the infamous king who had been murdered at Berkeley Castle, waiting for a message from Gramps or Gran or even God. It was all crazy; especially when it was about a sixty-year-old sleeper coach standing on rusted rails in the middle of a forest and valued at two hundred and fifty pounds. But Alice knew she had to do it this way; even Mum and Dad, Hester and Hattie, Val himself, expected it of her. If nothing happened this afternoon they would be thrown into disarray. This was a Pettiford project and it needed the blessing of Station Master Will Pettiford and his wife Patience.

So Alice waited.

After Perry had taken Nell and Mo back to Lypiatt Bottom, Edmund joined his mother in the sitting room where she was in a state of collapse in front of the open French doors. He sat opposite her on the piano stool and very gently played a few bars of the *Moonlight Sonata* with one hand.

'Darling, please don't.' Hattie was gazing sightlessly down the garden and did not turn to look at her elder son. 'You know very well it makes me cry.'

'Perhaps that's what I intended.' But he stopped and leaned his elbows on his knees. 'I want to sound you out about something and I want you to be all soft and squidgy.'

She looked at him properly now. She was smiling. 'You remind me of the days when I was crazy, Edmund. I'm still a bit crazy but nothing like then.' Her smile widened. 'All right, I think I'm squidgy enough. What is it?'

He considered his approach, then drew a breath and came straight out with it. 'I want to change my name, Ma.'

'You think I should have chosen something more original? Like Perry?'

'Lord, no! Everyone thinks he's really called Peregrine.'

'Only because you introduce him as such! You're very good at the innocent mistake, sweetheart. A bit like your father.'

Edmund snorted with laughter. Percy was not innocent ever; and he rarely made mistakes.

'Actually it's because of Dad that I want to change my name. I don't feel like him in any way whatsoever. I've been conscious of it for years. When I was twelve I went so far as to calculate the time between your wedding and my birth. I was quite disappointed to discover I was legitimate!'

Hattie was unshockable but she still protested at this.

He leaned forward and put his long fingers over her mouth. 'You admit you used to be crazy. That would have been round about your crazy period. During and just after the war.' He gave his small smile. 'It wouldn't have worried me, Ma. Not a bit.'

'No?' There was a small pause as if Hattie might be thinking this over.

Edmund did not wait. He blurted, 'I'd like to be a Pettiford, Ma. Your name. D'you realize that, after Ted, the name will go? We can't let that happen.' His smile grew. 'Close your mouth, Ma. It's not that shocking. But I thought I should sound you out in case Dad got the hump about it.'

Hattie closed her mouth obediently but continued to stare at him in disbelief.

'Shall I play some more of the *Moonlight*?' he asked. 'With both hands?'

'No!' She spoke sharply. 'I don't feel squidgy now and I don't want to feel squidgy if you don't mind.' He looked surprised and she swept on. 'In case Dad got the hump? In *case* Dad got the hump? You think he will enjoy his eldest son casting him off like an old glove? He's seventy-eight, Edmund! He can't take knocks like this.'

Edmund said calmly, 'You think I should wait until he is dead?'

'It's not funny!'

'But you are, Ma. Casting him off like an old glove, forsooth!'

'All right. Melodrama. Yes. But you understand what I mean, surely?'

'Yes. I understand perfectly. So I must wait until he is dead. And I am not intending that to be comic.'

Hattie made to get up, then sank back. Tears filled her eyes. 'What has made you think that Westbrook is not the name for you?'

'Oh Ma.' Edmund sighed. 'It's more positive than that. I'll keep Westbrook if it means so much to you. How does Edmund Westbrook Pettiford sound?'

Hattie managed an upside-down smile. 'A mouthful,' she said.

He looked at her. 'Let's drop it for now. I simply thought ... well, actually I thought you might be pleased. And I thought Ted and Doffie would be pleased too.' Hattie made a sound in her throat. He added quickly, 'It doesn't matter, Ma. But if ever I get a partnership in the firm, I would like Pettiford to be on the headed notepaper.'

He laughed to show her it was all a bit of a joke but as she watched him lope off to the tennis court to unhook the net and drag the gritted surface, she knew it was no joke. He would probably talk to his father quite soon; perhaps this evening. Perhaps he would hear him through the open window and go up any moment now and find him with Hester. Just as Nell had done. From the look on the girl's face, Percy and Hester must have been in rather compromising positions. Nell had looked . . . sick.

Hattie sighed and resumed her study of the garden. It had been quite an afternoon, what with Hester's tearful confidence and Percy's unexpected and enthusiastic re-action to Hattie's request to 'be nice to Hester'. Well, if anything was happening right now upstairs, she had only herself to blame.

Nell had wanted so much for Edmund to drive them home that she had nearly burst with disappointment when he had thrown the car keys at Perry and disappeared into his room. Yet she could not have talked to him about anything that had happened that afternoon, least of all finding his father in a clinch with his aunt Hester. And Hester, who would have been the obvious confidante – objective yet sympathetic – was also 'out of the frame', as Perry would put it.

She sat by Perry in the front and tried to respond to his banter. His attitude towards their particular part in the event-ful afternoon was to dramatize it out of all recognition. First of all it became a French farce, then a story from the Knights of the Round Table.

'Mo can be Galahad and I'll be Arthur. You can be Guinevere.'

'Do shut up about it, Perry. You're embarrassing me.' She was not really embarrassed but Perry did not know about the scrimmage in the cupboard under the stairs. She half turned in her seat. 'Mo, where can we drop you?'

Mo said, 'At your house. If that is all right.'

Perry said, 'Not many girls have a couple of blokes fighting over them. Not these days anyway. I think you should be flattered.'

Nell swivelled her eyes at him disgustedly then said to Mo, 'My parents will be back soon and I want to cook the meal. So it might be better if we dropped you now.'

Perry said, 'She wants to split us up, old man. In case we start pawing the ground again. Though I have to remind you that it was not me who was pawing the ground—'

'Will you shut *up*, Perry!'

Mo said, 'It is not worth dropping me off, Nell. I have lodgings nearby. I can walk there.'

Nell frowned. Surely he wasn't lodging with someone in the village? He'd started off in a disused signal box or something. Then her godmother, Helena, had offered him a room but he had found somewhere else. And now, somewhere else again.

Deciding not to ask him any more questions, she slumped in her seat and tried to ignore Perry and his absurdities. They reached the front door of the house and she fetched the key from beneath the second flower pot and opened up. Mo was so close behind her he was almost treading on her heels; Perry slammed his door and joined them. She went through to the kitchen and opened the back door so that there was a breeze cooling the house; they were still there. She rounded on them.

'Listen, I'm really fed up with this. Both of you go away and leave me to peel some potatoes in peace!'

Perry said, 'Right. We know when we're not wanted, don't we, old man?'

Mo said flatly, 'I'll hang on.' He looked Nell in the eye. 'We have a bargain, do you remember?'

Nell was bewildered; she remembered that Mo was trying to be 'a friend' but had there been some kind of bargain struck that she would give him time to prove himself?

Perry suddenly stopped being flippant and said, 'If you're staying, I'll stay too.'

Nell looked as if she might explode. Mo shrugged. 'Then I will go. Goodbye.' He turned on his heel and was gone.

Perry said, 'What the hell is the matter with him? What sort of bargain have you made with him, Nell? Don't put yourself in his hands, for God's sake, woman. He's obviously a complete nutcase.'

'Look, Perry. Thanks for the lift. I really do need to be by myself for a bit. Sorry and all that. I'll phone you. Tomorrow probably. After church.'

She almost pushed him out of the front door. Then she went back to the kitchen, turned on the tap over the sink and held her wrists beneath the water. It was all too much. Too much.

When she looked out of the kitchen window and saw Mo walking round Mrs Mearment's garden with Mrs Mearment on his arm, she left the tap running, ran her wet hands through her red hair so that it stood on end and marched to the fence.

'Are you doing this deliberately?' she asked as they stood admiring a particularly beautiful peony.

Mrs Mearment beamed across the fence. 'Oh, Nell! Isn't this marvellous? When this young man came to see me this morning and told me he was your friend, I was delighted to offer him my spare room! Since Bert died it's been lonely, you know. And lodgers . . . well, you never quite know where you are with them. And then Mr Checkers turned up like an answer to a prayer! The fact that he knows dear Doffie and Ted – what could be a better recommendation?'

She would have gone on except that Nell made a sound halfway between a laugh and a sob.

Mo said, 'You did not give me a chance to tell you about finding digs with Mrs Mearment—'

'He knows about the coats I made during the war. From

car rugs!' Mrs Mearment turned. 'I don't know what else Doffie has told you, my dear. We had some high old times then. Getting in the hay . . . I was a dab hand with a pitchfork, and Doffie could shin up a tree and pick the apples from the top!'

Mo said, 'If I am going to learn how to be a good friend, then I need to see you fairly often.'

Mrs Mearment said, 'I've got some lovely snaps – albums of them. Nell when she was a baby. Alice in her bridesmaid's dress when Hattie got married. I made the dress and though I say it myself it was beautiful.'

'I won't be a nuisance, Nell. I promise.'

Mrs Mearment's smile spread. 'I want you to feel it's your home, Mr Checkers. If Nell has told you all about me and my little foibles then you're practically one of the family already!'

'That is most kind, Mrs Mearment.' He smiled at her and patted the back of her hand as it lay on his arm. Then he looked at Nell again. 'You won't mind, will you, Nell? Mrs Mearment does need some help with the garden. I'm not certain about being one of the family but I do feel I am among friends. At last.'

Nell made some sounds, indistinguishable from Mrs Mearment's vociferous reassurances, then announced she was busy and left them to it. But as she peeled potatoes and washed a lettuce, she began to think more clearly and was quite certain she had never mentioned her mother's brides-maid's dress or the now-famous jackets that Mrs Mearment had made for nearly everyone in the village from a consign-ment of car rugs issued by the air raid wardens. She knew that Hattie had inherited old Gran Pettiford's second sight when it came to forecasting pregnancies; she knew that her own mother could get in contact with 'the other side'. Surely Mo Checkers could not see into the past? She shivered; it was quite horrible. There seemed to be no escape from him.

Alice almost gave up. It had gone six o'clock and she was conscious that Val had entered by the west door and was sitting quietly at the back of the nave waiting for her. She could not concentrate, knowing he was there. And in any case the intense efforts of the last two hours had not helped. She closed her eyes and drew a deep slow breath and spoke inside her head. 'All right, Gramps. I know exactly what you are saying. It's up to us. And of course you are quite right. I simply needed you . . . not for advice or anything like that. Just to know that you are still with me.' And his voice came back so clearly, just as she remembered it from over forty years ago. He said the same words too. 'There's a good girl.'

She waited for something else but there was nothing and she knew she should wait no longer. As she began to walk back down the aisle through the bands of coloured light, over the uneven stones and tombs, past the enormous pillars that soared to support the fan-vaulted ceiling, Val stood up and came to meet her. She went right up to him, encircled him with her arms and put her face against his.

He said, 'I take it he is here?'

'Not now. But he was.'

'And?'

'We're all right. We're doing the right thing.'

They walked out into the evening sunshine. The contrast between the empty, cavernous cathedral and the busy close outside, full of people meandering home from the shops, or sitting beneath the trees, was almost shocking.

Val said, 'Thank God for that.'

'What?'

'His blessing. The awful thing is, my darling, we would probably have done it anyway.'

'Oh, he knows that.' She held Val's arm and looked up at him anxiously. 'He doesn't ever give a blessing or anything like that. I . . . simply know.'

'What did he say? No! Don't tell me. It's between you and him.'

She hugged his arm and nodded. 'Thank you, Val. And thank you for believing me. When it started all those years ago – when he spoke to me first of all and the organist heard me . . . you thought I was going mad.'

He smiled. 'I did. But I hope you didn't miss the point, Allie. The point was that, mad or sane, I went on loving you.'

She smiled mistily. 'And I loved you all the time too and did not know it. Not until Joe set me free.'

He paused and turned to face her, his fine sandy brows raised questioningly. 'You have never put it like that before. I knew you had said goodbye. I thought it was . . . awful. For both of you.'

'It was an enormous . . . happening. Full of awe. But not awful in the sense of being frightful or terrible. I had been in thrall to Joe. We went to the Pumpkin Coach and it worked its magic.'

'As it did for us?'

She looked at him very seriously. 'Not in the same way, Val. When you and I swam together in the pool, we became one. I didn't know it and – whatever you say now – I don't think you did either. It was only looking back, after we lost that first baby, that we began to realize . . .'

'I knew,' he said stubbornly. 'I had known for ages. Nothing to do with the Pumpkin Coach and swimming in the pool.'

She smiled. 'Well, perhaps I knew too but could not see it because of Joe.' She pulled gently on his arm and they began to walk again. 'I was so worried about Joe. I loved him – yes, I did love him, Val – but I was terrified for him too. It seemed to me at times that he was too good for this world. When he went off to do his national service, I thought he would die. It was such an anticlimax when he caught venereal disease from a prostitute!' She shook her head. 'You saved me from all that despair, my darling. But I thought that the ties between Joe and me were still there, underneath our carefully cultivated friendship. And then he told me about his emergency teacher-training course and his wife being such a splendid nurse and . . . and he set me free!' She looked at a pair of lovers beneath one of the trees. 'I thought you knew this, Val.'

'I never thought of you being in thrall before. You were both so young and happy and carefree. Being "in thrall" conjures up a kind of Svengali relationship.'

She gave a gurgling laugh. 'You're right but I cannot think of another way to explain that day in the forest. I came out of somewhere dark and into somewhere light.' She looked up into the narrow, clever face of the man who had rescued her. 'I love you, Valentine Ryecroft,' she said simply.

Eight

For two weeks, past the longest day and almost to the end of the month, Alice Ryecroft spent a lot of time with her parents, Ted and Doffie Pettiford. She knew very well that Mrs Mearment's lodger was spending a lot of time with Nell. Nell informed her that she was actually teaching him something. When Alice enquired further, Nell said briefly, 'The subject is friendship. He has no idea how to be a friend.' This did not entirely reassure Alice but when she mentioned it to Val the next weekend, he said easily, 'I think it's all right, Allie. She's been away from home for a long time now. She can cope with this.' So Alice tried to forget it.

She bought an old-fashioned shorthand notebook and minuted all the discussions in her parents' flat. It was strange being back there again day after day; Alice had worked in Bishop Hooper's Mansions when the building had been leased by the Great Western Railway, and now she was back there on a new railway project. And taking shorthand notes then typing them up had been one of her many former jobs. In one way it came naturally, in another it felt odd.

Sometimes they were joined by an old colleague of Ted's, Dugdale Marsden, who was a genius with figures. Once Hattie and Percy joined them. Percy's eyes became very crossed indeed when he heard Duggie's estimates of costs, but Hattie said, 'You know very well that whatever we've got is yours. Ted and Val . . . my family. Could I deny them anything?' She looked at Percy and he said reluctantly, 'Of course not, my dear.' Hester was invited too but was busy with the end-of-term concert. She said much the same thing as

Hattie but without the passion; rather as if she no longer cared.

When Valentine was home for the weekend, he and Ted went to the forest together and spoke to some of the Gavelkind, who represented the dwindling mining community. One of the old Freeminers could remember his father talking about Will and Patience Pettiford. 'Will Pettiford did come to the court at Speech House and got a lease for a bit of land on the old Severn and Wye. One of the directors did want to stable a coach there. Hanky-panky, old Will Pettiford said. Just by one of the old pools down there, that's where it be. What were it called? . . . Bracewell's Pool. That were the name of the director, I remember. Sir something-or-other Bracewell. I reckon Will's daughter had more hanky-panky than old Bracewell did, though, cos he were killed in the first war.'

Ted interrupted quickly. 'Did you say the old Severn and Wye?'

'Coulda bin. Lost track of them old lines now, 'aven't they?'

Ted reported back to the 'committee', as they called themselves.

'If it *did* happen to be the old Severn and Wye, it would be going somewhere. We know it comes from Leadon. Thought it was just a spur to serve one of the open-cast collieries. But if it was going on . . . if it joined Leadon with, say, Coleford, there's just a chance we could do something really commercial.'

Val said, 'I'll get some maps.'

Alice said nothing. She had been in charge of the filing after Joe Adair left the office. In those days the cellars had been packed full of old files and maps. She and Joe had had to sort through innumerable folders, until Joe had labelled them all clearly. She thought everything might have been destroyed when the offices were made into flats. Next week, when Val was in London, she could have a good look down there. Perhaps her father would help her? But first she would investigate on her own. If the cellars had simply been abandoned, she might even remember in what order she and Joe had stacked the redundant stuff.

Doffie picked up the typewritten copy of their recent discussions.

'This is what we've got to do: sort out planning with the Department of the Environment. Make a copy of every letter to the Freeminers. There's still a working mine to the west of the Pumpkin Coach – we could approach them, outline our advanced planning for an extension to Coleford—'

'Hold your horses, our Doffie!' Ted laughed. 'It's more than likely that the line from Leadon went nowhere – that would be why Sir Richard chose it as a site for a love nest!'

'Even so . . .' Val smiled at Doffie; he had been wooing her good opinion for so long now it came as a matter of habit to stand by her in the smallest of arguments. 'Even so, we should let them know of our plans. Courtesy. Also it may elicit some information. There just might be someone there who had a grandfather who knew about the coach and Richard Bracewell etc.'

'We're talking over sixty years ago, Val.' His son-in-law was going a bit far if he expected yet another octogenarian to pop up with information from before 1914.

Duggie Marsden, poring over a column of figures at one end of the kitchen table, looked up. 'We might strike lucky again, Ted. And wasn't it Will and Patience Pettiford who actually dealt with Richard Bracewell? It all happened not that long ago if you look at it that way.'

Ted said, 'Trust you to stick up for Doffie! Just because you saved her from a fate worse than death!'

Duggie went back to his figures. He had never been able to make a joke of that terrible time when Doffie had been a victim of Reggie Ryecroft's madness and Duggie had saved her with a well-aimed blow from a frying pan.

He cleared his throat. 'It's impossible to give you any decent figures until I have talked to the people at British Rail. Cardiff oversees the forest area. We shall no doubt require an LRO—'

'Which is?' Alice asked, pen poised over her notes.

'A Light Railway Order. Though we have leased the ground, the track bed and any other remains – ballast, sleepers, maybe even rails – will be owned by them. Obviously planning permission must be obtained from the DoE – Department of the Environment, Alice. And then . . . we'll need volunteers. Enthusiasts who will clear the foliage, take up old track.' He looked up again. 'We're too old. Sorry, Ted, but that's the size of it.'

Ted pursed his mouth in a way that showed he did not necessarily agree but was willing to let the remark go for the time being.

'There's me,' Val said.

'And me,' said Alice.

'The boys will help – Edmund and Perry,' Doffie put in.

Duggie said, 'We need thirty to forty able-bodied men and women every weekend for at least two months. After that they can have a rest while new track is laid. And that means modern machinery.'

'And too much money,' Val objected. 'We've got to use most of our capital to buy a loco and stock.'

'All right, let me tell you what we've got so far.' Duggie held up a sheet of paper. 'You and Alice are suggesting mortgaging your house, and putting in Dorothy's money.' Dorothy Ryecroft, Val's mother, had unexpectedly left them a modest nest egg, and there had been Reggie's ill-gotten gains too. 'Hattie and Percy have not actually specified an amount but if they intend to borrow on Leckhampton House I would expect any figure up to fifty thousand pounds. That would depend on old Mrs Westbrook's permission, of course. Hester, who is far more businesslike, mentioned twenty thousand pounds.' He glanced at Val. 'How she has managed to save so much with all her holidays abroad and her expensive tastes . . .'

'Richard Tibbolt has been more than generous,' Val said briefly.

Duggie flushed slightly. 'Sorry. None of my business.

Finally, I am able to invest my house and my father's money—'

Doffie said quietly, 'Not all of it, Duggie. It's too risky.' Old Mr Marsden had been the original owner of the biggest department store in Gloucester.

'I've no one to leave it to,' Duggie said defiantly. 'I've done nothing with my life. To own a railway . . . That would be something.'

Val clapped him on the shoulder. Duggie had always been in love with Doffie Pettiford and still was, though they were both in their seventies. Everyone in the room knew it.

'Good for you, Duggie! When we go public you shall be our chairman. Is that a unanimous vote?'

Everyone cheered, and at that moment there was a knock on the kitchen door and Nell entered, closely followed by the 'new boy' with the unlikely name of Mo Checkers. Doffie enfolded her granddaughter in an enormous hug and Ted went so far as to clap Mo on the shoulder. Alice and Val looked on cautiously. Nell was laughing and seemed happy; that was something. She had been tetchy since April when she had come home from college.

Nell demanded to know 'the state of play' and was enlightened by her father in four terse sentences. 'We need to know where the track comes from and where it goes to. We need to see the Department of the Environment about planning permission. Also the man in charge at Cardiff rail headquarters about a light railway order. Finally, we need volunteer manpower to clear away the under- and overgrowth.'

Nell gave a sunny smile. 'Thank you, Dad, always succinct. Well, Mo and I will discover where the track comes from and goes to. I've got my bike and Mo has borrowed Mrs Mearment's – can you imagine it? Talk about sitting up and begging! Anyway, we'll go tomorrow, early. Yes, Mum, I know it's church but God will understand just this once. So that's one thing dealt with. Dad, you'll have to do the Cardiff thing because you're still working and know all the ins and outs. Uncle Duggie – Department of the Environment because he's the world's best diplomat. And Grandad Ted, you'll have to start a recruitment drive.'

Mo Checkers was grinning too. He said, 'You should put an announcement in the paper that you are forming a preservation society and need volunteers. You will have a queue outside this place! Everyone is interested in steam now that it has gone. It is human nature!'

Nell smiled congratulations. He was learning fast.

Doffie grinned. 'Well, you two have got us sorted out really well. I'll make tea. Nell, will you pop up to the shop and get some doughnuts or something?'

Val said, 'Allie and I will do that. Nell and Mo can sit down and draft the announcement for the *Citizen*.'

Duggie supplied paper and a pencil and moved over to the cooker to help Doffie. Alice and Val went off for the doughnuts. Ted looked unseeingly through the oriel window.

'We'll have to employ people . . . people with training and skills. So we must pay them. We need some of the men from the Swindon workshops. Men who are capable of rebuilding locomotives.'

Duggie said, 'Val would know about that. He could contact one of the old foremen. Put it to him.'

Ted nodded. 'But we need an engineer. Someone to take charge.'

Doffie said, 'Put the cups on this tray, Duggie. Mo, could you just move those papers—'

Mo said, 'I could do it.'

'Yes, of course you can, dear. Put them over here.'

'I mean, I could do it. My degree is in civil engineering. And this year I am researching metal fatigue in connection with air travel. I am working on an old prop two-seater at Staverton airfield. A local light-engineering works is offering stress facilities and any other back-up I might need. If I supplied drawings and specifications they could fabricate pistons or whatever was needed.' He looked round at the others; he had their complete attention. 'I could *do* it!' he insisted.

There was an awestruck silence then Ted said, 'My God.'

Nell squeaked, 'You never told me! Why didn't you tell me?'

'I didn't think it would count as – as conversation.'

'You idiot!' But she was smiling.

Doffie moved the papers herself and set the tray down in their place. 'When Alice hears this she will say that Gramps sent you,' she commented.

Duggie brought the teapot over. 'And she will be absolutely and incontrovertibly correct!'

Everyone laughed and relaxed, then started to talk at the same time. When Val and Alice came in it was like Babel. Eventually they grasped that by a stroke of sheer good luck the rather odd young man who seemed unable to leave their daughter's side had been sent to solve all their problems. So they had money, they had the beginnings of a strategy and now they had technical knowledge. Alice said predictably, 'Mo, I really think Nell's great-grandfather has arranged this. It's just too much of a coincidence.' Everyone laughed and she looked round, bewildered.

They drank tea and ate doughnuts in a state of near-euphoria and then it was time to come back to earth. Duggie got into his vintage car and started to chug back home to Hucclecote, then changed his mind at the top of the Pitch and turned down Denmark Road and into Worcester Street. He parked near Bishop Hooper's monument and made his way to the close and Hester's house. She should be acquainted with the events of the afternoon; after all, she was willing to invest quite a lot of money in this scheme of theirs.

Val and Alice offered to put Nell's bicycle and Mrs Mearment's 'penny-farthing' into the boot and drive Nell and Mo back to Lypiatt Bottom, but the two youngsters opted to cycle. 'It will be good training for pedalling all the way out to the forest tomorrow,' Nell explained rather deviously.

Val was very quiet as he took the car through the lanes. Alice glanced sideways and said, 'Anticlimax?'

'Perhaps.' He took his left hand off the steering wheel and

touched her knee. 'We could be heading for bankruptcy, Allie. You do realize that?'

'If we don't have a go we shall regret it,' Alice said positively. 'You will get more and more discouraged . . . What is happening with our transport system will – will *grind you down*. I couldn't bear that. These last three months you – you've come alive again, Val.'

He grinned. They drove on for a while in silence. Then he said, 'All right, neither of us minds too much about risking being broke. And Nell will be self-supporting so there are no worries there. But there is something else, my love. Might we be resurrecting ghosts that we laid to rest twenty-five years ago?'

She smiled at him. 'Oh Val, I do love you. You cannot really believe that, otherwise you would not have gone this far with the scheme.' She sighed. 'I've thought a lot about it. Of course I have. And do you know, I rather think that Joe is dead.'

He was startled; that possibility had not occurred to him. 'Why think that? He has written to negotiate the sale . . . everything.'

'We haven't seen his signature on anything, Val. It is all too impersonal. Joe was open and direct. He would have dealt with us himself, not through solicitors. I think his widow is settling his affairs. And he's talked about the Pumpkin Coach and the Pettifords. And you. Especially you. That is why all the correspondence has been for you.'

Val drove for a while, thinking. At last he nodded. 'I see what you mean. Does that make it more or less painful for you?'

'It's not painful. Really.' They turned at the village pump and bucketed down the lane. 'But we've always known that the coach is still there – Hester has kept us posted. And just to leave it there seems wrong. Joe and his mother were just left. It's not good to do that. After all, she was Richard Bracewell's daughter and Joe was his grandson.' The car crunched over the gravel and stopped opposite the back door of the house. Alice got out and leaned on the roof. 'If we can use it, make something of it, Val . . . that would form the circle. Nothing is ever finished but to complete a circle is the nearest we can come. Do you understand what I mean?'

He stared over the car at her. She had never been beautiful like her mother; she was pale rather than blond and her eyes were blue rather than violet. Sometimes, especially when she was being fey, he was almost frightened for her. She was too ethereal; too other-worldly. And he knew that life without her would be a void.

He said hoarsely, 'Sometimes you remind me of an angel, Allie.'

She grinned. 'All right, all right. I'm being pi and insufferable, you don't have to rub it in. All I wanted to say was that there are no resurrections going on. Just a few things that are obsolete. And if we could recycle them—'

He was round the car and had taken her in his arms. He did not kiss her; he held her to him as if he expected someone to kidnap her. He buried his face in her neck and inhaled the scent of her hair and warm skin. At last the moment of terror receded and he loosened his hold, his hands trembling.

She said quietly, 'It's all right, my darling. If it works it will be there for a long, long time. Our Pumpkin Line. Our very own Pumpkin Line.'

He tried to smile down at her. 'But . . . some time . . . midnight will come,' he said. 'Don't you remember telling me that we could never stay there past midnight because that was when the Cinderella magic disappeared?'

'Midnight can be postponed indefinitely.' She held his face and kissed his forehead, then the bridge of his nose. 'We shall be up and running long before then.'

'Who says so?' He waited until her lips reached his. He held her close again. Then he whispered, 'What a silly question. It was Gramps, wasn't it?'

She kissed him again.

Nine

Duggie Marsden sat at the back of the big hall of Whitsom Hall School for Girls and glanced sideways at the other relatives. There were grandparents as well as parents; he did not need to feel like a sore thumb. But he did.

The end-of-year concert was well under way. There had been tap dancers from the Lower Third; a spoof illusionist from the Upper Fourth; countless singers from young to old, a violinist who was excruciating and another who was very good. Hester had just introduced the school orchestra and there was a lot of shuffling going on as music stands and chairs were assembled on the stage. She came to the front and told the audience that the orchestra had been asked to play at a musical event in Gloucester Cathedral in September. This was a great honour and she was sure everyone would like to congratulate them in the usual way. She smiled and everyone clapped. Duggie suddenly realized that the gaggle of schoolgirls comprising the front of the audience were applauding Hester. They stared up at her adoringly. It had never occurred to him that she might be a popular teacher.

She stood there, making sure the applause lasted until the final music stand had been sited. She was wearing a dusky-red silk dress with some kind of crossover bodice arrangement and tiny cap sleeves. Duggie found himself clapping on; he was so used to Hester but now he saw her differently. She was very beautiful. And, apparently, very unhappy.

He had arrived at her small house in the close three hours

before. At first he had thought she wasn't in. He rang the bell, then knocked, and was walking away when a window opened upstairs and a voice called, 'Who is it?'

He had called back and she had said, 'Oh,' in a tone of disappointment. Then she had added, 'I'm in the bath. Wait and I'll be down.'

When the door opened she was half behind it and ushered him past her urgently. She was wearing a snowy-white bathrobe and her hair was coiled into a huge knot on top of her head. 'Don't want the whole world knocking on the door,' she said, brusquely and illogically. 'I take it you've come to report on the annual general meeting.' She almost pushed him down to the kitchen. 'I've got about half an hour and that is definitely all! If you remember, I couldn't come to the meeting because it's the school concert tonight. We had a dress rehearsal all afternoon and it was absolutely dreadful.'

He tried to apologize but she wouldn't listen. 'I must go and dress. Then I have to eat something, otherwise I shall pass out on stage. Why I let myself be talked into taking part in this Fred Karno circus production, heaven only knows!'

She had whirled away and taken the stairs two at a time. He could hear her above him bumping furiously around her bedroom. He had, of course, completely forgotten about the school concert. He thought mutinously that she never came to any of the 'meetings' anyway.

There was an extra-loud bump and then a silence, then something that sounded suspiciously like a sob. Duggie gnawed his lower lip and wondered what to do, and wished he hadn't come in the first place. His ears sang with listening; at last the bumping, subdued and slower, began again. He breathed deeply and looked round the neat kitchen. It reminded him of his own place, so neat it was almost sterile.

After a while he got up, filled the kettle and plugged it in. Then he looked into the fridge and saw salad and cheese. By the time Hester reappeared, dressed in the pink – or plum-coloured, or crushed-strawberry – silk dress, he had assembled a little meal on the kitchen table and was making a pot of tea.

She said, 'Oh Duggie.'

And he said, 'I do it for myself so it's no problem.'

'You must have some with me.'

'I will if I can. Alice and Val brought us all doughnuts. Come on, get started.'

She helped herself to lettuce and cucumber and said slowly, as if remembering things from the past, 'Alice . . . Val.' She looked up and forced a smile. 'Alice was my best friend. And I think I might have been in love with Val. Can you believe that? My own brother!'

He had always known that, of course, and said calmly, 'It happens. After all, it is one's first experience of the opposite sex. Don't be unhappy about it.'

'No. I'm not unhappy about that. At least not only that.' She munched her way through some salad then said briefly, 'I've finished with Tibbolt. I expect you gleaned that from Hattie.'

'Well, she did mention something about it.' Hattie had been full of it.

'Did she also mention that she has primed Percy to offer consolation?'

'Well . . .'

'And what about the fact that I grabbed at it! As if he were a lifebelt and I were shipwrecked!'

Duggie decided the time had come to be brutally honest. 'Her exact words were, "They both enjoyed themselves enormously." And if you want to hear the rest of it, Alice said, "Good for Hester!" And Val said, "You wouldn't be so chirpy about it if Percy decided to leave you!" And Ted described Percy in a very unfavourable way.'

'Oh dear Uncle Ted. I always wanted him to be my father and I think . . . Anyway, Duggie, I behaved like a tramp and I rather think Nell saw me! And I just hate myself and so does everyone else. No one has ever thought tuppence about me . . . Well, maybe Val. And Alice, of course. And darling Uncle

Ted. And Mother . . . oh Duggie, I miss Mother so much . . . so very much.'

Duggie could see she was about to break down completely, and if she had to be on stage at seven o'clock that was not a good idea.

He said quickly, 'Look. Have a piece of bread and butter and drink some tea and I will tell you all about the meeting. Then we can both have another cup of tea and you can take over. If you want to.'

'I don't. I've said all I'm going to say. Except that even the girls at school must hate me otherwise Sally Gold wouldn't have trapped me into doing this ghastly mistress-of-ceremonies thing!'

'All right. That's first on your agenda. First on mine is that we've made a sort of programme of what we have to do. And . . .' He began to unfold the amazing offer from Mo Checkers. He watched her carefully. She ate the bread and butter and nibbled some cheese and held her cup in two hands so that the steam soothed her tense facial muscles.

At the end he said, 'What do you think of that?'

'Too much of a coincidence.' She sipped judiciously. 'He's obviously besotted with Nell and he's oozing into the family like – like—'

'Golden syrup?'

'The mud in Bracewell's Pool.' She looked woebegone. 'I made Tib swim there again, you know, Duggie. He didn't want to any more. Said he'd always hated it and it wasn't magical at all. But it is and that is why he's left me.'

'Surely if it were magical he would have stayed?'

'I insisted on spending the night there. We've never done that before because after midnight the magic disappears, like in the Cinderella story. And we stayed and he's gone. That proves it.'

'For someone who is sceptical to the point of cynicism, that is the most ridiculous thing I've heard for a long time. Richard Tibbolt is crazy about you, Hester. Phone him – go and see him – apologize—'

'Never, never, never! That is not the kind of relationship we have!'

'You are a dominatrix?'

'Not – not like that. No. But I am in control. Always.' She sniffled suddenly. 'The truth is, I can't risk it, Duggie. I know I'm not a very nice person. I've got a lot of my father in me—'

'Rubbish! You are not a bit like Reggie!'

'Tibbolt is the one person who has loved me and stayed with me on my terms all these years. Ever since I was a student. If he should turn me down, Duggie . . . I couldn't take that.'

'Then just wait. Something will happen. You will find a way.'

'You sound like Alice.'

Duggie looked at her straight. 'I expect you know about Doffie and me. Alice could have been my daughter. So that is a great compliment, Hester.'

Hester, who knew 'everything' yet had understood nothing, said, 'Oh Duggie . . . oh Duggie, I am so sorry.' She put down her cup with a little clatter. 'That's why you have been so sweet to me. Because we are in the same boat. Sort of . . . leftovers.'

Duggie laughed. 'Oh Hester Ryecroft! You are no leftover. You are still young, and very beautiful. You are giving Percy Westbrook a new lease of life and probably frightening Hattie to death. You are a successful teacher in an excellent school. And you are going to be a great success this evening!'

She stared at him. When he started to get up and clear the table she said, 'I'm sorry, Duggie. You are no leftover either. You saved Aunt Doffie from my father. Everyone knows you are a hero. And . . . it looks as though you are going to be chairman of a railway! A railway all of your own!'

He turned on the hot tap and ran water into the modern sink. He said quietly, 'Yes. You're right. Whatever else happens, Hessie, we're going to own a railway!'

Later, as he watched her move confidently around the

stage, ad-libbing small intimate jokes, he wondered what had made him turn back and go to see Hester that afternoon. Alice would probably say it was old Will Pettiford up there keeping an eye on all of them. He thought it might well be because he had never forgotten the horrible clang of the frying pan as it connected with Reggie Ryecroft's head. Perhaps he was due to make some kind of recompense to the Ryecroft family. Or perhaps he was taking Ted's place for Hester. After all, Ted was fully occupied with Doffie . . . beautiful Doffie.

At the end of the concert he clapped until his hands were numb. And when Sally Gold, the head girl elect who had produced the whole show, came forward and hugged Hester, he could have wept. Wept proper tears. Which he hadn't done since Doffie had chosen to marry Ted Pettiford instead of Dugdale Marsden.

The next day, Sunday, dawned pearl-bright, just right for a long cycle ride.

Nell went into the garden, waved across at Mrs Mearment's in case Mo was looking out of his window, and walked through the lower gate into the field that separated them from the bluebell woods. She kept her eyes on the ground for mushrooms and began to pace slowly round the perimeter. She needed to think. It was an intriguing – even splendid – game she was playing with Mo and, true to his 'bargain', he had not once crossed the line from friend to lover. There were times when she met his dark, Asian eyes and quickly looked away, but that made the whole thing more interesting. After all, hadn't she wanted to lose her virginity this summer, as all her friends and colleagues had done over the past four years? Hadn't she intended to seduce poor Perry? And she could have done so easily – still could. Except for this ridiculous 'bargain'.

He was so different. If a seduction took place with Mo Checkers, it would be no summer affair to be ended whenever she was tired of it; she knew that much. Already he was inside her head; hardly five minutes went by without her thinking of him; she wanted to be with him, forcing him to laugh and talk to her and listen to her and just . . . be there. She knew that if she sustained one of their silent exchanges, she would be lost. She would go into his arms and then what would happen? She would become obsessed; she was already halfway there. She would attend no more interviews; she would not be able to leave his side; her degree would mean nothing. She probably would not even go to the ceremony.

She picked four more mushrooms and dropped them into her looped skirt. When she straightened, he was in front of her, his straight black hair standing on end, his T-shirt back to front, bare-footed.

He smiled apologetically. 'You waved and I thought you needed me. Was I wrong?'

She wanted to tell him that no, he wasn't wrong, that she needed him and thought it highly likely she would go on needing him for the rest of her life. Instead she smiled back at him. 'I'm glad to see you. Can you take these? There must be two or three dozen mushrooms. I'm going to cook them for my father's breakfast.'

'What about your mother?' He shovelled the mushrooms from her skirt, taking enormous care not to touch her legs through the thin cotton.

'If she will have them, yes.'

He said, 'She does not eat enough, Nell. She is too thin.'

'It's just the shape she is.' But she frowned anxiously. She knew that her mother went often to the cathedral these days and it frightened her father. Might her – her metaphysical side be sapping her physical strength in some way? She said, 'She's always been thin.'

He began to walk to the back gate of the garden and spoke over his shoulder. 'Not as thin as she is now.'

Her frown deepened. 'How would you know that?'

'Photographs. There is one of her in a dirndl skirt. She was not thin then.'

'I haven't seen that one.'

'Helena Maybury let me look through her album. They

101

went on a trip to Symonds Yat.' He pushed open the gate with his cupped hands and went through. 'There was a crowd of them. Toby Fletcher, Dennis Fluke, Helena, your mother and Joe Adair.' He laughed. 'I am getting the hang of conversation, Nell, don't you think?'

She moved past him slowly. 'I've heard them mention those names . . . You have an excellent memory, Mo.'

'Yes.'

But he appeared to have shot his conversational bolt because he said nothing more until he had put the mushrooms into a colander. And then it was simply, 'See you in an hour then?'

And she too had become monosyllabic. 'Yes,' she said.

It was as if he knew where to go. They left their bikes in the station at Leadon Markham and walked down the lane by the line until they came to an opening in the dense vegetation on their right. Before Nell could call to him that this was the place, he was striking sideways, holding back brambles to make it easier for her to pass. She remembered from her last visit some five years before that it was difficult to get through the undergrowth, but there were places where it fell back and they could search properly.

He was excited about it, taken up with the whole project; no longer concentrating entirely on her or their 'bargain'. She held on to a whippy alder branch and watched while he actually got on his hands and knees and tore at the nettles. She felt almost piqued.

'How did you know when to turn off the path?' she asked.

He did not even glance up. 'Obviously there has to be a spur from the main line. It might not be that one – we could be wrong.'

'Well, we're not. My father found this place first. And he told me to look out for—'

Mo interrupted her with a cry. 'It's here! Nell, come and look! See this – it's ballast. We should find some sleepers somewhere.'

'Dad always said they would have rotted away.' She did not move from the alder.

'Yes, if they were oak – and of course one would expect them to be oak with all these trees around—'

'Some of Nelson's ships were made from Dean oak,' she said.

'But what if they used stone? They were quarrying stone, clearing it like mad to get at the coal and iron. What if it was lying around and . . .' He stopped talking and dug frantically like a dog, then gave another cry. 'Look at this, Nell! My God, it's been practically sculpted. How marvellous – an industrial archaeologist would just love this site!' He looked up and his normally impassive face was split by a grin. 'We're on the right track, Nell! Literally!'

She released the alder and it sprang away and disturbed some birds, who clattered up to the canopy. She said patiently, 'Mo, we *know* there was a permanent way under this leaf mould simply because the Pumpkin Coach is sitting on railway lines and was obviously shunted along them. What we don't know is whether the lines continued on from the coach or whether there were buffers beyond it—'

'Listen, woman! We need to know exactly where in Leadon the track bed starts so that eventually we can relay it in its proper place! We shall have to trace it back the way we've come. Next time we must bring scythes or bill hooks or something to clear—'

'You don't touch anything in the forest without express permission. Either from the Forestry Commission or from the Freeminers.'

He grinned. 'There are ways and means of making footpaths, Nellie! If a man walks along a piece of land one hundred times, he makes a path with his body – no scything. If you and I do it together then it's fifty times. If we bring—'

'Kindly do not call me Nellie.'

He raised surprised brows.

'Look,' she swept on. 'If you want to trace the line inch by inch like this, let me go on and open up the coach. Get out the picnic.'

'All right. It's been a long morning. But we have come here to do a job, Nell.' He did not get up and she almost stamped past him and climbed over an enormous fallen tree trunk to reach the next thicket of fern. Here it was just possible to feel the old metalwork with her left sandal and she shuffled along it, swiping at the flies and brambles, knowing that soon she would emerge into what her mother called the forest cathedral. And then beyond that another barrier before the old permanent way emerged by Bracewell's Pool.

She felt her eyes fill with tears. She had wanted them to come upon the Pumpkin Coach together; she had wanted to see Mo's reaction to the total unexpectedness of it, to the magic of it. She had imagined that what followed would depend on that reaction. If it were the right one then they would do what everyone in her family had always done: they would swim in the pool and they would stop being friends and become lovers. Along the country roads, pedalling gamely to keep up with Mo on his ridiculously old-fashioned bicycle, she had let her imagination run riot. She was more than ready to surrender her virginity; it had become a very important issue. And it would happen today; she had been so sure of it.

And now she was not so sure.

Ten

Two weeks later Percy's mother, old Mrs Westbrook, died in her sleep. Hattie told Alice that it was a wonderful way to go; even so, Hattie herself could not stop crying.

Doffie, feeling helpless, was rubbing Hattie's back. 'I had no idea you were so fond of her, darling.'

'I wasn't. Not at first, anyway. But after I'd won her over – well, when I told her I was pregnant with Edmund – she would have done anything for me. When it turned out that Edmund was a boy . . .' Alice and Doffie exchanged glances but managed not to smile. '. . . she was so proud. D'you remember how Enid used to take Edmund in every night for his cuddle with her? And then darling Perry had his turn. She loved boys. They were going to carry on the Westbrook name for another generation.' Hattie's sobs grew louder and Alice joined her mother to hug the substantial shoulders and murmur comfort as best she could.

'She's missed her hundredth birthday by six weeks! Six little weeks! And she was so longing to get her telegram from the Queen. Percy had set up an interview with the radio people . . . Oh, he is distraught. Absolutely distraught!'

'Hattie, for goodness' sake, let her go! She's had a wonderful life in the bosom of this family you've made here. And she went to sleep last night not knowing she wouldn't wake up—'

Doffie was cut short by Hattie's wails.

'Edmund wants to change his name! That's the thing! Grandma would have hated it – just hated it! He's going to talk to Percy about it and he promised me he wouldn't. But he said this morning that now Grandma could not object surely Dad wouldn't mind.' She looked up at Doffie, tears streaming down her face. 'You understand, Doffie darling, don't you?'

'Not exactly. You're a little incoherent, dearest. Just slow down and tell us what this is all about. Really all about.'

'I've *told* you – anyway you already know. Edmund wants to change his name. Change his *name*, Doffie! He doesn't want to be a Westbrook any longer!'

Doffie looked shocked. She shared a terrifying secret with Hattie and one that could not be spoken of in front of Alice.

'We'll talk about it later, Hattie.' She leaned in close and tried to flash a warning glance. 'Alice, can you go and make a cup of tea and see what Percy is doing? I'll stay quietly here with Hattie.' She turned another meaningful look on her daughter. Alice, used to Hattie's histrionics, nodded once and left the room.

Doffie withdrew from Hattie's chair.

'How *dare* you, Hattie! You were within inches of blurting the whole thing out in front of Alice! She must never know – never ever know! Is that clear?'

'No – yes! Whatever. I wasn't going to refer to – but you and I – we know and now it seems as if Edmund himself suspects! He told me that at the age of twelve he looked up birth and wedding certificates just to check his legitimacy.'

'Well, he wouldn't get far there!'

'No, but he says he doesn't feel like a Westbrook. Which of course he isn't.'

'Lots of us feel we don't really belong to our mundane families. That doesn't mean a thing.' Doffie sat down on the edge of Hattie's bed. 'But if he wants to change his name . . . don't tell me he wants to take on Alice's name. He's always loved her . . . Too much, considering she's only an aunt once removed!'

'No. Not at all. He wants your name.'

'*My* name? Why, for goodness' sake?'

'I don't mean your maiden name, I mean Pettiford. He wants to be the last of the bloody Pettifords!'

Doffie was silent and dumbfounded for a while. Then she smiled.

'Oh Hattie. How marvellous. Gramps would be so – so happy.'

After the funeral Edmund managed to get Nell to himself in the summer house. The paint pots had been stacked neatly again and the chairs were all outside, arranged in the garden for the people who had come back to the house from the church service. It was hot inside and smelled of wood. Nell was still fed up. She had gone for an interview in Birmingham the previous week and had wanted the post badly. She had heard nothing and the new school year was almost upon them. It was nearly three weeks since the Sunday she and Mo had plotted the line from Leadon to Bracewell's Pool and then on for at least a hundred yards, probably further. Mo had kept up his wretched 'conversation' and they had not swum in the pool or made love in the ancient sleeping car. The Pumpkin Coach was going to be an office for the workmen and the committee. There was no magic left in it.

'Well, I'm sorry, Edmund,' Nell said, 'but I simply fail to see what all the fuss is about. Just tell him. Or don't tell him. Just do it. It's not as if you want to be called something amazing like Windsor or Guggenheim or – or Chiang Kai-shek.'

'I know. I didn't think I'd be like this. It all seemed so easy when I first mentioned it to my old lady. She went berserk. Honestly.'

'Well, she's so upset about your gran.'

'God, I told her ages before Gran died.'

'Oh, Hattie's like that. Drama queen.' Nell tried to concentrate on the problem and smiled slightly. 'Listen. Ask Hester to have a word with your father. No, seriously, I mean it. He's got a thing about Hester. He'll listen to her. And she'll just love the idea of you being a Pettiford.'

Val and Hester were also enjoying a tête-à-tête on the far side of the tennis court. Hester was wearing the dusky silk dress she'd worn for the school concert. It had brought her luck that night and she hoped it would continue to do so.

'The thing is, Val, I would prefer to take the train to Bristol. The car is such a nuisance and I shall need to explore some of these so-called squats on foot.'

'I'll come with you. You can't do this by yourself. It could be dangerous.'

'Rubbish. Anyway, I've got a companion so you need not worry.'

'Not Richard Tibbolt? Has he come to heel at last?'

'No. And kindly don't make fun of that situation, Val.'

'I didn't mean to. But I can't believe that the wonderful Tibbolt expects you to explore the seedier parts of Bristol to find his wretched kids.'

'Don't be absurd. He has no idea that I am going to do that.'

'But you will need him to know. Surely you're only doing it to get him back?'

'No! Not any more. I am doing something for him that needs no repayment. In fact, actually, I am doing this for myself. I can see I've been . . . unbearable as far as Tibbolt is concerned. Bossy and – and horrible. If ever he visits me again I want to be someone different.'

'For goodness' sake, Hessie! He fell in love with you as you are.'

'As I was. Then I made myself change – I used him. It was a revenge at first – because he seduced me when I was eighteen. Then it became – well, how our relationship was. A pattern. I need to change again, Val. In some ways I am very like Father. And you can imagine how I feel about that!'

He was silent. He knew exactly how she felt; he feared his father's genes more than anything else. They came to the far end of the court and turned sharply left into a natural maze created by out-of-hand rhododendrons.

Val said heavily, 'So . . . poor old Percy is going with you, is he? Be careful there, Hessie. I don't quite know what is going on and I don't want to know, but Hattie could be . . . difficult.'

She sighed. 'Not Percy. Duggie Marsden, actually.'

'Duggie?' He was surprised. 'You hardly know him, surely?'

'I suppose not. But I rather think he is taking Uncle Ted's place as my surrogate father.' She turned and smiled over her shoulder. 'He is the kindest man I think I have ever met, Val. And that definitely includes you!'

Val thought about it for some time. Then he said, 'But . . . you're still sneaking off round corners with poor old Percy! Don't deny it. I saw you last week—'

'I was comforting him. For God's sake, Val! He'd just told me about his mother dying.'

'All right. But don't tell me you've given him up on Duggie's advice because I simply won't believe you!'

'As a matter of fact, Duggie advised me to enjoy being an old man's darling. He thought it would do me a lot of good and be excellent therapy for Percy and wouldn't hurt Hattie one bit. In fact it might make her nicer to Percy. So there!'

She turned and looked at her brother, pouting coyly. And he looked back at her and saw what Duggie had seen: a very beautiful woman. Being wasted.

He said, 'Just don't get hurt, Hessie. That's all.'

'Right!'

They started to laugh.

Duggie fetched Doffie's cardigan and draped it round her shoulders, then fussed with the button at the neck. It was a little gesture that would not have occurred to Ted and Duggie knew that and made a meal of it.

Doffie sighed. 'Oh Duggie. I wish you could meet someone nice, you are such a caring man.'

'Only for one person.' But he smiled and stepped back. 'Perhaps two. I have taken young Hester under my wing, did you know?'

'She said you'd gone to her school concert.'

'And I'm going with her to Bristol before the new term starts. I'm standing in for Ted, actually. Apparently she was always jealous of Alice for having a father like Ted. We're trying for transference.' His smile turned to a grin. 'She says it is working quite well.' He took Doffie's arm and led her to some garden chairs beneath the crab-apple tree. 'Besides, she needs someone to stage-manage this thing with poor old Percy before it gets out of hand. It started as one of Hattie's jokey challenges to him. He called her bluff. And now he's well and truly hooked.'

'Oh dear.' Doffie glanced at him. It had been comforting to have Duggie's championship all these years; rather disconcerting to discover she had a rival in Hester Ryecroft. 'What about you, Duggie? You're not going to get hooked too, are you?'

He looked at her steadily then said, 'That linen frock suits you, Doffie. The lime green seems to give your hair some auburn shades. Your eyes are as clear as they were when I took you to that tea dance at the Cadena in 1925. I think I could still span your waist with my hands.'

She blushed. 'Yes. All right. You don't have to prove anything. I still wish you could meet someone who would appreciate you – look after you as well as you look after others.' She frowned. 'How do you feel about Enid?'

He turned and followed the direction of Doffie's gaze. Enid, Percy's sister, was carrying a loaded tray among the guests. She was wearing a black silk suit and black straw hat. Her face was marked with tears.

'I don't feel anything really. Poor Enid, always under her mother's thumb – and Hattie's thumb and Percy's thumb. I hope that's all there was to it as far as Percy went. He is a very devoted brother.'

'She is nearer your age than Hester is.'

'For goodness' sake, Doffie! I am a bachelor. I know now that I was born to be a bachelor. I was a disappointment to my parents because I did not go into the business. But I have been blissfully happy on the railway and now . . . well, their money will be put to good use.' He eyed her sternly. 'So stop being sorry for me!'

'All right,' she said peaceably, and resolved to have a word with Enid at the earliest opportunity.

Alice sat at the side of the summer house where the shade was deepest. She leaned her head against the back of her deckchair and closed her eyes and heard Nell advise Edmund to ask Hester to put in a good word with Percy. About what? And why Hester? Against her eyelids Alice could see rainbows of colour; she frowned and opened her eyes, intending to move away hastily. But Nell was already going back to the house with Perry and Edmund was striding off alone.

He met Hester as she emerged from the rhododendrons; he took her hand and put it to his lips. Alice smiled, remembering him as a boisterous baby boy; when and how had he acquired all the graces that so characterized him now? He walked his honorary aunt round the terrace and into the kitchen. Probably in search of a drink. Or taking her to see Percy. Alice closed her eyes again; she should go and help her mother with poor old Hattie, who was probably still weeping; but it was so pleasant sitting here watching everything happen around her, thinking about Nell and whether she might get this job and work in Birmingham, and whether she was in love with Mo and how nice he was and practically Val's right-hand man when it came to the railway project, yet . . . how mysterious he was too. She knew she was drifting into sleep and was almost there when Nell's voice spoke practically next to her. She snapped open her eyes and looked round, startled. But Nell was in the summer house again with someone else. Perry.

Alice started to get up; she could not play eavesdropper again.

Perry spoke and his voice was angry. 'Look, it was what you wanted, for God's sake! All the bloody summer – until that –

that *lummock* came on the scene – you were after me! Now, in three weeks' time you'll be gone and I'm suggesting a night at the sodding Pumpkin Coach and all I get is a big brush-off! There's a word for girls like you, you know!'

Alice was aghast. She lowered herself back down gingerly and put a hand over her mouth. How *dared* Perry speak to Nell like that! She waited, breath held against her palm, for Nell to scorch him with some well-chosen words.

Nell said, 'I've told you before, there is nothing like that between Mo and me. We are friends.'

'Have you seen the way he looks at you? Some friend!'

'Well, that's how it is, believe it or not. I don't care.'

'If it's true then why won't you sleep with me? You have as good as told me that's what you want to do this summer.'

There was a silence. Alice was pressing her hand so fiercely against her mouth that her eyes watered.

Nell said calmly, 'All right then. If that's what you want—'

'It's what *you* wanted!'

'All right. It's what I want. When?'

'Tonight.'

'Your grandmother's funeral was this afternoon, Perry!'

'So I need cheering up. Go up to my room as soon as poss. I'll tell Uncle Val you're looking after Ma—'

'But Hattie – they'll ask her—'

'She'll be OK. I'll fix her. If you're not there when I go upstairs, I don't think I can speak to you again. Ever!'

Nell said rather drearily, 'Bloody drama queen!'

Alice watched as Perry propelled her unceremoniously up the lawn to the kitchen door. Then she went to look for Val.

Duggie helped Enid to pick up the stray teacups and plates, and fold the garden chairs and stack them neatly in the summer house. The sun was going down over the city and skeins of midges were dancing over the evening-scented lawn. Duggie had made desultory conversation as they worked but Enid had said not a word. He suddenly realized she was crying again. He went to her, took a footstool from her hands and placed it on the ground, then folded her into his shoulder. She sobbed unrestrainedly for a moment, then tried to push away. He let her go.

'I'm sorry, Enid. I didn't mean to be ... forward.' He heard himself use the word and was glad Doffie could not hear.

She had her hands to her face and from behind them came a torrent of words. He leaned closer. He gathered that she was so ashamed of herself. He had seen her with Reggie Ryecroft, knew she was a – a – a – *whore* – dressed in the clothes Reggie had bought her, made up by Reggie, her hair done by Reggie – she had been a chattel, to be beaten whenever he felt like it. She had not minded Doffie seeing but when Duggie ... She was so ashamed, she had never stopped being ashamed.

Duggie whispered, 'But, Enid, that all happened in 1949. Twenty-five years ago! You have been a wonderful daughter, a wonderful aunt to your two nephews, a wonderful sister to Percy – and to Hattie. You must forget all that business with Reggie.'

She looked over the top of her hands. 'But you saw me. You *saw* me!'

'Yes. You came running out of the house, if you remember. Although Reggie had told you not to. You were brave enough to come out and tell me what was happening to Doffie. You saved Doffie's life, Enid. They say it was me, but really it was you. Don't you realize that?'

He went on talking to her, very gently, very slowly. He moved towards her and she did not back away. He held his arms wide.

'If you want to cry for your mother, please do,' he said.

She gave a little gasp and went to him. He looked over her head at the cathedral, outlined blackly against the sun. He hoped Doffie hadn't put some sort of potion in his tea. This was ridiculous.

*

113

Hester came downstairs with her hair loose and her lovely frock not quite the same. Edmund was waiting at the foot of the stairs.

'Well?'

'Good evening, Mr Pettiford,' she said. And giggled.

Edmund swept her off her feet and waltzed round the tiled hall with her.

'I love you, Hessie! You are beautiful and clever and persuasive! And . . .' He set her down and looked at her closely, then started to laugh. 'And wanton!' he added.

Val said, 'Did you have a jacket, Allie? Right. We're ready then. Where's Nell?'

Hattie said, 'She's staying the night, darling. She offered and I accepted gladly. I need her.'

Alice avoided her eye. 'That's all right then. I'll just say cheerio to Mum and Dad.'

'They're in the sitting room,' Hattie said cheerfully.

In the hall Edmund was dancing with Hester for some reason; it occurred to Alice that considering everyone had been to a funeral they were mightily cheerful. Val put his arm round her waist.

'What's going on?' he asked.

Alice said blandly, 'They're dancing.'

'I know, but—'

She turned and kissed him lightly. 'Nothing. Nothing is going on, darling.'

She hugged her parents and thought that this must be what Gramps meant about free will.

Eleven

In three short weeks Mrs Mearment felt she had got to know her young lodger as well as anyone ever could get to know him. She knew his eating habits; he wasn't one for meat and two veg, for instance. He would eat the meat, often as a sandwich, then he would eat each vegetable on separate plates. She had pointed out at first that this entailed three times the washing-up, so he had taken to doing most of that himself. He seemed to enjoy housework; a week ago there had been high winds and he had taken all the rugs out of the house and beaten them half to death on Mrs Mearment's clothes line. The garden had never looked so neat, and now he was talking about planting winter cabbage and purple sprouting broccoli. She wasn't daft, she knew what the out-door work was all about; it kept the Ryecroft house well in his view. If young Nell did not realize that Michael Checkers was head over heels in love with her, then she was the daft one.

That was another thing: she had told him straight off that she could no more call him Mo than fly. 'It's not your name – Nell told me you made it up from some Chinese general or something. I want to use your proper name. The one your mother gave you when you were a baby.'

He smiled. He often smiled at her and she appreciated that because smiling generally did not come easily to him.

'Call me Michael, Mrs M.,' he said. 'Though my mother actually shortened it to Mo.'

So for Mrs Mearment he was Michael and she thought of him as a grandson, and by the end of that windy autumn she loved him and it came quite naturally to her to lean on the dining-room table – taking care not to disturb any of the enormous maps or plans or whatever they were – and deliver a short homily.

'It's no good telling me you're all right. I can see you are not and, what is more, I know why.' She sighed sharply and carried on. 'Look. In three weeks' time it will be half-term and she will be home and you can show her all this stuff – maybe take her out to the forest.' She waxed enthusiastic. 'I could make you a picnic. Some sandwiches and a flask of tea. And there are apples.'

He edged a large diagram away from her hand. 'This is not the railway stuff, Mrs M. We are waiting now for a lot of things to happen and nothing much is.' His smile became wry. 'I think for a while it will become a waiting game.' He too sighed. 'Everything has a life. The Pumpkin Line is being born. The metal in my sample plane at Staverton –' he swept his hand over the diagrams on the table – 'is dying.' He looked up and met her eyes. 'My – relationship – with Nell was not born, yet I think it is dead already.'

She put a hand on her flat chest where she thought her heart might be. 'Oh my dear lord! You've known her – how long? Five months? How can you say a thing like that after five months?'

He lifted his shoulders. 'She has gone. For three weeks now she has not been here.' He tried to lighten his smile.

Mrs Mearment pulled another chair to the table and sat down heavily. 'She was lucky to get that job in North Heath, Michael. I was reading in the paper the other day that too many teachers are being turned out of training colleges these days. The population figures have fallen and there aren't the jobs around any more. You should be pleased for her. It could have been right up in Scotland or on the left-hand side of Wales or down in Land's End or—'

'I know what you mean, Mrs M. But it was more than that. She . . . removed herself from me. Somehow. I do not know why or how. But after old Mrs Westbrook's funeral she . . . wasn't there any more.'

116

'She went for the interview straight after that—'

'I do not mean physically. We were friends. She wanted us to be friends and we worked at it and she was right. It was good. It was really good. And then it stopped.'

She had no idea what he meant. Her best friend had always been Doffie Pettiford. They had moved into these houses within a month of each other and had been friends all through the war, and afterwards too when Alice and Val had gradually taken over the house and looked after poor old Gran Pettiford. Even now, when Doffie and Ted lived in the middle of the city, Doffie was still her best friend and she always would be.

She said, 'Real friends stay friends. Through thick and thin.'

'I would stay friends, Mrs M. But Nell . . . has gone.'

He looked so sad, sitting there surrounded by his precious paperwork. She knew he was clever. But not with people. Only with figures and sketches and scientific tests in a laboratory somewhere.

She said, 'She could have been ill. She could have been worried sick about the job. It's one thing to be told by these examiner people that you're qualified to do a job, and quite another to actually do it.'

'I know. I know all that. But it's more.'

'Then you have to play this waiting game you're talking about. You have to wait for her. Let her know that you're wait-ing and you'll go on waiting and she only has to lift her little finger and you'll be there.' Mrs Mearment spoke with some confidence and he looked up hopefully in spite of himself. She levered herself up. 'Now drink that coffee while it's still warm. It's made with all milk because you're looking real peaky lately.' She got to the door and turned creakily. 'I'll tell you one thing, Michael Checkers. Any of they Pettiford girls is worth waiting for.'

He looked down at his coffee; he was not fond of milk and there was already a skin crinkling over its surface. 'I know that, Mrs M.,' he said.

She left and he picked up his cup and drank the sickly brew in long painstaking gulps. Then he folded his diagrams carefully, laid his calculations on top of them and stood up. Perhaps there was nothing much he could do about Nell Ryecroft but he could have another try at finding out where the Pumpkin Line had originally gone.

Alice went to see her mother. It was an unexpected call and Doffie was delighted to see her.

'Your father has gone over to Wales after another wretched locomotive which may or may not be for sale.' Doffie was feeling gloomy and could not think why. 'And even if it is, it probably won't be possible to restore it. And anyway we've got nowhere to put it. We need sidings and a shed and . . . oh, just about every blessed thing!' She looked at her only daughter and saw how thin she was. Pale too. Gran would have said she looked washed out. 'Are you all right, chick?'

Alice smiled. Her father had called her chick when she was younger.

'I'm fine. Missing Nell, of course.'

'How is she?'

'She loves it. When she rings she talks about her class as if they were her family. One of the boys – Martin Trickett, his name is – has asked her to tea. The head says she'd better not. The other children will be jealous.'

Doffie said, 'I knew she'd love teaching. She gets that from Val's mother. I like to think that Dorothy Ryecroft's talents are still around and being used. Not stifled by some crazy man.'

'Don't think about Uncle Reggie, Mum.' Alice had been terrified for her mother after that awful business with Val's father. She changed the subject quickly. 'I thought I'd go and have another look in the cellar. It's an impossible task really, but you never know, I might hit on something.'

'I absolutely forbid you to go down in that filthy cobwebby hole again, Alice!' Doffie tried to look commanding. 'You did it that once and you came up looking like a sweep.'

Alice laughed. 'Mum, I have to do something. It was a mistake giving up my job.'

'You never really liked it.'

'True, but with Val in London and Nell in Birmingham, I feel a bit cut off in Lypiatt by myself.'

'Mrs Mearment is within shouting distance.'

'She's your friend, not mine. And anyway, she's fully occupied with that peculiar boy who was trying to insinuate himself into Nell's good graces.' Alice sighed. 'At least Perry managed to scotch that before it started.'

Doffie said, 'Perry?'

Alice shrugged. 'You know Nell had her eye on Perry when she finished at college. I think they might have come to some agreement.'

Doffie looked sharply at her daughter. 'You mean . . . you can't mean—'

'I don't know, Mum. But something happened and she just backed right away from Mo Checkers.'

'Oh.' Doffie looked nonplussed. 'I rather took to him. Mo Checkers, I mean. But . . . well, so long as it's Perry and not Edmund.'

'Why? What's wrong with Edmund?'

'Nothing is wrong with him. Except . . . he's a bit solemn for our darling Nell.'

'Mo Checkers isn't exactly a laugh a minute.'

'No. But Edmund . . . you know what I mean.' Doffie looked more nonplussed than ever. 'Perry is all right though.' She picked up the kettle. 'Shall we have a cup of tea? I feel shattered. I'm amazed you are taking this Perry thing so calmly. I mean . . . of course it might not be . . . but then again, it might.'

Alice laughed. 'Oh Mum, I do love you. But I don't really think I take anything calmly, especially where Nell is concerned. It's just that . . . Gramps has so imbued me with this free-will thing that I know there is nothing I can do about it. At least . . .' She frowned. 'Of course there is. But there's a feeling that non-interference is best.'

119

Doffie made tea, her lips pursed. This thing that Alice had with the other world worried her; it had made her ill before and she really was looking washed out now.

She said, 'I'm sure Gramps wouldn't mind if you pointed things out. I mean, still give Nell – well, anyone really – the absolute freedom to choose but simply point out various options.'

Alice smiled. 'Yes. That is exactly what Gramps means.' She placed mugs and spoons on the table. 'You're the only one who really understands that. But then you had a real rapport with Gramps, didn't you?'

Doffie sighed. At one time she would have agreed with that but since Gramps had been in touch with Alice, however sporadically, he was not her favourite person, dead or alive.

She said, 'Surely Val understands?'

'Up to a point. He knows that I believe in what is happening. I'm not sure that he believes it for himself. And you do.' She hugged her mother's arm and between them they almost spilled the tea, which made them laugh. They'd always been able to laugh together but not quite so readily since Alice's marriage to Val. When they sat down and sipped their tea, Alice said quietly, 'Mum, d'you remember the time you threw a cup of tea all over Dad and almost scalded him?'

'How could I forget?'

'I thought it meant the end of your marriage—'

'Darling, I am so sorry! You were only sixteen – I should have known better.'

'The point is, Mum, these things happen and in some ways strengthen a marriage.' Alice looked into her mug as if it were a crystal ball. 'Obviously there are things between Val and me . . . but we are just as close – more than close, inter-dependent . . . as you and Dad. Please believe that.'

Doffie stared at her daughter's downbent head; the pale hair had lost its shine and the nape of her neck was exposed and looked terrifyingly vulnerable. Doffie sighed again; she knew things that Alice would never know but she believed in

Val and she believed in the marriage. So she said, 'I do, my darling. I really do.'

Alice lifted her head and for a moment the two of them looked at each other and accepted all the things that must be left unsaid. Then Alice smiled.

'Don't worry about me, Mum. And don't worry about Nell either. She has a lot of your genes and you know – you must know by now – that you are a survivor!'

Doffie grinned back. 'I had lessons from Gran, remember. Now drink up, go down to that horrible old cellar and I'll make us a meal. How would you like to go to the cinema this evening?'

Alice had forgotten how eerily the single bulb lit the enormous cellars beneath Bishop Hooper's Mansions; especially as it swayed in the downdraught from the door beneath the main staircase. She gazed around her; the cellar was divided into alcoves and niches by the thick load-bearing walls of the building above. Four enormous bunkers underneath the pavement of Northgate Street had contained huge stocks of coal in her day. She had dug it out and filled the office hods with it, then lugged them back up the stairs to the main foyer and then up the grand staircase to the landing, where all the offices were situated. Nobody would do it these days; the staff association would call for an instant strike. She smiled slightly at the thought. She had received an enquiry only last year from a mature woman student in Brighton who was doing a paper on the evolving role of women in the twentieth century. She had wanted horror stories of Alice's time with the newly nationalized railways just after the war, and Alice could have provided her with plenty of ammunition for her argument: the primitive toilets, the lack of soap, towels, paper or disinfectant; the constant attention to the slow-burning stoves that heated each office; carrying the coal and cans of paraffin up at least forty stairs . . . But she had refused to do so, because she had been so happy working for Edward Maybury, dear Mr Berry and even the dreaded Reggie Ryecroft. Were people as happy now with all the rules and regulations to support them? Did they forge the kind of friendships she had had with Helena and . . . with Joe? Did they still have people like Duggie Marsden, who had run the Staff Office so well and so kindly?

The light bulb had stopped swinging and Alice walked further into the cellar to where the obsolete files continued to gather dust and probably constituted a fire risk. She pursed her lips: she had looked at the waist-high pile in front on her last visit; time to go deeper, through more dust, coal grime, rotting string and burst rubber bands. She gathered an armful of files and moved back beneath the light. She was looking for the magical initials S & W, which would signify the old Severn and Wye line through the forest.

After half an hour she was surrounded by discarded bundles of papers and she felt no nearer to finding anything useful to show to Val. She glanced at her watch and decided another half an hour would be enough; then she had to stack these bundles back in some kind of order, yet separately so that she wouldn't find herself going through the whole lot again. It was the only way she could do something useful, yet it seemed destined to prove that she was absolutely useless.

She said aloud, 'Oh Joe, come on. What would you have done? You were such an expert at finding lost files!'

She was speaking to herself; she had no intention of trying to get in touch with Joe as she did with her grandfather. This was an exasperated call to herself to be more efficient, to think before she took any more bundles beneath the light bulb. So when she heard a scuff on the stair it never occurred to her that Joe might be with her in the same way that Gramps sometimes was. She was not even slightly alarmed and only half turned to call over her shoulder, 'Is that you, Mum? Take no notice of me nattering to myself. Can't find anything useful. As per usual!'

It was a shock to say the least when Joe's voice said, 'Let me help.'

She gave a little yelp and spun round to face the stairs.

'Where are you?' she gasped. A figure, the same shape and size as Joe Adair's, came under the light. It was Nell's erstwhile friend, Mo Checkers. She gave another gasp, this time of laughter. 'It's you – I'm so sorry. I thought it was my mother, then I thought – I actually thought – you were a ghost!'

He did not smile responsively – Nell always said how po-faced he could be – but just stood there waiting for her shock to subside. She found herself talking simply to fill the gap.

'I used to come down here quite often. To fetch the coal and look out old files. And my friend – a colleague actually – was often with me and it was as if time was flipping backwards and I was sixteen again.' She shrugged. 'Of course you don't know what I'm talking about. How silly of me. But he was a bit of a genius – at least, I thought so – and he often found files that no one else knew about. And I was just – mentally, you know – asking him where the old Severn and Wye maps might be kept and – and – there you were!'

Her voice petered out. There was a pause; he seemed to be looking at her as if he had not seen her before, yet she always waved to him when she saw him in the garden. He had been to one or two of their meetings, when he had produced figures about weight and strain and ballast and sleepers that seemed to impress Val and her father. She was determined not to start chattering about Joe any more so she too was silent and still. Waiting.

He said at last, very quietly, 'I think maps would not be separate, would they? They would be contextual with something else.' She blinked, trying to follow this. 'Might there be a map enclosed with a request for a service from one of the collieries? Or to do with a derailment or an accident?'

She concentrated on his words; they made good sense. There had been many accident claims from the forest railways in her day. For the life of her she could not remember one of them. And then, out of the blue, she was transported to a day when Reggie Ryecroft had required a file to do with a claim from a firm on the Welsh borders. He had not remembered a name either and had expected her to search until she found it. Joe had come to her rescue, as he'd done so often before. He waited until Reggie was out of the office, then used the old bus line to phone a station master who had known the name of the firm.

Mo Checkers was watching her closely. His voice dropped nearly to a whisper. 'If you could remember a name, we would be able to search alphabetically. And with the two of us working together, we might well be lucky.'

She closed her eyes for a moment and saw Joe. Joe Adair with his round schoolboy face and his flop of hair; his kindness that was so fatally close to weakness; his pain flowed into her as it had done then. They had been much younger than Nell was now and the weight of their love had been too much for either of them to bear.

She breathed, 'Turner's. Turner's Iron Products. An accident. Reggie Ryecroft did them some kind of favour so that they could make a successful claim against the railway. Eventually they gave him a directorship in return.'

She opened her eyes. He was there. But it was Mo. Mo who was lodging with Mrs Mearment next door and fancied Nell.

He moved to the pile of discarded bundles and picked one up. 'You've got to D. Davis and Son. So . . .' He moved along the wall of papers. 'Turner's are going to be right behind these.' He began to lift piles neatly and replace them against another wall. 'If I make a tunnel, can you reach in and pull out a sample?'

They refilled that tunnel and made another. And another. And then she pulled out a file headed 'Thomas: opencast mine: application for extra wagons'. The next bundle was very thin; Reggie had decimated it a long time ago in an effort to cover his tracks. But from the middle a roll of fine cartridge paper spilled on to the dusty flagstones of the cellar. Reverently, Mo Checkers unrolled it, looking for all the world like a medieval knight delivering a message. It was a detailed map of the Severn and Wye Railway, showing its connection with the original Severn Bridge.

Mo Checkers breathed, 'Alleluia!' and Alice, very suddenly, wanted to cry.

That evening, she went to see Helena Maybury. Helena had been Reggie Ryecroft's personal secretary and had watched Alice and Joe fall in love and had warned Alice, right at the very beginning, that it would not last.

Alice had telephoned her as soon as she got home that afternoon and Helena had immediately invited her to supper.

'Now that Nell is away, you really must come up more often.' Helena hugged Alice warmly and led her into the little sitting room overlooking the Devil's Chimney. The October sun was coming low through the window but a small fire burned in the grate.

'I always sit here for an hour before supper,' Helena said. 'I don't read or watch television or listen to the radio. I just sit. I think it replenishes me.'

'I've done a lot of that lately.' But Alice smiled because she did not mind her own company. And Gramps had never spoken to her at home, only in the cathedral.

'Tell me all,' Helena said cosily. 'Has that clever lad proposed to our Nell yet?'

'No. I think that may well be over before it started. Nell is keeping in close touch with Perry, apparently.' She waited; so did Helena. Alice smiled. 'All right, I'll come clean. I had a funny experience today. That clever lad, as you call him, Mo to his friends, turned up in the cellars at Bishop Hooper's.'

'What on earth were you doing down there?'

'Hunting for a map of the old Severn and Wye. I want to help and it seemed the only thing I could do. So I was there. And suddenly, so was he. And he nudged my memory into working properly. I remembered that file – that wretched file – really old, from the nineteen twenties—'

Helena said instantly, 'Turner's Iron Products. A wagon came off the rails and they lost a load. They claimed. They got compensation. Reggie dealt with it. Years later –

forty-nine, was it? – he became a director. Bit of hanky-panky there.'

Alice was amazed. 'Your memory is terrific! I could have asked you about it – that would have been much simpler.'

'Sounds as if you and this Mo Checkers did a pretty good job anyway. Aren't you going to tell me that you found the file and it contained a detailed map of the lines as they were in the twenties?'

'Well, yes. But that's not quite . . . Oh Helena, it was so odd. I was thinking of Joe, you see, and there was Mo Checkers. And then he seemed to know . . . what had happened. He sort of led me to the file . . . Helena, it was as if Joe was in him.'

'Don't go too far, Alice. Please.'

'But, Helena, you know I can do this—'

'Only with your grandfather, my dear. And he is dead!'

'I think Joe is dead. I think his widow must have handled the so-called sale – which really was a bequest. And now . . . this boy from the other side of the world turns up—'

'Steady, Alice, as far as I know he's never been out of England.'

'But half of him is from another race, another culture . . . Helena, I'm sorry. Am I having another crazy period?'

Helena said stoutly, 'You never had a crazy period, Alice. You were weakened, ill even, after that miscarriage. But once you had said goodbye to Joe – you were all right.'

'You make it sound so simple.'

'It was, darling. You were so in love, the two of you. If he hadn't had to do his national service – if his mother had not died so tragically – maybe it would have been different. But your love became such a burden, Alice. Too heavy for a seventeen-year-old girl. Too heavy to have borne all through the years.'

Alice said, 'You don't think he was trying to help me today? As he helped me so often in the old days in the office?'

'No, darling. I think it was sheer coincidence that brought Mo Checkers down there at that time. He saw the cellar door was open, he saw the light below, he came down to investigate . . .'

'Yes, probably you're right.'

'Darling, Edward says I'm always right!'

'Oh Helena . . .'

'Let's go and eat, Alice. Edward will be starving. He's been repairing the drystone wall – did I tell you he's taken up walling in his old age? Guess who has been helping him? Hattie's eldest. Edmund. He's got a week's holiday and thought he would like to learn something different. Strange young man – very clever law student. Wants to do stuff with his hands all of a sudden.'

Alice smiled, remembering that Val had left Oxford to do something 'real'.

She said, 'He's following a precedent, of course.'

Helena raised her delicate brows but did not pursue the subject. They went into the kitchen, where one of Helena's lame ducks was stirring soup. And Helena, as usual, took over.

Twelve

Duggie Marsden still drove his pre-war Flying Standard, so it was not a very speedy journey down to Bristol. Hester could not admit to feeling just a bit scared; she made a great show of being a passenger in a veteran car and wore a scarf over one of her mother's wide-brimmed hats even though the Standard was completely wind- and waterproof. She held the top of her hat as if it might still fly away and gasped out her remarks without daring to turn her head to look at Duggie. They chugged sedately down the A38 and along Falcondale Road and Westbury Lane to the Downs and Clifton Village, where Duggie drew up outside a brass-framed window and suggested coffee.

'We should get down to St Paul's. It's gone eleven. They might go out.'

Duggie said, 'Listen, if they're the drug-crazed pair you've been led to believe they won't get out of bed till mid-afternoon, if then. And anyway, I need a fix of caffeine before I can go any further.'

'I didn't realize.' She struggled with the door handle. 'You seemed so relaxed and everything.'

'I was perfectly relaxed until I saw your get-up! You were obviously not happy with my driving—'

'Oh, I was! Honestly! It's just that the car is so old and sort of hiccups now and then. And when I looked down at one stage there was a hole in the mat and I could see the road about two inches from the heel of my shoe!'

'Why on earth didn't you say so? I would have stopped and adjusted the mat.'

He came round and opened her door without trouble and she got out feeling absolutely ridiculous now about the hat. They went into the old-fashioned coffee house. He handed her up a flight of stairs to a tiny landing with a table and a potted palm and went back to decide which blend of coffee they would like. She sat there feeling conspicuous, wishing she had accepted his offer to take her during the summer holidays so that it would now be over and done with, still rather bewildered that she had achieved enormous popularity at school after the end-of-year concert, wishing it had been Uncle Ted driving her instead of Duggie Marsden who was so protective and proper; in fact, in a state of total mental disarray, as was usual these days. She recalled the old Hester, cool head of department at school, fully in control of a passionate affair that had lasted over twenty-five years – had that Hester really been herself?

Duggie said, 'I ordered Brazilian – hope that is all right?'

'I really don't mind, Duggie. Thank you.'

She sipped and thought that the Hester of today seemed to be very happy to be told what to do. Well, if Duggie Marsden wanted the role of surrogate father, she more or less had to accept the counterpart and become his compliant daughter. Trouble was that Duggie was not Uncle Ted; Uncle Ted had always seemed to know her. Almost as well as he knew Alice; in fact sometimes better.

Then Duggie said out of the blue, 'I bet school is a different place this term, isn't it, Hester?'

She was surprised. 'Well, yes, it is actually. What made you ask that?'

'It was obvious at that concert that you were the belle of the ball. The little girls were wide-eyed and adoring, planning how they could save your life several times over. And the older ones were seeing you differently. Respecting you in a different way.'

'Really? All I could see was the sheer horror of it. You saved my life that evening, Duggie. I can never thank you enough.'

'It was a wonderful affair.'

'My God, they weren't even as good as they were at the dress rehearsal and they were terrible then!'

'The mistakes made it endearing. And the way you acknowledged the girls and presented them to us as something special . . . which they were.'

'Oh Duggie, is that how it seemed? What a stroke of luck!'

'More than luck. Skill. You have an innate skill which is completely unconscious but it comes to you in moments of crisis.' He nodded judiciously. 'That's what makes you such a cracking teacher, of course.'

Hester felt her colour sweep from neck to forehead. In an effort to regain some kind of control she said, 'I'm a bit worried about Sally Gold. Do you remember her? She was the Sixth Form girl, the director of the whole thing.'

'I remember her well. Attractive. A minx. But seriously in love with you, Hester.'

'Oh dear God. I was trying *not* to take it seriously. She told me yesterday she is a lesbian.' Duggie put his cup down hurriedly and choked on a laugh. She said, 'It's not funny, Duggie. It puts me in a most difficult position. She is now head girl of the school and has requested the head for personal tutorials with me.'

'Ah.'

'Quite.'

'Drink up, my dear. Let's get on. Perhaps after we've talked to Richard Tibbolt's twins, the whole thing will gain a little perspective.'

'I really don't see how—'

'Try to be totally objective, Hessie.' Duggie grinned. 'Next to the proposed Pumpkin Line, this thing with the twins is the most interesting situation I have been involved in for some time. Life, my dear Hester, is full of possibilities even when one is old and doddery.'

He handed her down the steps again and she reflected that he might be old but he certainly was not doddery.

Val traced the map with his long fingers. 'This is great, Allie!

See all these small coal sidings – the mines they served have long gone and we'd never have found them again. But they will be invaluable to us for stabling stock—'

'When we get any stock,' Alice put in gently.

'Darling, these things take time. We have to feel our way. If we go in with all guns blazing, we shall put everybody's backs up – especially the Freeminers, who can be awkward cusses at the best of times. We'll ask Ted and Duggie Marsden to go down to the Miners' Arms and get into conversation . . . bide their time and then produce this map and ask for help. We need to know who owns this land so that we can get a lease. Buy it, maybe.'

'Why Dad and Uncle Duggie?'

'It must be someone called Pettiford, of course. And when Ted loses his rag he'll need Duggie because he's the ultimate diplomat.'

'Dad wouldn't—'

'All right, he wouldn't lose his temper but he's got a way of projecting a kind of sullen silence that is just as aggressive.'

Alice remembered the times Dad had sent Mum to Coventry when she did something to annoy him. She smiled and shook her head at her husband.

'You're right. He can do it at home too.'

He was surprised. 'I've always thought he was the perfect husband and father.'

'Haven't I ever told you about Dad's secret weapon of total silence?'

He seized her suddenly and kissed her. 'No. But I've a feeling you're about to do so!' He looked into her eyes, willing her to come with him to that other place . . . Nothing happened. He released her and said lightly, 'What else haven't you told me about your past?'

She knew him as well as he knew her and put a hand to his face. 'Val . . . dear Val. I love you.'

He stayed very still. 'I know,' he whispered. Then, when he sensed she would move away, he held her hand against his cheek and said, 'Don't leave me.'

'Never. Not ever. Why did you say that?'

'I've been away five days. As usual. And in that time, something has happened.'

'I found the map.'

'You and Nell's boyfriend.'

'He's not—'

'All right, Mo Checkers. Did he say something? About Nell?'

'No. I think he's given up on Nell. He was trying to move things forward – like I was. It was such a coincidence that we decided to look through the cellars again at almost the same time.'

He searched her face for something; then held her close. 'It upset you going down into those ghastly old cellars again.'

'A bit. Not really though.' She breathed in the familiar scent of his shirt and closed her eyes. Val had rescued her; had kept her safe all those years ago. She spoke into his neck. 'Val, before winter comes – before we start to unearth the Pumpkin Line and change Bracewell's Pool beyond recognition – let's have a day at the coach. Tomorrow. Let's take a picnic and go to Leadon tomorrow. Let's paddle in the stream and trek down to the pool and – and—'

'And what?' he teased her.

'See what happens.' She laughed.

He held her away from him, laughing too but still watchful. 'Are you being a brazen hussy? I seem to remember the first time I took you there—'

'That was because it was tradition – no, really, I mean it! Bracewell and Rose's mother first of all, then Mitzie – and there were others too, you could tell. There was no escaping that magic – you had to surrender to all that romance—'

'So it was really nothing to do with you and me! It was the ghosts of seduction from way back . . .' He was still laughing, then realized she was not. He held her close again. 'I'm joking . . . oh darling Alice . . . it was our first time and we made our first baby there. How could I forget?'

She said steadily, 'We made our second baby there too. Our lovely Nell.'

'I know. I know.' His hand combed her hair and felt its brittleness. 'We'll take a picnic and see what happens, my love.' He picked her up and carried her upstairs, and much later he said into the dark room, 'Afterwards . . . when you and Mo had discovered the map . . . what did you do then? Did you take him to your mother's for tea?'

'Yes. But he would not stay so I drove him back in the car with Mrs M.'s bike in the boot.' She sighed. 'Mum wanted to cook a meal. Never mind.'

'And then? What did you do then – walk in the woods? Telephone Nell?'

'I had supper with Helena and Edward.'

'Thank goodness. Sometimes the thought of you here on your own all week long . . .'

'Don't be silly, darling. I love it. I didn't want to admit it but I never enjoyed that job in the college library.'

He began to kiss her all over again. 'That's all right then,' he said comfortably, and made plans to see Helena as soon as possible.

The address given to Hester by Tibbolt's wife, Hermione, was in an insalubrious area of the city where modern high-rise flats jostled with soot-encrusted terraces from another era. In the middle of it all was a small Victorian park, its boating pool and bandstand broken-edged and covered in graffiti. Duggie and Hester sat between the two, staring alternately at the cracked mud in one and the advice to f— off on the other.

Hester said, 'I spent three years in Bristol. I never knew this area existed.'

'Thank God for that. This is the perfect place for getting one's throat cut.'

'Oh, I came near to that until I found a way to enslave Tibbolt and then use him.'

Duggie glanced at her, shocked. He said nothing.

She said, 'I was eighteen when he took me to Provence as an unpaid nanny to his kids. He was going to coach me . . .

James Joyce was leaving me cold. He coached me all right. Then Hermione decided she was in love with a woman and he decided he was in love with me. He had made me desperately unhappy. Revenge was very sweet.'

'When did you realize you loved him?'

'I suppose when he left me. And I'm not sure that I do love him, actually. He made me feel very . . . special. And Percy is quite good at doing that.' She glanced at him and said, 'So is Sally Gold, incidentally.'

Duggie smiled. 'Don't try to compete with Hattie. I don't mean for Percy. I mean in the amorality stakes.'

Hester smiled too. 'No. All right. Though I don't think she is like that any more. Not since she lost that little girl all those years ago.'

'I wouldn't put money on it. She wants me to bed Enid.'

'Oh my God.' Hester stared at him. 'Would you?'

'I would have to marry her first, Hessie. After eloping with your father, Enid has had no self-respect whatsoever. If I suggested bed without offering wedlock . . .' He left the rest to her imagination.

After a moment she said, 'Dugdale Marsden, you are a very good man.'

'Not a bit. This trip, let me tell you if you have not already guessed, has been undertaken in the spirit of voyeurism. I am good at that—'

'Not only that, Duggie.'

He knew she was thinking of the time he had attacked her father with a frying pan and a rolling pin, and he hardly knew what to say about that. After another small silence he stood up.

'Come on, let's get it over with.'

She was momentarily panic-stricken. 'I don't know what I'm supposed to do! They won't remember me! I won't remember them! And anyway, what right has their father's mistress to interfere in their lives?'

He shrugged. 'None. Except that their father asked her to do just that. So he must have great faith in her persuasive powers.'

'But what am I persuading them to do?'

'I don't know. Wait and see. Possibly nothing at all. You will see them, that is the important thing. Decide whether they should be left to their own devices or shopped to the police.'

'Duggie!'

'Come on. I'll hang around if you want me to.'

It was all too reminiscent of the time twenty-five years previously when he had 'hung around' outside the house in Newport until Enid had rushed out to inform him that Reggie Ryecroft was raping and killing Doffie Pettiford. He sat outside the soot-stained terrace now in the same car as he had had then and sent up a little prayer for Hester Ryecroft, who had thought for so long that she had sorted out her life better than anyone else and then discovered she was quite wrong. He watched as Hester knocked ineffectually on the boards nailed across the front door, then felt his heart jump – as hers must have done – when the window above the door opened and a head emerged. Words were spoken – he could not hear them but the tone seemed amiable enough – then Hester approached a ground-floor window that was also boarded up but that magically opened, boards and all, and after a moment's hesitation she climbed through and disappeared. And Duggie realized his heart was thumping with a well-remembered terror.

Hester followed a pair of bare heels up the scuffed and uncarpeted stairs. She had recognized Toby immediately because he looked so much like his father but when she was led into the room over the front door she did not recognize Evadne. For a moment she thought that the girl in the dressing gown sitting at the scrubbed kitchen table was someone else entirely.

Then Toby grinned. 'You were right, Evie. It is her. Hester the whore.'

Hester visibly flinched. Nevertheless she said, 'That is most unfair, Toby. Whores sleep around for money. I have only slept with your father.'

'But you made him pay,' Evadne accused.

She must look like Hermione, Tibbolt's ex-wife. Hester could barely remember her; short with a mass of frizzy curls, probably very pretty because Evadne certainly was.

Hester said, 'Yes, I suppose I did. It's over now though. I've had enough of revenge and I suppose he'd had enough of me. He's gone anyway, for whatever reason.'

They exchanged glances, surprised and definitely nonplussed.

Evadne said, 'You mean he dumped you – my father actually dumped you?'

'Yes, Evadne, that is what I mean.'

They exchanged glances again; they might not look like each other but there was such an affinity . . . She shivered.

Toby moved to the table where Evadne sat, hands in front of her. He said, 'You don't care?'

'Yes, I care. I miss him terribly. But I can see now that it could not last. It was wrong.'

He said triumphantly, 'My God, I see it all now! You can see the error of your ways and you've come to show us ours!' He tipped his head back and laughed. 'Oh Evie, this is rich – this is really rich. Hester Ryecroft has seen the light and she wants us to see it too!'

Hester spoke through their mingled laughter. 'He asked me to come and see you. It was last April actually.' She remembered the daffodils . . . and the birds singing in the close. 'It has taken me too long. I am sorry.'

They both stopped laughing and did their exchange-glance again. Evadne's face screwed up with concentration.

'He asked you to come to see us last April . . . you didn't . . . he dumped you? So you've come here simply to get him back?'

'No. I don't think so. As a matter of fact, he dumped me – as you so charmingly put it – last April. It's taken me all summer to realize that I had to do this.'

'Do what?' Evadne said sharply.

Hester managed a smile. 'That's the trouble. I don't know. I suppose that's why I've put it off.'

'You had to phone Dad to get the address of our squat though. You had to get in touch with him and we were a good excuse for doing that.'

'You think I had to have some kind of motive? Perhaps you're right. I don't know that either. I got your address from Hermione.'

'And she *gave* it to you? You could have been going to turn us in!'

She found her teacher's voice at last. 'I still could,' she said levelly.

They were silent. Toby reached across the table and put his hands over Evadne's.

Hester said, 'However, I don't think that is what your father had in mind, otherwise he would have done it himself by now. He may well have needed an objective opinion.' She got up and went to the window. On the other side of the road she saw the Flying Standard waiting. She said, 'Maybe he did not require that much objectivity either. You see, he knew that when I was . . . younger, I was in love with my brother. He married my best friend and I was glad because it meant I could still have a small share.'

They were dumb with shock. She said, 'It's because of my brother that I understand about you. Recognize your feelings.' She turned. 'No one else would know.' They were still silent and she came back to her seat at the table. 'Is that why you use . . . what do you use, heroin? Does it help you to accept that you are twins and sleep together?'

The continued silence was assent. Hester let it build for a while and looked round the room. They had tried to make it presentable; the mattress in the corner was covered with a clean white sheet; she wondered about bathroom and kitchen arrangements. She could almost taste the despair and said, 'What are you going to do? You are nearly thirty years old . . . How long can you go on like this?'

Toby spoke as if by rote. 'We shared a womb. We were together then, before birth. What is more natural than to want to stay together always?'

'But your way of life is acknowledging that it is not natural. And to inject yourselves—'

'We do it for each other,' Evadne said.

'Somehow that is worse. I don't know why.' She stared down at the ridged grain of the table. Alice's grandmother had had a similar table, ridged by constant scrubbing. The twins were obviously clean enough. 'Do you eat?'

'Of course. We have social security money. And Dad . . . is good.'

Toby said, 'He comes to see us. Makes sure we're not paralytic. People expect us to die, you know. Nobody really understands about drug-takers—'

'Don't be too reasonable about it, Toby.' Hester used her teacher's voice again. 'You know very well heroin is terribly addictive and does in fact kill eventually. It takes away certain normal incentives too. Like working. Or at least doing something besides . . . this.' She swept her hand round the room. 'Didn't you have a pottery over in Provence?'

'Hermione's little hobby for us!' Evadne sneered.

'She might patronize you but that wouldn't matter. It's there. And in an area quite used to unorthodox relationships. I take it your mother still lives with a female partner?'

'So we'd be a little enclave of nutters? Is that what you're saying?' Evadne was really angry. 'Hermione might be patronizing but you take the bloody biscuit!'

'Sorry. You'd rather I told you to go and find conventional partners?' Hester sighed. 'Sorry again. You shouldn't have let me in. Nothing to do with me. I am just thankful to see that you have a table and chairs, a bed with clean sheets . . . Perhaps that's why your father wanted me to visit you.' She stood up. 'I'll go. Forgive me. I would dearly have loved to do what you are doing. Since your father left me I have been consoling myself by flirting heavily with my friend's husband, who is over seventy years old. Believe me, I did not mean to patronize or interfere.' She moved to the door and looked round again. 'There is a part of me that almost envies you.' She forced a smile. 'Goodbye. Good luck.'

Evadne looked at her challengingly. 'Have you got any money?'

'Yes.' She went back to the table, removing her purse from the pocket of her jacket. She opened it and tipped it upside down, then pulled out the notes. There was probably fifty pounds. She turned and left.

Thirteen

Nell met Perry at Birmingham New Street and they immediately caught a slow train that would stop at North Heath. Nell had spent the morning at a union meeting, listening to a debate on the latest pay increase.

She kissed Perry briefly and by way of greeting said, 'Some good news at last! Wilson might have a narrow majority but we'll make it work, you'll see.'

'And now – here I am.' He put his hand on her bottom and pressed her hard against himself, kissing her enthusiastically. 'God, I can't wait to get to your flat!'

She looked annoyed. 'Honestly, Perry! Can't you think of anything but sex? We're living in a rather large world, you know.'

'But we can only inhabit a small one at any one time,' he said, rolling his eyes suggestively. 'Come on, let's get a corner seat.' He leaped up the steps of the last carriage, which was empty, pulling her after him. 'I tried to get Ed to let me have the bloody car, but of course no joy. He's becoming self-obsessed lately. This name-change thing has got to him. He's ferreting around among the old papers – birth and death certificates – spent a day in the booking office at Leadon looking through the monthly returns for the last thirty years—'

'The monthly returns? Whatever for?'

'Apparently, when your father worked there he couldn't seem to balance them and Hester used to do it for him. Edmund has sneaked out each one she wrote, photocopied it and returned it the next day.'

'But – but *why?*'

'I've got a theory. Tell you later. Sit down and pucker your lips.'

He was over her like a rash; gone were their days of friendly banter, all he ever wanted from her now was physical contact and what he called 'the whole works' as soon as it was sufficiently private. She had intended that strangely awful night at the end of August to be an experiment not to be repeated but Perry had thought it made them a couple. She wished so much, so very much, that she had never gone to his room that night. Hattie had appeared to take it for granted, and even Uncle Percy had said to her, 'Sleep well, my dear. If you can.' It was all horrible. When she saw her mother and father leaving she had almost banged on the window. But . . . well, this was what she had wanted all summer – as Perry was quick to remind her. And as she kept reminding herself, if Mo didn't want her, there were others who did.

The train took twenty-two minutes to reach North Heath and Perry did not stop kissing her in all that time. She could not resist him; he was so much part of her life now that she sometimes wondered whether she might be in love with him and not know it. Was that possible?

They walked down the station steps and crossed the old village green where the stocks sat in full view of the ancient church. To one side of the murky pond was the start of the Guy Fawkes bonfire for that year. She thought of her class of seven-year-olds, especially Martin Trickett, who still wanted her to go to tea with him. She thought of her parents, who did not maul each other about but were so obviously deeply in love. Her eyes filled with tears.

'Darling, try to keep in step with me otherwise we're going to fall over!' Perry hugged her so tightly to his side that her hip was in danger of dislocating. Then, as they entered the narrow snicket that led up to Acacia Crescent, he suddenly stopped, turned her to face him and began to kiss her again.

She said, 'Perry, for goodness' sake! People are coming down this way all the time. The children in my class. It's not

141

the sort of thing they expect their teacher to be doing at the weekend!'

'This damned thick overcoat . . .' He was actually trying to unbutton it. 'It's only October—'

She brought her knee up sharply, then walked on at a very brisk pace in case he should tear after her and get his own back. She heard him when she got into the crescent and she actually ran up to the house and opened the front door before he could reach the gate. No one was in; on Saturdays the population of North Heath seemed to leave the old village. She raced upstairs and opened up her flat, then turned in the doorway and enfolded Perry when he reached her.

'You little . . .' he breathed as she kissed him.

'I know. Sorry. We've never been touchy-feely before and I can't get used to it.'

She made it up to him for the rest of the short afternoon but was glad when the light faded and he suggested a cup of tea. She sat on the edge of the bed and dressed slowly while he was in the bathroom. She thought of that time in the theatre; the first time she had met Mo Checkers. She began to cry.

Perry came out of the bathroom and knelt by her, full of concern.

'Darling, what is it? Tell Perry. Please.'

'I'm homesick. That's all it is.'

'Another three weeks, sweetheart. Don't cry.'

'I'm sorry, Perry. So sorry.'

'Tell you what. Let's get married. Dad will find us a cottage somewhere and you can write poetry and I'll work on the land and we'll make love all night long.'

'Don't be silly.'

'All right. Let's get married. Is that sensible enough?'

'You haven't even got a proper job, Perry!'

'I'll get one. Just say you'll marry me and you can leave Birmingham and never come back again!'

'Darling, I just love it here – the school is marvellous, the kids are super. There's this little seven-year-old called Martin Trick—'

'You never talk about it, which means you're bottling all the hatred up inside you, waiting for each weekend and the total release I give you!' He was only half joking.

'You – you're such a buffoon! Of course I don't talk about it – or anything else! I never get a chance.'

He was instantly, charmingly, contrite. He let her tell him about Martin Trickett and the new maths she had to teach. Then he told her about his theory that Edmund was in love with Hester and had changed his name to Pettiford so that she would love him. Which was so ridiculous that Nell laughed at last and then, in the middle of it, started to cry again. His comforting ended up with him licking her tears, which seemed to inflame him once more. They made love.

She said, 'Perry Westbrook – or, to give you your proper name, Persival Westbrook—' He growled menacingly and she smiled. 'I give up. I really do. You are incorrigible.'

'In that case, say you will marry me.'

'You will marry me,' she mimicked.

He sat away from her and looked stricken. 'You don't take me seriously, do you?'

'No. And it's just as well. Edmund in love with his aunt who is eighteen years older than he is. Me marrying you and living on air . . . You're crackers.'

'I'll show you. I'll get a job and you'll be proud of me.' He grinned. 'Or maybe I won't. And then you won't!' He went through to the kitchen and she heard him making tea. She finished dressing; at least she did not feel as dreary as she had done. That was something.

He brought tea in to her. 'My train goes in an hour. I'll get the car from Edmund and fetch you for half-term.'

'If you're busy with your new job he could fetch me himself,' she teased, wishing he would.

He helped her on with her sweater, holding her gently, kissing her ear.

He murmured, 'Listen, I'm serious. I don't think I've told you this. I love you.'

'Oh Perry.' She hugged him. 'I wish you wouldn't.'

He leaned away to look at her but he said nothing. When they were seated sedately in opposite armchairs – pre-war Rexine – he said, 'I've saved the best bit till last. Dad is having an affair. With Hester. What have you got to say about that?'

Nell had done her best to forget the scene in Hattie's bedroom. She did not want to recall it now so she shrugged.

He stared, 'God. You knew. Since when?'

'Since that awful doubles match. With you and Edmund and Mo.'

'Since then? I've only known since I caught them in the shrubbery.'

'Right. It's nothing really. I'm sure of that. A bit of slap and tickle perhaps—'

'Slap and *tickle*? They're hardly the squire and the parlour maid, Nell!'

'Well, I don't think it's serious at all. Really. I think Hattie must have threatened your father with instant death if he wasn't nice to Hester, so he pushed the boat out a bit just to show her – Hattie, I mean.'

Perry considered that. 'Ye-es. I can see that happening. But I reckon poor old Dad might be smitten. Dugdale Marsden has taken Hester to Bristol today on some private project. Dad doesn't like it at all.'

As Uncle Percy hardly ever spoke and rarely changed his facial expression, Nell was puzzled. 'How can you tell?'

'His eyes, of course. Haven't you ever noticed? When he's upset in any way, his eyes become crossed.'

She said gently, 'Darling, your father's eyes are permanently crossed.'

'Not really. He has a cast in the left one. But sometimes, quite suddenly, they both go into the middle. Ed and I picked that up when we were quite young. When his eyes met over the bridge of his nose, we scarpered.'

She laughed affectionately. 'Oh Perry. I do love you.'

'Really? Do you mean it?'

'Oh darling, do shut up! Of course I love you. And Edmund. I always have. You're the nearest thing to brothers that I'm going to get!'

'Oh Christ. If you love me like a brother, I've had it!'

She reached for her thick coat and began to button it in spite of his slapping hands. 'Listen, let's get fish and chips on the way to the station. I'm ravenous.'

'All right. Do you want to bother to come to the station though?'

'Not really. But the fish-and-chip shop—'

She screamed as he got her arm behind her back and pulled it painfully. She thought he would start kissing her again and when he didn't she was deeply thankful.

Val and Alice drove all the way to Leadon; they had intended taking the train but the Sunday service was almost non-existent. They left the car at the station and called on Mrs Seth, the porter's wife, where they were plied with tea and tatties. Val had lodged with the Seths when he had been a lad clerk at Leadon and he spent some time reminiscing with Seth's widow. Her memory was phenomenal.

'Seth showed you the old coach, din't 'e? You took your sister there, I d'remember. Several times that were. She was a beauty, she was. Married with half a dozen kiddies now, I expect. Then you brought this young'un and got 'er into trouble!' She roared with unembarrassed laughter. Alice looked at Val, startled, but he shook his head helplessly.

'You didn't think no one knew?' She chortled. 'The bus lines was a-buzz with it. 'Ow you had to get married, then you lost your baby.' She stopped laughing and looked over her glasses at them. 'Din't let it stop you though, did you? Lovely daughter you got. Lewis was down the other day and 'e showed me a snapshot.' She concentrated her gaze on Alice. 'Tole me you named 'er after that sekertery in the office . . . Helena something. The one what married the super-intendent.'

145

Alice, who had known in her heart that everyone in the Gloucester district would have known about everything, said simply, 'Yes. We shorten it to Nell. Helena is her godmother.'

'All nice and proper now. Everything comes right in the end.'

Alice said, 'You mentioned Lewis. Would that be the old station master down at Awre?'

'That's 'im. Thought the world of your grandad, did old Lewis.'

'It was Mr Lewis who first gave me the name of that firm . . . Turner's.' She smiled at Val. 'We've come the full circle, by the sound of things.'

They eventually made their farewells and walked on, parallel with the line, until they came to the boulder that marked the spot where they had to strike into the forest itself. There had been no big clearing as yet; they had advertised for voluntary help and had a bundle of eager letters, but until they had talked to everyone concerned they did not want to be seen to be tearing the undergrowth to pieces. Even so, it was possible to see that some clearing had taken place.

'You didn't say anything?' Alice called ahead as another piece of rail came into view.

'No. I didn't know a thing about it.' Val stopped and turned. 'D'you know, I think Mo has been here.'

'What makes you say that?'

'He's such an undercover man!' Val laughed. 'He's uncovering bits, just to check on that map. I reckon he's keener than most of us!'

'He's trying to forget Nell,' Alice said on a sigh. 'I feel rather responsible for her sudden shift to Perry. It did not occur to me that it might break Mo's heart.'

'How were you responsible?' He held aside a long bramble.

'I overheard them. After Gran Westbrook's funeral. Nell agreed to spend the night there.'

'Well . . . that was all right, wasn't it?'

'With Perry. I could have stopped it. I didn't.'

He was silent, pushing a way through the fern till they reached the 'cathedral'.

Then he said, 'It was her decision, Allie.'

'Yes. I know.'

They came to the dark pool and the coach at its side. They left their stuff on the steps of the coach and walked round the pool, then undressed and entered the water. It was so different from that first time, yet it was the same. They floated on their backs and listened to the autumn wind blowing high up in the tree canopy, then they swam quietly back to the muddy bank and lay together where a spotlight of sunshine warmed them.

Alice murmured, 'We're getting old, Val.'

'Do you mind?'

'No. I like it. We take time to – to . . .'

'Savour the moment.'

She laughed. 'Yes. That's it.'

He rolled on to an elbow and kissed her again. She closed her eyes and savoured that very moment. And then something happened. Suddenly, frighteningly, the years disappeared. She was with Joe again. Here, by the coach that his mother had left him so unknowingly. She opened her eyes and across the pool, emerging from the coal-coloured water, she saw him. Still young, his stocky, schoolboy body as lithe as it had been . . . before. She was terrified. Her fingers dug into Val's shoulders and she crushed her cheek into his. She could not manage this . . . she could not bear it. Gramps spoke in her head; she had heard him but never seen him. Now, seeing Joe, she had a very real sensation of drowning. Then he disappeared into the thick foliage round the pool and she closed her eyes again.

Val was all concern. 'What is it? Darling, are you ill?'

She sobbed a little laugh, drew a deep breath; everything was all right.

'I thought I was. Oh Val, I thought I was going mad –

properly mad. More . . . out of my mind and into someone else's. I'm so sorry, darling, so sorry.'

'What was it – Gramps again?'

'No.' She managed another laugh and it sounded natural. 'Darling, someone else is here. Mo Checkers. You were right, he must be looking for the old lines. He's just got out of the water on the other side of the pool and gone off . . . presumably to find his clothes!' She focused on Val's face. 'We've been discovered in the act, Val!'

He studied her face. 'You're not worried? My God, I would have thought – knowing you – you would have wanted to go straight back to the car!'

She touched his nose. 'Not a bit worried. Just so glad – so *thankful* that we're here. You and me. Val and Alice.'

He went on looking at her, then said at last, 'Helena told me. That you thought Mo Checkers was speaking for Joe Adair.'

She said, 'Oh Val! You shouldn't have asked her and she shouldn't have told you. I know it worries you—'

'It worried you, by the sound of it.' He held her tenderly. 'But you don't know that Joe is dead. And I don't think he is. So stop worrying.' He helped her to sit up. 'Let's go and get out the picnic and Mo might reveal himself to us – even share some food. And then we can offer him a lift back home. Come on. He's just a young man who is in love with our daughter and wants to get close to her by helping us with the railway. He must have been mortified to see us actually making love. An elderly couple like us!'

But Mo did not appear.

While Alice tidied up the food and left the coach in its usual state of disrepair, Val walked round the pool again. He saw no footprints in the mud. As they made their way back there was no sign that another human being had followed them. He examined the few places where the line had been uncovered; it had not been on that day – the earth was dry and hard.

He said, 'Darling, when Ted and I go to see the Freeminers' council next month, I'd like you to come too.'

She seemed happy about that. She seemed happy about everything now. He resolved not to leave her alone so much; he would involve her absolutely in this whole scheme of the railway. He looked up at the tree canopy and sent a message to whoever was around: leave her alone . . . just leave her alone.

Fourteen

Half-term came at last. Nell tidied her classroom and went to the staff room for a cup of tea. The other teachers sat in attitudes of exhaustion; the head – Scottish, thick lisle stockings and tweed skirt – was giving them a pep talk for the run-up to Christmas. 'Carols of course. Four traditional, at least two from the new book – can you cope with that, Shirley?' Shirley, head of music, nodded resignedly. 'And a play. Doesn't have to be Christmassy. About fifteen minutes. I thought you would like to have a go at that, Nell.' Nell felt her brain click into action.

'May I work with Shirley and do something musical?'

The head beamed. 'Excellent.'

Shirley looked less enthusiastic. Nell's class was notoriously unmusical.

'Let's meet next Friday and see what we have come up with,' said the head. 'We'd better go now. I see two husbands in the playground already.'

Nell glanced through the window and saw that one of the 'husbands' was Edmund. Her heart leaped; no Perry.

They struggled into anoraks and gathered bulging briefcases and handbags. Shirley said, 'Can anyone in your class hold a tune?'

Nell grinned. 'Me.'

'Very funny.'

'I thought your class could provide a musical accompaniment.'

Shirley snorted. 'Even funnier.' She sighed deeply. 'If it

150

weren't for Christmas planning we could have had the full week off. Bloody Christmas.'

Nell laughed and ran out to meet Edmund; she would have gone into his arms if he had extended them but as usual he did not. She slowed and they walked through the gate sedately to where the car was waiting. Martin Trickett was also waiting, lingering with his mum, apparently looking up at the elms for mistletoe. He smiled shyly. 'I wanted to wish you a happy half-term,' he announced, glancing suspiciously at Edmund. 'And we were wondering, Mum and me, if you could come to tea on Monday.'

Mrs Trickett surged forward. 'He's really keen, Miss Ryecroft, and you would be more than welcome.'

'You are very kind.' She smiled at Martin. 'I don't live in North Heath, you know, Martin. And I'm going home for the holiday. This is my cousin and he has come to drive me.'

Edmund held out his hand. 'Edmund Pettiford,' he said. 'Pleased to meet you.'

Nell glanced at him, surprised. She had forgotten their conversation in the summer house about his name-change. Only two months ago and he had already floated his rather odd idea.

Edmund looked at the small boy so obviously in love with his teacher. He said, 'May we give you and your mother a lift back home?'

Nell could have hugged him. The Tricketts were delighted, and some of their attention was diverted to him and the car. He insisted that Mrs Trickett sit by him in the front while Martin shared the double seat in the back with Nell. Unfortunately, Martin was unable to speak for joy and Mrs Trickett did not stop. When they got out at the big council estate on the edge of the railway line, they said their good-byes almost tearfully. Nell transferred to the front seat and wound down her window to wave until the first bend. She said, 'Now can you see why I enjoy my job so much?'

'I never doubted you would.' Edmund coasted down the long hill on to the A38. 'Although after listening to Perry's tales of abject homesickness, I did wonder if it was all you were cracking it up to be.'

'Perry's an idiot,' Nell said shortly.

'That's true. He's also lazy and a sponger.'

Nell was surprised. 'Edmund! He's your brother, for goodness' sake.'

'Brothers are allowed to be brutally honest. And while we're being honest, you're a bit of an idiot too, young Nell. I do realize you needed to get some sexual experience, but Perry? He's boasting about it quite openly. Apparently, you're insatiable.'

She screamed out at that. 'I'll kill him! All he can think about is . . . and then he has the gall to blame me!'

'I'm joking, woman! I would have killed him for you if he'd so much as breathed a word about it.'

'Then how did you know?'

'I didn't. Till now.'

She turned and swiped at him; he ducked and the car swerved and she screamed again.

'Stop the car! Let me out! I refuse to sit by you and listen to this horrible manipulation of the truth. How dare you, Edmund! I expect Perry to behave badly but not you.'

He was silent, driving carefully now, ignoring her demands to stop. By the time she had simmered into a furious silence they were well on their way. At last he spoke.

'Sorry, Nell. I didn't realize it was quite so awful. Are you in love with Perry?'

'Of course not! It was to have been a summer fling, that's all. I sort of bet myself that before I started work I would lose my virginity.' She forced herself to say the words; her face flamed. 'Perry seemed ideal. I didn't realize he would think it was something . . . ongoing.'

Edmund glanced sideways with a tentative grin and she reciprocated unwillingly. 'Honestly, Edmund, it's . . . awkward. I mean, he's so intense and I don't want to commit myself to anything even semi-permanent. I'm sorry. It sounds so terrible when I say it, yet it just happened like that. And I can't hurt his feelings by telling him I'm really rather bored.'

Edmund's smile exploded into laughter. But then he sobered.

'He's like his father. Poor old Mum. Mind you, she's as bad. When she was young – in the war – she probably behaved very badly indeed. But then she met Percy Westbrook. And she fell for him like a ton of bricks. Strange, isn't it?'

'We've always thought so.' Nell was enjoying this conversation; it was the kind of idle gossip she had shared with her mother – and with Perry too before he became so ardent. She said, 'Why did you refer to Uncle Percy as Perry's dad? He's yours too, you know.'

Edmund gave her that sideways glance again.

'Actually, he's not. That was one of the reasons I wanted to change my name. No . . .' He pre-empted the next question. 'No, I *don't* imagine I am a Pettiford. Uncle Ted would never have looked at another woman. But I didn't want to be a Westbrook any more. And Mum was a Pettiford so I didn't see that Percy could be angry about that.'

'I wasn't going to ask that. I was going to ask how you know Percy is not your father.'

'I think I've always known. So many small things don't add up. But I haven't got proof, if that's what you mean, and I don't particularly want it. One day I shall get Mum to admit it and tell me who my father is. I'd like it to be Dugdale Marsden actually.'

'Or Edward Maybury.' Nell really was enjoying herself. 'Hey, I bet it's Edward Maybury! Because of the name. Edmund. Edward.'

'I thought of that too. I'm going to see him next week. Ask him to approach the chairman of the British Rail Board. To donate a locomotive. He's got some clout and if I go with him as his adviser – don't laugh, Nell, I know I'm only a junior in the firm at present, but I am qualified to give advice about things like that. And the name will stand me in good stead. I think I'll be able to tell from his attitude whether or not—'

Nell interrupted suddenly. 'It will break Helena's heart! You can't do it!'

'I know. That's the trouble about trying to find out. Somebody might be wounded beyond repair.' He took a breath. 'I think I'll have to wait for Mum to tell me. It won't be long now. She is pretty vulnerable at the moment.'

'Percy and Hester?' Nell hazarded hopefully.

'Absolutely. Silly old fool has fallen for Hester, I'm afraid.'

'Oh . . . poor Aunt Hattie. There has always been a rivalry between them. So there's no chance Hester will discourage him?'

'It's all right. I've got a plan.'

'Really?' They were passing through Cheltenham and Nell craned her neck, thinking she recognized someone. A man on a bicycle – the bicycle looked like Mrs Mearment's. It was almost dark; she couldn't be sure, but – no, the man on the bicycle wasn't Mo. Nell relapsed into her seat.

Edmund said, 'Yes. I'm going to offer some competition to the old man. I'm going to make Hester fall in love with me.' He fiddled on the dashboard and switched on his lights.

Nell looked at Edmund incredulously. 'Don't be ridiculous! She's old enough to be your mother.'

'Just about. Yes. Eighteen years between us. I find that quite interesting.'

'Edmund, I'm . . . shocked. Seriously. You sound really calculating.'

'I'm doing it for Mum, remember. Also . . . she might know something.'

He turned off the old Cheltenham road and darkness closed in on them. The headlights picked out dear, familiar sights; the church tower, the line of yews, the old pump. They turned down the lane and bumped round the side of the house. There were lights on in Mrs Mearment's. Nell felt her heart thump.

'Oh, it's lovely to be home, Edmund. Thank you!' And she cupped his face, which shone dimly in the darkened car, and kissed him.

He said, 'Now who is being calculating?'

She laughed like a schoolgirl and got out of the car. 'Bring my briefcase, there's a dear!' she called over her shoulder. The kitchen door opened and there stood her mother and father. They enclosed her. Edmund, following more slowly, looked at them and knew a moment of pure envy. For a long time now he had not felt he belonged to the Westbrooks. His mother, yes; he had always been close to Hattie. But Percy, Aunt Enid, his grandmother – even Perry – did not belong to him or he to them. He had wanted to meet Nell and bring her home because he told himself it was his duty to protect her from Perry; but that was not the real reason. The real reason was that he felt so easy with Nell. Always had done. Surely he wasn't in love with her? He didn't want to be in love with anyone. It got in the way of everything and never made anyone happy. Look at that idiot Mo Checkers, working himself into a stupor so that he didn't have to think about Nell. Even Perry paced the floor at night . . . No, he didn't want that. He thought about Hester Ryecroft. He thought about the Ryecrofts generally. They interested him.

Hester was thankful that it was half-term. She felt completely exhausted from just six weeks of teaching. Sally Gold had – thank God – distanced herself after her confession of lesbian tendencies; even so, Hester was only too conscious of her presence in a room, her fleeting smiles, the enormous improvement in her work. She was a very clever girl and had never felt the need to work; now, suddenly everything had changed and her essays not only revealed her amazing imagination but also the amount of reading and research she was doing. One of them had even been illustrated! It was just too much.

And then this silly business with Percy seemed to have got completely out of hand. She could not believe that back in the summer she had thought the horrific cast in his eye was so attractive; now, when it swivelled very obviously over her figure, she could not suppress a shiver. The really awful thing was that Percy saw the shiver and thought she was trembling with desire. And Hattie did not find it amusing any more – if she ever had. Instead of getting angry she was looking much thinner and smaller and totally miserable. Hester told Duggie that she didn't enjoy being an old man's darling after all. And he lifted his brows and said, 'There you are. You now know something about yourself that you didn't know before. Where does this leave you with Richard Tibbolt?' She did not even answer that one.

She arrived home that Friday afternoon, promising herself that pleasure of the middle-aged: a nap before supper. The house was positively shining after Mrs Marvel's ministrations and a note informed her that the fish pie in the fridge would need an hour on number four. Hester made tea and took it into the sitting room. Outside the wind was blowing the leaves in heaps around the close. She sat away from the window and closed her eyes. For two pins she could have wept; but really there was nothing to weep about.

She was managing to relax when the phone rang. She should have let it ring but it might be Alice or Val. Nell was coming home tonight; it could be Nell though it was rather early . . . She went into the hall and picked up the receiver. It was Tibbolt.

Nell said, 'That was the best high tea I've had since – since—'

Val grinned. 'Since yesterday afternoon, I imagine. You've told us how wonderful your landlady is, remember.'

'She is. But even the tea tastes better at home.' She put her hand over her mother's. 'That does *not* mean I am homesick, darling. No more than I was at college. It simply means that home is . . . home.'

Alice smiled and Nell continued, 'I'll tell you something else for nothing. The tutors at college didn't get across what jolly hard work teaching is. All this guff about short hours and long holidays is a load of—'

Alice interrupted. 'May we consider the word "jolly"? Dad

156

and I get the impression that you are having fun and we imagined it was because of seeing Perry every weekend.'

Nell made a hideous face. 'Perry is boring. And uses up a lot of precious time too. But he has driven me round the district so that I know where I am.' She squeezed Alice's hand reassuringly. 'No, the jolly bit is definitely at school. I've got so much to tell you that won't go into letters or phone calls. Some of the little ones are so ... marvellous. Such marvellous creations – they're complete, all there, and they find their own solutions to problems if you give them space. One of them wanted to know why she wasn't getting through to God each morning at prayers. I made some silly suggestion like thinking about angels – can't remember now. The next day she brought her toy telephone in and used that. And now all my class, even the older ones, plug in to God each morning. Don't you think that is absolutely marvellous?'

Val and Alice looked at her shining eyes, her hair which was almost back to its normal colour, and smiled contentedly. Nell had found a place in the world.

After the boiled eggs, bread and butter, caraway seed cake and enough tea to 'drown a horse', as Nell put it, she told them she wanted to 'beat the bounds'.

'Yes, I know it's dark and windy and everything. But I need to settle in again. Besides which, I don't want to interrupt the two of you while you wash up. Washing-up time is quality time. You enjoy it.'

'Put on a coat!' Alice called. 'And don't be long!'

Nell went first into the front room, little used since Gran had inhabited it so comfortably. She peered through the open curtains and saw the trees blowing against the moonlit sky. The lane was empty; no cyclists anywhere. She went upstairs and stood in the doorway of her bedroom, which looked over the front door. It was her mother's old room. Nell had a single bed behind the door and a desk and chair in the window; her mother had had a double bed there. Sometimes she had shared it with Aunt Hester. The walls had absorbed their conversations, their laughter, their tragic tears.

Nell looked into her parents' bedroom, where her mother had so often slept with Grandma when Grandad worked the night shift. She tried to imagine it and then stopped abruptly. She did not envy her mother her special gift and she had no idea how it might be passed on to her; she took no chances.

She went back downstairs and quietly opened the front door. The night was not welcoming, though Martin Trickett had told her that he loved the wind. 'It comes to play with us, miss. Takes my cap off and plays football with it. It makes me laugh.'

She closed the front door behind her and braced herself against the coldness of it; that was the trouble with being stimulated, you often felt cold as well. She had wanted to wander down the garden and up to the bluebell woods, but it was too cold and dark for that. She went round the house, watched her parents in the lighted kitchen, washing up, smiling, talking. She felt herself on the point of exploding with love for them.

Another light came on, this time in Mrs Mearment's house; she crouched as if she could be seen, then straightened and went down the path to the fence and peered at the lighted window. Suddenly, shockingly, Mo appeared in its frame. She gasped and crouched again. He stood there a moment, then turned his head and spoke to someone, and reached up and pulled the curtains across.

Tibbolt's voice was achingly familiar. He did not introduce himself.

'They told me you'd been. That was a marvellous thing to do. Thank you, Hester.'

She bit her lip and felt her eyes stretch wide. So the Tibbolt twins had got in touch with their father, had told him of her visit.

She stammered, 'I – we – found them easily. I telephoned Hermione.'

'You could have asked me.'

'You did not leave me an address. And – somehow – I

thought you didn't know it. I didn't know what to do. We contacted social services . . . and then my – my friend – thought that their mother must have an address. And she did.'

'I see. Well, I am very grateful, Hester. They have actually been to see me. You made a very good impression.'

She said weakly, 'That was not the intention. In fact I have no idea what the intention was. *Your* intention.'

'So you did it for me?'

'I think I did it for me, actually, Richard. Because I realized I'd given nothing at all to you or your family. I wanted to make a start at . . . getting straight with myself.'

There was a pause and she began to think they had been cut off. Then he said with peculiar intensity, 'When can I see you? It's your half-term. I'm lecturing at the end of the week but until then – I could be with you in just over an hour, Hessie.'

She was shaken. She had forgotten the depth of their physical intimacy; it was nothing like the small thrill of Percy Westbrook's devotion.

She said, 'Wait. I did not go to see Toby and Eve in the hope that you would come back to me, Richard.'

'You always call me Tibbolt!'

'It was to show you that I had the upper hand in our relationship – surely you understood that? We have always been engaged in some kind of sexual duel, Richard. Always. We cannot go into old age fighting a duel.'

'Hester, has it not occurred to you that I have reached old age? I could retire in three years' time. If I so wished.'

She thought of the age difference between herself and Percy Westbrook. What was the matter with her? Of course she knew exactly what the matter was . . . She needed a father to replace memories of the sadistic maniac who had been Reginald Ryecroft.

She said feebly, 'You have a young mind.'

'Hester, listen. Let me come to you. Now.' He waited and she said nothing yet her resistance to him was obvious in her silence. He said, 'All right. Let us go to Leadon. Let's do the Pumpkin Coach again.'

'Don't be ridiculous—'

'I know it's almost winter – I know. But I don't care. Let's swim. Let's pretend we're both young again. Let's see if we can resurrect the magic. Let's—'

'Richard. The family have bought the Pumpkin Coach and leased the land all round it. We're going to run a private light railway. First of all as a tourist attraction and then, possibly, as a commercial goods-carrying line. I haven't been down there since . . . you and I went. But it could be full of voluntary workmen clearing the growth, renewing the ballast and rails.'

He seemed stunned. 'My God. How wonderful! This is down to your brother, I imagine.'

'I suppose it is. And then Alice's first boyfriend let her have the coach and the land it was on. And then darling Uncle Ted and Val went to see the Freeminers and the Forestry Commission, and Edward Maybury pulled some strings with the British Rail Board and . . . it's taken ages but I think it's going to happen.' She did not realize that her voice was energized with enthusiasm. She had not taken a great deal of interest in the step-by-step development of Val's original idea; now, as she listed it all for Tibbolt, she understood how enormous it was.

'Darling. Hester. Sweetheart. We must see it one more time. Let's go down there. Tomorrow? Have a look. What do you say?'

'For old times' sake?'

'And the new times. Darling, there's got to be new times for us. And when we remember the old times – especially down there – you will know that. For certain sure!' His chuckle came over the line. 'Do you remember when I put you in that flat in Clifton Village and you withheld all favours, sexual and otherwise, and then suddenly relented and rang me and asked me if I would like to see the Pumpkin Coach?'

'Of course I remember. How could I forget?'

'Last time . . . it was my fault it was such a fiasco—'

'No. It was because we stayed. After midnight the magic finishes. Just as it did with Cinderella's pumpkin coach.'

'You sound the image of Alice Ryecroft.'

'Yes. She is my best friend. My closest and dearest friend. And she is married to my brother.'

'And you still love her?'

'I do. I could not have borne it if anyone else in the world had married Val.'

'Hester, you are a very complicated person and that is why I love you and cannot live without you.' She said nothing and he hurried on. 'I will be with you as soon as I can. I'll leave Bristol at eight ack emma and hopefully arrive in time for breakfast.'

She said, 'All right. But, Richard ... don't expect too much. I think I am changing and I don't know what I am changing into.'

She put the phone down. At one time the call would have filled her with triumphant joy. What on earth *was* the matter with her?

Breakfast at Lypiatt Bottom started at 8.15 and was still being enjoyed an hour later. Val flapped the newspaper and decided aloud that this Muhammad Ali or Cassius Clay or whatever he called himself deserved the title if he could spout poetry in a boxing ring.

Alice said, 'He's got a nice face too,' and Nell nodded agreement.

Val said, 'My God. Women's judgements!'

Nell said, 'I think I'll pop over to Mrs Mearment's and see how Mo is doing.'

Val glanced at Alice. 'Actually, Nell, Mo and Edward Maybury intended to go to Newport today to see about an engine in the sheds there. Steam. Edward has pulled some strings and it could be donated to us. But Mo needs to see whether restoration is viable.'

'Oh.' Nell felt peculiarly flat. 'Perhaps I'll slip over quickly now and—'

'They planned to leave at seven.' Val cut a fourth piece of toast in half. 'They'll be back at a decent time. Mum and I wondered whether you'd care to come and see progress. You'll be surprised at how far we've got in the six weeks since you were there.'

'Longer than that. I went with Mo to plot the lines – well, uncover them really.' Nell swallowed. She hadn't wanted to go back to the Pumpkin Coach but if she stayed home there was a risk Perry might come to see her.

She accepted the other half of her father's toast. 'I'd love that,' she said, smiling. 'Yes. Let's wash up quickly and go, shall we?'

Later that morning Helena Maybury greeted her guest with much pleasure.

'Edmund! How very nice to see you, my dear. Is everything all right – your parents – Perry?'

'Absolutely, Aunt Helena. I brought Nell home last night. On my way to see her now. Thought I'd pop in for a word with Uncle Edward.'

Helena ushered him into her small sitting room overlooking the Devil's Chimney.

'He's already left, my dear. Have a coffee and tell me how you're getting on down at Smithers and Jameson.'

Momentary disappointment at Edward Maybury's absence made him pause on the threshold but then he smiled and sat down.

'I'm having a close look at company law just now. With a view to representing the Pumpkin Light Railway in future!' She clapped her hands and made to go into the kitchen to make the coffee. He said, 'And of course, one of the reasons I changed my name to Pettiford was because one day I hope to add it to the headed notepaper. "Smithers, Jameson and Pettiford" – Gramps would be proud of that, don't you think?'

Helena paused. She had known old Will Pettiford only by reputation, but even now the name still meant something. And here was his grandson – his *great*-grandson – offering his work as a tribute to the old man.

162

She said, 'I wonder what your great-grandfather would make of the Pumpkin Line? By the way, that's why Edward is out today. He and Mo are looking at an old steam engine in the Newport sheds. Mo is hoping he will be able to assess what needs doing to make it a working locomotive again.'

She went out then and Edmund sat very still and looked through the window at the ancient rock formation and the view beyond. Mo Checkers, the stranger who had come among them, had taken Edmund's idea and brought it about.

Edmund prided himself on his objectivity, his ability to stand aside from all family matters and comment on them sparsely and with amusement. Suddenly, objectivity had gone; he was in at the emotional deep end. Disliking Mo Checkers very much indeed.

Fifteen

By the time Edward Maybury and Mo Checkers had reached the old sheds at Orchard Junction, it was almost light and the wind had dropped to reveal a typically grey English day.

'Clocks go back next weekend,' Edward commented, parking his Armstrong Siddeley on a rough piece of ground almost next to the sheds. 'Nights will be darker but at least the mornings will start at a proper time.'

Mo, mindful of Nell's adjurations about making conversation and feeling relaxed in the company of this elderly man, said, 'I quite like the dark mornings. Christmassy. My father always got up very early to do his paperwork and we would have a cup of tea together before Mother got up.'

'Ah. Special times. Private times.'

'My mother was frightened of the dark. Dreadful things always seemed to happen at night in China. Father and I . . . we found it protective.'

'How interesting.' Edward glanced sideways; he had never given much thought to the boy's foreignness but he knew Helena had tried to winkle information from Mo before now and got nowhere. He felt that for her sake he should make an effort but could think of absolutely nothing to say that might elicit anything more. He was surprised when Mo met his glance and smiled.

'Thank you for not asking. For taking me in as you have done. For taking me to the theatre that night.'

'That was Helena, of course.' Edward huffed a little and was thankful to see a figure coming towards them out of the greyness. This would be the chap who would unlock the doors for them. Edward realized suddenly that, Helena or no Helena, he did not wish to be a father confessor to Mo.

He opened his door and slid out of his seat. 'Good morning to you,' he said much too heartily, then held out a hand. 'My God, is it Lewis? Awre Junction?'

They shook hands heartily. Edward, suddenly garrulous, began to reprise Mr Lewis's career for him.

'Well, sir, I were actually at Awre Junction just a coupla years. Then I transferred up here to Leadon for a few more and finished up messenger in the Newport office when the rheumatics got a-'old of me!' Lewis grinned. 'Been retired the last ten years but I can't keep away, and when I heard about your little railway I kep' an eye open. This engine, *Devonshire Belle*, she bin in the sheds over ten years an' I thought she might just do for you.' He turned to Mo. 'And this is your engineer? They gets younger all the time, cleverer too.'

Mo shook the proffered hand and let the staccato speech flow round him and carry him along to the shed with its rusty padlock and dungeon chains. He wondered whether Nell would class this as 'conversation' and grinned in spite of himself. Mr Lewis saw the smile and misconstrued it.

'I might be old, young feller, but that's something in my favour when it comes to little schemes like yours and Mr Maybury's here. Cos I remembers. I remembers when these railways covered the old forest, when the first Severn Bridge was still up and running. And the viaduct over the Wye.' He turned to Edward and suddenly his face was split by a hideous grin. 'I remembers old Will Pettiford. An' his son, young Ted Pettiford. An' I've had plenty of contacts with 'is granddaughter – Ted's daughter – Alice, weren't it?' He turned back to Mo. 'Yes, I know the Pettifords.'

It was his trump card and Mo, though understanding the need to talk, also knew when to be quiet. He beamed at Lewis and clapped him on the shoulder, and it was obviously the right thing to do because the grin came back wider than before and revealed some stumps that might well have been teeth a long time ago.

'You'd better call me Bert, young man,' he said. 'I think I might be in your company often in future.'

Mo continued to beam. 'My name is Michael,' he said.

Edward, standing back now, his influence and introductions over, tried to store this small exchange in his mind. Helena would find it interesting. Most interesting. He followed the other two into the blackness of the shed. To the left of the old hand-cranked turntable, the *Belle* was stabled on a short rail right against the buffers. Sidelined; ready for the scrapyard. He looked at her: she was silhouetted against the cracked skylights, the familiar outline suddenly heart-wrenching. There were the front buffers and the small ledge round which the ganger would go with his oil can, and the lamp boy with the flickering front lamps. Above that, dim in the darkness, was the front of the boiler, the steam valve, the squat stack – was that a gleam of brass after all this time? – the round portholes in the driver's cab, the square tender . . . Edward felt himself transported back in time, remembering a trip on a ganger's trolley through the forest . . . Who had been with him? Ted Pettiford, he thought, and someone else, a new recruit, a lad clerk called . . . Joe Adair.

Mo was already in the cab, on his hands and knees.

'Firebox seems intact. Hardly any rust and no splits that I can see by this torch.'

Lewis's voice was almost contented. 'You'm right there, lad. Bin through it with a toothcomb. Sound as a drum.'

Mo raised his head to the level of the cab opening and looked down to meet Lewis's eyes. They both smiled.

The sound of Richard Tibbolt's car was unmistakable as it echoed hollowly through the tunnel of Elizabethan houses and into the close. Hester checked in the hall mirror that every hair on her head was gathered into her chignon, then opened the front door. Her hand shook slightly and her throat was dry. The sensation was familiar: she had felt like this at the farmhouse in Provence. Every time Richard had approached she had thought she might faint.

He came up the path looking as she must look – apprehensive. She realized how grey was his hair, how stooped his long figure. And she had insisted on him swimming in Bracewell's Pool . . . What was the *matter* with her? Was it something to do with her father's sadistic streak?

He did not hold out his arms to her and she found herself backing away from him, holding on to the front door. He came into the narrow hall and leaned against the wall and looked at her.

'Oh Hester,' he said.

She closed the door carefully, her back to him. She knew she could turn and kiss him now and they would go upstairs and everything would be as it had been. Maybe even better because Percy had been so ardent . . . Oh God. Percy.

She turned but did not move towards him. 'Richard,' she said.

He became alert; he knew something really had changed; she had forgotten how agonizingly sensitive he had always been to her moods. She almost smiled at the thought because she was no longer moody. At least that was one good thing.

She said, 'I waited breakfast. There are croissants and honey and coffee on the stove.' She edged past him and went into the kitchen and he followed her and sat down at the table without a word. She poured coffee and took the croissants from the oven.

He said in a low voice, 'You have tried to re-create the kitchen in Provence – that first holiday.'

'The only holiday. I never went back again. The checked tablecloth . . . I counted the squares, you know. So that I wouldn't have to look at you and know that you didn't really love me. The napkins. The big coffee cups.'

'I'm sorry, Hessie. I'm so sorry. I cannot imagine how I could have been so utterly selfish. I actually thought I was helping you!'

'You did! I am not reproaching you, Richard – I didn't mean to, honestly! I had always thought of myself as some

167

kind of second-rate citizen. You taught me about sex – the sheer power of it. When I got back home thinking I was nursing a broken heart, I realized what you had given me. Suddenly, I had confidence, Richard. I knew you'd come back at some point. And I knew what to do.' She smiled wryly. 'And I did it. Didn't I, my dear?'

He reached across the table. 'Hessie ... you know I love you, don't you? The question is, do you – can you – love me?'

She avoided his hand and broke her croissant. 'I don't know either of those things, Richard. As I said on the phone, I cannot continue to use sex as a weapon and I need to know what else there is besides. And as for you loving me ... you left me that day after we'd been to the Pumpkin Coach. You didn't love me then. And if you love me because I did what you asked and went to see the twins, that is not enough for me.' She looked up at him. 'I'm sorry, Richard.'

There was a long pause. Then he picked up his cup and sipped thoughtfully.

'What has happened, Hester? Can you tell me?'

'So much. A great deal is internal and I haven't even sorted it out yet. But as for events ... I am having what I thought was a flirtation with Percy Westbrook.' She ignored his indrawn breath. 'I think he thinks he loves me. It's ridiculous. But it has made me realize that I love Hattie and I am hating the fact that she is hurt and it is my fault.'

'It takes two people to—'

'I have always wanted a different father. Uncle Ted was first choice but he had Alice already. At first I imagined Percy ... but that relied on sex again, you see. No good. Duggie Marsden has stepped in. He took me to Bristol. He lets me talk rubbish. He is ... reassuring.'

'Well, that's good.'

'Yes, it is. Because school has somehow changed. I discover that I am popular. The girls call me Tough Piecrust because they like me being tough with them. The head girl, a beautiful creature called Sally Gold, tells me she is a lesbian and that she is in love with me. She is a brilliant English student. We are together a great deal of the time. That is not good, Richard.'

'Rather like you and me. Only . . . different.'

She met his steady grey eyes and suddenly they were laughing.

She spluttered, 'That's what Duggie said – well, not quite. But he said it's a classic relationship and very precious and I must jolly well learn to deal with it tactfully, which he is quite sure I will do because I have an innate skill where young people are concerned!' She pulled a handkerchief from the sleeve of her cardigan and wiped her eyes. 'Oh Richard . . .'

He took his own handkerchief and held it to her nose and she blew into it like a child.

'He is quite right too. I should have been the one giving you these words of wisdom, Hester. Perhaps you are right about the sex . . . I'm not sure whether it has been a weapon though. Perhaps – perhaps it has got in the way sometimes? Perhaps we have been unable to see past it?'

She lifted her shoulders wearily. 'I don't know any more. I am . . . such a mess, Richard. Percy . . . he is desperately missing his mother. Edmund has changed his name from Westbrook to Pettiford and that is breaking his heart. He still takes Enid out and about but he did that for his mother and now she's not here . . . You know, Richard, when you stop thinking about life entirely from your own point of view . . . when you worry about how other people feel and react . . . I wonder whether you can ever be happy again.'

He cupped her face in his hands. 'You mean that being unselfish and sentient is jolly hard work?' He grinned persuasively. 'I do understand that, my love. But if we did it together, what then? Would that make it easier?'

'But you're not like me!'

'Hermione would not agree with you. And when you and I first met . . . I wanted you and I made sure I got you. Wasn't that why you wanted to avenge yourself? Wasn't that the start of it all? Come on, Hessie. We've both been out for everything we could get. We've thought of ourselves as top dogs for so long.'

She shook her head. 'I'm not thinking straight.' She swallowed the last of her croissant and dusted the flakes from her fingers. 'I know I'm glad to see you.'

'That's enough to be going on with.' He smiled. 'And I'm looking forward to seeing the Pumpkin Line.'

'All right. But . . . our old relationship is over, my dear. And if there is to be a new one, then it must be different from when we first met. I cannot be – I cannot *allow* myself to be – vulnerable again.'

He frowned slightly but nodded. Looking at her standing up, tall, slim, like a ballerina with her hair strained back from her face, he wanted her quite desperately.

'May I kiss you, Hessie? As friends?'

She looked down at him and then shook her head slowly. 'It's not that I don't want to.' She waved a hand helplessly. 'I've tried to explain. I am a mess. I must sort myself out first.'

'Do you mean your feelings for Percy Westbrook?'

'Not *my* feelings. But yes, I do mean Percy. Somehow I have to finish things with him. So that Hattie isn't hurt. And he isn't hurt. And I rather think Edmund might have seen something so I have to do something about that too.'

'And then?'

'And then everything will be clearer.' She looked at him. 'Won't it?'

He took her hand and put it against his face. He did not know whether it would be clearer or even more muddled, but he knew he would wait for her.

Valentine, Alice and Nell arrived at the Pumpkin Coach just before midday. A dozen volunteers were still working on clearing the line and it was a simple matter now to walk from sleeper to sleeper through the high walls of bracken and emerge into the vastness of the forest cathedral. As usual Alice sensed all the other women who had come here since the coach was first stabled by the pool. Joe Adair's grandmother, pregnant after one visit; Mitzie, careless and wanton and so soon pregnant with Hattie; herself . . . and Val. She cut off her thoughts quickly before she could begin wondering whether Nell and Mo had discovered the 'magic'.

When Hester and Richard arrived it seemed the most natural thing in the world. Val pumped Richard's hand and immediately began to tell him about the plans for the railway. Hester was obviously delighted to see them all and she and Alice set to immediately to clear out the rubbish from the old coach. Edward came crashing through the undergrowth soon afterwards and crowds of them gathered near the pool to eat sandwiches and to make a careful fire of the old blankets and deckchairs from the coach. Nell was very happy to see Edward; they sat with a group of the volunteer diggers and were caught up with their enthusiasm. Alice and Hester sat on the steps of the coach and watched Richard and Val pushing their way deeper into the forest in an effort to find a continuation of the railway line. Val held the map in front of him like a talisman and Richard reached across and pointed and then urged Val further round the pool.

Hester said, 'I'm happy.' She looked at Alice wide-eyed. 'Alice, just at this precise moment, I am happy. How can that be? The magic has gone, my life is definitely in its second half, I've done nothing with it . . . yet I can be happy!'

Alice smiled, knowing exactly what Hester meant. 'The fleeting moment,' she murmured. Then, in a stronger voice, 'Perhaps the magic did not always bring happiness, Hessie. Now it's the after-midnight time. Real life. Nothing to do with magic. A lot to do with – with—'

'Appreciation?' Hester suggested.

They met each other's gaze; brown eyes looked into blue ones; suddenly they were laughing. 'We're getting old and pretentious,' Hester spluttered.

'Isn't it great!' Alice said. 'We're renewing our best-friends vows!'

'D'you remember the time you climbed out of the common-room window on to the laboratory roof to sunbathe?' Hester could hardly speak for laughing. 'And you actually argued with Doc Grey that if we'd done fire practice out there, then we should be entitled to use it for sun-bathing!' They clutched each other helplessly.

Helena had a delightful after-lunch nap then prepared a high tea for 'the boys', as she thought of them. They duly returned, Mo in need of the newly installed shower, Edward as immaculate as ever. They had had no lunch because Mo had been unable to tear himself away from the *Devonshire Belle*. 'I really think that the pistons will need no more than greasing . . . It's amazing. Those old locomotive engineers were . . . amazing!' He looked at the two of them, at the laden table and the darkening view outside. 'And this is . . . amazing.'

'Have some more cake, dear,' Helena said fondly. 'I am so glad you have found us and become one of us. After what you have gone through . . .' Mo looked at her, brows raised, and she added quickly, 'Well, you know, we gather that your child-hood was not happy and . . .' Her voice faded at Mo's obvious astonishment.

It was Edward who said uncomfortably, 'We've got the wrong idea, I think, my love. Mo – Michael – was telling me earlier how close he was to his father.'

'And to Mother.' Mo looked at Helena. 'I am so sorry. I was pretty desperate when I came here. I should have told you – told you all about my family. But somehow I could not speak.' He bit his lip, looked away and then when Helena began to blanket everything with soothing chatter he looked back and blurted, 'When I fell in love with Nell, everything else seemed . . . irrelevant. Even my work on metal stress. Until the Pumpkin Line. The Pumpkin Line has always given me strength. It has magical properties.'

Edward cleared his throat. Helena nodded doubtfully. 'The Pettifords have always thought so, of course. It is very damp down there. That pool—'

Mo laughed. 'It is mysterious. Exciting. My father would

have wanted this to happen. I am so close to him down there.' He waved a hand at the view. 'I am close to him here.'

Helena stared. Edward said something about closing her mouth. She did so and swallowed. Then opened it to speak.

Mo looked at her and nodded slightly. 'He is dead. So is my mother. They were in a car driving to Alnmouth – they loved it there, the beach is magnificent, you know. Very quiet. Except for one of these . . .' he spat the words 'boy racers.' He shrugged. 'He was killed too. And at least they went together. They were very close. I cannot imagine one without the other.'

Edward and Helena reached out to him automatically and offered what comfort they could.

Percy Westbrook drove his mother's ancient car into Gloucester that morning, desperate to see Hester and finally take her to bed. The house was empty, he knew before he rang the bell. He sat in the car and thought about what a fool he was; then how much he missed his mother; then how he wished – had always wished – that he had personally killed Reggie Ryecroft for taking his virgin sister and making her the broken being she was now. He turned the car in the close – he had never been able to reverse it – and drove slowly home, feeling very much older than his seventy-eight years. He was nearly eighty. But he did not feel eighty when he was with Hester. She was so beautiful, and had seemed so attainable at first.

He drove into the garage at Leckhampton House and revved the engine before switching off. Hattie hated him doing that; she always said the fumes came into the kitchen. He smiled faintly. Hattie. He needed Hattie, she would solve all his problems . . . She had made a dynasty of the Westbrook family. Edmund and then Perry . . . and baby Mitzie. He got out of the car, tears in his eyes because it seemed to him that Edmund wanted to opt out of the dynasty. He went through the kitchen and into the big sitting room with its baby grand and windows opening on to the garden and the tennis court . . . and there they were. Hattie, Perry and Enid. He opened his arms and Hattie went into them.

He whispered, 'You're so thin.'

She said, 'That's the best compliment I've had for years!'

Perry snorted and Enid said, 'Shall I dish up now?'

Percy said, 'We'll do it, sis. I'm back home now. Everything is going to be all right.' He kissed Hattie. 'I must have been mad, darling.'

She whispered, instantly forgiving him, 'But you really are back now?'

'Yes.'

Perry snorted again as they left the room. Enid began to cry. Perry said, 'There, there, Aunty. Don't be upset. Something has happened and everything is all right again. No need for Edmund to seduce Hester . . . this is how Ma and Pa have always been and we ought to know it by now.' Enid continued to cry and Perry said, 'Look, let's have that drink. Then we can eat together and everything will be . . . back to normal. How does that sound?'

Enid accepted the glass that Perry handed to her and managed a watery smile.

That night, in the big bed, where Hattie had so often imagined herself the archetypal earth mother and Percy had been able to forget his squint and his age, they made love with a deep understanding and acceptance of each other, far removed from all posturing or role-playing. Percy told Hattie that she had made his family strong and good, that her kindness to Enid had saved her from a complete breakdown, that his mother had always doted on her . . . He told her how sorry he was for letting Hester's beauty go to his head and assured her that through it all he had never stopped loving Hattie. He said that it was something to do with second childhood and she laughed and kissed him and said it didn't matter; not a jot. And then he lay on his back, smiling contentedly, and was asleep within a few minutes. She lay listening to his gentle snores and then was gone too.

She woke at first light. Neither of them had moved. She knew instantly that he was not there. For a few minutes she did not even raise herself to look at him and confirm that he was dead. She accepted it within her physical body before her brain could accept it into her mind. She stayed perfectly still within his lifeless arm and felt deep thankfulness for his easy departure and for the fact that they had made love one last time. Then she carefully disengaged herself, slid out of bed and put on her latest black negligee before going downstairs to tell Enid and Perry.

Sixteen

They got back from the church at midday.

Leckhampton House looked as it always looked, a big family home, welcoming, generous; yet, now, strangely different. It had been dark when Hattie arrived almost thirty years before, heavy with plush and mahogany. The garden had huddled around the tennis court as if trying to break the wire and take over. Gradually Hattie had changed all that. The shrubs were contained into a sort of maze, the lawn exposed and kept green and mowed, a perfect gallery from which to watch the tennis. The house was opened up, French windows installed in the sitting room, door curtains removed so that light flooded into the hall and highlighted the tessellated floor. All the paintwork was changed to white and the heavy flock wallpaper replaced with the new pale colours of the latest Walpamur paint. Hattie had kissed old Mrs Westbrook and said, 'I know change is not always welcome, darling. But I want it to be bright for the children . . . Darling Percy wants a big family . . . well, you know that of course.' And Grandma Westbrook had somehow colluded with her and had chosen pale pink for her own room.

Perhaps that was it; the curtains drawn until after the funeral made the house dim once again, reduced the walls and doors to greyness. It was a bit better when Edmund went round opening the curtains. But not entirely.

It had been an early funeral because the nights were long now that the clocks had gone back. 'If we're all milling around here in the dark, I think I shall go mad,' Hester had informed the undertaker. 'Besides, my niece has to go back to Birmingham the same evening . . . She could only get the one day off.' She stopped, realizing how irrelevant all this was. The undertaker had told her to leave it all to him.

So they arrived in ones and twos; the same group who had gathered for old Mrs Westbrook not long ago. Percy was replaced by Richard Tibbolt and Enid had to go to her room. As far as anyone knew, she had not stopped crying since Percy's death; Perry told them it had started before that.

Hester had persuaded Mrs Marvel to take on the brunt of the catering, and the kitchen and dining room seemed heavy with food. They stood in groups in the hall and sitting room; nobody quite liked to make themselves comfortable in any of the enormous armchairs. Edmund sat at the piano and lifted the lid. Hattie said, 'If you dare play the *Moonlight* I'll leave the house!' Edmund looked up and smiled fleetingly. 'Neither of us will leave, Ma. We're a unit now. You, Perry, me. The last of the Westbrooks.'

'And Enid,' Hattie reminded him.

'Of course.'

They continued to stare into each other's eyes. Hattie said, 'Do you mean you're going to be a Westbrook again?'

And he said again, 'Of course.'

'Oh Edmund. Thank you.'

Nell was at her elbow. 'Come on, darling. A stiff drink. As mixed by your baby son. Your hands are like ice.'

'Oh Nell . . .' Hattie felt her whole body was full of tears. 'Thank you. And – and I'm so glad, so very glad, about you and Perry. It would have been lovely if it could have been Edmund but of course not. Perry and you . . . marvellous.' She drifted away, smiling, remembering when Nell had come home from college last spring and practically asked permission to seduce Perry. They had all laughed together then. She had not known what was in store . . . It seemed now like another life.

Nell looked at Edmund, brows raised. 'What did that mean?'

He shrugged. 'Did you hear what I said? I'll go back to the

177

Westbrook name. Maybe later, probably much later, I can have another go at being a Pettiford.'

'Thank goodness! It was one of your less than wonderful ideas.'

He looked down at the piano keys and began to pick out a tune. His mother had heard what he'd said all right; and he had heard what she'd said too. He bit his bottom lip and tried to make sense of it. Nell had gone, passing drinks round and urging people towards the numerous quiches and sandwiches. In her place stood Hester. He glanced at her and put both hands on the keys. He had been going to try to come between Hester and his father and now there was no need. But she still might know something about his parentage.

He said quietly, 'This was Dad's favourite tune. An old music-hall number, I think.' He began to play 'April Showers'. She watched his fingers; her expression was completely blank and he wondered whether she had in fact loved Percy. When he finished she nodded slowly.

'Yes. I can imagine he would enjoy something sentimental like that. By the way, it was sung by Al Jolson. A long time ago.'

'Thank you, Hester. Are you all right?'

'As all right as everyone else – a bit more all right than your mother, I imagine.'

'You remember persuading Percy that it was OK to let me change my name – I suppose you sold it to him as a young man's fancy?' She shrugged and he went on, 'I've just told my mother that I am changing it back to Westbrook.'

'Ah. That would please your father.'

'Would it?' He played a chord very softly. 'Do you know who my father is, Hester?'

Her blank look sharpened into alertness. He smiled.

'So you do? Tell me.'

'I don't know what you're talking about, Edmund. Obviously—'

'Obviously you either know or you have had your suspicions.'

'I must go and find Richard.'

178

He played another chord, hard. She jumped and her hands on the piano clenched into fists.

'What did Percy do for you, Hessie? Were you an old man's fancy? Did you see him as your sugar daddy?'

'Edmund! How dare you speak to me like this!'

He pressed his lips together, knowing he had gone too far. 'I'm sorry.'

'I'm going—' She half turned and his hands crashed on to the keys again.

'I still want to know, Hessie.' He took a deep breath. 'Why won't you tell me?'

'Stop bullying me, Edmund! You remind me of—' She stopped speaking; looked at him as if she had never seen him before and walked out of the room.

In the hall Hattie stood holding the newel post, tears streaming down her face.

'It's all right,' she forestalled Hester. 'It's just that damned song. Nell was humming it too just now. It was one of Percy's favourites.'

Hester said angrily, 'Edmund knew that. He was playing it purposely.'

'He thinks it's good for me to cry.' Hattie smiled through her tears. 'Oh Hessie . . . d'you know, I'm so glad you got to know and understand Percy in the last few months. You can see why I am going to miss him so much. Lots of people thought our marriage was odd, you know. Ted tried to dissuade me – he called it Beauty and the Beast—' Hester was certain Ted would never have said that, but she let it go. '—but you know how persuasive my dear Percy was. There was no turning your back on him. Was there?' Hester was conscious that her reply was crucial; Hattie needed to know how far they had gone.

'I didn't know him that well, darling.' Hester produced a wisp of a handkerchief and mopped Hattie's face. 'He told me you wanted him to be kind to me because of – well, you know, Tibbolt and everything. But I was so wrapped up in my own misery . . . Oh Hattie, I'm so sorry.'

179

She could have been sorry for a number of reasons but Hattie did not question that. She buried her face in Hester's neck and sobbed helplessly.

'Thank you, Hessie. Oh, thank you so much,' she gasped.

Hester said later to Richard Tibbolt that it was the most ambivalent conversation she and Hattie had ever had.

'But you spiked Edmund's guns anyway.' Richard stroked her long hair, buried his face in it, drank her in.

'I'm not at all sure about that. She and I – we want to believe each other. That doesn't mean we do. Edmund could destroy that very easily.' She sighed. 'The trouble is, I've nothing to go on except tiny little bits of evidence and an enormous amount of intuition. And the end result is rather . . . appalling. I shall have to keep it to myself.'

'He has got a right to know, darling.'

'Only if it doesn't hurt – damage – anyone else.' She stood up and he realized that she had hardly noticed that he had been caressing her for the past ten minutes. 'Let's have a cup of tea. That was all pretty ghastly – I'm sorry, Richard, I shouldn't have let you come.'

'You couldn't have stopped me.' He came behind her. 'I needed to see that the whole Percy episode was finished. Fate obviously means us to be together.'

She sighed, still not registering his mood. 'You've hit it on the head, my dear. Fate. I wanted it to be me, not fate. I wanted to turn him round, show him that Hattie was there, waiting. Oh God. I feel I'll never be rid of him now.'

He stayed where he was and watched her as she moved expertly around the cooker. Then he sat down again and drank the tea she poured, nibbled the biscuits she put before him. If he had hoped to stay the night he was sadly disappointed because as soon as he had emptied his cup she took it to the sink and spoke over her shoulder.

'It's dark already, Richard. You will ring me when you get home, won't you?'

'Of course.' He fetched his greatcoat from the cupboard

under the stairs and struggled into it. She dried her hands and turned, smiling a forced smile.

'What are you going to do for Christmas? It's not far off now, is it?'

'No.' Obviously he had hoped to spend it here with her. But he said suddenly, 'I'm going to take the twins over to France. Hermione will be there – she's had a bust-up with her partner. We might be able to give Eve and Toby a family Christmas.' He laughed, making it sound ridiculous, but as she stood in the doorway and watched him climb into the car she thought that it wasn't so ridiculous after all. Christmas and families; she must never forget that Richard had a family and perhaps this was a good chance to back away and let him be with them.

Nell had hoped to see Mo but of course he had never met Uncle Percy. He wasn't there and she did not have time to ask her mother about him; or so she told herself. In view of what Hattie had said, she felt bound to let Perry drive her back, come into her upstairs flat and do 'the whole works' – though in fact it did not happen like that, and when he rolled away from her she realized that he was crying. She comforted him as best she could but he refused tea and sympathy and was still sniffling helplessly when he got back in Edmund's car and drove off. She watched his rear lights till they disappeared round the bend, and then went indoors. Her landlady called out that there was a cottage pie in the oven. She took it upstairs on a tray with a pile of bread and butter and ate ravenously, a book propped against the cruet. It was Thursday tomorrow. Carol practice first of all, then numbers work until playtime and after playtime a rehearsal of 'The Owl and the Pussycat' with Shirley and her class. Nell smiled to herself. It was good to get back to real life. Christmas would be here all too soon and she was bound to see something of Mo then.

Mo spent the whole of that Wednesday with Bert Lewis at

Orchard Junction. He was supposed to be using one of the firm's welding guns to test the pre-stressed aluminium in the laboratory. Instead he packed the gun and a mask and took them with him. He was fitting new valves to the *Belle*'s piston sleeves. Bert had been cleaning the *Belle* for the past three weeks and in places her dark green livery glowed like jewellery in the darkness of the shed. Today it was the turn of the smoke stack.

They paused at midday to devour Mrs Mearment's sandwiches.

'We'll be able to try a fire in the box this weekend,' Bert mumbled, champing into a doorstep with his half a dozen teeth. 'We'll fill the boiler. See if those pistons will bite.'

'They'll bite,' Mo said confidently, though there was a flutter in his stomach. You never really knew what would happen. A piece of metal was one thing, an intricate assembly of pieces quite another.

'Thought you'd be going to that feller's funeral,' Bert commented, picking up another sandwich, discovering it was beef and replacing it in favour of the soft cheese. ''E's as good as a Pettiford, 'idn't 'e?'

'He married Hattie Pettiford. Yes. But . . . well, I'm a hanger-on really, Bert. They wouldn't want me at a family affair.'

'You did ought to get in with that Alice's daughter. Fancy name.'

'Helena. They call her Nell.'

'Nellie, eh? I knew a Nellie once. Round as a butter ball, 'er were. An' even tastier. Then I married 'er and she soured off a bit.'

Mo put his head back and laughed. 'I thought I would marry this Nellie. But she preferred her cousin. That's another reason for not going to the funeral – the cousin will be there because it's his dad they're burying.'

'Never mind, lad. We're better off without marrying them. This is the life for the likes of you and me.'

'I think you're right, Bert. Have this last sandwich. It's cheese.'

'Don't mind if I do. Your landlady do know 'ow to make sandwiches, don't she? Half a pound of butter to a pound of cheese and stick it together with piccalilli. Not bad.'

Mo laughed and got back beneath the old locomotive. Yes, this was real life all right. And he'd be seeing Nell soon; at Christmas.

Alice and Val went to bed early and held on to each other very tightly. Val whispered, 'She'll be all right. You see.'

'It's Perry and Enid too. I think Edmund is coping. But Enid has gone completely to pieces. And Perry isn't a lot better.'

'D'you know what he told me? That they – Hattie and Percy – went upstairs together before supper. Percy had been out in the car and he came home and just went straight into Hattie's arms and then they went upstairs. He might even have died while they were making love.'

'Well . . .' Alice tipped her head back to try to see his face in the darkness. 'I don't know what to say to that, Val. Is it meant to make us feel better about Percy's death? Or very much worse?'

'Better, idiot! They hadn't been themselves for ages – since Hessie came on the scene. But then, at the end, everything was all right. He turned his back on Hessie and went home to Hattie. Don't you see? It's wonderful!'

'I'm not sure. But I'll take your word for it. It's just been such an awful day, I can't see any silver linings in the clouds whatsoever!'

'Well, there are. Edmund has given up on trying to become a Pettiford. Dear old Duggie took some tea up to Enid and reported back that she drank it. Hester was with the Two-timing Tibbolt. Mo telephoned to say he has fitted the valves into *Belle*. Perry pulled himself together long enough to take Nell back to school.'

'That's what I don't like. Mo fitting valves when he should have been with Nell. And Perry taking her back and no doubt in bed with her at this precise moment!'

'You've changed your tune, Allie. I thought you weren't keen on Mo Checkers.'

'I still don't like the fact that we know nothing whatsoever about him. Have you noticed he tells us he comes from the North – what part, for goodness' sake? He never mentions his parents, his school . . . and this research work, presumably funded by his university. Which university?'

'He's not a great talker, sweetheart. And anyway, he's proved himself. Why should he have to tell us anything at all about his background?'

'No reason. And that is why I've changed my tune, as you put it. There's something . . . *staunch* about him. True. And he does talk – if I run into him in the garden he mentions the weather. And – and – he loves Nell. I know it. And in spite of all this malarkey with Perry, I think she loves him.'

'Malarkey? That's a new one for you, Allie.' He smiled into her hair as he felt her relax. For a long time after she was asleep he lay looking into the darkness and wondering how Hattie felt about being alone.

Ted and Doffie were worried too and Doffie offered to stay the night.

Hattie dried her tears yet again and tried to focus through puffy eyes.

'You know you are both my favourite people, next to the boys and Enid of course. But I want to be alone. Really. I want to think and think and think about Percy. I've still got his family with me and we can talk about him. I want Enid to tell us all about when he was young – remember, he was fifty when I met him.'

'Surely not tonight, old girl.' Ted thought of Enid upstairs, probably in an exhausted sleep. He wouldn't put it past Hattie to wake her and drag her downstairs to be given the third degree.

'No. Tonight is just for me and Percy. Twenty-nine years we've been married and I want to remember every one.'

'Oh Hattie,' Doffie mourned.

'I know. It's not long enough. But I'll tell you this, Doffie darling. I know I'm selfish and I know I haven't been completely faithful to him but I made him happy. You have to admit that, Doffie. I made him happy always.'

Doffie, remembering her angry criticism in the past, knelt by this wayward niece of Ted's and clasped her hard. 'I do know that, darling. I do.'

'And if he'd really wanted Hester, I wouldn't have stood in his way. That's how much I loved him.'

At this, Doffie began to cry too and Ted, shifting from foot to foot, said, 'I'll find Duggie. Time we went home.'

He found Edmund in the kitchen, eating some of the leftovers and frowning at the dark window. At least he wasn't crying.

'Duggie? Nice chap. Typical railwayman.' Edmund spoke absently. Ted thought he was probably crippled with grief. 'I think he must still be upstairs with Enid.' Edmund focused on Ted. 'I say, that would be funny, wouldn't it? If they made a match of it.'

'Not very,' Ted said and made for the stairs.

Duggie was coming out of the bathroom; he looked haggard.

'Enid's asleep. I persuaded her to take some pills with a cup of cocoa. She's totally exhausted.'

'For God's sake don't start feeling too sorry for her, old man. She'll have expectations beyond man's imaginings – even Edmund has just said you two might make a match!'

Duggie smiled wryly. 'I don't think so. Doffie put it into my head and if it would help . . . well, I could manage it, I think. But Enid will never forget that day in 'forty-six. The Reggie Ryecroft day. I am the last person she needs.' They walked downstairs and both hugged Hattie and then went out to the car. Duggie said as if there had been no gap, 'D'you know what she said in between all that ghastly sobbing? She said something about being free now.' He leaned forward so that they could hear him. 'I've got a feeling she'll leave. Not just Leckhampton House but Cheltenham. Perhaps even

England. She's just over sixty and she's been in her much older brother's shadow all these years, lapdog to her mother, nursemaid to her nephews . . . I think she might break loose.'

Doffie said, 'What about money?'

'She's got plenty apparently. Her father left her a large sum which she hasn't touched and Percy bought her a substantial annuity . . . She'd be very popular on one of those cruise liners.'

The three of them sat in the enclosed car and thought about Enid. And then Hattie.

Hattie waited up until Perry drove Edmund's car into the garage. The two boys joined her and they held on to each other, Perry sobbing openly again, Hattie weeping quietly into his shoulder. Edmund hung on to the two of them, staring over their heads, his eyes narrowed. When the crying had exhausted itself he said levelly, 'We'll have to get rid of Gran's old car. It's a danger, not even Dad could put it into reverse. We'll get a family saloon and you can learn to drive it, Ma.'

She lifted her head, at first shocked and then interested.

'I used to drive, you know. Your father had a smaller car when he was still working and I could drive that. Yes. It's not a bad idea, darling boy. We'll go down to the garage and look around. Maybe even tomorrow.' She kissed him. 'Thank you, Edmund. You have given me something else to think about.'

Perry said dully, 'What about me, Ed? Got anything else for me to think about?'

Edmund broke the circle of three and lowered his mother into a chair. 'You should get a job, Perry.'

'Yes. Yes, you're right.' Perry frowned to stop more tears. He remembered saying something about a job to Nell not all that long ago. 'I should have talked to Dad.'

'What about your uncle Ted?' Hattie said quickly before any of them could begin to see the endless view of life without Percy.

'Yes. Yes, I'll ask Uncle Ted.'

They escorted their mother upstairs and looked in on Enid; she was fast asleep and snoring lightly. They left Hattie to undress while they went downstairs to make her a drink. 'Cocoa, darlings. Lots of sugar. Like Gran used to make for me when I was small.'

Edmund fetched a milk saucepan, Perry a beaker and the tin of cocoa.

Edmund said, 'Is this how it's going to be? You and I looking after two older women until they die too?'

Perry was shocked. 'God almighty, Ed! Thanks a lot. Could we see how it goes? After all, Ma's doing fine and Aunt Enid is always a bit of a wet week.'

'Ma needs to be something else. A bit wacky. A bit crazy. Way out. You know exactly what I mean. Widowhood . . . doesn't suit her.'

Perry mixed cocoa and sugar and milk into a paste as if his life depended on it. Edmund poured on the boiling milk.

Perry said, 'Let's take up a couple of slices of that quiche.'

'She won't want it.'

'Tell you what. If she eats it, then she's going to be all right. If she doesn't we'll have to think of something else.'

Edmund gave a wry grin. 'All right. I don't know what, though.'

But Hattie ate both slices of quiche, drank her cocoa, kissed her sons and lay down.

Seventeen

In spite of everything, Nell enjoyed the half-term before Christmas. Between them, she and Shirley encouraged, cajoled, even bribed their two classes into a humorous version of 'The Owl and the Pussy Cat'. Shirley adapted the lyrics from a popular musical and the finale, with Shirley's class as writhing cats and Nell's class as owls providing a rhythmic backing of tu-whits and tu-whoos, went down very well with school and parents alike. Even Shirley, a confirmed pessimist, remarked that they had invented the first non-singing musical and it had worked.

Beneath the excitement of Advent, Nell knew that Mo was there; in her mind, dangerously close to her heart. She had foreseen this kind of takeover and fought it tooth and nail. She knew so little about him; not his birthday, not his age, not even where his home was. Any information at all seemed to come from someone else. Aunt Helena had told her that he was an orphan, his parents killed in a car crash. Mrs Mearment had told her mother how hard he worked; about the laboratory at Staverton, the pieces of aeroplane that lay on the table in his room, the yards – miles – of notes and algebraic squiggles all over his specially wide notebooks. But Nell did not need these details; she knew him instinctively, more than that. She knew him as if they had been together in another life. When Edmund had played 'April Showers' on the baby grand at Uncle Percy's funeral, she had had to lock herself in the bathroom and hang on to the washbasin for dear life. That time, that first time, in the theatre, she had known even then that the sentimental old-fashioned tune would always haunt her. She fought it as best she could, parcelling up all thoughts of home and mentally sitting heavily on the parcel. And the Owls helped a great deal. They had to learn to swing in time to Shirley's music, to click their fingers and make suitable owl noises. Then they had to get used to the stiff cardboard costumes and the large papier-mâché heads which at the very end of their song they could swivel round completely. Well, most of them could. It was the pièce de résistance and brought the house down. She had gone to tea with Martin Trickett and the whole family had pitched in to help make the owl heads, Mr Trickett mashing down the paper with flour and water, Martin getting himself plastered as he moulded the resulting mush on to a balloon. Even the head had understood that it was a necessary tea party.

Nell was fairly certain she was mistress of her own life; besides which, she would be seeing Mo at Christmas.

Val and Alice had brought Hattie as well and afterwards Nell had dinner with them in their hotel and stayed the night. The hotel was called the Lynx and commanded an excellent view of the local golf course.

'Wait until tomorrow. You can see for miles across the Lickey Hills. People don't realize how beautiful Birmingham is,' Nell told her mother.

Alice nodded. 'Shakespeare's country,' she commented.

Val said, 'Next summer, let's go off for two or three weeks. Explore this area. Mo was telling me there are some lakes west of here. Beautiful.'

Nell said nothing.

Hattie lifted her brows. 'Mo actually volunteered some information? Does that mean he knows Birmingham?'

Val said, 'He was at Birmingham University. Did a placement at Longbridge. That's when he decided to specialize in metal stress.'

Nell swallowed and said, 'Anyway. How come you're not at work, father dear? Don't tell me you had a day off to come to see a class of infants doing their Christmas play?'

He smiled at her. 'Actually, that's my news, daughter dear. I have retired from British Rail. I am now managing director of a company with the rather delightful name of the Pumpkin Line. Your uncle Duggie is chairman. Your mother is company secretary. Mo is chief engineer. Bert Lewis is in charge of maintenance . . . we have taken the plunge!'

Everyone laughed and clapped their hands. Hattie said, 'I'm a sleeping partner – of course you knew that.' And they laughed again and Alice suddenly hugged Hattie and told her she was marvellous. They ordered champagne and toasted the new company, then each other.

Much later, Alice went to Nell's room and they talked for some time about things that did not matter. It was getting colder and they sat in the small tub chairs with their backs against a radiator.

'This is nice,' Nell said contentedly. 'We break up in another week and I'll be home. I can do cards and presents then. Haven't had time for anything like that.'

She looked at her mother, longing to ask about Mo and determined not to. 'How are the boys? I think Perry's seen the light. He's not been up at all since he brought me home from the funeral.'

'I meant to tell you. He's got a job! They all went to look at cars – Edmund was determined to get rid of old Mrs Westbrook's and find something that Hattie could drive. And Perry got a job at the garage! Just like that! Apparently he's always been a bit of a genius with cars but his grandmother didn't want him to be a mechanic – too menial! He did some kind of deal with Grandma's car – let them have it so long as it was used as a kind of advertisement. Then showed the owner round the engine – how it should be greased, the belt and so on; he knew exactly how it worked – and they offered him a job! That's why he couldn't come today. He sent love, best wishes, good luck.'

'That's wonderful!' Nell was genuinely pleased. 'And how is Edmund?'

'I'm not sure.' Alice frowned. 'He's taken Aunt Hester out a couple of times. Your father asked him about it. He said he was sorry for her, that she was grieving for Percy as much as they were.'

'But – but the great Tibbolt is back in the running, surely?'

'I don't know.' Alice smiled at her daughter. She knew Nell loved this kind of chat but Hester was her best friend and if she was unhappy then Alice would be unhappy as well. 'He was at the funeral, as you know. Apparently he intended to spend Christmas with his children in France. And he's gone over with them already. Hester assures me it is a good thing.'

'Oh.' Nell reached for her mother's hand. 'Don't worry about her, Ma. Hester is well able to take care of herself.' She shook the hand gently. 'It's high time I came home and sorted everyone out! Not to mention the Pumpkin Line!'

Alice smiled lovingly. 'Don't look at it like that, darling. You're spreading your wings now. You might want to visit friends after Christmas . . . anything.'

Nell thought of the friends she had made at college and shook her head decisively. 'My friends are still at home, Mum. You know that.'

Alice held tightly on to her daughter's hand.

'Nell, forgive me if I am assuming wrongly. I rather think Perry has found someone else. It probably won't last but—' She stopped as Nell interrupted her.

'Mum – stop there! I am delighted for Perry. It didn't work for me. Not at all. It was just an experiment. And I thought it was the same for Perry and then when he got so possessive I hated it. I might even have hated him eventually!'

'Yes. Yes, you might.' Alice did not release Nell's hand. 'The thing is . . . Mo is going back home for Christmas.'

Nell stared but said nothing.

Alice repeated, 'I could be making stupid assumptions, darling. But I had to tell you before you came home. Forgive me.'

Nell still did not speak for some time. Then she said in a low voice, 'Is it – has it been – that obvious?'

'Well, everyone could see he was besotted. But then when you and Perry were so together . . . Mrs Mearment said it was just as well because he works all the time and could never be a proper companion in life. Those are her words, darling, not mine, but they make sense.'

'Yes. Yes, I suppose they do.' Nell released her hand and looked down at it. She remembered the day in the forest when Mo had almost ignored her in his excitement at finding the old sleepers and fishplates. 'The thing is . . . he was so terribly *randy* at first – sorry, Mum, but he was. And I slapped him right down and told him he must learn to make conversation and be – be *normal*.' She glanced up and tried to smile. 'Looks as though I shot myself in the foot, doesn't it?'

'Tell him, darling! Don't be unhappy at this stage. Take it a stage further and see what happens. You might still be unhappy. But then again, you might not.'

'No . . .' Nell took a deep breath. 'Perhaps some things are meant not to be. You should understand that, Mum.'

Alice wondered how much Nell knew about Joe Adair. Helena could have told her; or Hattie. She hoped it was Helena. She said, 'Of course I understand. Most people would. But –' she smiled – 'the other side of the coin is that some things most definitely *are* meant to be! There's something about Mo. His feel for the Pumpkin Line. His feel for us – the whole Pettiford thing. He seems to know things about us—'

'Mrs M. shows him old photographs. And when he's being so damned silent he's probably listening his head off!' Nell caught her mother's eye and smiled unwillingly. 'Sorry, Mum. I do know what you mean. But I rather think it's an optical illusion. Something like that anyway. I'm not going to push it, darling. And I would much rather you didn't. Is that all right?'

'Of course. Of course, Nell. But—'

'Let's talk about Hattie. She really is marvellous, isn't she? I quite thought she would somehow . . . sink.'

'Yes. So did I. She's much quieter, of course. But she's

running the house superbly. Pouring a sort of loving-caringness over the boys. And Enid. She's wonderful with Enid. Enid is talking about booking a cruise for the whole of January and Hattie is gently encouraging though she will miss her like mad. Grandad and Grandma go up often, of course – keep an eye on her. She doesn't have time to feel lonely.'

'Coming up here with you is good. She's still interested in everything – she's always been so interested in whatever is happening.'

'Especially where you are concerned. You are the daughter she didn't have.'

'Oh Mum. Poor Hattie.'

Alice stood up with some difficulty from the low chair. 'It's getting colder all the time.' She pulled the curtain aside. 'Oh Nell! Look! Oh darling, how marvellous. It's snowing.'

They stood by the window, watching the flakes whirl through the darkness. Already the ground was white. Nell wondered whether Mo was looking through his window at Lypiatt Bottom and seeing the snow too. She clamped down on the thought and put an arm round her mother's shoulders.

'I love you, Ma,' she said.

'I love you too, Nell,' Alice said, and thought of Hattie's poor deformed daughter who had died within an hour of birth and who had been named after Hattie's own mother, Mitzie. And quite suddenly, Gramps was with her, just as he was when she stood by King Edward's tomb in Gloucester Cathedral. And she knew. She knew that Hattie's father had been Reggie Ryecroft.

She closed her eyes and Nell chuckled and said, 'My kids are going to love this! I dread Monday morning.'

Alice opened her eyes; the contact was gone. There was the snow, not really mysterious, probably horribly slushy by Monday. She noted that Nell had used the possessive pronoun when she spoke of the schoolchildren. She too chuckled and said, 'You liar! You're looking forward to

Monday and that first snowball fight!' and she was thankful that at least Nell could think of other things besides Mo.

Hattie did not see the snow until the morning. Something quite amazing had happened when she went to her room that evening. She had been sick. And she was never ever sick.

She got ready for bed and sat, bolstered by pillows, hugging her knees and thinking. Six weeks since Percy had died. Six weeks. He had been almost eighty, seventy-eight to be exact. And she was fifty-one. She probably had another twenty years to live, maybe much longer. Supposing she lived as long as Granny Westbrook? She was only halfway through that kind of lifespan. She shivered and hugged herself as tightly as she could and tried to imagine her arms were Percy's arms.

She knew he hadn't left her. That was why she was so tranquil. After those first few days of weeping she had discovered something about herself. All right, she was behaving like Enid, weeping a great deal during the day. But in between the bouts of grief, she stopped weeping and cleared the kitchen of the last of the funeral meats, made a casserole for that evening, polished the baby grand. Then she allowed herself to weep again and instead of despairing she let the tears flow through her, washing her, soothing her. She tried to find ordinary words for what was happening and came up with 'medicinal baptism'. She liked the words and repeated them often. After all, she was in fact being constantly baptized. And it was something to do with Percy. It could actually be Percy. She gave that thought due attention, but Percy the Baptist did not sound right so eventually she left that. It was enough that her tears had a purpose, a reason, an end result. And the periods of calm were quite wonderful. She moved round the house, feeling graceful again – she had lost a great deal of weight, of course – setting things to rights, polishing photographs in their silver frames and arranging them so that wherever she went she would see an image of Percy. When Duggie called to see Enid, she made coffee and

194

took it to them and smiled at him approvingly. She did not believe that Enid would go on any cruises; she thought that Duggie would marry her and they would live quietly together in Duggie's house in Gloucester and Enid would find contentment – nothing ecstatic but the sort of contentment she had known with her brother. Safe, secure.

Hester called and tried to talk to her about Edmund and she had no difficulty in fending off her questions.

'Darling Hessie. Edmund hoped he had been born out of wedlock – can you believe him! He actually went through the birth and marriage certificates! I think he wanted his father to be a peer of the realm or something a bit more exciting than a railwayman. Poor darling. He'll learn to be proud of Percy eventually. He was such a wonderful man, Hessie. I am so thankful that you got to know him properly just before his death. And now your Richard Tibbolt has come back and everything is as it should be for you. I am really pleased, Hessie.'

Hester had not looked pleased. She had told Hattie quite shortly that Richard was now in France, that the head girl at school had confided to Hester that she was a lesbian and that Edmund was rather difficult about everything.

Hattie was mildly surprised. 'Surely part of that problem is easily solved? Introduce your lesbian to my Edmund. He will be fascinated. And I bet you a hundred pounds – I mean that, Hessie: one hundred pounds – that, lesbian or no lesbian, she will fall for Edmund.'

'How can you say such things at a time like this?' Hester said, waving her hands helplessly.

'Because I can see things I couldn't see before. I don't mean like Alice. But like Gran. I've got Gran's gifts, Hester.'

Now, sitting on her bed at the aptly named Lynx Hotel, after a wonderful evening when darling Nell had done so well, she could almost hear her own voice announcing that she had inherited her grandmother's gift. It had been a very special gift: Gran had known immediately when a woman became pregnant.

She straightened her legs and drew the covers up to her chin and lay down very carefully. She felt her breasts; they were not particularly tender. Yet she had been sick and had only just reached her bathroom in time. That could be the champagne, of course. She was fifty-one and as regular as clockwork still. But there had been nothing since Percy's death. Could it be the change of life?

But she knew, with Gran's strange foresight, that it was not the menopause or the champagne. She knew that, just before Percy died, he had given her another baby. It was going to be a girl. She would have a girl at last. And she would be special again; outrageous as she had always been. Maybe she would qualify for an entry in the *Guinness Book of Records* as the oldest mum in Britain? It would be such fun. The boys would boast about her and Doffie would throw up her hands and say she was indefatigable and disgraceful and they would all love and admire her.

She lay very still in the strange bed and let herself be baptized yet again with her own tears. Percy's love made manifest. Baptism and birth. She was most probably the luckiest woman on earth.

And Nell, who could not sleep after the terrific excitement of the day topped up with a rich meal and champagne, wrapped herself in a blanket and pressed herself against the radiator to watch the snow and do her own thinking. She thought about Martin Trickett and a girl called Esme Leach, both from the council estate, both listed in the head's private notebook as 'disadvantaged' but both cherished deeply by their families. They were slow learners certainly, but they had shone in the play: she must remember that and find ways to teach them the basics through other projects. When the spring arrived she could take the whole class to do some pond-dipping and then appoint monitors to record the results. Her thoughts flowed easily and then suddenly, abruptly, snagged on something else. Mo Checkers had gone to university in Birmingham. On the railway line between North Heath and the city, there was a stop especially for the university. Students got on and off, easily identified by backpacks bulging with books, jumble-sale greatcoats, John Lennon glasses. They were all nationalities and he had been one of them, his mixed race probably acceptable for the first time in his life. He had got his degree – she was willing to bet it was a First – and at some time during a placement at Longbridge . . . *Longbridge,* a mere cycle ride down the road from North Heath . . . he had become interested in metal fatigue. She already knew that when he was interested in something . . . or someone . . . he became fixated. He hadn't left her alone at first; his dark eyes had watched her all the time. And that day at the Pumpkin Line . . . She closed her eyes and shook her head; her father had told her how he had worked on the ancient locomotive acquired by Uncle Edward.

She took a breath. So Mo Checkers had been here, in this area, where she now worked and had her life. And he was in Gloucestershire too, often one jump ahead of everything that had happened to the Pettifords. It wasn't just Nell Ryecroft who held his 'interest', it was the whole family. He had wormed his way into . . . everything.

She expelled the breath and noted that the window was misting. It was double-glazed, which was supposed to stop condensation; so much for technology. She rubbed a clear space and looked out. The snow was no longer falling, stars were out and a half-moon reflected on the thin white coating that lay in folds all over the Lickey Hills. It was exquisite. She made herself think 'traditional Christmas'. A man and a woman dressed in Arab clothing; a donkey; a stable . . . Martin Trickett and Esme Leach . . .

Someone emerged from a doorway below and walked across the virgin snow. A man in a padded anorak with a hood, very Chinese. He trudged towards the dim shape of the clubhouse that served the golf course and stood there beating his arms round his own body, obviously staring out at the night view of the hills.

Nell held her breath and kept polishing the window. It couldn't be. Yet hadn't she just decided that he was everywhere? She reached behind her for her clothes, slung over one of the tub chairs. After all, if Longbridge was one of his old stamping grounds, he might well have . . . He might even have been in the audience tonight. Oh God. It was the sort of thing he would do. She couldn't bear it. She began to dress frantically.

She was dragging on her jeans when he turned and started back to the hotel. He moved more quickly now, using his own tracks, almost running. He must be freezing out there. He looked up and saw her outlined in the lighted window. His hood fell back and he was blond and Scandinavian-looking.

She closed the curtain abruptly, furious and desperately disappointed. If he had followed her here it would have proved something . . . Oh, if only he had followed her here. If only he had come secretly to the school and watched her children do their stuff so well . . . If only he had been *there*!

She flung off her clothes and left them on the floor and pitched herself into bed. Then she began to wonder whether she had hurt him irreparably by sleeping with Perry. Oh God, she couldn't bear that either. She remembered that first dreadful tennis match when he had pinned her against the wall of Helena's house and kissed her and she had begun to relax against him and . . .

She slept at last.

Eighteen

It was Christmas.

After the various church services, they all congregated at Leckhampton House for Christmas dinner, which was eventually served at three o'clock. Hattie did nothing, quite literally. Helena had made the shopping list and had everything delivered on Christmas Eve. Alice, Doffie, Hester and Nell did vegetables, made sauces, cooked, allowed no one past the kitchen door except to deliver more drinks, nibbles and the occasional mistletoe kiss. The boys laid the big table in the little-used dining room, made a tower of crackers in its centre and sniggered about Sally Gold and Aunt Hester.

'D'you think—?' Perry said for the third time.

'Of course not!' But Edmund was not as emphatic as he had been the first time he discounted Perry's theory.

'She's quite avant garde when it comes to sex,' Perry said, polishing a fork on a starched napkin. 'I mean everyone knows she slept with her prof when she was a student. And that must have been quite something in those days.'

'Days of yore, d'you mean?' Edmund mocked.

Perry ignored that. 'And then . . . well, Dad of all people. Can you imagine—?

'I'd prefer not to, if you don't mind,' Edmund said firmly. 'But I do agree with you about Hester. Dark horse and so forth.' He looked at Perry as he lit the candles. 'You fancy Sally Gold, don't you?'

Perry said, 'She's gorgeous. And she's bloody clever. She's been offered a place at St Hilda's. She doesn't want to go because of Aunt Hester.'

'Good Lord, you've been having some pretty heavy conversations with her!'

'Yes.' Perry put down the fork and picked up a spoon. 'It nearly drives me mad. I'm crazy about her, Ed.'

'You were crazy about Nell five minutes ago.'

'That was . . . I dunno . . . a sort of experiment. For both of us. She went off me before I went off her, so you needn't think I'm breaking her heart. It was sort of friendly sex. This is different.'

'Because you just talk?'

'Well, yes. But more than that. Nell is . . . Nell. You know, up front, no nonsense. We've known her all her life, seen her through nosebleeds and wet knickers and—'

'Shut up, Perry. We look after Nell. Whatever happens to us or to her, we keep an eye on her. All right?'

Perry put down the spoon, surprised. 'All right. Of course. I've always felt like that. I'm surprised you do too.'

'Well, I do.' Edmund stepped back and counted out the place settings yet again. 'D'you make it fifteen? That's with Mrs Mearment.'

Perry treated this as a rhetorical question. 'What I meant was, Sally is different. Different from any girl I've ever met – and I've met quite a few, you know, Ed – she's mysterious and—'

'Because she says she is in love with Aunt Hester.'

'That's ridiculous of course but—'

'What's ridiculous? Aunt Hester is beautiful, classically beautiful. She could make anyone fall in love with her.'

Perry went to the sideboard and poured himself a drink. He chuckled. 'My God, anyone being you by any chance? You're always round there lately – is that what it's all about?'

'You know bloody well I'm on the trail of my parentage—' Edmund advanced menacingly as Perry mimicked him. 'And anyway, the boot is on the other foot, my lad. I could take Hester to bed any time I wanted to!'

Perry spluttered into his glass even as he retreated round the table. When he could speak he gasped, 'You haven't met

Sally yet, have you? You've got some competition there, Ed old chap! Plus Richard Tibbolt, who might be in France at present but is very much in Hester's mind. You think you know it all, don't you? You think you're my bastard brother! Well, you are in one way of course!' He dodged a cushion. 'But can't you see how like Dad you are? You're following in his footsteps! Whether you know it or not, you're bloody well falling in love with your own aunt! How's that?'

Edmund caught up with him and they both fell on to the carpet and grappled, laughing and gasping helplessly. Hattie stood in the doorway and surveyed them with a kind of resignation. They were going to be elderly brothers to her new daughter; but at heart they were still little boys.

She had been to see her family doctor only last week and he had confirmed what she had known from the moment she was sick at the Lynx Hotel. He had thought she would be horrified and completely incapable of looking after a baby at her age, so he had offered her an abortion. 'All legal and above board, my dear. I know a very good clinic, in the country, like a four-star hotel. It would make a little break for you—' He stopped speaking because she was laughing.

When she finished telling him how delighted she was he was cautiously pleased. However, after she had pre-empted all his objections, he nodded slowly.

'I can see what you mean. In the event of . . . illness . . . your sons would be able to . . . make arrangements . . .'

'Absolutely. Should I die in childbirth, fall under a bus in the next twenty years, go right off my rocker – and after all, I'm halfway there already – or simply be declared an unfit mother . . . my family will rally round.' She leaned forward. 'None of that will happen, doctor. Don't you see, my husband has arranged all this. He knows exactly what I want and he's going to be with me through the pregnancy, the labour . . . and absolutely right there when our daughter is born.'

'Daughter?'

'Yes, of course. It's a girl, doctor. I shall call her Millicent again, but I won't be shortening it to Mitzie. That would not be fair to our first daughter, who was also a Mitzie. I shall call her Millie. Millie Westbrook. Don't you think it sounds absolutely, wonderfully *right?*'

The doctor nodded slowly. 'Absolutely,' he agreed.

So Hattie planned to tell them all. Today. Probably during the short break between lunch and tea. But no, because they would be all over the house then and she herself had planned a short nap on her bed. She would wait until the pudding was *flambant* and then tap her spoon against her glass and say that she had an announcement . . . No, she would play it down; right down. So that later, years later, they would say, 'Do you remember the way Hattie told us about Millie's imminent arrival?'

She wandered back to the drawing room, smiling secretly, and there were dear Ted – more of a brother than an uncle – and Edward Maybury and darling Val looking so distinguished these days, and Duggie Marsden who would soon propose to Enid and stop all this freedom nonsense; and there was Helena fussing round old Mrs Mearment, a mince pie on a plate and a glass of sherry at the ready, and Enid gathering up glasses and wiping her eyes surreptitiously. Hattie loved them all. And their warts.

Nell, skimming downstairs from the bathroom, met Perry and Edmund emerging from their labours at the dining table. Edmund, anticipating difficulty for Nell, said swiftly, 'Come and see what we've done, Nellie-belly. It's looking good, really good. But we need your seal of approval.'

She told them she was needed in the kitchen more than here but allowed herself to be led into the austere dining room.

'Very festive.' Nobody seemed to remember that Percy's coffin had been on this very table only two months ago. 'I like the balloons. Oh, and the crackers.' She looked from one to the other. 'Is your mother all right?'

It was Perry who answered. 'You've seen her. What do you think?'

'I don't know what to think. She's exactly as she used to be. More so.'

Perry said, 'Is she having an affair with Duggie Marsden, d'you think?'

Edmund said, 'Shut up, you little fool! Two months since Dad died!'

'Ed . . . be sensible. It wouldn't matter if it made her happy.'

Nell said slowly, 'Actually, that's how it is, isn't it? It can't be, of course, but it's as if she's in love all over again.'

They were drawn together, sharing the intrigue. It couldn't be Duggie, of course, because he was dancing attendance on Enid all the time. So who could it be?

Nell said slowly, 'Oh God. I hope it's not the Pettiford curse.'

'What are you on about now, woman?' asked Perry in exactly the tone of voice he had used to Nell before their 'friendly experiment'. He heard it himself and was pleased.

'You know.' She looked from one cousin to the other. 'My mother. Going to the cathedral to talk to Gramps Pettiford. And apparently Gran had it and could foretell all sorts of things. I'm wondering whether Hattie . . . no, it couldn't be, she's far too down-to-earth. But just suppose she *thought* she was in touch with Uncle Percy. More in love with him than ever . . . you know what I mean.'

They did. They looked back at her and then at each other. They all felt extremely uncomfortable.

Perry said, 'Go and talk to her, Ed. Play the piano or something. Make her live in the present.'

Edmund, frowning prodigiously, did not argue. He forgot that he had not intended to leave Perry and Nell together. He went.

Perry said, 'I'm sure you're wrong, Nell. Not even Mum could have an affair with a ghost. I mean . . . we should know.'

'Yes but . . .' She realized what he had said and bit her lip. 'Are you all right, Perry? The last time I saw you, you were so terribly upset.'

'I know. And I am all right. I've got a job and . . . actually, Nell, my dear cousin Nell . . . I think I've fallen in love. Properly this time. You don't mind, do you?'

'Oh Perry. Of course not. We were just experimenting. Both of us. Weren't we?'

'Yes. Although – Nell – I'll always love you, and if you're an old maid when you're forty and if I've got divorced by then, we'll get married.'

Nell grinned. 'That would be nice.'

Perry grabbed a spray of mistletoe and held it over his head and she went into his arms.

So it was that Hattie made her wonderful announcement at the end of their Christmas lunch, when it was already almost dark and the dining room was lit by candles and the paper hats had slipped incongruously to the backs and sides of heads and the table looked as if a bomb had landed in the middle of it. The chatter was dying down and Enid had just mentioned that she would go upstairs in a few minutes for a rest but that she would – definitely – be up to get the tea in two hours, maybe three. In the lull that followed, Hattie said, without preamble, 'By the way, I've got some news. Percy and I are having another baby and I know I'm much too old and Percy isn't here any more, but I am so happy about it and I want all of you to be happy too.' She looked round. It wasn't quite as she had imagined. She had intended to stand up and hold her wine glass aloft and utter the words triumphantly, defying Percy's death and her own age. She had considered looking out Perry's old Union Jack and hoisting it above her head. But this . . . it sounded like a plea.

The awful thing was that no one reacted for what seemed like ages. Most of them had had too much to drink and wondered whether they had heard correctly. And some thought this must be Hattie's menopause kicking in.

Then Nell began to giggle; she looked across at Perry and Edmund and said, 'We were right. She's having a love affair! Isn't it wonderful?' Because, after all, this was no affair with a ghost. Nell had already worked it out. Percy's last few hours on earth had been spent doing what he was so good at: making Hattie Pettiford very happy.

Doffie, closer to Hattie than anyone, scraped back her chair. Tears clogged her voice as she rushed round the table and put her arms tightly round Ted's wayward niece. 'Darling, it's rather frightening but it's also marvellous! Have you seen a doctor? Will it be all right?'

Hattie turned to her and smelled the familiar lavender water; it triggered a hundred memories of when Doffie had held her like this, ostensibly giving comfort but asking too for reassurance. And Doffie had never been slow to show her disapproval either. If she thought Hattie was making this up or had been up to something with someone else, Doffie would tell her so.

Hattie said, her voice strong, 'I can do it – I want to do it more than anything I've ever wanted before. Percy has given me something of himself. Can you understand?' She lifted her head from Doffie's silk blouse and addressed everyone. 'Try to understand. I would have been so pleased . . . before. But now, oh God . . . now, it's like being involved every day in a miracle. I want you to be involved too – all of you.'

An absolute chorus broke out. Nell and Perry could not stop laughing – Edmund hissed at them that they were drunk – Duggie grinned and of course Enid wept. Helena clasped her hands and Edward encircled her protectively because they had never been able to have children. Mrs Mearment's voice piped up saying, 'What did Harriet say, Ted? Someone is having a baby? That's rather nice on Christmas Day and everything, isn't it?' And Ted said with ill-concealed pride, 'Typical of Hattie. She should be past it. But she will never know that.'

Sitting very still between Edmund and Nell, Hester was also doing her sums and realizing that Percy had already said goodbye to her before he died. She had thought of him as a kind of unfinished business, cut short by untimely death. Now . . . now it seemed quite different. This baby was Percy's way of telling Hester that he had dumped her. She looked across the table at Hattie, who seemed to be glowing in the candlelight. She remembered Hattie coming back from the war with Percy in tow, looking like a gypsy with her mass of black hair and dark eyes; remembered how horrified the family had been at this older man with thick glasses and a squint, and one eye that always seemed to be staring down the front of Hattie's blouse. They had thought Hattie wanted a father figure, a big house, plenty of money. And all the time Hattie had been in love with him. In her peculiar way she had been faithful to him, in spite of various flings. And now she was able to tell the world that, right up to the last, he had loved her.

Hester felt as if an enormous weight had been lifted from her. She was about to raise her glass and say in her resonant teaching voice, 'Here's to Hattie and Percy!' when the front-door bell rang and Edmund pushed back his chair.

'I'll go,' he said.

He appeared to be the only one who was not hysterical with joy at his mother's news. He couldn't believe it. They would be a laughing stock. How would the senior partner at work take this news? Smithers and Jameson were practically Victorian.

He went down the hall and tugged open the heavy front door. A girl stood there, someone he'd never seen before. She was small, just a kid really. Dressed in a beret pulled right down over her ears, a leather jacket above her jeans, Doc Martens. Probably broken down, no petrol, wanted to use the phone.

She said, 'I'm very sorry to call on Christmas Day. I wanted to see Miss Ryecroft and I went to her house in the cathedral close and her neighbour told me that she was here.'

'Oh.' Edmund was unusually nonplussed. She looked up at him and he saw she was in extremis. He said, 'Please come in. We're only just finishing our meal. Shall I get her to come out to you? Or will you come in and be introduced and have a drink?'

'Oh no. I couldn't do that.' She came in sideways and looked at him again. She had blue eyes . . . or were they green? He couldn't tell. But she was pretty. In fact she was probably beautiful, but not beautiful like Hester, not classical. She said, 'I expect you know all about me and what a bloody nuisance I am. And I know I am but I've sort of lost control. And that's horrible because . . . because I've always been in control. I've always known exactly what I was doing. And now, oh God, all I can think of is old Piecrust and her gorgeous hair and I know it's unnatural and she will eventually hate me for it, but what can I do? It's Christmas Day and I just had to see her even if she does hate me!'

It all clicked into place. He said, 'Oh . . . you're Sally Gold. My brother is in love with you!' It came out like that, carelessly; and Edmund was always so careful. He strove to assume his normal manner. 'What I mean is, I'm Edmund Westbrook and you know my brother, Perry. He works at Jennings' – the garage on the London road.'

'Yes. Miss Ryecroft introduced us. He took me for a spin in that lovely old car.'

'It was my father's. My grandmother's before that.' Edmund could not seem to regain his usual aura of control. He was blabbing everything out to this kid as if he wanted her to know the whole family history. 'He talks a lot about you. And I can see why.' Edmund swallowed, trying to restrain his runaway tongue. 'You really are very beautiful,' he said.

She managed a wan smile. 'Thank you. You and your brother . . . you seem so . . . open. So uninhibited. I wish Miss Ryecroft had that trait too. She's buttoned up so tightly you wonder she can breathe.'

He grinned. 'That does describe her very well.' Just then the general babble from the dining room died down and Hester's voice rang out, 'Here's to Hattie and her extraordinary womb! Not to mention dear Percy and his—' She shut up suddenly and Perry shouted, 'You're drunk, Aunt Hester! Pass me that mistletoe, someone – I'm going to kiss my aunt – properly!' Sounds of bursting balloons and screams of laughter followed this.

Edmund said, 'But obviously she's well and truly unbuttoned at the moment!'

Sally Gold raked her fingers through her red curls and grinned.

'Some party,' she commented.

Edmund took her elbow. 'Come into the sitting room. I'll get Hester and you can have a chat.'

'She'll send me packing,' the girl said gloomily. 'But even that will be better than not seeing her.' She let Edmund pilot her into the sitting room, which was also looking wrecked, with glasses everywhere and the fire dying in the grate. Edmund set to, putting logs on the cinders and gathering up the glasses. Sally wandered around, touching the piano, the baubles on the tree.

'Is she here often? You seem such a close family.'

Edmund did not ask who she meant.

'Fairly often. She and my mother are good friends. And in the summer she comes to play tennis.'

'She is amazing, isn't she? I don't know how I'm going to bear to leave her and go off to university. She is everything to me. Everything I do and think and say and feel is . . . just for her.'

He was kneeling, reaching under a chair for a plate holding half a mince pie. He looked up at her and saw the raw emotion on her young face. He wondered what it might be like to hand your whole self over to another person. He remembered how he and Perry had sniggered about her so-called lesbianism and he felt ashamed.

She stroked the raised lid of the piano. 'Does she play?'

'Not much. I'm the one who tickles the ivories most.'

'Oh.' She closed the lid and straightened herself, looked down at Edmund and gave a wry smile. 'This wasn't a good idea, was it? She's going to hate me for disrupting the party like this. I think I'll give you a message for her and just go.'

Edmund stumbled to his feet. 'You've come all this way—'

'Dad gave me a car for Christmas. I wanted to try it out.' Her smile turned to a grin. 'The poor old parents will be doing their separate nuts. I failed my driving test last week. I'd better get back.'

'Oh God. What if you're stopped?'

She shrugged. 'I'll be done, I suppose. Doesn't matter. Don't look like that – I always get away with things. Spoilt only child . . . you know how it is. I get everything I want. Until I fell in love with my dear Piecrust. I've got a feeling I'm not going to get Piecrust.' She raked her curls again and tugged her leather jacket over small hips. 'Listen. Just tell her she's won. I'm going to take the place at St Hilda's. I'm going to get a good degree. She's going to be proud of me even if she loathes me!'

He stammered, 'She doesn't. No one could loathe you. You've got such terrific . . . guts!'

'Oh . . . sorry, what is your name?'

'Edmund.'

She laughed. 'What a mouthful! I'll call you Ed. All right? Thanks for being so nice to me.' She tipped her head to one side. 'Funny, you've got a look of her about you. You should grow your hair really long.' She made for the door.

He said, 'Shall I see you again?'

She opened the door and looked round at him. 'D'you want to?'

'Oh yes.'

'Well . . . I suppose . . . I have to warn you, I'd only see you to try and make Piecrust insanely jealous! Or even to reduce you to an emotional pulp and tell her that I will release you from my spell only if she goes to bed with me!'

She was laughing but he was shocked.

She said, 'I'm sorry. I was forgetting you were her generation – I would never say anything like that to her. So it's most unfair of me—'

He blurted, 'I'm twenty-seven! Hester is forty-five!!'

She laughed more. And then she heard the dining-room door opening and she was gone. Across the tiled floor of the hall and through the heavy front door. It closed softly after her and no one would ever have guessed she had been in the house.

Except Edmund. He went through to the kitchen, clutching glasses and plates, and opened the back door to gasp in the dark air. What had she said so tellingly? 'Everything I do and think and feel . . .' The words echoed in his head.

He knew exactly what she meant.

Perry shouted for him. 'Who was at the door, Eddie?'

'Someone who had lost their way.' Edmund turned to the sink and ran hot water on to the dishes. 'I'll wash. You can dry,' he said.

'What a Christmas. What do you think?' Perry asked, straddling a kitchen chair.

'Yes. Quite a Christmas,' Edmund agreed.

'No, not that!' Perry was impatient. 'About Mum, for God's sake! The bloody baby.'

'Oh. Sorry. I'd forgotten.' Edmund stopped swilling glasses and frowned. 'Funny thing. I didn't like it at all at first. You know, the thought of all the cracks we'll be getting. But now . . . it sounds rather . . . I dunno . . . fun – is that the word?'

'Sleepless nights. Smelly nappies. Yes, I guess it will be fun!' Perry started to laugh. 'What *is* good is that we can talk about Dad. Not as being dead but as being . . . well, a dad. Again!'

'They were always . . . weren't they?' Edmund said fondly, quite forgetting his teenage disgust at his parents' practically public love-making.

'You mean, at it?' Perry was convulsed with giggles. 'Good old Dad. Good old Mum. I say, what a way to go! I wouldn't mind that at all! I'm not going to wait for the cracks – I'm going to boast about this.'

'Right.' Edmund threw a tea towel at him. 'Get wiping.'

Edmund thought that he had probably never been as happy as he was at that moment.

Nineteen

Nell worked hard that spring term. The pond-dipping was a great success and the nature table supported a range of specimens from snail shells to snowdrops, catkins and empty pale-blue thrushes' eggs. Martin brought in a 'pressed frog' found beneath the tyre of the headmistress's new Renault; the girls gasped and put their hands over their eyes and for an instant Nell almost did the same. Then she announced in a matter-of-fact voice that they would all try to draw the frog while they had the opportunity. 'This is our chance to get to know what a frog really looks like and how cleverly he is designed.' She glanced at the item lying on a piece of kitchen paper then quickly averted her gaze. 'It's a way of – of – appreciating this particular species.' One of the girls, Janice Morgan, was making quavery groaning noises. Nell said with quiet emphasis, 'And it will mean the poor thing did not die in vain.' She could almost hear Perry laughing at her. She wondered what Mo would make of all this and then cut the thought off quickly; she dared not let him take over her head as he had done before Christmas.

When the primroses appeared she and Shirley cycled out to the lakes one Saturday morning. Shirley wanted to talk about another non-musical musical for Easter. Nell simply wanted to spot primroses, smell damp earth, become part of the regeneration process that was spring.

'I thought I was meant to show the children . . . things,' she said vaguely when Shirley stopped talking about another of Lear's nonsense poems. 'But so often *they* show *me*. Our roles are completely reversed. I mean, Jason Smith looked me in the eye when I said we were hearing a cuckoo and he told me it was a dove and that we wouldn't be hearing no cuckoos, miss, till April.'

Her impersonation of Jason's Brummie accent made Shirley laugh. 'That's nothing. You wait till you take the sewing group. Martina Lammas taught me how to do feather stitching. I mean, have you ever *heard* of feather stitching?'

'Well, yes. But I didn't think people actually did it any more.'

They burst out laughing and free-wheeled down the next hill, then stood on their pedals to get up the next. Exhilarated, out of breath, they stopped at the next crest and looked back at the smoky pall that was the heart of Birmingham.

'It's an exciting place to be,' Nell said.

Shirley nodded gaspingly. 'But then, most places are,' she added.

'You're right.' Nell propped herself against her handlebars. 'Did I tell you that my parents are buying a railway that runs through a magic forest? And that in the forest there is a pumpkin coach? Like Cinderella's. It stands by a coal-black pool. It can weave spells.'

Shirley laughed. 'Oh, shut up and save it for the kids,' she said amiably. 'Let's find a pub for lunch and then get home. I've got masses to do and it'll be dark before we're halfway back if we start telling fairy stories.'

'All right.' Nell mounted her bike again. 'In two weeks the clocks go forward and summer starts.' She pushed off, lifted her feet from the pedals and shouted, 'Yippee!'

Mrs Mearment was so pleased to see her lodger that she hugged him, and was glad when he hugged her back.

'I began to think you was going to stay up there for ever,' she said. 'Two postcards. Oh, and the Christmas card of course. You said you would keep in touch.'

'There was nothing to say. Not really.' He lugged in his backpack and looked round the kitchen. 'It's good to be back. Have you let my room to anyone else?'

'Course I haven't! I told you it was your room till you gave me notice.'

'So you knew I'd be back, postcards or no postcards.' He grinned at her and she grinned back.

'Those conversation lessons 'ave stayed with you, Michael.' She nodded approvingly. 'When you first arrived you couldn't have teased me like that.'

'Who said I was teasing?' He hugged her again and she told him that March was a treacherous month and he shouldn't be out in a thin jacket and a T-shirt.

'Are you wearing a vest? I thought not. I've got some upstairs. Belonged to my husband but I've kept them in mothballs and they're as good as new.' She drew out a chair for him and went to the stove to make tea. 'Sit and tell me all about it before you go up. Did you get your certificate or whatever it's called? What did they think of all those funny sums and the bits of metal? If you didn't get top marks I've a good mind to go and see them myself. Just tell them all the work you did, night after night at that table—'

'It's all right, Mrs M. They loved my funny sums. And I've got it. It's a PhD and if I like I can be called a doctor.'

She was delighted though she did not really know what he was on about. He told her about a presentation he'd had to do on a machine that stressed metal to breaking point. He talked about tutorials and a professor from some space agency, who had offered him a job in America. 'He knows Neil Armstrong, Mrs M. I would meet him and talk to him. They have facilities over there for all kinds of research . . . It's a wonderful offer.'

She poured tea and it filled the saucer. She righted the teapot. 'You won't take it?' It sounded like a plea.

He looked at her, reached out and took the tea, emptied the saucer back into the cup and sipped. 'Lovely,' he said. Then, 'I have to earn a living, Mrs M.'

'You've got a job. You're chief engineer. For the Pumpkin Line.'

'Yes.' He sipped again. 'That's what I want to be. But it's

part-time. And I think I've probably done my work by getting the *Belle* up and running. Other people will do the rest.'

She sat down carefully. 'But you're back. Here you are. Back.'

He nodded. 'I have to see that everything is going well down in the forest. I thought Val would write, keep me posted. But I've heard nothing.'

'No one knew where you were.'

He looked at her. She was the same age as Doffie Pettiford; they had been friends for decades. She looked years older than Doffie. He had read somewhere about 'rheumy eyes' and had not known what it meant until now. Mrs Mearment's eyes were definitely rheumy. He reached over and took her hand.

'You knew where I was.'

'I promised not to tell anyone,' she protested.

'You did.' He kept her hand, acknowledging her faithfulness.

She said, 'It's not just the railway you've come to see, is it?'

'No. I've got some unfinished business.'

'With Nell Ryecroft.'

It was not a question but he shook his head. 'No, Mrs M. I've got Nell out of my system now. It's with her parents. Once that is over I shall go.'

She swallowed painfully then said, 'Nell has finished with her cousin, you know. When his father died he seemed to go off her. Nell is on her own again now and I wouldn't be surprised if she was very pleased to see you.'

'Oh, I'll be gone before the Easter break.' He saw the pain in her face and said quickly, 'Tell me what has been happening.'

She took her hand back and stirred her tea. 'Such a lot. I don't know where to begin. Hattie Pettiford – Westbrook I should say, shouldn't I – she's having a baby this summer—'

He interrupted tactlessly. 'You're joking, Mrs M.! She's old – and her husband is dead . . .'

Her voice became cold. 'She is fifty-two. It has been known

214

before. And it is her husband's child. Like a gift from the other side.'

'I'm sorry, Mrs M. It's all rather . . . unlikely, you must admit.'

'Unlikely or not, it's happened. And she is very happy about it and so is everyone else. She was out mowing the grass in that dry spell. Wants to start her tennis parties early this year.'

'Good Lord.'

'And Doffie and Ted – and Alice and Val, of course – are out at Leadon every day, weekends included. I miss them.' She looked up again from her tea. 'I'm lonely, Michael.'

'I'm here now, Mrs M.'

'For a week. Easter is a week away.'

He paused, then shook his head and said, 'I'm sorry, Mrs M.'

She sighed sharply and stood up. 'I'll get those vests and put them on your bed.'

They had planned to do an inaugural trip on Easter Monday. The line from Leadon to the coach had been cleared, the track relaid and reballasted. The old connection to a siding at Leadon had been hastily reconstructed so that the *Belle* could be shunted from the shed at Orchard straight on to the Pumpkin Line. To get this done, Edward Maybury had gone to Paddington and pulled every string in the book. 'I had to sign away my own life!' he joked. 'That connection is purely temporary and must never be used again. In fact it must be removed – no trace left.'

Val said, 'In other words, perhaps three people know of it.'

'One. Maybe two,' Edward corrected.

Val said, 'Obviously we don't remove it. We've got a hold over the chairman now. You didn't sign your life away, Edward. You signed his!'

Edward was shocked. 'It was a gentlemen's agreement, Val. A personal favour. No way can the line be left in situ.'

Val said soothingly, 'As soon as we can spare the manpower, it will be taken up.'

When he recounted this to Hester later on, she said gloomily, 'I can quite see that there will never be manpower to spare. Oh Val. You've got a lot of our father in you!'

Val looked grim for a moment then said, 'If you mean sheer cunning, then that is something to thank him for. We'd never have got this far without a bit of cunning, Hessie. And you know it.'

So they were almost ready for the trip. The renewed track was just under one mile long, probably the shortest railway line in the country. The line that meandered on from the coach was still to be tackled.

'This is not public,' Ted said at one of the meetings in the flat. 'This is just for us and for the volunteers who can come that day. We'll do a trip from Leadon. Sandwiches and drinks at the coach. Then a trip back.'

'Yes. We can't invite the press or anyone else just yet. Hester, of course.'

Duggie said, 'Hattie and the boys. And Enid.'

Doffie said, 'Mrs Mearment. And Nell will be home by then.'

Alice said, 'Mo should be there. After all, it was he who got the *Belle* going. Does anyone have an address?'

Val said, 'Probably Mrs M. but she's not saying.'

Ted burst out, 'Why all the mystery, for God's sake? What's he got to hide? It's just about a year since he arrived and all we know is that he is doing some work on metal stress and went to Birmingham University!'

Helena said quietly, 'His parents were killed in a car crash. He was – still is – absolutely devoted to them.' She glanced at Alice. 'He came here because he got a placement with GlosPlanes. Got to know us and felt at home.' She shrugged. 'Rather a compliment in my book.'

'He feels so at home he's gone for good, by the look of things!' Ted, always the bluff protester, marched to the cooker and poured tea angrily. 'He should be here. The university term is over and he ought to come and see his bloody engine that he was so besotted with!'

Alice got up to help her father and smiled at him gently. 'He'll be here,' she said with certainty. Ted's face creased into a frown; if Alice had been in touch with his father again he did not want to know. He had never really believed in these get-togethers they had in the cathedral – did not want to believe in them – and if there was some kind of afterlife he had every intention of talking very sternly to his father and telling him what he thought of him for getting in touch in the first place and draining Alice of her strength each time.

Alice touched his arm. 'It's all right,' she said. 'I saw a light in his window last night. I think he's home.'

He covered her hand with his. 'Good girl,' he said. 'And what about Nell? When does she come home?'

'Tomorrow. They have a week before Easter and a week after. She sounds tired to death. I don't know whether she will want to join in our shenanigans.'

'They're not shenanigans, Alice! This is a very important occasion. A test run, if you like. Mo Checkers did all the calculations, granted. But until a loco actually runs along the line . . . well, who knows?'

'I simply meant that Nell might not be up to much for a bit. Her friend, Shirley, rang the other evening. Apparently Nell has had a rotten cold for two or three weeks – they went for a cycle ride, she didn't have a jacket – and it rained . . . you know. Anyway, they did another play – just for the other children this time – and Nell only just got through it. I'd like her to rest.'

Ted handed her the teapot. 'That means you won't come either. The whole thing is going to be a flop.'

'Oh Dad, do stop it. Of course I'll come. Get another bottle of milk from the fridge. And stop buttoning up your mouth like that!'

He unbuttoned and smiled. Only Alice could speak to him like that. He remembered . . . ah, how he remembered. He opened the fridge door and smiled into the interior. He was an old man. God, he really was. An old man. His smile widened as he reached for the milk. Because right inside himself he knew that he was just the same: Ted Pettiford, short fuse, no good at talking, but good at doing . . . The Pumpkin Line would prove that. The Pumpkin Line would give them all new life. Alice too. Please God, please Dad, Alice too.

Perry went early to collect Nell. He had acquired another vintage car for the garage and insisted on giving it a good run. It was an Austin Seven, draughty and very cramped, but he had been tinkering with it for a week now and it went like a dream. It almost compensated for the fact that Edmund had taken Sally Gold to the Odeon last week. Edmund had assured him that all she wanted to do was to talk about Hester but Perry still envied him deeply. The Austin Seven alleviated the envy; perhaps he was going to be one of those blokes who loved cars better than women.

He discussed this at some length with Nell. She had an amazing cold and sounded as if she was speaking underwater so he was doing her a favour really. 'Ed reckons I only fancy her because she's a lesbian. But that can't be right because I don't think she is. She's so bloody feminine for one thing. No offence to you, Nell, but she's perfectly proportioned. You haven't met her, have you?'

'Doh,' said Nell.

'Don't try to speak, darling. And blow your nose, for God's sake. That's better. She's got this wonderful red hair, just a mass of curls, and her hands and feet are just perfect. I couldn't get her out of my head—' Nell made a sound and he glanced round at her. She shook her head, holding a tissue to her nose. 'Well anyway, then I bought this car and I'm all right now. She's gorgeous, I can't think of anything else now I've got her . . . call her Mad Hatter after Ma . . . My God, listen to me! I must be one of those crazy blokes – and I don't care!' He chugged through Bromsgrove and pulled up at a chemist's shop. 'Hang on – got to leave the engine running in case . . .'

He came out of the shop with some pastilles. 'Here, suck

these. Bert Lewis reckoned he'd got a cold last week, got rid of it in a few hours. These things burn it out.'

Nell lifted her brows.

'You remember Bert. Worked with Mo on the *Devon Belle*. Knew your great-grandfather. Pipe. No teeth.'

Nell said something that Perry correctly interpreted as 'charming' and began to suck one of the sweets. By the time they were driving through Cheltenham her eyes and nose were pouring and Perry was still assuring her that her cold was 'burning itself out'. She tried to ask after Hattie.

'Cat? We haven't had a cat since – oh sorry. Hattie. Ma. Yes, she's fine. Tons of energy. Mowed the lawn. Doffie came over and warned her about doing too much and she said there was no chance anything would go wrong this time because Percy is in charge. Can you believe it? She's going like your ma, all mystical and peculiar—' Nell made furious gurgling noises and he said, 'Sorry – sorry, sweetie. But you know exactly what I mean so don't pretend . . . *Nell*, into a hanky, for God's sake! I'll share anything else with you but not your cold!' He pretended to wipe his face with a piece of cotton waste; Nell saw with great pleasure that he now had a streak of oil along his jawline.

'Anyway,' he resumed, 'Aunt Doffie came back with a slammer. She said that this one was going to be different from the others because Mum was actually working instead of lying on the bed all day ordering people around!' He chuckled appreciatively. 'It's true too. I've never seen my mother move around so much in the whole of my life!' He turned his mouth down. 'Not that there's anyone much to order around now. Once Enid's gone, it'll just be me and Edmund.'

He drove carefully past Staverton airfield, where Mo had done so much work. Nell stared out of the window and wondered whether she would ever see him again. Not that it mattered any more; she loved all her children, the school and the staff. Especially Shirley. She made gurgling sounds at Perry and he nodded.

'I haven't forgotten. But we don't have to wait till we're forty.' He chuckled. 'Now that really would please Ma. A daughter-in-law already in the family. I said *family*! Not family *way*!' He roared with laughter and then suddenly exploded in a sneeze. 'My God, you've passed it on already! Oh well, you'll have to sleep with me now.' He went on laughing in spite of Nell's explosive splutters of 'Shut up!' and 'You absolute idiot!'

That morning, also quite early, Alice received a telephone call from Mo Checkers.

'Is that you, Mrs Ryecroft?'

'Who else would it be?' She wondered why he was so obviously distancing himself from all of them. 'And we were Alice and Val when we worked together.' She did not think he had called them anything at all, but was determined to make a breakthrough.

'Oh . . . well. Perhaps. I was wondering whether I could have a word.'

He would have seen Val drive away half an hour ago, so he knew she was on her own.

'Of course. As a matter of fact, I was going to come over. I'd seen the bedroom light on so I guessed you were home and there's quite a bit to tell you about the Pumpkin Line.'

'I'll come to you. Mrs Mearment is making a cake.'

She frowned slightly; they had included Mrs Mearment in all the plans. Alice had known that she would be an ally in persuading Mo to join them next Monday.

She began to say something of this but he interrupted hastily and said in a low voice, 'I'll be with you in two minutes.' The phone clicked a goodbye in her ear. She put the kettle on and opened the back door.

He slid in like a character in a spy film; Alice laughed at her own thought and he flashed a look at her that was only just short of dislike.

She said, 'Mo, whatever is wrong? Are you all right? Didn't

they like your paper? Val was absolutely certain you'd walk away with a PhD on the presentation alone.'

'Yes. I did. And I've been offered a job in America on the strength of it.'

She was making coffee so could not hug him, but her face lifted in one of her special smiles. 'Congratulations, my dear. I know you won't want to take it but what an honour—'

'I've accepted. I'm going.'

She paused, surprised, then making herself pleased for him. She carried the coffee into the living room and they sat at the familiar table, staring out at the late daffodils and early tulips. She wanted to mention Nell's name and could not. Nell had told her it was over and Mo himself had not left them an address . . .

She stopped telling him how much he deserved this opportunity and said, 'Well, at least you can come with us on Monday. Val will be so pleased. And my father . . . he was most insistent you should be there. That was why I was coming to see you.'

'Where are you going on Monday?'

She smiled again. 'We are running the *Belle* along to Leadon where we have opened a temporary connection with the Pumpkin Line. We've got a mile of track that is operational and we're doing an inaugural run. It wouldn't have been the same without you.'

'Oh, I'm sorry.' He did not sound sorry. 'I have to be back in Birmingham tomorrow morning.'

'Birmingham?'

'My university. You knew that.'

'Yes. Val told me. I did not realize . . . but of course. We should have known that's where you were.' She frowned. 'Nell's school is in the south of Birmingham. She did not say . . . anything.'

'She did not know. Why should she?'

She was in no doubt now: he was angry. He was being deliberately unpleasant. Still she faltered, 'I thought you were friends.'

221

He shrugged. 'Apparently not.' He downed his coffee, stood up and went to the window. 'Sorry. We were friends. Then Nell decided . . . we were not.' He kept his back to her. 'Give her my best wishes anyway. And I hope Monday's inaugural run will be successful.' He paused, then said, 'Who will drive?'

'Bert Lewis. Half of us are going down to the coach, then he's shunting back to pick up the others. We're having a picnic and returning the same way.'

'Sounds . . . just right.'

She said impulsively, 'Mo, you must be there! Can't you phone excuses? You should be there. You're the engineer! If anything goes wrong—'

He said, 'Nothing will go wrong. Remember the Pettiford magic.'

They were both fraughtly silent. His body was stiff as a ramrod.

She said at last, 'You know about the magic, then?'

'Yes. Everybody knows. It's simply to do with sex, isn't it? There's no real magic except that.'

Her voice was a thread. 'You saw Val and me. That day. You must have been working there and when we arrived you hid. And then you swam across the pool and I saw you get out the other side. You were . . . disgusted.'

'Only with myself.' He sounded almost weary. 'Disgusted that I had let my resolution falter. You had all got under my skin, my defences. I thought I was so clever, getting to know Helena and Edward. Meeting Nell. Almost managing to seduce her on our second meeting – that would have been enough. I could have left then. It would have set everything straight. But I didn't seduce her. Instead, I fell in love with her.' He swung round. 'That was partially your fault, you know, Alice! I met you and I could see why . . . could under-stand how . . . that early evening in the cellar of Hooper's building . . . I understood then.'

She stared at him. 'Who are you?' she breathed.

'You know who I am. You have felt it all along and not

faced it. History has been repeating itself, Alice. First you turned away from my father and went to Val. And then Nell turned away from me and went to Perry. Neither my father nor I could fight that. It's the other side of the Pumpkin Coach, isn't it, Alice? It's after midnight when the bad things happen.'

She gripped the edge of the table. 'Joe. You are Joe's son.'

'I am Joe's son. And I am Julie's son. They are dead, and, as you well know, Alice, that means I have no family. So I came looking for you.'

'He told you.'

'No. Not my dad. Because he was happy. And successful. He was a well-known educationalist in the North, Alice. Respected. Loved. He did not need to tell me anything. I simply knew him, through and through. As you knew him.'

She made a sound of protest.

He said, 'My mother told me. She knew. She knew how unhappy he had been lying in hospital in a strange land, hearing of his mother's death, knowing that you had turned from him.'

'That's not true, Mo! He turned from me!'

'He gave you a chance to leave. And you took it.'

She was silent, recognizing the impossibility of making him understand about Joe. He sat down again slowly, waiting. And at last she said, 'So when they died you wanted . . . revenge?'

'Yes. I wanted to even things up. I used the coach. And Helena, of course. Dear Helena. She loves you devotedly.' He blinked. 'It seems that everyone does.' He paused and added clearly, 'Even the dead.'

She looked him in the eyes; he blinked and dropped his to look at the table. She said steadily, 'My grandfather has been with me. Perhaps five or six times. That is all. No one else. At first I thought – was afraid – that Joe was speaking through you . . . but even before you told me today who you are, I knew it was not Joe. We had said our goodbyes a long time ago.' She put out a hand and touched his arm. 'I can imagine how you feel, Michael. I expect your mother disliked the very thought of me. But I was never a threat to her. Your father and I were very much in love. But we were not meant for each other. We married other partners. And we grew to love them.'

He kept his head down. 'You went to the Pumpkin Coach. That day. Dad came down to see exactly what his mother had left for him. And you went with him to Leadon and showed him the way through the trees. He told my mother he could feel the old track beneath the soles of his feet.' He lifted his head and said angrily, 'He may well have been an educator – an innovator in his field. But in his heart he was always a railwayman.' She said nothing; her blue eyes were wide and full of memories. He stared into them. 'And – and – he was like all the rest. He always loved you.'

'And I always loved him. And always will. But I lived without him as he lived without me. Happily. Very happily, Michael. Please don't forget that. Maybe he felt as I feel, that he could not have lived without his wife. Just as I could not live without Val. He did not have to. Please don't forget that either.'

Mo choked on a sob, then gasped, 'They had a way of looking at each other. As if they could never look away again. I tried it on Nell. In the theatre. Oh God, what have I done?'

She said swiftly, 'What *have* you done? Exactly?'

'Not what you think! Tell me one thing, Alice. The truth. I deserve the truth. Is Nell my father's daughter? Is she my sister?'

Alice's hand was still on his arm; she clutched it convulsively.

'Is that what you thought? Is that how you were going to – what did you call it – even things up? Seduce her and then tell her she was your sister?'

He shook his head but said, 'Is she? Tell me!'

'No. She belongs to Val and me. Thank God. She is nothing to do with Joseph Adair or any of the family who owned the Pumpkin Coach. She takes after my mother and my husband's mother. She is kind and true and fearless and intelligent.' She withdrew her hand and put it in her lap. 'And . . .' She paused. 'I rather think she is too good for you, Michael Adair. I rather think it is a good thing you are going to America. We should say goodbye now.'

He said, 'Alice. Forgive me. I had to know.'

'And now you do.'

'Mrs Mearment seemed to think that she and Perry were not . . . together . . . any more.'

'He has gone to fetch her today. They are very good friends. I don't know more than that.' She stood up. 'I have to get on.'

There was a sound from the lane; it could have been a tractor. Then gravel crunched beneath tyres. Alice ran through the open door and stood in amazement as the Austin Seven chugged round the corner of the house. There was a flurry of greeting. Perry said, 'She's absolutely soaking wet, Aunt Al. All over my shirt and tie—'

'I can see oil on your face,' Alice interrupted, all too conscious of Mo in the kitchen behind her.

Nell got out of the car and flung herself on her mother. 'Ibe so bleased to be home,' she said and sneezed into Alice's shoulder.

'Let's get you to bed,' Perry said in a proprietorial way. 'Poor old thing. Not used to hard work . . . too much for her.'

Nell tried to hit him but he ducked and said his goodbyes.

'See you Easter Monday!' he called as he leaped back into the vibrating car.

Alice supported Nell into the kitchen.

It was empty.

Twenty

Alice said nothing. That night there were no lights in Mo's bedroom. She tried to recall whether she had told him to go immediately but could not remember. She devoted the rest of that pre-Easter week to Nell, who continued to leak tears of all kinds for another twenty-four hours and then was suddenly better.

'You must have been run down,' Alice insisted, bringing in the friar's balsam and a shawl. 'I've a good mind to write to your head and ask her to keep an eye on you. I know you and this Shirley are young and enthusiastic but she should not allow you to burn yourselves out before you've begun.'

Nell waved the steaming basin away. 'Don't you *dare* do any such thing, Mum! Every other teacher in Birmingham has got this identical cold. It's a germ that I could have picked up from the children or—'

'I *knew* this would happen. All that talk about it being an easy job to teach young children – Hester was right, it's not a job, it's another life!' She ignored Nell's waving hands and placed the basin securely on her lap. 'This will get rid of any fluid you might still have. And if you don't do what I say I will definitely telephone your head and—'

'All right. All right.' Nell pulled the towel over her head and breathed fiercely while Alice tucked the shawl around her to ward off any tiny draught. She wanted to wrap her arms round this only child of hers and hold her tightly against all the terrible things waiting for her in the world. Nell's voice was muffled from beneath the towel. 'I will obey you entirely, oh matriarch, on the strict understanding that I can come to the grand opening of our railway on Easter Monday. Is it a bargain?'

Alice smiled. Mo Checkers, or rather Michael Adair, would most definitely be in America by then.

'It's a bargain,' she conceded and put another log on the fire.

Sally was thankful to have broken up for a whole fortnight. It was a refined type of torture to see her beloved Piecrust every day and not be able to talk to her personally, or touch her. Yet as soon as she told herself she was free for two weeks, she wanted to be back in the Sixth Form sitting room, watching through the glass door for a glimpse of the tall slim figure with the bundle of hair seeming to hold her upright. When Edmund took her to the pictures for the second time, she sat in his car afterwards and told him exactly how she was feeling and he seemed to understand.

It was nearly dark and the moon came and went behind clouds that were moving fast in a typical April breeze. Edmund said nothing while she blabbered on about Hester; he closed his eyes and consciously relished being with this brightly coloured, exotic creature; he was still happy but now he wanted her quite desperately.

She slowed down and peered at him through the darkness. She did not need to see him distinctly; he was the opposite of Perry, fair with light blue eyes and high cheekbones above a long jaw. Perry took after his mother; they could have gypsy blood in them. Edmund took after . . . who? She realized suddenly that his eyes were closed.

She said, 'Wake up, Ed! You love her too. I know that. It's why I like to be with you. We both want a bit of the Piecrust and we can't have it.'

Her voice was light and Edmund thought she could probably sing rather well.

'Don't be revolting,' he said. 'She's my aunt and I love her and admire her as an aunt.'

'She's no relative whatsoever,' Sally said. 'I've been doing my homework, you know. She and your real aunt, Alice, were best friends at school. And still are. You spent a lot of time with Piecrust – you told me so. I think you fancy her as much as I do.'

He said unguardedly, 'I think she might know who my real father is. I was working on her.' He peered back at her. She looked about twelve and her loose-knit jumper was off one shoulder, which probably meant she was not wearing any underclothes. Somehow it all irritated him; probably she didn't even realize he could be aroused. He said, 'Sometimes I wish you'd . . . grow up, Sally. I know there are a lot of years between us but when you talk about Hester, you sound completely . . . immature.'

She ignored that. 'Your real father? Are you illegitimate, Edmund?' She came close and laughed in his face. 'Are you a *bastard*?'

He said slowly, 'Yes. I really think I am.'

She shrugged. 'Ask your mother. Obvious.'

'I intended to. But at the moment . . . the baby and everything.'

'Then go back to Piecrust. What are you doing, taking me to the pictures like this? You could be with her, asking her things about the past!'

'I tackled the whole thing the wrong way round,' he admitted. Her honesty brought out his own. 'I sort of threatened her. Put her right off.'

'Then go back and unthreaten her! Gosh, if I had an excuse like yours I wouldn't be hanging about here hoping for a snog with someone as completely unsexed as me.' She frowned. 'Does that make sense?'

'I know what you mean. And that isn't why I'm here. I like you. I admire you even though I think your ideas are half-baked. You're honest. And brave to the point of being stupid—'

'Piecrust says I've got a good brain and an intellectual depth too!'

'Hester. That's her name. Hester. Not bloody Piecrust.'

'Funny, everyone thinks you're so calm and collected – Piecrust says you're a cold fish – yet you always fire up when we're together. Now that is interesting.'

'Oh shut up, Sally! You're being immature again.'

'No, I'm not actually. I'm opening my mind to you, Ed. I come out with you now and then for one reason only, because you're Piecrust's pseudo nephew. And just then you stopped being that and you were Edmund.'

He gave her a suspicious, sideways look and she burst out, 'Now be fair, Ed! I might be immature and have nasty per-verted inclinations, but I am always honest.' She paused and then went on, 'Gosh. That's what you like about me, isn't it? That I speak the truth and I speak it all the time – I never stop! You couldn't ever trust me with a secret, Edmund, because it would be out in a flash!' She scrambled on to her knees – no mean feat in the confines of Edmund's car. 'I am honest. I stand by that. But . . .' She cupped his face in her delicate hands. 'I am also open. Open to the world, Ed. So please do not trust me. I like you. I do not want to hurt you.'

He was rigid, pressed back against the driver's seat, conscious only of her closeness, her small palms on his cheeks, her fingers just beneath his eyes.

'I don't care,' he said hoarsely.

'You would. And then you would hate me. And I don't want you to hate me. Ever.' She leaned closer and put her mouth against his and it was her sheer inexperience that woke him up.

He took her wrists and pulled her hands away and very gently pushed her back into a sitting position. She whispered, 'It's all right, Ed. I want to. Really. For you, because you are so special. I know what to do. I do. Really.'

He smiled at her in the thick darkness and held her still.

'Well, I don't. Not with you anyway. I was about ten years old when you were born, Sally. I think that was when I tried my first kiss. On a little kid who then thought we were engaged to be married.' He chuckled. 'I've been very careful who I kiss since then.'

'Edmund, you know you are safe with me because I am in love with Hester. If you want – anything – then I'm the one. Don't you see?'

'Oh Sally, Sally. Obviously you are acquainted with the word sex. Have you also heard the word love?'

Suddenly, to his amazement, she was crying. He let her go and she twisted round and opened the car door, swung out her legs and then turned back to spit at him, 'How dare you patronize me! How *dare* you? I love Hester. I love her with my soul as well as my body! Haven't you listened to a word I've said? And however "open" I am, it is only you I tell about my feelings for Hester! Because if I let myself be . . . *open* . . . it might get her into trouble. It would certainly make her a laughing stock. That's how I know I love her, because it goes against my nature not to tell the world how I feel! That's why I come out with you – that's why I kissed you – that's why I would sleep with you! Because I am grateful to you for being here. Don't you *understand*?'

She scrambled out and ran up the road. They were parked in the middle of Gloucester town and she lived near Painswick. He had to go after her but for an overlong moment he was stunned by her outburst. She was so damned . . . unexpected.

His headlights picked her out halfway along Stroud Road and he parked the car and got out to run after her. When she realized it was him she broke into a run, so that when he caught her at last they were both suffering from stitches and had no breath for any arguments. He had to hold her; she would have fled if she could. In any case he needed something, someone, to hang on to. He dropped his head – beside her he was enormous – and kept gasping, 'Sorry . . . sorry, Sal . . . so sorry.' And then, quite suddenly, she capitulated and was in his arms, weeping freely and telling him that she too was sorry and it was all her fault and she was no good to anyone, and why on earth she was going to St Hilda's she did not know except that she had to get right away, at least she knew that.

'You're going to St Hilda's because you're the cleverest girl at Whitsom Hall and my aunt is proud of you and you're doing it for her!' He scooped her up and her feet left the ground and she gave a little shriek. He laughed into her face, which was now just above his. 'You'll always love her but when you come back you'll see it's not perverted at all. And that's when you'll marry me and we'll settle down and have children and you'll probably become the headmistress at Whitsom Hall and all the Sixth Form girls will fall in love with you!'

She laughed with him and very gently he put her down, bending his head and brushing her bare shoulder with his lips. She said waveringly, 'Oh Ed,' so that he knew that if he kissed her now she would respond completely. But she was eighteen and he was twenty-eight.

He said, 'I've got a treat for you. Are you busy on Easter Monday?'

'A treat! There you go again, mistaking me for someone who needs treats!'

'Are you busy on—'

'No, I am not! What is the bloody treat?'

'The opening of our railway. The Pumpkin Line. D'you want to come? Hester will be there.'

'Oh Ed. I do love you.'

'No, you don't. Not yet. But you will. You made the mistake of opening your mind to me. And now I'm inside I won't come out.'

'That's what I mean. I just *love* you! And I'll do something for you too. I'll find out who your father was.'

He laughed. 'My God. It gives you an excuse to get under Hester's skin. I'm beginning to feel sorry for her.'

'Save your pity for yourself, old man!'

He led her back to the car and held the door. He watched her slide into the passenger seat, her sweater falling lower, her tiny feet neatly side by side. He thought she was probably right and that he would need . . . perhaps not pity but certainly sympathy from someone, even if it was only

231

himself. He smiled quietly into the night. In a strange way he welcomed the heartbreak that might well lie ahead.

During the afternoon of Good Friday, Duggie Marsden proposed marriage to Enid Westbrook. He had planned it very carefully; his best suit – which unfortunately was also his funeral suit but Enid would not notice that – a rather splendid tie with his family crest embroidered on the royal blue in gold thread, a plain white shirt of course and black shoes polished to within an inch of their lives. He bought flowers the day before in case the shops did what they were supposed to do on Good Friday and closed down. Obviously they weren't quite as fresh as they could have been – they were yellow tulips and tulips had a habit of hanging their heads. (He should have asked Doffie what to do about that, though Doffie was pretty hopeless when it came to flowers.) However, he had tugged the paper sheath right up to their necks and Enid would know how to revive them. He had been horrified at the price of engagement rings and had come out of the jeweller's empty-handed because, after all, Enid must be well over sixty now and he was into his seventies and engagement rings were totally unnecessary. He had a rather good garnet that had belonged to his mother but he wasn't sure about the size. He pocketed it just in case.

Ted's phone call had precipitated this preparation. The boys – Perry and Edmund – were driving Hattie, Doffie and Ted to some airfield over by Cirencester to see an air display. Hattie had 'performed' there during the war – in fact Ted thought she might have met Percy there. He wasn't sure because Hattie had been gabbling on the phone, and though he wasn't deaf he didn't always hear exactly what people said. Duggie had said he quite understood all that and if Ted was about to invite him along then he could forget it. Easter Monday with all the family at the opening of the Pumpkin Line would be enough for him. He was looking forward to a quiet few days before all the shenanigans. 'Is Enid going with you?' he had asked suddenly. And Ted had replied, 'Edith who? Oh, you mean Enid. Speak up, old man, your voice is quite frail. No. Enid is still making lists of things to take on her cruise. She'll never go, of course. But it makes her feel good.'

So Duggie had known that Enid would be alone at Leckhampton House for the whole of Good Friday afternoon. And he had planned accordingly.

He wasn't absolutely certain how this had all come about. Doffie had suggested it in the first place, he remembered that. And he had felt a kind of kinship with Enid. The outsider, the hanger-on. Just as he was. Or had been. Now that it was mostly his money financing the Pumpkin Line, he was by no means a hanger-on any longer. But Enid . . . Enid had lost her mother and then her brother. She adored her nephews and they adored her, but they were men now and had their own concerns. Perry was totally selfish, just like his mother. Edmund was a bit of an enigma; he opened up to no one, least of all his maiden aunt. And Hattie . . . Duggie sighed sharply. Hattie was Hattie. She professed to adore Enid – 'the sister I never had' – but she was having another baby and would expect Enid to fill the role she had so ably filled with Edmund and Perry. And Enid was now over sixty. Perhaps this was the time to marry Enid and take her out of that particular equation. She would fit into Duggie's life somehow, surely? He would hardly know she was in the big old town house.

He had tried to talk about it with Hester but she always seemed to have things on her mind lately. School mostly, but also the fact that her blessed Richard Tibbolt had gone to France for Christmas to try to weld his ghastly family together, and had not yet come back. He telephoned and wrote – he had sent her a poem last week that she would not show to Duggie, so it was special. But he did not return.

Duggie told himself that this whole thing was meant to be. He could not marry Doffie, who, after all, was the love of his life, and Enid needed him. She needed her own home and a husband and . . . damn it all . . . she needed some kind of

status! And he could give it to her. And here was the opportunity. And he must take it.

He chugged sedately up the drive of Leckhampton House
and parked well clear of the garage; Hattie had maintained
for years that the garage leaked exhaust fumes into the
kitchen.

Nobody answered the doorbell, which was no surprise
because the house absorbed sound like a sponge. Granny
Westbrook had told him once how Hattie had screamed and
screamed when her baby girl was on the way and Granny had
not heard her for ages. Poor Hattie, the most . . . *unexpected*
. . . of all the Pettifords.

He went round the side of the garage into the back
garden, with its shaven lawn and the tennis court ready and
waiting for the summer. The kitchen door was locked. Also
the French windows into the sitting room. He backed
into the garden until he could see Enid's window; it was well
protected with net curtaining but it was open, and he called
and gesticulated and felt incredibly foolish when nothing
happened. If anyone could see him from next door they
would wonder what was going on: an elderly man,
respectable-looking, yelling for his sweetheart, waving his
stick . . . Now there was an old-fashioned word. Sweetheart. A
lovely word. Not really applicable to Enid.

He sighed and walked round to Hattie's window, which
overlooked the tennis court. No curtains there. No Hattie
either. He sighed again. She was not only unexpected, she
was exciting. He had stood in this self-same place in the past
with the boys, once with Doffie, and listened, all of them with
a kind of embarrassed and wry resignation, as Hattie had
made audible love to Percy. What a woman. What an amazing, beautiful, bountiful woman.

Then quite suddenly she was standing there in the window,
seeing him, opening the casement and calling, 'Is that you,
Dugdale? Hang on a minute and I'll let you in.'

It wasn't Hattie's voice, of course, because it wasn't Hattie. It
was Enid in one of Hattie's dresses that did not fit Hattie any

more: low cut with a built-in support that thrust her breasts almost under her nose. Duggie sighed as he trudged back to the door; honestly, if Hattie thought she was doing Enid a favour by giving her something like that, she was sadly mistaken. Hattie looked daring and seductive in that dress; Enid looked . . . well, cheap. He remembered the last time Hattie had helped her sister-in-law to pack and leave home. Percy had been so angry, so terribly angry. And Hattie had said brazenly, 'You should understand that she needs sex just as you do.' And Enid had gone to Reggie Ryecroft and he had dressed her in clothes rather like the dress she was wearing now. And then he had used her and beaten her afterwards to within an inch of her life. Oh God. Surely she was not dressed like that for Dugdale Marsden?

The key turned in the lock and the door opened. Enid was smiling. She did not look as if she were reliving a nightmare.

She said, 'Come on in. No one else is here. Did you come to see Hattie?'

'No. I came to see you. They told me you were packing.'

'I am, I am! Hattie gave me this frock and told me I could take any of her stuff – anything at all. She is so good to me, Dugdale, so good. I shall have to come home often to see her. And the boys. But I don't want to be here when Millie is born. Just in case . . . you know. It would be like history repeating itself. If anything happened again I don't think I could bear it.'

He followed her up the stairs. 'But Hattie will need you, Enid.'

'That's what I thought. But she had a good talk to me the other day. She told me how awful she felt about . . . last time. That it was all her fault. And that if I stayed just to help her out she would feel worse still. And she gave me the dress and told me to go for it! That's what she says to the boys sometimes when they're going to do something not quite . . . straight. She says, go for it, my darlings, and let the devil take the – the—'

'Hindmost. That's probably when they're after unsuitable girls. Or something,' Duggie said lamely.

235

Enid laughed. 'Well, that's what she expects me to be doing! That's what they do on cruises, you know. Single ladies look out for single men and vice versa. It's terribly exciting.'

'It sounds ghastly to me.'

'Well, Dugdale, forgive me, but you have never seized an opportunity in your life, have you?' He thought of Doffie and said nothing. 'And you've never travelled – and it's not for lack of money. You really do need to broaden your mind, my dear. When I get home I'll tell you all about it and then you can do something similar.'

They went into Enid's pristine bedroom. A large case was open on the bed. Another, obviously packed to capacity, was strapped and stood by the window.

'Have you actually booked a cabin on one of these cruise ships?' Duggie enquired.

'Oh yes. It sails from Falmouth to the West Indies. Edmund is going to drive me down and Hattie will come too if she is feeling up to it. I'm going to have a royal send-off.'

'That's nice. I must say, you do sound so much better. Cheerful.'

'Bereavement is like that, you know. There are stages you go through. I read all about it. I am in the acceptance stage which immediately precedes the receptive stage. By the time we reach Barbados I shall be able to mingle freely with the other tourists, talk to them about Percy. Accept their sympathy.'

She would be a sitting duck. She would wear this dress and give out all the wrong messages: it would be obvious she had private means, that a man had loved her – he bet his bottom dollar she wouldn't tell anyone that Percy was her brother so they would assume she was a rich widow – and that she was absolutely available.

He said, 'Just what do you hope to gain from this cruise, Enid?'

'A man,' she said bluntly. She smiled. 'Hattie told me to be quite frank about it. You're the first one I've said it to. It's quite easy really.'

He swallowed. 'Well then, you don't have to go looking. I came here today knowing you were alone. I wanted to propose marriage to you.' He sat down suddenly on the end of the bed; he was too old for this sort of thing really. 'Will you marry me, Enid?' As he spoke he removed the tiny ring box from his waistcoat pocket and snapped it open. The garnet was very small, only just visible. She stared at it.

'Is it a ruby?'

'No. A garnet. My mother's.'

'So you haven't bought it?'

'No.'

She went on staring and then recovered herself enough to say, 'How sweet. Perhaps your father gave it to her one moonlit evening in Queen Victoria's Jubilee year. Or something.'

He looked up, surprised. 'Actually, she bought it herself. After he died.' He smiled, remembering his down-to-earth mother. 'It was her birthday and she said he would want her to have something nice.'

'Oh.' She smiled too, apologetically. 'I'm such a romantic, you know. I remember when Valentine used to come here to see Hattie. He was so attentive to me. I thought he was wonderful. I still tremble when he comes into the room.'

She seemed to have forgotten the proposal. He said, 'Do you tremble when I come into the room?'

She laughed aloud. 'Oh Dugdale! Of course not. I've never been frightened of you.'

He was astonished. 'Were you frightened of Val? And Percy?'

'Oh yes. Of course. They're men. You know, proper men.'

He wondered where that left him. 'But . . . frightened?'

'Women are of men, you know. Just a little. That's how I made the terrible mistake of succumbing to Reggie Ryecroft. He frightened me and I thought that was because he was a real man.'

'Oh Enid! Oh my dear girl! You cannot go on this cruise thing looking for a man and dressed like that. Something awful will happen to you. You are still a child, you don't know what true love is. Marry me, Enid. Stay at home and be my wife. We'll move house and you can choose everything. Just imagine that!'

She laughed again, then sobered.

'Oh Dugdale, I am sorry. You are the last man . . . the very last man . . . I could never even consider marrying you. You do not make me tremble, my dear. And more than that, you saw me that day . . . You know what happened. I couldn't bear to live with someone – sleep with someone – who had seen me like that. Don't you remember I told you that after Mother's funeral? I thought you understood then. You have been so kind – you have come here and sat with me through my pain and sorrow. I did not know that you could feel for me. But I can never feel for you. I am so sorry.'

She began to cry again. He couldn't bear it, it was such a mess. He suddenly wanted her to go so that he never had to deal with her tears again. It was as if she understood that.

'Please go, Dugdale. I don't want this. I want to be happy. I want to pack and try on Hattie's dresses and – and just dream.'

It was the saddest thing he had known. He left the house, got into his car, waved through the window in case she was watching, though he was 99 per cent sure she was not, and drove off. She was in the acceptance stage, was she? And next would come the receptive stage. He shivered with terror for her.

Twenty-one

On the morning of Easter Monday, Michael Adair was up before five o'clock and on Mrs Mearment's bicycle pedalling hard for Gloucester, and then crossing the canal and river and heading towards the forest. By the time he reached Leadon Markham the air was golden with light, the ground with daffodils and primroses. He turned off into a lane that would eventually take him to the old engine shed where the *Devon Belle* was stabled. It was eight thirty when he dropped the bicycle into a bush, crossed the spur line and put the key into the padlock on the shed doors.

He pulled them wide and propped them with the old buffers they had found. The sunlight flooded into the darkness of the shed and there, shining green and gold, was the locomotive.

'Hello, my beauty,' he said in a low voice. 'They've groomed you well – you look a thoroughbred. I had to come and see you on your big day.'

And a voice replied, 'I bluggy-well knew you would!' And Bert Lewis's head appeared from the side of the cab, wearing his old canvas-and-patent-leather driver's cap, his face one big toothless grin. 'Hello there, Mike. Given you a heart attack, 'ave I?'

Mo grinned back. 'Well worth it, Bert. Don't tell me you slept in the cab overnight?'

'Why not? It's the truth.' He stood up. 'I couldn't leave her. Not on the night before her run. And these days . . . there be 'ooligans about who would enjoy wrecking what we've done. Not having that.'

'What would you have done then, Bert?'

'Conked 'em on the 'eads with this.' He lifted his shovel, then climbed down. 'I've kept it shiny. Thought we could have a bit of breakfast together. Mr Ryecroft and his wife will come 'ere. No one else. They'm all going to wait at Leadon till we get there.' He limped over to Mo's side. 'She dun't look too bad, does she? That firm you sent round to do the sandblasting – that's what really brought her up.'

'You painted her afterwards.'

'That I did.'

'What about the axle boxes?'

'Said they was as good as new. We've been lucky. I 'eard they was trying to restore a loco in Wales. Springs 'ad gone, wheel tyres 'ad to be machined . . . turned out to cost a fortune.'

They walked round the engine, touching the newly painted metal, standing back occasionally to admire the brass funnel, the letters picked out, the sheer beauty of the old machine.

Bert Lewis said quietly, 'Your dad would be proud of you, my lad.'

Mo took a deep breath. 'So. You know, do you? It got round quite quickly. I told Mrs Ryecroft less than a week ago.'

'No one's said owt to me, lad. I knew 'oo you were straight off. Joe Adair knew me well. Mostly from the old bus line – that was the railway telephone line connecting all the stations and departments – but I met 'im during his first month with the company. Mr Maybury took 'im all round the forest lines on a ganger's trolley. An' I was the one what druv it.' Bert chuckled. 'Nearly lost the use of my arms that day. Your dad thanked me specially. 'E was a good boy. Like you.'

Mo tightened his mouth and frowned prodigiously to stop the tears. The thought of his father at sixteen entering these very woods with this man was almost too much to bear, yet was – somehow – all of a piece.

Bert Lewis said, 'Reckon everything 'as come round full

circle. I dun't know whether you know this, my son, but your father and Alice Pettiford, they worked together in the old General Office. Then your dad went away in the Navy and met your ma, and little Alice – she weren't really little at all but everyone did always call her little Alice – she'd known Val Ryecroft all 'er life. His sister were her best friend. And she and 'im . . . well, they got together. As you know. And now there is you. And there is Alice Pettiford's daughter. I reckon that 'ud make a perfect circle.'

Mo cleared his throat.

'It's not quite so . . . simple, Bert. I don't think I would be very welcome in the family circle.'

Bert was genuinely astonished. 'And what gives you that idea, lad?'

Mo shrugged and looked at him with a grin. 'Your eyes must be bad, Bert. My mother was Chinese.'

Bert's expression changed to one of bewilderment. 'What's that got to do with a basket of eggs?'

Mo's grin exploded into a puff of laughter. 'Oh Bert . . . Well, maybe nothing at all. To you. But there are other things anyway. Nell – Alice's daughter – she is very attached to her cousin, who will probably be coming today.'

'I knows him. Daft bugger. Black hair all over the place and roving eyes likewise.'

Mo laughed again and wondered how he was managing to keep up this conversation. Except that Bert Lewis had pumped the ganger's trolley that had taken a very young Joe Adair through these ancient woods. Mo had felt a kinship with Bert and thought it was because they had worked side by side through last autumn. He said, 'That's him. He's all right, actually. I think they will be all right. Together. As a couple.'

It was Bert's turn to tuck his lips into his gums and frown. But then he said, 'Come on. Let's fire up and fry some bacon on that there shovel. We need a decent head of steam for when Mr Ryecroft do arrive.'

So they went to it, laying the kindling and feeding coal carefully and then beginning the slow alternate shovelling:

the rhythm that came from another time, learned over the years by Bert Lewis, probably in Mo from birth. There was great satisfaction in working together so expertly, watching the sweat gather on each other's foreheads, grinning occasionally as the fire began to roar in its box. It was ten o'clock before everything was to Bert's satisfaction, the valve hissing steam gently, the fire red and glowing. Then he wiped off his shovel again and fished in a tin tucker box for bacon more fat than lean, bread cut into enormous doorsteps, tin plates and cutlery – eatin' irons, Bert called them.

'Best meal of the day,' he announced as the thick rashers sizzled on the shovel. 'Take that bit there, my son. Make room for the fried bread.'

They closed the door of the firebox and sat on the foot-plate, feet dangling, chewing contentedly. A mist hung at the top of the trees but already they could see it was going to be a wonderful day. Mo pushed back his thick black hair and it fell over his forehead again immediately.

Bert said simply, 'That's your ma's hair, I reckon, son. Your dad was mouse-brown. But his flopped as well.'

Mo nodded, realizing how good it was to talk of his parents. 'Yes. Apparently I've got my mother's hair and eye colouring, my dad's shape and size.'

'True. If I d'remember aright, Joe Adair looked like a schoolboy.'

'There are a few photographs. Yes, I suppose he did. When you knew him he wasn't much more than a schoolboy.'

'We grew up faster then. He'd lost his dad in the war and he was looking after his ma. I think she died young.'

'Yes. Not a happy life. She did not even know she had inherited the Pumpkin Coach. So it was some time before my father knew it was his. He told me about it. And the forest. And my mother told me . . . other things.'

'And you came here to find out about the rest.'

'I suppose I did. And now I've laid all the ghosts and I'm going to America.'

Bert looked round, rheumy eyes as wide as they would go.

'No. That can't be, son. You b'long here. With the Pettifords.'

'Ted and Doffie? They are the only Pettifords left now. America will employ me, find me work – stuff I can do.' He looked Bert in the eye. 'I have to do this, Bert. They are researching metals that can withstand terrific stress. The sort of stress they might find on Mars. I might be able to help, Bert.' He smiled faintly. 'What is it they say now? I might make a difference!'

'I don't doubt that, not for a minute. No good laughing about it either. 'Tis true. But . . .' He looked away from Mo's dark gaze. 'I'll miss you. That's all.'

'Yes.' Mo swallowed. 'I'll miss you too. Thank God we've got the *Devon Belle*, eh?'

Somewhere beyond the old engine shed they heard a car. They both crammed in the last of the food and got into the cab, opened the firebox and shovelled again. By the time Val appeared beneath them there was a satisfying roar and a hiss of steam.

He was not over-surprised to see Mo. 'We thought you wouldn't be able to stay away,' he assured him, climbing the footplate to shake hands enthusiastically. 'Well done! Great to see you! We must talk – when we have the Grand Picnic perhaps.' He wedged himself into the back of the cab, pumping Bert's hand, clapping them both on the back. 'How long have you two been here?'

Mo was grinning in spite of himself. So Alice had kept their conversation private. He said, 'Bert slept here. I've been here a couple of hours . . . not sure. It's going to be a grand day!'

' 'Tis that!' echoed Bert.

Val said, 'How long before there's enough steam to get to Leadon?'

'It's there.' Bert jerked his head at the boiler. 'When you're ready.'

'I've left Alice and Nell at the junction to work the points. They're all right. Let's have a cup of tea first – what d'you say?'

Neither of them said anything. Mo knew he must avoid seeing Nell and her mother at all costs; Bert produced his enamel canister and eased it under the valve. Steam hissed everywhere. Through it, Mo said, 'I'll let you fire for Bert. I've got my bike here. Mrs Mearment's bike, that is.'

Val assembled tin cups on the cab's sill. 'It can go in my boot. No need for you to cycle all the way back. If we'd known you were here . . .'

Mo almost told him that Alice had known since last Friday. That was the trouble with conversation, you could so easily spill things that were best left contained. Instead he said, 'I have to get back. Sorry.'

There was a pause. Val frowned and looked up and Mo refused to meet his eyes. Val was as sentient as his wife. Bert began to run through the specialities of the *Belle*.

'Mike and me, we fired her up and took her two or three yards before Christmas. Since then we've had all kinds of inspections. And Mike found a two-man firm who sand-blasted 'er so's I could start the painting. I was saying to 'im about that old engine in Wales what was donated but is proving to be more money than what she's worth.'

'Oh yes.' Val held out his cup and sniffed ecstatically at the steam. 'My God, scalding hot tea out of doors. Nothing like it.' He went on to elaborate about other engines that had proved too much for the restorers. 'We were just lucky – Edward Maybury has pulled enough strings to crochet a vest!'

Mo choked into his tea. If only Val had not brought Nell today, it would have been perfect. Yet . . . hadn't he known all along that somehow Nell would be here? Wasn't that why he was here too? So why was he so intent on getting back on Mrs Mearment's bike and pedalling as fast as he could back to Gloucester? He pushed back his hair for the umpteenth time and clutched a lump, pulling it until his eyes watered. And still he was no clearer about any of this. It had been so much simpler when he had started on this odyssey last year: find the woman who had wrecked his father's life and punish her in some way. But then there had been Helena and Edward Maybury and Nell . . . Oh God, there had been Nell.

Nell stayed very close to her mother as they sipped flask-flavoured tea from the thermos and eyed the hastily installed ground frame with some trepidation.

'No need to worry,' Alice said as comfortably as she knew how. 'I've changed the points using these kind of things before. We'll practise in a minute. It will probably need the two of us but we shall cope.'

Nell said, 'I'd be happier if you were at least two stone heavier, with some sign of muscle in the upper arm.'

'Yes. Well. Of course I was much younger when your grand-father showed me how to . . . but it's a knack rather than brute force.'

'Anyway, they'll all be here before then. Grandad and Uncle Duggie can surely manage it between them.'

'Duggie's not coming. But your grandfather will manage. He's probably here already. Down at the station. They'll be in the waiting room. Run and see, Nell.'

'In a minute.'

They were sitting on a pile of sleepers at the side of the track and Nell moved even closer to her mother.

'All right.' Alice had not wanted Nell to come today but of course there had been no stopping her. She wasn't properly well yet; that was obvious. Alice took her hand and held it gently against the plastic thermos beaker. Nell must not catch another cold.

Nell shivered as if in response to her mother's thought. She would never admit it but she had felt most odd since that awful streamer of a cold. She had wandered to the bluebell woods and noted that it was going to be a wonderful year for the flowers; she had walked around the church and sat in a pew to say a couple of perfunctory prayers. She had not asked about Mo and she had not gone across to Mrs Mearment's house for a chat. There was never a light in his window and Mrs Mearment did not pop in to ask how Nell was. It was as if the Berlin Wall had suddenly appeared between the two houses. Yet she knew he was near and she had been certain that he would be at the opening of the Pumpkin Line. Hadn't he been the one to find that first map? Hadn't he torn at the undergrowth to discover the original permanent way? Hadn't he worked like a Trojan on the locomotive that Uncle Edward had 'rescued'? He would appear with the others. He would be in the waiting room on Leadon platform with Hester and Hattie and the boys . . . He was here, she was sure of it.

Her grandparents were the first to appear, closely followed by a few of the volunteers, who were pulling a luggage truck stacked high with food.

Doffie said, 'Hester came to help me make the picnic. And I've put your frozen stuff in one of those insulated bag things, Alice.' She pointed to a very large plastic box. 'That's the cake . . . no, I didn't make it, Nell darling. And if you're being horribly sarcastic, then shame on you! I ordered it from Brunner's and they supplied the candles too.'

'How many?' Nell asked.

'Sixty-five.'

Nell was surprised. 'Is that all? Somehow I think of the coach as being hundreds of years old.'

Hattie appeared. She had been sitting on the end of the truck. She stood up with some difficulty. 'Time is so very, very relative, Nell,' she said, coming over to peck Nell's cheek. 'For instance it has almost drawn to a stop for me. If I expand much more I shall pop, then it really will have drawn to a stop!' They all laughed; so often Hattie made them laugh.

Ted went to the ground frame and showed them how easy it was to pull the lever so that the points connected the Leadon line with the Pumpkin Line. In the distance a puff of smoke appeared above the forest canopy and then they heard the unmistakable sound of a train whistle. The others emerged at Leadon level crossing and ran towards them; Hester slipped on the rails and was saved by Sally Gold. Edward, who had got there first, hung back, smiling. Perry brought up the rear; he was wearing a red bandanna and an eyepatch. Alice murmured, 'He's such a happy human being, Nell. Like his mother.'

Nell glanced round in surprise. 'D'you mean Perry? Mum, I thought you knew. It was just . . . It's over. It was over when Uncle Percy died. Perry is absolutely besotted with that girl in Hester's class. Sally Gold. Look at them.'

'That will come to nothing, Nell.'

Nell shook her head. The *Devon Belle* came alongside Leadon platform; Bert was waving his cap from the cab; Val was the other side, making a strange whooping noise. Mo was not there either. Everyone started to cheer and jump. Unexpectedly, Edmund went berserk, running in circles and punching the air. Sally released Hester and doubled up with laughter. Perry seized her and whirled her into a dervish dance. The volunteers yelled and ran to meet the engine and then run back with her. Doffie put her mouth close to Ted's ear and said, 'I'm suddenly thinking of your sister.' He nodded; he had heard that perfectly well. 'Mitzie.' He glanced at Hattie, who was smiling placidly and holding her abdomen. 'She would have loved this. She was wild and kind. Rather like Hattie.' Doffie hugged his arm and remembered what Gran had told her before she died. Nobody else need ever know. Not now.

Val jumped down and handed up the two of them. Everyone began to pack the rear of the tender with the picnic boxes. People climbed on to the footplate and the buffers. Bert whistled again and the *Devon Belle* passed slowly over the points and entered the forest on its very own line, followed by a gaggle of walkers. And then came the surprise: from tree to tree was strung a line of red, white and blue bunting that lasted the full mile from the junction to the coach. And Nell knew then that Mo had been home and had been at work here every day. With the thought came her cold again; her eyes filled and overflowed down her face.

Edmund skipped over the ballast and produced a handkerchief.

'Perry told me you were dripping at every pore,' he said. 'But this is ridiculous.' He lowered his voice. 'Pull yourself together, Nell. He's gone to America. So what? Brilliant job but he'll be back.' He shoved her sideways and she half fell through head-high fern. He grabbed her and held her hard.

She choked, 'America? What do you mean?'

'Thought Mrs M. would have told you. She told me.'

'But . . . America?' She had stopped the tears somehow and gazed up at him incredulously. 'And why did you . . . You barely know Mrs Mearment.'

'Of course I know her. And of course I would try to find out. You're the sister I never had, or will be till July. Besides, I wanted to talk to her. Still haven't discovered my real father. Thought she might know something. Can I have my hand-kerchief, Nellie? You seem to have stained my shirt.'

'There's something so infuriating about you, Edmund Westbrook or Pettiford or whatever you call yourself. You think you're so damned clever—'

'If you mean because I understand how you feel about Mo Checkers, you're absolutely right. I do understand. And that makes me damned clever.'

She was still, staring up at him, completely misunderstanding. He grinned.

'It's not that surprising, Nell. It was completely obvious from the word go. You just gawped at him all the time like a schoolgirl. I didn't realize he felt the same way because he hardly spoke and his facial expression was always the same – miserable. Then he went for Perry in the summer house, and so I knew that it was mutual.' He frowned at her expression then added, 'Just why did you go off with Perry? If you were trying to make Mo jealous, I have to tell you it doesn't work like that. He simply retired from the field.'

Her cold had completely dried up again; she ran her tongue round lips that felt chapped.

'Nell? It's not that bad, you know. You could go out to see him. Write to him.' He made a face in an effort to snap her out of this paralysis. 'You've still got me. And Perry. We'll love you for ever.'

She whispered, 'Edmund. Are you serious?'

'Of course.'

'You remember kissing me? I was a kid.'

'Of course. How could I forget?'

She stared a moment longer, then she said, 'Thank you, Edmund.' She pushed through the ferns. Everyone was well in front of them. She said, 'You're wrong. Mo was here. He decorated the trees.' She glanced around. 'He's probably still here somewhere. This is his railway as well, remember.'

'Maybe. But he's landed a job in the States. Mrs Mearment was definite about that.'

Nell measured her strides to the space between the sleepers. She was certain he was here.

Hester spread a rug just above the reedy edge of Bracewell's Pool; it was where she and Tibbolt had made love. She sat down and pulled her maxi-skirt to her ankles. It was the last time they had made love. The day Percy had died. Six whole months ago.

Sally said, 'This is marvellous. Sort of primeval in some way. Is it just the trees?'

Hester said, 'Trees, coal, iron. Ships, war, death.'

Sally squatted comfortably like a Bushman in Africa. 'I see. A cycle.'

'Everything is a cycle. We all come full circle and find we've learned nothing, done nothing. In fact we're back where we started.'

'Not quite. Fashions change, for one thing. Age changes, for another. In your particular cycle I wasn't around before. Now I am.'

'Why are you? You're not interested in restoring old railways. You're not related in any way whatsoever to the Pettifords.'

'Edmund asked me to come.'

'Edmund? We thought it was Perry.'

'So you do talk about me?'

'Not like that. I was worried because you're eighteen and Perry is twenty-seven. Edmund is a year older.' Hester had twisted to look up at Sally. Her dark eyes mirrored the pool. Strands of still-dark hair had escaped from the chignon and curled around her face. Sally was staggered, as always, by her beauty, which was better than perfection because of the slight imperfections: a mole beneath her eye, lines from nose to chin that were not laughter lines.

She said, 'You were worried. You care.'

Hester unclasped her ankles and banged her knees. 'Of course I care, you little idiot! You are one of my pupils and you are exceptional! You need to concentrate solely on work for the next three years and you insist on frittering your energies away with—'

Sally interrupted ecstatically. 'Of course! That's one of the circles! Don't you see – I am about to repeat your experience when you went to Bristol! With poor old Prof Tibbolt!' She saw Hester's expression change and straightened her legs abruptly to sit by her as close as she dared. 'Don't be angry. I found out because I wanted to find out everything about you. *Everything.* And I'm good at finding out things. That's why I'm going to be all right at St Hilda's. I store tiny little fragments of things and then fit them together. Like a jigsaw puzzle.' She tried a persuasive smile and went straight to the point, as was her wont. 'Edmund asked me here today because he hoped I could find out something about his real father. And I have been out with him – just a couple of times, that's all – because I might find out stuff about you.'

Hester said tensely, 'Edmund would not have told you anything about me.'

'Listen. Keep calm. Everyone at school, practically, knows about you and old Tibbolt. You've never made a secret of it. Some of the girls have followed you home on their bicycles and seen him arrive in his car—'

'You mean *you* have followed me home on *your* bicycle!'

'All right. Yes. But it is known. We're proud of you! We think it's marvellous. Honestly.'

Hester continued to stare into the violet eyes for another few seconds, then sighed and turned away. 'For goodness' sake. What does it matter anyway?'

'Quite.' Sally made herself more comfortable. Behind them Alice called, 'Hester, come and help with the food!' Sally said, 'You're right about Edmund. He would never gossip. Especially about you. He – he – reveres you.'

Hester barked a laugh. 'Like heck!' And Sally echoed the laugh delightedly.

'That's what I adore about you! You are ethereal and magical and then you are so down to earth! Oh Hester, please be nice to me. Just for today.'

'I'm always *nice* to you, Sally! Today I shall continue to be *nice* to you. But kindly accept the fact that whatever fragments of information you gather today or any other day, they'll never make a true picture. Time and wisdom are very necessary ingredients.'

Sally said slowly, 'So the circle never ends in quite the same place, does it?'

Hester was silent. Alice called to her again. Hester smiled and said, 'No. That is true, Sally.' Her smile deepened. She turned and began to get up. Sally leaped to her feet and held out a hand, and after a moment Hester took it.

Sally said, 'Edmund said he'd got off on the wrong foot. That's the only reason he thought I could help.'

Hester laughed. 'Oh Sally.' She looked up at the hole in the trees surrounding the pool. She said, 'Tell him I don't know anything. But I might well have worked something out by trying to make a jigsaw from the pieces we all have in the family. And if I can do it, so can he.'

She walked up the bank then turned and looked at Sally, who was standing very still staring up at her. She smiled. 'You see, Sally, you and I are probably sisters under the skin, aren't we? We both make jigsaws and then wonder why we can't get the sort of picture we want.' She held out a hand. 'Come on. Let's go and help lay out the food and drink and try to learn from Alice. She's

251

never had to rely on making jigsaws. She does it all by instinct.'

The picnic was riotous. The *Devon Belle* breathed quietly against her buffers while Bert stayed in the cab and heated sausage rolls on his diamond-bright shovel; Val and Ted opened champagne and proposed toasts; Edward Maybury made a speech; a man called Thomas Wood said that, on behalf of all the volunteers, he just wanted to say what an honour it had been to work on this restoration and how he hoped they would be able to trace the line right up to the old Severn Bridge and restore that too and . . . His friends pulled him down because it was obvious he was drunk. Perry decided they must all swim in the pool but no one else seemed keen, so he stripped to his underpants and ran in and immediately out again. The water, which had frozen over that winter, was still icily cold.

Alice and Nell joined Bert for a return trip to Leadon; both firing for him, laughing and exhausted at the same time. Bert told them about the difficulty of feeding the fire-box in the first place.

He looked straight at Nell. 'Couldna done none of it without young Mike acourse,' he said. 'Even this morning he turned up and helped me fire 'er up. Wanted to know how 'is sandblasting lot 'ad done.'

Nell was frozen, staring back at him.

Alice said, 'He's gone to America. A really good job . . .'

'Not till Wednesday, little Alice.' Bert switched his gaze. 'D'you remember how 'e got me on the bus line that time? To find out about the accident on the old Severn and Wye railway?'

Alice said quickly, 'That was Joe. Joe Adair.' She glanced meaningfully sideways at Nell.

'Aye,' said the old man heavily. 'That were someone else quite diff'rent.' He rubbed his hand on some cotton waste and took the driving handle. 'Back we go then, eh?'

Nell said, 'But you said . . . what did you mean?'

Bert chose that moment to blow the whistle; Alice shovelled as if her life depended on it. After a moment, Nell joined her.

Someone had built a fire outside the Pumpkin Coach and people were grouped around it finishing off the leftovers. Doffie and Hester were waiting on Hattie, whose boys had regressed completely and were playing hide-and-seek with Sally through the undergrowth. Ted and Val were yet again following the track further into the forest. The volunteers formed a queue for a train trip with Bert.

'Well, everyone looks happy enough,' Alice said, trying to sound pleased about it. She wished the last half an hour had not happened and they could sit with Hattie and then go home. But Nell, hot from the firebox, suggested a walk round the pool.

'We can't get right round, but we could probably make it to the alders over there.'

Alice had known this would happen, if not now then when they were driving back to Gloucester, but she still said reluctantly, 'The undergrowth is going to be wet. Your cold—'

'Is better, Ma. Come on. You obviously knew that Mo was here. My God, I've felt him here all the time! He might still *be* here. It would be just like him to watch us from the other side of the pool.'

'Darling, he's not. And if he is then he clearly does not want to see us. But he's not. He told me.'

'You've seen him. When?'

'The day you came home. Nell, please don't let us talk about Mo. I can't lie to you and it's better just to forget him. Believe me.'

Nell was already giant-striding to the pool's edge. She was so certain . . . so sure. He was here because he could not keep away from her. His long silence did not matter now; her frantic efforts to keep all thoughts of him at bay seemed so ridiculous. He was part of her as she was part of him. She

253

remembered the man on the snowy golf course before Christmas; perhaps that had been Mo keeping watch over her . . . She had seen his face and knew it had not been him, yet anything was suddenly possible. Anything at all.

She turned and held out a hand for her mother. 'Darling, I heard what you said back there. He's gone to America. But I heard what Bert said too.'

'Nell, he was mixed up. Didn't you realize that? He must be in his eighties now and the generations blur into each other.'

'He was talking about someone else. The boy you worked with in Gran's flat – when it was a railway office.'

Alice said heavily, 'Joe Adair.'

'That's right.' Nell tried to jolly her along. 'You had a fling with him, didn't you?'

'Is that what it was? That's not the point. The point is, my dearest girl, Mo has gone to America. He was offered a wonderful opportunity—'

'Mo is here, Ma. I know it.' Nell noted her mother's ashen face and led her along the edge of the pool to a fallen tree. They perched themselves on it. Nell said, 'Just sit for a while. Let this place work its magic. You've overdone it looking after me this week.' She waited, watching the other bank for any movement. He could be there, among the alders, watching her. She said quietly, 'What do you think of when you come here, Ma?'

Alice did not reply for a long moment, then she said, 'I think of my aunt sometimes. Your grandfather's sister. Mitzie. She obviously fell for the wrong man. He never acknowledged Hattie as his own.'

Nell could have sworn the alders swayed; there was no wind.

She said, 'You think I have fallen for the wrong man, Mum. Don't you?'

'Yes. Just as I did.'

'You?' Nell took her eyes off the alders for a second and looked at her mother with surprise. 'You mean that boy? Joe

254

wotsit? You didn't exactly fall for him, did you? It was always Dad.'

'I suppose it was. But I didn't know it. At the time. I wouldn't want it to happen to you, Nell.' Alice was watching the alders now. They were still again. Someone moved across them. She whispered, 'He's dead now. He's *dead.*'

Alarm flared in Nell; she had never been with her mother when Gramps had got in contact. In the past Nell had treated it as a bit of a joke. Now she was frightened for her mother. This was how it happened: the sudden tense awareness; the splitting of the dear and precious persona that was Alice Ryecroft. It was happening now . . . Nell put her arms round her mother and held her tightly. 'Mum!' she called as if Alice were a long way off. There was no answer. Nell sobbed. And her mother reached round and touched her shoulder comfortingly. 'Can you see?' she whispered.

Nell looked. The alders were not moving but someone was there. Someone standing very still, deliberately melting into the background. Nell squeezed her eyes tightly shut and opened them again.

And then she knew it was no ghost. Whatever her mother thought, whatever she said, the figure against the alders was Mo. Just as Nell had known . . . he was there. Nell felt her heart leap and then settle. It was all right; Mo might be going to Timbuktu but at this moment – now – he was as close to Nell as he dared get. And this time she would tell him; she would apologize for the fiasco that had been Perry; she would admit that, try as she would, she could not get Mo out of her head. And then she would tell him that she loved him.

Her mother was shaking in her arms.

Nell put her lips to her mother's ear. 'It's all right, darling. It's Mo. He's been here all the time. I knew it.'

Alice did not hear. She spoke suddenly, loudly. 'You are dead! I cannot bear it! To send your son to torture me like this – I cannot bear it, Joe! I cannot bear it!'

Nell stopped looking at Mo and turned her gaze on to her

mother. In the shadow of the alders the shape moved, looked across to them and then vanished. Very gradually Alice subsided against Nell's shoulder.

She said, 'He's gone. It's all right, my love. He's gone.'

Nell said, 'It was Mo. You knew it was Mo. Why did you tell him he was dead? He's not dead. He was there.'

Alice sighed deeply. 'Yes. He was there. I'm sorry, Nell. He was there – has been with us – to find out . . . things. He is clever and very deep. Not like his father. Joe was always open. It could not have been his idea to – to plot some kind of revenge. And Mo himself . . . he cannot be all bad. He was angry for his mother – I can understand that.' Alice straightened. 'Nell, I'm sorry. We should have talked about this before. But you were so ill when you arrived and I thought Mo was leaving for America immediately. There seemed no point.' She sighed again.

Nell stared at her, incredulous that her mother was telling her these things, incredulous that there had been some kind of plan – no, *plot* – behind Mo's arrival in their midst as Aunt Helena's latest protégé. She moved back, dropped her arms, stood up.

Alice said, 'I'm sorry, darling. So sorry. Did I frighten you?'

'Yes. You did. You are frightening me still. I cannot believe that Mo is the son of the man you . . . you so obviously loved. *Loved*, Mum. Have we been living some kind of arranged scenario for the past . . . what is it now – a year? A whole year. How long have you known that Mo is the son of your – your – whatever this Joe Adair was?'

Alice's face twisted. 'Nell . . . please . . . don't. Joe was not – never could have been. We were children, darling.' She looked at Nell's face and stopped speaking. Then she said quietly, 'Just over a week. I've known just over a week. I promise you, Nell. Until then I liked him, not at first, but then, later—'

'Here's Gran. Don't talk about it any more. Please.'

'But I have to tell you . . . things. About Joe Adair. And his wife Julie.'

256

'I don't want to hear. Sorry, Ma. It's the way I cope. Head in sand and all that sort of thing.' Nell tried for a laugh. Her brain was reeling. Joe Adair . . . Alice Pettiford's 'fling'. But it had been more than a fling, much more than a fling.

Nell turned thankfully to her grandmother. 'Is it time to go home, Gran?'

'Yes. Are you all right?'

'Yes. Mum was having one of her psychic turns. But she's fine now.'

Doffie tried to be matter-of-fact. 'She gets it from Gran, of course. I didn't think Gramps would get in touch out here . . .'

Alice glanced from one to the other. She felt a million miles away from both of them and – quite desperately – she wanted Val.

Nell said something; she did not remember what it was but her tone was reassuring. They stood up and made their way back to the picnickers. The party was over. And – Nell said the words in her head very lightly – she seemed to have acquired a brother. She swallowed. It could not have happened, of course. Her father was called Valentine Ryecroft. Joe Adair was someone in her mother's past. Hardly ever mentioned. And why not? Because – could it be? – it *must* be – because he was Nell Ryecroft's real father.

Twenty-two

It was difficult to avoid her mother for the next two days. Nell had, in any case, planned to return to North Heath on the Thursday of Easter week; there was a teachers' meeting at school on the Friday and she and Shirley had decided to get together that weekend and make a plan for the final term of the year.

Alice said, 'We haven't had any proper time together! You were so ill for the first few days—'

'I had a cold, Mum!' Nell protested.

Val tugged her hair familiarly just like any father might do to his daughter.

'We'll take you back. Make a day of it. You can show us round.'

Nell improvised quickly. 'Dad, I'm really sorry. It would have been fun. But Shirley is picking me up so that we can talk over our lesson plans.'

'Well . . . not to worry. It's a short term and a decent break at the end of it.' He grinned at her. 'I'll say no more than that in case your aunt Hester gets to hear of it. I understand that you need every minute of your long summer break for planning next year's work, assessing the year before . . .' His voice went into a drone and Nell picked up a cushion menacingly. It was so much easier being with him than with her mother.

She telephoned Edmund as soon as she could talk privately.

'I want you to pick me up – any time on Thursday will do – and pretend you are taking me to Tewkesbury to meet

Shirley Fellowes – she's another teacher – who will then take me on to Birmingham.'

'Hang on, old girl. Thursday is a working day for me. Solicitors do not get school holidays, you know.'

'Shut up, Edmund! You said you would look out for me. I am asking you to do that. You can be in North Heath in under an hour so I am asking for two hours of your time.'

'North Heath? You just said Tewkesbury—'

'For God's sake, Edmund, I'm desperate! My parents want to take me back and I cannot bear that. So I've told them that I'm meeting Shirley Fellowes at Tewkesbury. But of course I'm not!'

'What's going on? I don't get it.'

'I will explain in the car. What time will you come?'

'I suppose I can get an afternoon off. Say, two thirty?'

'As late as that? Make it twelve thirty and we can have lunch somewhere.'

'What the hell is happening, Nell? Are you all right?'

'No, I am not *all right*. I'll see you at twelve thirty on Thursday. Thanks.' She replaced the receiver as the shape of the family car wavered through the bottle-glass window in the hall. Her parents had been shopping and were back. She rushed upstairs and was reminded of the time she had climbed into the cupboard to escape Mo Checkers. She lay on her bed and told herself firmly that everything was all right. She was still herself, Nell Ryecroft . . . or maybe Nell Adair . . . Who the *hell* was she?

Edmund arrived early, at midday, and she loved him for that. Alice, who had realized over the three days since Easter Monday that something was terribly wrong with Nell, was looking white and pinched and it was left to Val to do a swift check of Nell's luggage.

'Dad, for goodness' sake! I can SOS you on the phone if there's anything vital I've forgotten. Just say goodbye and go back inside. It's cold.'

Val frowned. 'Yes. But you're coming in to say goodbye to Mum. Edmund won't mind hanging on—'

'I've said my goodbyes to Mum. Now I am saying them to you. Best of luck with the Pumpkin Line. Don't work too hard.'

She almost flung herself into Edmund's old car and slammed the door. Edmund wound down his window.

'Cheerio, Uncle Val! It was great last Monday – thanks. And to Aunt Alice for the super food!'

Nell said through gritted teeth, 'Drive away, Edmund. Now!'

He waved through the open window; Val put his hand up in a salute. He was still frowning.

She refused to explain anything until they were at Worcester. He told her later that if they hadn't been almost at their destination, he would have turned round and driven straight back to Lypiatt Bottom and 'thrashed it all out'. But even as he spoke, he knew that she had gone too far for any reasonable discussion. He could listen; he soon discovered that that was all he could do. She could not listen to him. She was so tense that when he put his hand over hers she withdrew sharply. He recalled his own state of mind when he first began to suspect that Percy Westbrook was not his father; he had been unable to stay in the same room with poor Percy. But he had not turned against his mother as Nell had.

They went to a pub just outside Stourport and he ordered a ploughman's lunch for the two of them, hoping that at least she would pick at some cheese. He tried to look at her objectively and noted that her hair needed a comb and she seemed to be falling apart in some peculiar way. Her clothes appeared not to fit and her movements were clumsy – not that she moved a great deal, her tension was ghastly and could be infectious as he could feel his own muscles tightening in sympathy. He thought of Sally Gold, so small and neat; he thought of her frank – brutal – honesty.

'Listen,' he said, making another attempt to hold Nell's hand and being rejected again. 'Start from the beginning.

260

Never mind all this revenge business. Go back to the Pumpkin Line. I talked to you – d'you remember that? You were absolutely certain that Mo Checkers was there – in hiding – watching us—'

'Not Mo Checkers! Michael Adair. Son of Joe Adair. Who was my mother's boyfriend when she was sixteen and is, apparently, my father!'

'So you keep saying. Which would mean your mother had you when she was about eighteen, which, in its turn, would mean you are now twenty-seven. The same age as Perry. Which, of course, you are not.'

'I've done all those sums, thank you, Edmund. I've no proof but I'm pretty certain that Michael Adair is a year older than I am. So this Joe Adair left his wife with a newborn baby and came to see the Pumpkin Coach at some point. Probably he did not know for some time that it belonged to him – solicitors take a while to sort out wills and things—'

'Be careful, Nell!' He had made several attempts to jolly her out of her intensity and this one was no more successful than the others.

'He knew the Pettifords had a connection with the coach so he looked Mum up and she took him down to the forest and we all know about the coach and Bracewell's Pool and – and – everything.' She put her hands to her face. 'Oh God!'

He said quietly, 'Have you had a look at your birth certificate?'

'I don't know where it is any more. I had to have it for my college application and then I got it back and it's probably in the attic with my thesis and stuff. Anyway, that's not the point, Edmund. The point is that Mo knew all this. He knew. And when his parents were killed he decided to find out what sort of a girl his father fell for. And when he got to know us, there was his revenge, ready and waiting to fall into his lap.' She tried to grin. 'The sacrificial lamb, Ed. You never thought of me like that before, did you?'

'But if you're not his sister, then the whole perverted and sick plan falls on its face, Nell.'

'Not really. The whole plan would have gone on. He was getting at my mother, don't you see! My God, he deliberately made her think – two or three times to my knowledge – that he was a ghost of his own father. She looked absolutely ghastly when we were at the pool, white as a sheet. And Aunt Helena told me of another time . . . So I was a tool. That was all. He pretended to love me in order to . . . He does not feel anything for me at all.' She leaned back slightly as the waitress brought their food, then she stared at her plate while Edmund unwrapped the napkin round her cutlery. 'That's what I cannot bear, Edmund. Mo is me. I thought I was Mo. It's like losing an arm or a leg . . . No, no, it's worse than that.' She looked up from the plate. 'It's like losing my soul!'

He would have smiled at her melodramatics had he not been looking into those sea-blue eyes and remembering another beautiful, scatty, dishevelled girl who had opened her heart and mind to him so recently.

He said gently, 'But at least – if you weren't his sister – it would make your relationship with Aunt Alice – your mother – all right again?'

He could almost see the terrible loop of her misery snag at that. She stared down at a tomato which he had cut up for her and stuck her fork into a segment of it. Then she said, 'I – I suppose it should. Yet . . . I rather think that she must have treated Joe Adair abominably if Mo was so intent on avenging his father.' She looked up, bewildered. 'That makes sense, doesn't it, Edmund? He – Joe Adair – must have told his son what my mother did. It was so awful that Mo was consumed with this – this *necessity* – to hurt my mother.'

Edmund was eating a large piece of cheese; he was hungry and saw no reason why two of them should waste their meal. Nell waited for two seconds and then went on, 'And it must have been really awful for him to – to *use* me! I cannot help but – but – see her behaviour as – as the root cause—'

Edmund swallowed and said quietly, 'There are a great many ways you can look at this, Nell. The only right way is to talk to your mother. Not run away from her.' She shook her head decisively. He went on in his persuasive voice. 'One of the ways is that Mo Checkers – Michael Adair – came down, as you say, for revenge. On your mother. Not on you. He had made a very devious plan, offering the Pumpkin Coach to your father, instructing his solicitor to make no mention of the death of his parents, presenting himself first as a kind of third world drop-out, eliciting our sympathy. For a short while – a very short while, Nell. Because – eat your salad but listen hard – because he met you and fell in love.' She made a sound of total rejection but he went on inexorably. 'You both fought it at first but it was obvious, Nell. The family knew and were afraid for you.'

Very slowly she ate the tomato. Edmund watched her for a second then resumed his own meal. His mind was racing now on parallel lines: Nell and himself, neck and neck. Terribly, inevitably, unsuitably in love; both of them in turmoil about their paternity. But he was . . . curious. And not unhappy about Sally, prepared to wait. Whereas Nell was rejecting everything and everyone, like a child thrashing about, determined to hurt someone else.

He waited until she had put down her knife and fork and then said softly, 'Nell, are you pregnant?'

Her head came up with a jerk, staring at him wide-eyed. Then she laughed scornfully. 'Of course not! He never had any intention of risking that, Ed! He'd be saddled then, wouldn't he?' She laughed again with bleak bitterness. 'We went to the pool. For me it was a way of telling him that I wanted him.' She sighed and looked past Edmund's head at a row of tankards above the bar. 'Bracewell's Pool, Ed. Nobody realizes what significance it has for the Pettifords, do they? I was such a – a *kid* – then. When I discovered that the reason he was with me at Bracewell's Pool was so that he could try to uncover the old railway track, I had a fit of pique that was simply . . . ginormous!' Her laugh held ruefulness. 'See? Not much better now, am I? Anyway . . . that was when I turned my back on him and went off with Perry. Just like a schoolgirl. Only much worse than that.' She even managed a wry smile. 'You see, Edmund, I was a virgin. All the other girls managed to get rid of theirs at college. Not me.' She sat back and said with self-loathing, 'I wanted sex. If I couldn't have it with Mo I would have it with Perry.' She leaned across the table when Edmund said nothing. 'You didn't know I was like that, did you, Ed? Your little cousin.'

Edmund said calmly, 'I've always known you were very desirable, Nell. Now I admire your honesty. You didn't hurt Perry. You probably hurt Mo a great deal, which was the object of the exercise.'

'Oh Edmund . . . what am I going to do?'

He smiled and took her hand again and this time she did not reject him.

'Nothing, dear coz. Except what you are good at. Teaching. Working hard. Getting on with your life as best you can.'

'But Ma? And Dad? Oh Edmund, I do hope he is my dad. I love him so much. I don't want Joe Adair to be my father! I hate him!'

Edmund smiled and put her hand to his lips. 'I'll find out, Nell. I'm already hot on the trail of my own father, so I'm quite good at going through parish records and dusty old papers.'

'Oh Edmund . . .'

He stood up. 'Listen, if you want to have a decent cry on my shoulder, let's get back in the car.' And she smiled gratefully and followed him out of the pub.

It wasn't too bad after that. Somehow Edmund had taken the load of her terrible emotional mess and she trusted him to deal with it. He had given her some kind of hope, though hope for what she could not say. It was only later that she realized she had not asked him how his own search was going; she thought then how grief – any extreme emotion – could make you selfish.

Shirley was excited and happy. After the staff meeting on Friday they caught the train into Birmingham and followed the canal into the heart of the city, where Shirley took her to a coffee shop. 'We're in the middle of one of the most industrialized places in the world, the furthest we can actually be from the sea in this country, yet you can smell water! That is important to the Saxons and the Danes – and you're bound to be one of them, Nell, with your colouring—'

'Lack of it,' interpolated Nell.

'And the bluebells are out and summer is coming and it's the best term in the whole year – though Christmas is pretty good – and I am going to Corfu in the holidays – and . . . I'm in love!'

Nell listened and remembered last year when she had come home and started applying for jobs and waited to fall in love. Was that it? Had she wanted to be in love so much that she had imagined half of it? Was her hurt all down to damaged pride? Shirley was so happy she was practically incandescent; Nell did not remember being like that. Shirley produced a photograph and they pored over it together.

Hester arrived home after the first day of term feeling as if she'd been down a coal mine all day. Sally had enlisted her help with a large poster announcing the school garden party, which had involved copious use of marker pens and charcoal sticks. 'It's not exactly on your job description, Miss Ryecroft.' Sally was a mixture of joy at being back in the vicinity of her idol and desperation to be nearer to her than in the formal setting of a tutorial. 'But I can't seem to get the proportions large enough.'

Hester had let down her guard sufficiently to say, 'Are you suggesting that my physical size makes it possible for me to produce big art?'

Sally giggled. 'I hadn't meant it like that but I suppose it is a possibility!'

Hester had found herself helping the girl and entering into the sort of repartee they had shared down by Bracewell's Pool. Of course, Sally read more into it than was intended and asked with her usual frankness why she was helping out.

'Could it possibly be that the student–teacher barrier is slowly but surely disappearing?' she suggested.

Hester pretended to consider the question, putting a finger to her chin and leaving a smudge of marker.

'As you know, child,' she said portentously, 'I consider you to have the makings of a future prime minister. In other words, you have a certain cunning, a low approach to life which could get you there . . .' She resumed working. 'And I believe in making a friend of a future prime minister.'

Sally gazed at her. 'You are saying . . . what?'

'I am saying that as long as I hear no more nonsense about lesbianism then I see no reason why we cannot be friends.'

Sally was ecstatic. 'Oh . . . oh *Piecrust*!' she breathed.

'Not that friendly, actually. Get on with the smaller lettering. I need a decent time this evening to make some lesson plans for the Lower Fifth.'

'Sorry, Miss Ryecroft.' Sally said no more. She was frightened to break the spell. But when Hester eventually put down the marker she did say, 'Thank you ever, ever, ever so much. And I did tell Edmund what you said. He's going to have another word with you, I'm afraid.'

So Hester was forewarned. But that did not help.

It might have been better had she found time to have a bath before his arrival, but Sally had not mentioned that he would be parked outside her house in his grotty old car and that he would get out of it, smiling, his fair hair and blue eyes making him look like a younger edition of Val.

'What a splendid day for the beginning of the summer term,' he said, pecking her cheek then arming her up the short path to the front door. 'And why are you not your usual pristine self? What is this . . . stuff?' He touched her face and examined her hand. 'A leaking pen, no less! What do you make of that, my dear Watson?'

'Oh God. I didn't realize it was on my face!' She went into the tiny hall and stacked her book bag under the stairs. 'Put your coat on the banister, Edmund. I'd better go to the bathroom.'

'You don't seem surprised to see me.'

'Sally told me you would be coming. I didn't imagine it would be today. However, I suppose the sooner we get it over, the better.'

He watched her go up the stairs, then ducked his head and went into the little sitting room on the left that looked out on to the close. Mrs Marvel had been, and the smell of lavender polish was everywhere. He thought of poor Percy coming here to see Hester; enjoying the tidy bijou house, the immaculate classic beauty of Hester. Edmund smiled slightly. After all was said and done, Percy had always returned, even at the last, to the chaotic gypsy attractions of Hattie Pettiford. Edmund wondered whether Percy had always known she had been unfaithful to him; whether Hester had been a kind of late retaliation. But no. Percy had loved Hester in a different way . . . that was all it was.

Hester came back after a while; she had showered and was wearing a kimono thing, white silk covered in enormous orange circles. He stood up and said without thinking, 'My God. No wonder Dad fell for you!'

She said almost wearily, 'For goodness' sake, Edmund! Your father was leading Hattie on. I've told you all this before. You have no need at all to dislike me quite so intensely. I was the idiot!'

He was genuinely surprised. 'I don't dislike you, Hester. Not a bit. I admire you more each time I see you. All right, I tried to threaten you last Christmas but then Sally was there and I saw that you were being badgered on all fronts and—'

'Sally was at Leckhampton House? At Christmas time?'

'Yes. She had a car for Christmas – she's hopeless actually, failed her test twice already – and she needed to see you – came here – neighbours told her where you were so she—'

'But then she left?'

'She saw it was the wrong thing to do.'

Hester said, 'Yes. I think she understands now. It could have been awkward at school.' She paused then said, 'In many ways she is very . . . thoughtful.' Another pause and she added, 'I could never pass a driving test either. Strange.' She looked at Edmund. 'You probably thought I was the cause of your father's heart attack. I thought so too. And then . . . well, the baby.'

'Exactly.' Edmund held her gaze. 'It was how he would have wanted to die, Hester.'

'It was . . . it was such a muddle, Edmund. But I was terribly selfish. Percy built my confidence – made me feel desirable again. Richard had left me and I – I needed . . . Edmund, I really am sorry.'

He sighed. 'I'd like to use all that guilt to make you tell me about my real father. But I find I cannot even do that!' He sat down heavily. 'Go and get dressed. I'll take you out for a meal and we won't talk about this any more.'

She made for the door. 'Mrs Marvel has left me something in the oven, I expect. And there's always too much. Share it with me, Edmund.' She opened the door. 'Come and sit in the kitchen and I'll dish something up for us.'

He trailed after her and laid the table with the cutlery she passed to him, then he stood by her and made coffee in her new percolator and found proper demi-tasse cups and sugar crystals. The meal was all in a French cast-iron casserole, plopping now and then like Vesuvius and revealing chicken, carrots and baby potatoes. He discovered he was hungry. Things had been fairly lax at home since Enid's departure; his mother nibbled all the time, Perry brought in fish and chips and Indian meals and he himself had worked through lunch hours, unwilling to remember Nell's face opposite him in the pub at Stourport.

Hester put out a cheese board and some biscuits he had never seen before; he poured the coffee. They sat back and he told her about Nell's unhappiness, though not its cause.

Hester said, 'Ah. So it is not to be. Not one of those things that burns itself out quickly. Alice fell for someone in the same way.' She sighed. 'I was insanely jealous because I thought I was losing her.'

He almost told her that Mo Checkers was in fact the son of Joseph Adair. But it was not his secret.

'And then she married your brother and all was well.' He sipped his coffee and smiled. 'Perhaps I'll have to marry Nell and make it well for her.'

She was startled and didn't realize he was joking. 'You can't do that!' she said.

'Because of Sally? You're right. I've already proposed to her and she didn't exactly say no.' He smiled and registered that her smile was slower to come. He said carefully, 'Not because of Sally? Because of something else?'

She looked down at her coffee and stirred in some more sugar. There was a long pause. Then Edmund said, 'How could that be? Are you saying that Nell and I are brother and sister?'

She took a deep breath. 'Have you noticed that crystals do not sweeten as strongly as granulated?'

'Hester. Are you saying that Nell—'

'You told me we would not speak of it and I am refusing to do so!' She looked up and said fiercely, 'I do not *know* anything, Edmund. One or two coincidences and that is all. And if I had concrete proof it would make no difference. Alice and Val were always meant for each other. When we were children – sixteen – we thought we would live together – the three of us! When they married I was so happy – it was what I had always dreamed of. I could not have shared Val with anyone else in the world. Just Alice. And there's an end to it. I mean it, Edmund! I do not wish to speak of it ever again. It is supposition!'

He returned her fierce glare with one of total blankness, but she knew that behind the pale blue eyes his brain was computing, just as hers had done. And there was more than that; he would know because he was so like Val.

She hiccuped on a sob and said, 'I think you should go now.' He did not move or speak. She stood up and took the tiny cups to the sink so that her back was to him. She clattered the dishes unnecessarily.

At last he levered himself up from the table. He said, 'I agree on two counts. That it is supposition and that I should go. The other count – that we do not speak of it again – is ridiculous. If we are the only two people, besides my mother, I assume, who know this, or rather *suppose* this, then we have to talk about it. You must see that. All right, not now. Perhaps not for years. But at some point.' He went through into the hall and picked up his jacket from the banister. He returned to her and put his arms round her shoulders. She stayed very still. He spoke into the back of her head, where her hair was knotted thickly.

'All that emotion. All that love and fear and hate . . . sometimes I wonder whether we are better off without it.'

Her breath was catching in her chest and he could feel it. She whispered jerkily, 'Perhaps other families could do without it. Not the Pettifords. Not the Ryecrofts.'

He put his lips to the nape of her neck. 'No,' he said. 'And I am both Pettiford and Ryecroft. Am I not, Aunt Hester?'

'Oh Edmund . . . I am so sorry.'

'Well, I am not. I would be proud to be either. To be both is very special.'

He hugged her shoulders, turned and left. And Hester sat down again, put her head on the table and wept. Then realized it was not for Edmund or herself or Val and Alice. But for Richard Tibbolt.

Twenty-three

May Day and Whitsun came and went and Nell did not come home.

At the beginning of July, Val was working in the forest clearing the line with the other volunteers, drawing up agreements with Edmund's firm, Smithers and Jameson, initiating legal searches into ownership of the land beyond the Pumpkin Coach, accompanying Edward Maybury on his 'diplomatic' visits to London. The illicit connection with the line at Leadon Markham was still in place and Edward was extremely uncomfortable about it.

'It was a gentlemen's agreement, Val. If I break it, no one will trust me again. And there may yet be other favours we need. There's some rolling stock from the old S & W stabled down in South Wales that would be invaluable if we decide to open up as a tourist attraction—'

'What about our plans to make it a working line?'

'Not really enough coal mines left to make it viable. And the whole area has been designated a tourist site. So there will be grants and we might be eligible.'

'No reason why we couldn't do both. A single load once a week would be enough to remind the industries that we exist.'

'Perhaps. And that's another argument for keeping my friends in high places on our side.'

Val smiled at Edward's caution; Val himself had never been cautious. But he knew that Edward was right. He clapped the older man on the shoulder and then said in a neutral voice, 'I suppose you haven't got an address for the boy? Mo Checkers. Michael Adair. Whatever he is called these days.'

'Michael Adair,' Edward replied instantly, which surely meant he had got an address. 'I think Helena might have dropped him a card. You know, just wishing him well. That sort of thing.'

Val tried to sound careless. 'I wouldn't mind asking his advice about using the Orchard shed. Laying fresh track parallel with the main line.' He glanced quickly at Edward. 'It would get us out of this situation with the illegal connection at Leadon.'

He had struck the right note. Edward said eagerly, 'That would be a good thing to do, Val. And the boy certainly knew his onions. It was as if the railways were in his blood.' He laughed at such a coincidental idea then fished in his breast pocket. 'As a matter of fact, I may well have it here . . .' He fumbled through a small notebook. 'Helena likes me to duplicate various addresses in case one of us loses . . .' He found the place. 'Michigan. That's it. It's only temporary. He is expecting to move out to the desert, wherever that might be.'

'He writes regularly then?' Val asked idly as he copied the address on to the back of an envelope.

'Well, not really. I think Helena writes more often. You know what she's like.' Edward's voice descended fondly.

Val gave himself a moment in which to conjure up an image of Helena: daughter of a signalman but, with her fine features and statuesque bearing, more aristocratic than any aristocrat. The sort of woman his own mother might have described as 'thoroughly county' and with standards to go with it. Helena had always championed Michael Adair, as if she had known from the beginning just who he was.

He said resignedly, 'Yes, I know.'

Edward was enthusiastic. 'He could provide us with data to convince the board. Might even agree to test the ground. That would please Helena. She's been saying that until he comes back and sorts things out nothing will be right again.' He laughed, embarrassed. 'You know how Helena is.'

Val said again, 'Yes, I know how she is. And she's been talking to Alice. Of course.' Val sighed. 'I might have guessed Alice would never simply forget Joe just because he has died. Perhaps he is more real to her now he is dead than when he was alive.'

Edward, who was not as bluff and insensitive as most people imagined, said quietly, 'It is always devastating when we lose old friends, Val. It is natural that Alice would be sad.'

Val glanced again at the man who for so long had been his superintendent and who knew the Pettifords as friends as well as employees. He would have liked to question him further; what had Helena confided to him all those years ago when she and Alice were so close?

He said, 'Of course. But why would that drive our daughter away from us, Edward? Can you understand that?'

Edward took another deep breath and let it go despairingly. 'No,' he said.

That afternoon, Val sat in the Pumpkin Coach, now the official headquarters of the Pumpkin Line, and wrote to Michael Adair in Michigan. He opened with the plan for a completely new line to run parallel to the existing main line, attributing the idea to Edward, who thought that the adjacent land would be owned by the company and would therefore be accessible for leasing or purchasing. It was a question of coming up with some technical details – figures – for the board and they were wondering whether Michael would be willing . . . Val paused, gazing through the window at the dark pool below the coach, wondering what had happened to split his family in two. Wondering whether Joe Adair had somehow come back to claim Alice. She was thinner than ever, her blue eyes taking up most of her face. Doffie was nagging her to see a doctor. But she knew as well as Val knew that this was not a medical matter.

Val put down his pen and pressed his hands to his eyes. If Michael Adair would not come home and sort it out, then he would have to break all the rules about personal privacy that he had laid down years ago to protect himself from his father.

He would have to go to Birmingham and force Nell to talk to him properly.

He picked up the pen again and scribbled frantically. 'I no longer understand what is happening here with my family. Nell has detached herself completely from her mother and me. Please find the time to come home and help us.' He folded the letter quickly and sealed it in an envelope before he could change his mind.

Later that afternoon, Hester sat in her tiny sitting room trying to finish her weekend marking early so that she could drive over to see Harriet, whose time was drawing near.

This summer Mrs Marvel was not coming in every day and, since Richard Tibbolt had left her, Hester rarely bothered to make a meal for herself – but without that mandatory break the evenings seemed very long. She had decided to give more time to Hattie and Alice. To go out and about in the evenings got her right away from the school environment and the adoration of Sally Gold. Certainly Sally no longer pestered her to death, but her self-discipline was so obvious it had become a pressure of another kind.

Hester finished reading an essay on a selection of Shakespeare sonnets, put the twenty-five facsimiles in a folder – had they passed one copy around or had all twenty-five of them sat in a circle and taken dictation from the twenty-sixth? – and decided that a cup of tea was in order before she went out. She went into her pristine kitchen and made it very precisely, in a silver teapot on a silver tray, and carried it back into the sitting room to watch the world go by. Richard had always liked to do that after they had made love. 'Tibbolt', she had called him, not even giving him the intimacy of his name. And now, here she sat, the same person, the same teapot, yet . . . sterile. Too old for children, too young for retirement. If she got in touch with Richard, what on earth could she offer him? There he was, still in Provence, struggling with his peculiar children – probably Hester herself constituted one of the reasons for their peculiarity – and doubtless bonding again with the awful Hermione, long divorced yet not forgotten, who might well have decided that she preferred her ex-husband to the woman artist she had lived with for so long.

Hester took a gulp of tea and almost scalded the roof of her mouth. Her eyes watered, her nose ran, yet she was not weeping because weeping implied emotion and she was a . . . cold fish. She dabbed and blew and pushed the tray to one side of the table, picked up her pen again and found a notepad in the concealed drawer. 'Dear Richard,' she began. Then stopped. She had tried to write to him several times since the business of Edmund's parentage had cropped up but got no further than 'Dear Richard'. This time she was determined.

> You've heard of wet blankets obviously. Have I been a wet blanket in the past, Richard? If so, then what is happening now is only fair and just and I must learn to live with it. This wet blanket is heavy and cold and presses down on me almost all the time and its other name is Guilt. I have been guilty of using another human being and what makes it worse is that the human being is you. I am probably guilty of breaking up your marriage too and therefore alienating your children. I tried to apologize to you before Christmas but it is more than likely that you did not notice because it would have been a very grudging apology. Therefore let me write it down here and now. I am sorry, Richard. Terribly sorry and remorseful for the way I have always behaved towards you – as if you owed me something when in fact the debt is entirely mine. I am not asking for forgiveness because I do not see how that is possible when you are still trying to clear up some of the mess I have made. My deep regret is now on record. It is not enough but I do not know any way of making amends. I wish you well for the future.
>
> Yours, Hester Ryecroft.

She read it through twice. She had wanted to tell him that she still loved him and found life difficult without him but that would put more pressure on him. She thought that the fact that she had written, very clearly, 'Yours', would tell him everything. Or would it? She gnawed her lip and picked up the pen again. Then put it down, reached into the drawer for an envelope, thrust the single sheet inside and sealed it quickly. She would post it on the way to Leckhampton House.

Hattie sat in a hard, high chair and stared out of the window at the tennis court with its drooping net, the wide sweep of the lawn defined by the crescent of rhododendrons, giving the house its privacy; the summer house where poor besotted Mo Checkers had knocked Perry down a year ago; all of it bathed in sunshine, which was absolutely marvellous if you happened not to be heavily pregnant, the size of a house, with legs like tree trunks and a sudden terror of being all on your own when labour began.

She said aloud, 'Sorry, Percy darling. I know I am not alone because you are always with me but . . . well, I don't have to explain, do I? It's after last time, obviously. And even then your mother took ages to hear me and you didn't think it was serious at first, did you? I'm sure that can't happen twice, darling. But you will make sure it doesn't, won't you? I mean, I take it you have some kind of . . . kind of *pull*, haven't you, Percy dear?'

She waited for a reply though she had never had one yet, and nearly jumped out of the chair when the telephone pinged and then went into a steady ring. Perry had had extensions put in every room and she had only to reach sideways but she stared at it for a moment, wondering whether – of course not seriously – but just for an instant wondering whether it might be Percy.

It was Doffie.

'Darling, I'm so *pleased* to hear you!' Hattie carolled. 'You are the answer to a maiden's prayer – though you could hardly call me a maiden! I'm sitting here on my own – no Enid of course, Perry is off chasing that girl from Hester's school though it is clear she prefers Edmund. Edmund has gone up to see Nell because she's doing something special . . . I know, darling, she never tells us anything these days, does she? But at least she told Edmund and he will represent the family. My two boys have always been so close to dear Nell.'

Doffie said, suddenly anxious, 'You don't think he's getting too fond of her, do you, Hattie? I mean, in the circumstances . . .'

'What circumstances? Oh. You mean *that*. I never think of that now. And neither should you. Edmund has given up the silly idea of changing his name. That is all in the past. And it must stay there, Doffie.' Hattie's voice sharpened. 'It would break Alice's heart if she thought . . . and it wasn't like that. A fling. That's what we used to call it, didn't we? Just like you had with poor old Duggie.'

That stopped Doffie in her tracks; Hattie adored her aunt-in-law but if she was about to get holier-than-thou she must think again.

Doffie recovered and said briskly, 'I was ringing to see whether you were all right, and in spite of being on your own you clearly are. I could come over if you need me. I realize you are not due until the end of the month when Ted and I will be staying anyway, but as you tend to be early—'

'Darling, that is so sweet! I'd simply love to see you. I'm a bit worried about Mrs Marvel.'

'Who on earth is . . . oh, you mean Hester's daily?'

'You remember she came here at Christmas? She simply adores the boys. She said to me the other day that this house is full of love. Isn't that wonderful? But of course she hasn't told Hester that she comes here three times a week and I don't quite know how to broach the subject.'

'What you are saying, Hattie, is that you have poached Hester's daily help—'

'It wasn't like that, Doffie!'

'But that is how Hester will see it.'

'Well, she might. You know how funny she can be and she

might think this is some kind of revenge for the way she annexed poor darling Percy.'

'I see. So exchange is no robbery. Percy for Mrs Marvel.'

'Doffie, how can you!'

'Well, honestly, Hattie. For goodness' sake, just tell her. If she is "funny", as you put it, she will get over it.'

'I wondered whether you would mind awfully if I told her that it was your suggestion in the first place. When you saw how alone I was and how tired and—'

'Why don't you simply leave it all to me, Hattie? I could tell her myself, take the blame, ask her to slap my face—'

'Now you're being silly. But actually, Doffie dearest, I would so appreciate it if you could tell her. Sometimes Hester can be so ... caustic. Thank you, darling, so much. Now listen, if you're coming over now, could you stop and pick up some fish and chips at that place in London Road? I've got a real yearning for fish and chips—'

'Not very healthy. But all right. Ted and I haven't eaten yet so we can share a helping.'

'Oh Doff. Can't you come on your own? I adore Ted, as you well know, but I thought you might be able to massage my neck. Like you used to when I was expecting Perry and Mitzie. And if Ted's here he gets all anxious about you over-doing things.'

Doffie sighed audibly. 'Hattie, you are incredible. I'll be with you in half an hour depending on the queue at the fish-and-chip shop.'

'Dear Doffie.'

Hattie replaced the receiver and smiled through the window. 'I knew you were listening all the time, Percy. It's going to be all right. I know it.'

Hester was the first to arrive. She came through the kitchen door and cooeed her way to the sitting room, where she discovered Hattie sitting on a Windsor chair dragged in from the kitchen, her legs stuck out in front of her very in-elegantly, her wild gypsy hair bunched up in a rubber band, her cheesecloth smock sticking to her in places and tears rolling down her face.

'Good God!' Hester rushed over to her. 'Has it started? Oh God, what shall I do? Bag? Hospital? What?'

Hattie pushed herself upright and scrubbed at her face with the palms of not-too-clean hands. She emerged, smiling but definitely grubby.

'Hester! What a lovely surprise. Doffie is coming in a minute with fish and chips. We can have a midnight feast. I'll show you Enid's latest letter. She's having a simply marvellous time and playing the field just as I told her to!'

Hester was annoyed. 'Good Lord, I thought you had gone into labour. Why the hell are you sitting here bracing yourself like crazy and crying your eyes out? Where are the boys?'

Hattie told her, then said, 'I was thinking of Rose Adair. And her mother. Who was probably on her own when she had Rose, ostracized by her snobby family. Alice told me once that Rose never knew she was illegitimate until after her mother died and her aunt came to tell her. It was a sort of excuse for Rose not inheriting anything. Though of course she did have the Pumpkin Coach. But she never knew about that either because she died as well. And then it went to Joe.'

Hester rose from her crouching position, pulled the piano stool forward and sat next to Hattie.

'What on earth are you talking about, Hattie? I suppose this is part of being pregnant. It wouldn't have suited me.'

Hattie smiled fondly. 'Now you expect me to agree with you and then we can bicker about that. But as a matter of fact, Hessie, I think you would have been a wonderful mother. Nell thinks the world of you – you know that.'

Hester shook her head and stood up. 'I'll make some tea, shall I? You will need something to wash down the chips.'

'Oh, that would be lovely! I've been having that primrose tea. You'll see it on the shelf. It's supposed to be good for the skin and I don't want too many stretch marks. A few are interesting but when you look like a map of Russia—'

'Don't look at yourself then!' Hester came back tartly as

she passed the piano and noticed that on the closed lid was the sheet music for 'Sally in Our Alley'. Poor Edmund.

'I wasn't thinking of the effect on me. It's other people.' Hattie gave a little chuckle as she adjusted her position in the chair. She knew she was quite capable of making the tea herself and most certainly would have done if Hester hadn't turned up. She grinned as Hester made a sound of incredulous disgust and said something about middle-aged exhibitionists. Dear Hester, so easily riled. But she was always glad to see her; and glad too in a way that Percy had recognized that quality in Hester that bound her so closely to the Pettifords; not just her beauty, nor her caustic wit. Her – her *staunchness*. When the chips were down, Hester would be faithful and loyal to the end. Chips. Hattie felt her mouth water; she yearned for chips, and fish fried in deep batter and very crisp. Not even Mrs Marvel could cook it like that at home. Thank God for Doffie.

In the event Doffie took Hester aside and was almost completely frank with her. 'Hattie is feeling simply dreadful about it,' she said. 'You can imagine, can't you? She went overboard about what a marvel Mrs Marvel was at Christmas and probably made her laugh, and then Enid left and Mrs M. came up on a temporary basis and Perry and Edmund did their charm stuff on her, and before you know it she's almost part of the household.'

Hester shook her head, smiling slightly because, yes, she could imagine it. Hattie was like one of those natural geysers, she gushed at all times. But she gushed warmly.

'If Mrs M. can manage it all, then who am I to begrudge Hattie all the help she can get just now. I can't get over the way she is coping, actually. One minute the house is full to bursting and she's organizing everyone so that she doesn't do a damned thing. The next it's just her and the boys and they're out most of the time and she's pregnant! Edmund told me she was mowing the lawn the other day.'

'Yes, I know. Ted worries, of course, but she's always been

like that. A creature of extremes. And while she's busy with the baby and the house at least she isn't trying to marry Nell off to Perry or Duggie to Enid – or even organizing another affair for you! Oh Hester, I hope you're going to be all right, darling. Why don't you go and see your Richard and patch up whatever needs patching up?'

'For one thing, he is not "my" Richard. And for another . . .' She gave the deepest sigh. 'I wouldn't know where to begin. How many patches to find.'

Doffie said eagerly, 'I know exactly what you mean. It used to be so awful when Ted and I had one of our rows . . . We don't do that much any more. Perhaps age has got compensations. But, Hester, when we'd said and done unspeakable things, we – we sort of cut our losses and didn't bother with patches.'

Hester nodded. 'Yes. But, you see, I'm not like you and Alice. I'm not really . . . *lovable*. I attract people for a time. Then they realize that I'm hard and they drift away . . .'

As Doffie said later to Ted, it was the saddest thing she had ever heard in her life. And though Ted told her that, as usual, she was exaggerating, he privately agreed with her. But then he had always had a soft spot for Hester and she for him.

At that moment a blood-curdling scream came from the sitting room; came, in fact, from Hattie. Both women abandoned the greasy fish-and-chip paper and dashed from the kitchen.

That summer Dugdale Marsden had taken to walking round his native Gloucester, trying to imprint various landmarks on his mind before they disappeared for ever into the archives of the planning office. Sometimes he took a camera with him, sometimes he did not. He had quite a collection of photographs of cupolas, sprouting on the skyline or tucked neatly between buildings. He poked around Cromwell's old lodging, crossed the road and stared hard at the monument to Bishop Hooper, then sat in the library and read up about both men. He wondered what had happened to the ironmongers who used to ply a brisk trade in Barton Street, so he made a few enquiries about them. Ted told him he was a magpie; Doffie smiled kindly. The only person who was fascinated by his random trawl was Hattie. Last time he had been at Leckhampton House she had said, 'I'd love to scurridge around like you do, Dug. All that area close to the spa . . . I remember going to a dancing class there. I wonder . . .'

And he had said gladly, 'I'll find out. If anyone mentions that they are "wondering" about something, that's when I feel my nose begin to twitch!'

She had laughed unreservedly and he had thought how relaxing it was to be with her. After Enid's constant misery, Ted and Doffie so emotionally entangled it could be tiring just to watch them, poor old Alice haunted by her ghosts and Val agonizing on the sidelines, it was good to be with some-one so . . . not exactly superficial . . . someone as basic as Hattie was.

He had said, 'By the way, I've never heard that word before. Scurridge. But if it's not in the dictionary it should be.'

He now thought of himself as a scurridger and that's what he was doing that summer's evening. He was scurridging along the old railway line that ran by the side of the park and landed up practically in the docks. And this time he was scurridging with a purpose. He was scurridging to find out how and when these parallel lines had been laid.

As the sun made the War Memorial rose-red, he decided to give up; not all his scurridging could turn out successfully and he really needed the Guild Hall records, or perhaps a word with Edward Maybury – or even Ted. Though of course if Ted did know anything about the building of the old line to the docks he would be insufferably condescending about imparting it. Duggie trudged home to his tall old town house that looked drabber every year, put his hat and cane on the hall stand, glanced into the front room that caught the evening sun, then made for the darker regions where he kept the phone.

He dialled Hattie's number three times and it was always engaged. At the fourth failed attempt he decided to take action.

He drove out to Leckhampton slowly and sedately. In London Road he stopped at an excellent fish-and-chip shop and bought two helpings of best haddock. No chips because Hattie was quite plump enough, what with the baby and her eating habits. When he bounced up the drive of Leckhampton House he was surprised to see two cars outside the garage, and his heart sank when he identified them as belonging to Doffie and Hester. Three women. One of whom he would adore till his death. The other who saw him as a father figure. And Hattie. He sighed, left the fish and chips in their polythene sack and went through the garage to the back door. He was inside the kitchen when the scream rang out, followed immediately by Hester's voice, shrill from the hall. 'The doctor is still out on rounds, Doffie. Try again to persuade her to let me call the ambulance.'

He flung his hat on to the kitchen table, dropped his stick anyhow, and launched himself towards the sitting room. He glimpsed Hester grimly hanging on to the telephone receiver at the bottom of the staircase; she looked as if she had been there for ever – no wonder he had not been able to get through.

The scene in the sitting room was like a Victorian classic. Hattie lay on the floor, bolstered by cushions, a Windsor chair upturned behind her. Doffie knelt beside her, holding one hand, supporting her head with the other. The scream, Duggie thought, had probably been one of sheer effort as she bore down; she was now relaxing, eyes closed, breathing deeply. Doffie was making soothing noises. Duggie knelt by her and put his face close to Hattie's.

'Only me, old girl. D'you mind?'

Her eyes opened wide. 'Duggie? Oh Duggie darling, how sweet. You're so good at coping. Will you just tell these girls that I am not – definitely not – going into hospital! I am having this baby right here on the floor. So if you could get

Doffie to find towels and things – and Hester to ring the mid-wife instead of the doctor – we'll be fine. It's coming again! Stay here, Duggie, don't leave me!'

Doffie said, 'She shouldn't be bearing down! I've been to the classes with her and she can't possibly have reached the second stage already!'

Duggie took Hattie's hands and Doffie moved away.

'She knows what she's doing,' he gasped as Hattie reared up with that same gurgling scream. 'Get the towels, Doff.' And for the first time in his life he felt intense irritation with Doffie Pettiford as she hesitated, apparently needing a physical shove to get her going.

For a long moment Hattie remained half upright, her grip painful, her eyes bulging with effort, then she subsided again.

'Bloody hard work, Duggie,' she panted. 'But we're nearly there. Can you bear it, my dear? I'd rather you were here than anyone else.'

'Of course I can bear it,' he said firmly. 'Christ, if you can bear it then so can I!'

She summoned a grin from somewhere. 'You're an old man,' she reminded him. And then the next contraction came. And the next.

In the hall Doffie snatched the phone from Hester and dialled her own number. 'Ted? Get over here quickly. I know I've got the car. Just get a taxi – anything. And pick up the midwife as you come. Her address is . . .' She flipped through the book, found it underlined, told him then slammed down the phone.

'We need someone here with a bit of oomph,' she told Hester briefly before taking to the stairs. 'Boil a kettle or something, Hester. Make yourself useful.'

Hester looked into the sitting room and then made quickly for the kitchen.

'Bloody Pettifords,' she muttered as she filled the kettle. 'Who do they think they are?' Then she thought of Ted speeding past Staverton and through Cheltenham. As a child Ted Pettiford had been her ideal father-figure. She smiled at herself, then filled a saucepan and stuck it on the cooker.

Less than five minutes later, in the sitting room, slithering on to the Chinese rug, Millie Ryecroft arrived. Duggie supported Hattie with an arm round her still-heaving shoulders. Together they surveyed the slime-covered infant with a kind of awe. Doffie arrived with the towels and, as if he had been trained for this very moment, Duggie took one and rolled the baby into it, scooped her face clear and looked at the hooded eyes.

'I think you're meant to cry, Millie,' he whispered. 'It shows your lungs are functioning properly.'

The tiny button mouth worked as if smiling agreement; then the whole face crumpled, the lips parted and a thin wail drifted through the house.

Hattie said contentedly, 'She's going to be such a good baby. Thank you, Duggie darling. You've been simply splendid. If you want to be her earthly father, you know you are so very welcome.'

Hester, coming in at that moment with a steaming kettle, wondered what to make of such a peculiar invitation; Doffie chortled. A car door slammed, the back door opened and the midwife arrived.

'My goodness, Mummy! You don't believe in hanging about, do you?' She peeled off her coat, opened her bag, grabbed the kettle and put on an overall. 'Show me where I can wash my hands, ladies. Let us just leave Mummy and Daddy together with baby, shall we?'

Suddenly they were all gone. There were sounds of Ted arriving. Duggie whispered hoarsely, 'I've done it again, Hattie. Pushed myself in where angels fear to tread. Did you mean what you said?'

Hattie held her baby with expert tenderness. He realized that here was a woman who knew exactly what she was doing, who would give him freedom to do exactly what he wanted to do, who would make sure everyone around her was happy and comfortable and well fed.

He said, 'Oh Hattie, please say you meant it. Please say you will marry me and let me have a share of your life. Please, Hattie. I think I must always have loved you.'

She threw back her head, exposing the still-magnificent column of her throat, and then she laughed.

'Of course I meant it, dear Duggie. When I told you that you were the one I wanted to stay by me . . . that was when I knew. Oh Duggie, just look at her! We might not have made her together, my dear, but we brought her into the world together. She's ours, Dug! Our Millie!' She looked at his profile as he bent towards the baby. 'Who knows, Dug? We could make a baby between us, couldn't we?'

He turned and smiled. 'We can try, Hattie.' He could actually feel life opening up all round him. He might have only a few more years; perhaps only a few weeks. But he was already in heaven and he knew it. Then he stood up.

'Darling, I've got two pieces of haddock in the car!'

She sighed happily. 'Oh Duggie, how absolutely perfect. I'm terribly hungry. Let's just wait for Aunty Midwife to cut the cord and settle Millie. And then we'll gorge!' She giggled. 'I am so happy, Duggie. I asked Percy to fix it for me. And he has! Even to the haddock!'

Twenty-four

The news of Millie's arrival made Nell smile and then suddenly weep. She was in the school office, the secretary tactfully working at her desk, a sick child sitting in the visitor's armchair holding a plastic bowl at the ready. It was raining outside, a summer rain barely dampening the heads of the hollyhocks that the children in Nell's class had tended lovingly this term. Nell used all the telephone cable so that she could look outside and have her back to the rest of the office. She felt a pang of pure homesickness which she swallowed with her tears because it was her mother on the other end of the line.

Alice was making a determined effort to sound 'normal', whatever that might be.

'Aunt Hessie and Grandma thought they were in charge, but of course Hattie was holding the reins the whole time as you might imagine.'

Nell swallowed again. 'I thought she had booked to go into hospital,' she said hoarsely.

'She did. Fooled us all because she had no intention of going apparently – or so she says now.' There was a pause, then Alice's voice said firmly, 'She thought Uncle Percy would be closer to her at home.'

Nell tried to remember how she might have responded to this two or three months ago and said in a similarly firm voice, '*You* should understand that, Ma! Only with you it's always the cathedral!'

Alice said nothing; Nell waited and still nothing. She said quickly in an effort to close the gap, 'So – knowing

Hester – Grandma actually delivered the baby?'

'No. Actually it was Uncle Duggie.'

'Uncle *Duggie?*'

'He had brought two pieces of haddock from that shop in London Road and –' she paused as Nell repeated, '*Haddock?*' then went on, 'And just happened to be the only one with her when . . . As a matter of fact, Hattie told the others to go. She preferred Uncle Duggie because he's so good in a crisis.'

Nell breathed, 'Of course. The famous time when he rescued Grandma from the clutches of crazy Grandad Ryecroft!' She tried to laugh and almost choked.

Alice said doubtfully, 'Yes, I suppose so. Anyway, everything is fine and Millie is beautiful. You know that terrible posed photograph of Gran when she was about sixteen? Well, Millie looks like that.'

'Oh. Jolly good.'

There were sounds of vomiting behind Nell and she added quickly, 'Must go, Ma. I'll get a card and so forth.'

'See you at the end of the month?'

Nell replaced the receiver and turned to hold the plastic bowl and make soothing noises. The trouble with the summer hols was that they were so long.

A week later, Alice was telephoning again.

'Ma, I'll phone you from a kiosk. This isn't really on. Yes, I know it's playtime but I'm on playground duty and . . . all right. I'm listening but make it quick.' She glanced through the window. Shirley was kneeling by one of the boys, who had kicked a football and almost gone with it. She heard her mother's words but at first the meaning escaped her. It was too ridiculous. She said, 'Hattie won't marry again. She adored Uncle Percy.' Her mother's voice went up a register and Nell frowned. 'Yes, but he's old! I know, so was Uncle Percy. Yes, I know Hattie is fifty-something which of course is old but not as old as . . . I can't believe it, Ma. A new baby *and* a new husband? It's ridiculous! Anyway, I have to go. I'll ring you tonight.'

Nell turned and stared at the secretary. 'It's my aunt. She's just had a baby and she's getting married again!'

The secretary looked bewildered. 'What about her husband?'

'He died last October. Less than a year ago.'

'And is the new husband the father of the baby?' The secretary sounded suddenly avid for details.

Nell said, 'No, of course not. Her old husband is – was – is the father. The new husband is an old family friend. I call him Uncle Duggie. He must be about ninety!'

'Oh my God!'

'He delivered the baby then they ate haddock together and now he's marrying her! I can't believe it!'

The secretary said, 'Nowt so queer as folk.'

Nell could hear the shocked delight behind the platititude. Suddenly she began to laugh.

The secretary said, 'Would you like a glass of water?'

Nell spluttered, 'No, thanks. I'm not hysterical, honestly. It's just that my aunt always does things which surprise everyone – well, everyone in our family anyway. And now . . . this.' She made for the door and said as an afterthought, 'I think my family are very special. I can't help loving them even when I don't want to!' And she was gone.

Shirley was still 'on cloud nine, or even nineteen', as she put it, but she did manage to enquire about Nell's plans for the holidays and was genuinely pleased when Nell said she was going back home.

'Thank God for that. What made you change your mind?'

'I can't quite explain. There's a new baby in the family who will probably be famous one day. And there's going to be a wedding too.'

'So it has taken a wedding and a baby to send you back home. Does that mean that whatever they did – and it must have been awful from the way you've acted this term – you've forgiven them?'

'Have I been that bad? Sorry, Shirley. And I don't know

whether I've forgiven them or not. All I know is that I would expect them to forgive me – they have forgiven me over and over again, all my life. So . . . I suppose I have to try to take this . . . *thing* . . . on board.'

'And you still can't talk about it?'

'No. Sorry again. But no. I can't even think about it, actually. I'm going to have to wrap it up in some way and shove it to the back of my mind.'

'How poetic.'

'Well, I'm like that.'

They both laughed. Nell could feel happiness creeping up on her again; it might well be a long way off but at least it was there. It was no good re-examining the whole thing about Mo being her brother; that line of thought would lead inevitably to bitterness and despair; but just to be back home, seeing her parents, Grandma and Grandad so explosively in love still, and of course Hattie. Crazy Hattie. It occurred to her that it was still good to be alive. She hadn't had that thought for the whole of the term. She must never waste time again.

It was Sunday afternoon and Edmund telephoned Sally at her home. He was using the extension in the dining room; Mrs Marvel had taken over the kitchen as her own personal domain, his mother was resting after a large lunch, Millie likewise. Perry was watching television in the sitting room. The telephone in the hall was much too public.

Sally's voice interrupted the ringing tone.

'I bet that's Ed. And I bet he's going to say why don't I come for a spin on this dreary Sunday afternoon.'

'Right on two counts,' Edmund said pedantically. 'But it's glorious sunshine here, not a bit dreary.'

'Sunshine can be dreary. Unless you are suggesting a spin.'

'I'll be with you in an hour. And just because you have left school doesn't only mean an end. It means a beginning.'

'Oh, shut up. You left out two words that make all the difference. I have left school *for ever*.'

'Shut up yourself. And be at the gate. I cannot bear the way your father looks at me over his specs.'

'He can't help wearing specs—'

He put down the receiver, grinning. She would use him as a punchball, he knew that. And considered it a privilege.

She was wearing khaki shorts, a halter top, canvas shoes and nothing else as far as he could tell. Her red hair sprouted out of two plaits.

She said, 'I am so bored I could scream. I spent all morning fiddling with my hair, painting my nails. Mother said in her day she would have done something useful. I mean, what help is that?'

'You might have enquired further. Asked if she had any spare tapestry work around. Offered to peel some potatoes. Weeded the garden.'

'I hate you,' she said dully.

'I don't hate you. But sometimes I disapprove of you. Strongly. Mostly for your lack of self-discipline. What your mother meant was—'

She wailed suddenly, 'I won't see Piecrust. I've seen her every day except Saturdays and Sundays – oh, and bloody Whitsun of course. Now the holidays go on for ever and then . . . what am I going to *do*?'

'I'll wangle an invite to Hattie's wedding for you. She'll be there. And probably for Millie's christening too. And she'll want to know how you get on at university.'

Sally was silent. Then she said at last, 'How is Millie?'

'Gorgeous. As you would expect a sister of mine to be, of course.'

She did not react to that but said just as glumly, 'Everything seems to happen in your house. Nothing does in mine. Not ever.'

'You happen.' He grinned sideways. 'I am amazed at how your parents cope. They're so . . . sedate. Such thoroughly good people. And you exploded into their midst. I wonder whether you are a changeling.'

If he hoped to divert her gloom he was disappointed. She

said, 'What difference does it make? We're stuck with each other.'

He thought of Nell and himself. 'You're right there. I'm pretty certain I'm a changeling myself. But I am well and truly stuck with Percy as a dad.'

'Have you dropped all that then?' she asked with minimal interest.

'Yes. Too many hearts to break.'

'So you know? You actually . . . know.'

'Not actually. No. But Hester and I reached the same conclusion, so we're most likely right. But it doesn't matter.' He looked at her and smiled. 'It really doesn't, Sal. I know Ma is my mother. And Percy didn't do a bad job of being a father. I wish you'd known him.'

'I'm glad I didn't. He must have had something going for him – your mother and darling Piecrust loved him to bits. But Alice told me – seriously – he hardly said a word and he was cross-eyed.'

'Alice? You've been talking to Alice about my father?'

'I talked to everyone I could about him. Remember I told you I would help you—'

'I thought you would limit your enquiries to Hester. I thought that was the object of the exercise – to give you an excuse to talk to Hester.'

'Well, I talked to Alice. You sound miffed. Did I do the wrong thing?'

'Try to remember exactly what you said. Exactly.'

'You are miffed. You're really angry. You didn't tell me that Alice was out of bounds. Why? She must have been around when you were born. Your mother is much more than a cousin to her. She could have confided in Alice. Besides which, everyone seems to think Alice is psychic. So she might have some kind of information line direct to your father – always assuming he died.'

'What are you on about, Sally? You know my father died! He died a couple of months before you rolled up at Leckhampton House in that car of yours!'

'No. I mean your real father. Your blood father.'

'For God's sake! What makes you think *he's* dead?'

'Isn't he?' She stared at him. He had a classic profile. She breathed, 'He's still alive . . . someone you know . . . that's why it could hurt him to be exposed . . .'

Edmund stopped the car with a jerk. 'Get out,' he said.

She was bewildered and alarmed. 'Are you kicking me out to walk back? Where are we? I haven't been looking at the road—'

He got out himself and cut her short by slamming his door. She scrambled out and came round to him.

'Edmund, I'm sorry. I know I'm impossible. Nobody puts up with me like you do and now I've ruined that! I'm really sorry.'

'What for?' he snapped, going round to lock the doors.

She wailed, 'I don't know! That's the trouble – I never know. Just being me, I suppose!'

He took her arm and propelled her towards a stile.

'In answer to your previous question, we're at the top of the cheese-rolling pitch at Coopers Hill. There's a big area . . . Look, here we are. See the view? What do you think?'

She stared from his face to the view. It spread before them like a child's pictorial map. Brockworth, Shurdington, distant Cheltenham . . . Gloucester to the left . . . Chosen Hill. She clasped her hands beneath her chin and was silent for a long time. He did not break the silence. She spoke at last and with awe.

'Oh . . . oh Edmund! Dear, dear Ed. It's wonderful . . . It makes me feel small and insignificant and yet part of something huge and magnificent. Oh Ed, how did you know that this was exactly what I needed?'

'Because I needed it too.' He sat on a mole hill, pulled her down beside him and held her head against his waist. 'You got it in one, of course. I knew you would. It's huge, isn't it? The world and the universe and . . . everything. Makes us feel small. Yes. But we have to believe that we are vital to that hugeness. That it wouldn't be like it is if it weren't for each one of us. So – right again, Sally Gold – we are not in-significant. We're part of a pattern. And my father – whoever he might be – may or may not know that he has me for a son. But I've been woven into the pattern with Percy for my dad and if I start upsetting it now, where might it end?'

Her small face, with its crazy aureole of red hair, turned up to his. He continued to cradle it in the crook of his arm, smiling at her, willing her to be happy. She said, 'I know you're right. I love you for it.'

He brushed her forehead with his lips, then gently turned her face back to the view. 'Start from the left,' he suggested.

'All right. Cows. In that field halfway down. Black and white ones – oh my God, three of them are lying down! That means rain.'

'Good. We need it. What's that building beneath the cows? Huge aluminium roof.'

'Used to be the Gloucester Aircraft Company. Don't know any more. But go out to the edge and then in a bit . . . Is that the cathedral?'

'Yes. And the river. Apparently my great-grandmother used to live in one of the hamlets along the river. We could go there one day.'

'Could we swim in the river there?'

'I don't know. If we can swim in Bracewell's Pool I suppose we could swim in the river.'

'I haven't swum in the pool, actually. Perhaps we could do that.'

'Perhaps. I'm not keen. I used to have an awful dream when I was a kid. About someone drowning in the pool. I've never swum in it.'

'Who was it – the person who drowned?'

'I don't know. The whole place is thick with stories. I must have heard some of them and my subconscious did the rest.'

'I bet I know who it was. I bet it was your grandmother. Mitzie.'

'Maybe.' He tried to sound uninterested. 'I rather think she died of drink and licentious living.'

She ignored the joking tone and said, 'Yes, but despair gripped her. Don't you see? She had to give up her little girl – your mother – to her parents, but she never forgot her. She came back to end it all.'

'Don't muck about, Sally!'

'I'm only half mucking about. Perhaps after having your mother, her whole life was a time of after-midnight.'

'Oh, so you've heard that one, have you? From Alice?'

'As a matter of fact . . . yes. Don't be angry again. Alice told me stuff that was common knowledge anyway.'

'I know. But Alice is a bit whimsical. I wouldn't want you thinking we're all like that.'

'I don't.' She scraped her nail along his jeans, setting his teeth on edge, then said quietly, 'There's one really good thing to come out of this. The after-midnight thing. You and Hester . . . you're related. Properly. I know she's always been Aunt Hester to you and Perry but it was an honorary title before. And now . . .' She looked up at him anxiously. 'You know I'll never ever say anything to anyone else, Ed.'

He gazed into her eyes. 'You told me once you could not keep secrets.'

'I can keep yours. And Hester's. Till I die.'

'We can't be sure. But we are both inclined to think that we might be related.'

'And that has to be good.'

'It does. I needed to come here to fully realize that.' He smiled. 'And of course I needed you to point it out for me!'

'Of course.'

He saw her eyes were full of tears. She said, 'I wish I could love you like you love me, dear Edmund. And not just because you are related to my dear Piecrust.'

He stood up and drew her to her feet. 'Come on. Let's go and find a nice tea shop and plan our trip to France.'

'What?'

'That's why I came to see you this afternoon. I thought we might take Hester over to France. To see her old prof. You know about Richard Tibbolt, I expect. He's living over there with his kids at the moment. Hester thinks he's forgotten all about her but no one ever forgets Hester Ryecroft, as well you know. I've got my annual leave coming up and I didn't know what to do with it because I was quite certain your parents would not let me take you away. But if Hester is with us . . . and the only reason Hester would go on holiday with us is to see . . .'

'What about if he doesn't *want* to see her?'

'That's why I need to talk to you about it. The possibilities and the probabilities and whether we can pre-empt any of them and whether I should leave my mother so soon after Millie's birth. And . . . whether you are big enough to do this thing for Hester and not try to keep her for yourself.'

She got into the car and sat there, considering. 'I don't know about being big enough . . .' She grinned. 'I'm such a squit anyway. But I want Hester to be happy again. More than anything I would like her to be . . . settled. And if that means pushing her back into Richard Tibbolt's arms, then so be it.' Her grin widened to a proper smile. 'As for leaving your mother with Millie . . . well, she'll be married by then and only too glad to have the house to herself.'

'True. You see, you have already sorted out two problems!'

'Oh Ed . . .' She reverted to being a little girl and rubbed her forehead against his sleeve. He put his hand over hers. He ached with love for her.

Nell was determined to make this holiday a success, and her first port of call was Leckhampton House because she needed to tell Edmund that she was determined to cope and might need his help. It was disappointing to find Edmund not there and Perry watching some rubbish on television with his bare and rather smelly feet on Hattie's footstool, the rest of his body sprawled all over the now-famous Chinese rug, which Hattie had been reluctant to send to the cleaner's.

'Glad to see you, old girl, but need to find out what is going to happen to Gary Cooper. So why don't you pop upstairs and see Ma and Millie? Duggie will be along for dinner so you're just in time. Once he's here it's all canoodle and lovey-dovey.'

'I take it Hattie will be cooking dinner during all this display?'

'No. Haven't you heard? We've filched Mrs Marvel from poor old Aunt Hessie. She's got no lovey-dovey, no Mrs Marvel, no nuthin'!'

'Oh shut up,' Nell said, making for the door and wondering whether she was following in Aunt Hester's footsteps. 'And by the way, Gary Cooper shoots the baddie and gets the girl.'

'You miserable bitch!' Perry called after her. But he did not move because she could be wrong.

Nell enjoyed the next hour. Hattie was a tonic, with her strangely amoral codes, her overweening pride in producing Millie – 'For us all, darling, not just me! Percy arranged it so beautifully and he knew I could do it. Hester is years younger than me but he knew she couldn't have managed it.' She looked at the sleeping child. 'I should try to get in touch with other posthumous babies. It's a fascinating subject, Nell. And I would love to know if there are other mothers in my position who have then felt free to fall in love again.' She frowned and tried to explain the inexplicable. 'I know it's a shock to the family, sweetie, and it was a shock to darling Duggie. I fully appreciate that. But it wasn't to me. I knew he could love me at the drop of a hat! If I'd looked at him in a special way . . . There have been amazing moments when I knew he wanted to kiss me. But he was sort of bound to poor Enid. He is so kind, Nell. And when your darling grandmother – when Doffie asked him to look after Enid . . . well, he would have married her instantly if she had agreed to it. But she didn't. So she was out of the picture and darling Percy is out of the picture. And Millie needs a father – I don't want to burden the boys too much in that direction.'

'Hattie. Dearest. You don't need to explain. Hattie

Westbrook is above petty explanations. Hattie Westbrook lives instinctively and is nearly always right.'

'Remember that it was Hattie Westbrook who encouraged her sister-in-law to have an affair with Reggie Ryecroft. And she has never forgotten that.'

'Well, Enid is obviously doing her best to forget it!'

'I've got her last postcard here, darling. Have you seen it?'

They gloated over the brief message. Enid had won the deck quoits tournament. It was the first time she had won anything in her whole life.

'I love that girl,' Hattie said sentimentally.

'You love everybody,' Nell commented. 'Is there a man?'

'Oh, several. She is having a whale of a time.' Outside a car door slammed and Hattie smiled. 'That's Duggie. He's coming to dinner. Darling, would you be an absolute angel and take Millie downstairs so that I can give Duggie my undivided attention?'

Nell scooped up the sleeping Millie. A wonderful smell of milk and talcum surrounded her. Nell dropped a kiss on the wide forehead. 'You are completely brazen, Hattie,' she commented.

Hattie started to protest, then stopped. 'Well, perhaps I am.' And she smiled.

Downstairs the film had come to an end and Perry had switched off the television. Duggie looked in, crooned over Millie then went upstairs with a familiarity that obviously did not surprise Perry. Nell sat in a low chair near the open French door nursing the baby, cradling the downy head and marvelling at the rosebud mouth, tiny nose and perfect miniature fingers, each with its own mother-of-pearl nail. She so rarely allowed herself to sit still doing nothing; she knew this was special, dictated by Millie, enhanced by summer . . . being home . . . coming to terms with whatever was the truth.

Perry said idly, 'You look pretty good cuddling our Millie like that. You're a natural.'

Nell said nothing, enjoying the moment. Perry continued

to stare up at her from the floor. He said, 'We had something, didn't we? It wasn't just a fond embrace, was it? Talk to me, Nell. What happened?'

She looked away from Millie for an instant and smiled at him.

'Actually "fond embrace" describes it perfectly, cousin. In spite of everything, I've never really regretted it. And we're still good friends. Edmund was afraid we might not be . . . Where is Edmund, by the way?'

'Oh, I know you came to see him, not me, not even Ma and Millie. Everyone suddenly comes to see Edmund.'

She tore her gaze away from Millie again and glanced at him, surprised. 'Come off it, Perry! Of course I came to see everyone. Especially this little one here . . .' She gloated over the still-sleeping face. 'You're already used to her. Remember I'm not.' She was going to ask about Edmund again, then knew she shouldn't. 'As for Duggie's defection from Enid to your mother! Well, we're all absolutely flabbered and gasted.' She chuckled. 'Isn't it great? Have you chosen your room in Duggie's house yet? I'd have the one at the top overlooking the square and the library and museum. I'll help you decorate it if you like.'

The ploy worked. It had not occurred to Perry that he might be gaining territory with his mother's alliance; he knew it had probably not occurred to Duggie either, so that gave it added zest.

'Would you? Could be a sort of project for the summer, couldn't it?' He took his legs off the footstool and rolled on to his stomach. 'I say, Nell, you're obviously falling in love with that baby. How about if we went on with the shocking bit and produced one of our own? We could make a flat in Duggie's house and have a ball! What d'you say?'

'Absolutely not! For goodness' sake, Perry, don't you learn anything from events? We've done that. It's over.'

He wasn't sorry; immediately the words had left his mouth he had known they were absurd. But he couldn't let it go immediately.

'You'd do it with Edmund, wouldn't you? I know about him taking you back to Brum at Easter. He told me.'

She was very still, staring at Millie with a new intensity.

'What else did he tell you?'

'What else was there? Go on, tell me! Did you take him up to your room? Where we . . . I thought that was special to us, Nell.'

She relaxed. 'No. I didn't take him up to my room. He was in a sweat to get back home, apart from anything else.' She turned and risked a smile. 'Come on, Perry. D'you think I sleep around or something? Of course Millie is adorable but that doesn't mean . . . Anyway, we've got our pact still, I hope?'

'Pact?'

'You've forgotten already! You said that if I was still on the shelf at forty, you would marry me.'

'Oh yes. Of course.' He grinned at last. 'Sorry, kiddo. I'm in a bit of a state and you haven't even noticed so I'm being my usual self. Awkward as hell.' She looked surprised. He tried to shrug, failed and sat up. 'Oh, it's just this Edmund and Sally Gold thing. I was the one who fancied her in the first place. And Edmund just steps in . . . He's taken her for a spin, whatever that might mean. She's eighteen and he's thirty. Well, nearly. It's not good enough, Nell. My nose is right out of joint in any case, what with Duggie Marsden in prospect as a stepfather. And Edmund isn't in the least bothered by any of it!'

'Neither are you. Not really. In fact, it's a marvellous thing to be happening, Perry, my lamb. You like being completely free and there would have been times when you couldn't have been. Duggie's filthy rich so he's obviously not after the Westbrook money. You're used to him. He's got that lovely old house that is crying out for your attention—'

'All right, all right.' Perry sighed. 'I feel all the time as if I'm waiting for something to happen, Nell. And it doesn't.'

She sighed too. 'I feel the same. And I rather think nothing else will happen. This is it, Perry. Millie arriving in our midst, needing us, loving us because we're *us*. Duggie at last becoming part of the family . . . This is real life, Perry. And it's enough. It really is all right.'

He scrambled to his feet, came to her and put his arms round her and the sleeping baby. He said, 'Christ, you'll have me in tears in a minute, coz! But you're damned right. If this is what it is, then it's more than enough. The jolly old cup is jolly well overflowing!'

She laughed, turned to him and planted a kiss on his face. Then they both looked down at Millie because her eyes were open and it was as if she knew . . . everything.

Twenty-five

Hattie was unexpectedly conformist when it came to Millie's christening.

'We must be married first,' she told Duggie. 'I'm not having you hanging around like a spare part at Millie's do. I want you to be my husband by then.'

'Sounds all right to me,' Duggie said comfortably.

'And me,' Edmund agreed. 'I'll give you away, Ma. Then Hessie, Sally and I can go off the next day and leave you in peace.'

'And be home for the christening,' Hattie stipulated.

'Should be. I've only got two weeks' annual leave,' Edmund reminded them. 'It will be nice to know that Duggie is here.'

'Has everyone forgotten me? I'll be here too!' Perry poked his head round the kitchen door. 'And as I'm still one of the breadwinners in the family, may I enquire what there is to eat?'

'Mrs Marvel's at Hester's today,' Hattie said. 'I thought someone might pop down to the fish shop. And, Perry darling, can't you have a few days with Nell? Remember it's going to be my honeymoon.'

'Hell's bells!' Perry came into the kitchen and flopped into one of the chairs. He glanced at Duggie. 'Nell said she'd give me a hand doing up my room in your town house, Dug. I suppose I could sleep on the job, as it were.'

'Your room? My house? You want to live in my house in the city? I thought you'd expect me to get rid of that.' Duggie glanced at Hattie; she looked absolutely marvellous, sitting there nursing Millie. She said nothing so he was bound to assume that she was very much in favour of Perry 'doing up a room' in the old town house. And surely that would be a small price to pay for two weeks alone with Hattie and Millie?

'Not the downstairs,' he stipulated. 'And my bedroom is at the back, first floor.'

'Nell thought the attics might be good.' Perry grinned. He had told Edmund he was 'cut to pieces' at the way Sally had been practically seduced away from him, but there was still Nell. And the town house of course.

The wedding was a quiet affair at the register office but of course the family congregated at Leckhampton House afterwards. Hattie wore a grey linen suit for the actual ceremony. 'Darling Doffie, I know it doesn't do much for me but just in case my dear Percy is watching, I wouldn't like him to think I'm trying to repeat our unique experience.' She carried Millie over one shoulder, where the baby wobbled her head quite happily and dribbled regurgitated milk down her mother's back. Duggie mopped and held the baby in place when Hattie released her left hand for the ring. Sally said it was really touching. Perry, Edmund and Nell exchanged expressionless glances.

When they were all disposed round the house and garden with Mrs Marvel dispensing sherry and tea, Hattie disappeared into her room and emerged in full wedding regalia, white satin dress, full-length veil and orange blossom. Duggie was absolutely delighted.

'Is this my special surprise?'

'Nobody knew, darling.' She kissed him fondly. 'Not even Doffie. I wanted to wear my original dress but I couldn't quite fasten it at the back. So I got another one! What do you think?'

'I think you are the most beautiful girl I have ever seen. And when I think – after all this time – that I have found true love . . .' He kissed her back and Doffie, standing by Ted, smiled and shook her head – but without any real regret. Duggie deserved every bit of happiness he could get. Hester, standing on the other side of Ted, said, 'Do you remember me saying to you that Hattie performed for Percy?' He nodded and she went on, 'She's still doing it, only this time for Duggie.'

Edward put his tiny sister on Sally Gold's lap and took his place at the piano. 'The first dance for the newly-weds!' he called and broke into the strains of 'April Showers'. Nell stopped fiddling with her camera and looked up quickly. She did not catch Edmund's eye; he was grinning at his mother; but as she looked away again she saw a movement in the garden and for a moment thought that someone was watching them.

Hester walked sideways round the perimeter of the room to avoid the dancers and stood by Sally. The girl was dressed in a brown silk shift with what looked like a gold-coloured curtain tie at her waist. Her wiry red hair was strained back behind her ears where its bushiness was contained in a sort of netted snood. She looked marvellous.

Hester said, 'Do you need any help there?'

Sally looked up from the baby in her lap, her face alight. 'Oh Hester! Isn't she wonderful? Hattie, I mean. But Millie as well! All of you. I adore you all! And I can't wait to have a baby. Just look at Millie, isn't she God's very own miracle?'

Hester chuckled. 'Literally. You realize Hattie is over fifty?'

'Yes. But she's Mother Earth too, isn't she? I mean, if she were sixty she could still do it.'

Hester laughed again. 'Steady on there! She's not that much of a miracle.' She sat by Sally and leaned over to tickle the baby's chin. 'But this one is special, isn't she? She's going to be spoiled to death between all of us.'

'Nothing the matter with that. I'm spoiled and look what a charmer I am!'

'True.' Hester stopped smiling and looked at Sally directly. 'Why are you coming to France with Edmund and me, Sally? Are you hoping to see me humiliated, rejected by the man who – as you well know – was my lover for over twenty years?'

Sally was horrified. 'No! Never! Oh Hester, how could you

think such a thing of me? Edmund asked me because he knew how dreadful I felt at leaving school . . . leaving you. He invited me here today so that I could see you. He thought it was a chance for me to be with you again – daily – just for a little while. Oh Hester, don't begrudge me that . . . please.' The big eyes were full of tears, the baby forgotten. Hester leaned across and picked up the little bundle and held her gently.

'Do you see me as barren, Sally?'

Sally was almost frantic. 'Oh God, no! I see you as a sort of – of – goddess! Wonderful, unattainable, wise . . . oh Piecrust, don't put me through this!'

'I am barren. Of course I am. But I've worked with children, as you know. And Nell has been so special to me. Edmund and Perry too. But if I had a choice now of staying as I am or having a child, I would stay as I am.'

Sally nodded fervently.

Hester smiled. 'All right. I accept that you are coming for good reasons. I had hoped it was to be with Edmund rather than me.' She held up her hand as Sally opened her mouth. 'Now, have you any idea why Edmund has arranged this trip?' Sally continued to stare at her with a kind of horror, then shook her head. 'Do you think he needs a valid reason to take a holiday with you?'

Sally took a breath. 'Perhaps. I don't know. I grabbed at the chance because of seeing you every day—'

'Yes. Quite. Has he said anything more about his parentage?'

Sally's eyes seemed about to drop out of her head. 'No. Nothing. He's given up the whole idea, I think.'

'And you spoke to no one else about it?'

'No. I didn't realize it was a secret of course. But . . . no.'

Hester sighed. The poor girl had already been through this with Edmund, that much was obvious. And she had in fact told someone about it . . . Who could that be? Surely not Alice? Hester's heart jumped at the thought that Alice might well come to the same conclusions she and Edmund had

305

drawn for themselves. It would kill her. She glanced across the room; Alice was one side of Val, Nell the other. Though dear Uncle Ted Pettiford was still nominally holding the reins, Val was the real strength of the family these days. It was his enterprise, imagination, brains and often brawn that had launched the Pumpkin Line. If anybody else discovered that he might well be Edmund's father, he would lose all that. And Alice, who depended on him so much, what would she lose? It was clear to Hester that Edmund's motive in getting Sally right away from Gloucestershire was to separate her from Alice.

She said comfortably, 'That's good. If Edmund is happy, let it drop, my dear. If you'd known Percy Westbrook you would realize he must have been Edmund's father. It hurt Hattie very much when Edmund began this silly quest. We don't want to spoil things for her now. She is so happy.'

Sally swallowed. 'Yes. She is, isn't she? I just love your family, Miss Ryecroft. They are all so interesting.'

'Not really. Most families have a Hattie tucked away some-where.' Hester sat back in the chair and made Millie more comfortable. 'Why don't you go and have a chat with Nell, my dear? You hardly know her and she is probably wonder-ing why on earth you and Edmund and I are off to Provence next week. You have my permission to tell her our reasons!' She smiled at Sally, who got up feeling dazzled and bewildered. Sally was quite certain why *she* was going to France and she knew why Edmund was going, but why on earth was Piecrust going? Surely she was not willing to throw herself at the ungrateful wretch who had ditched her over a year ago? It was ridiculous. She could have anyone . . . Sally's own father had met her and called her a 'humdinger', what-ever that meant. She tilted her head to smile widely at the tall ash-blond girl clinging to Valentine Ryecroft's arm.

'Hello,' she said. 'I'm one of your aunt's students and she thought we should get to know each other. I wondered whether you could show me where the bathroom is?'

Nell smiled and her face was transformed. She released

her father and made for the door. 'You're Sally. Hester says you're brilliant. Come on. Hattie's got her own bathroom and no one will be there. Then we can sit in Hattie's bed-room and have a chat if you like.'

Sally followed Nell's long legs up the stairs and breathed a sigh of relief. At last she had found someone in this compli-cated family who knew exactly who her father was and appreciated him to the full. That was the only trouble with the Pettifords and the Ryecrofts; some of them seemed unsure about their parentage; they must have been quite an incestuous lot in the old days. Sally grinned and Nell said, 'We must seem so strange to you. But honestly, we're quite ordinary.'

Sally let the grin turn to a giggle. 'That's exactly what Piecrust said.' She disappeared into the bathroom and closed the door. 'But actually it's not true!' she called.

Val and Alice took a turn round the garden. It was very still and midges were dancing. Val loosened his tie and undid the top button of his shirt. Alice took off her wedding hat and swung it by the brim. 'What a really happy day,' she said. 'I know Percy turned out to be just right for Hattie but the day itself . . . d'you remember? You came to that wedding too. I remember seeing you and Hester sitting in the church and feeling absolutely flabbergasted!'

'Oh, we came all right. Hester was curious. So was I. I'd been in at the beginning if you recall – I came round to tell you about leaving Oxford, and Hattie had brought the new boyfriend for your inspection. It struck me as a very unlikely match.'

'We all felt that. And of course it wasn't a terribly nice day for it. And we were afraid old Mrs Westbrook was going to completely dominate Hattie. Whereas in fact—' She waited for Val to chuckle and when he did not she thought she knew why. She went on deliberately, 'Joe came too. He was staying in Wainlodes on holiday with his mother. Rose. And he had cycled over to see me in my bridesmaid's dress.'

He stopped in the middle of the shaven lawn and turned to face her. 'So it should have been a happy day for you. You loved him then, remember.' He smiled. 'It's all right, Allie. I can face that now. You were a child – so was he—'

She interrupted him. 'I was happy. Yes. But not like this. Not like today. Not with such certainty, such security for the future. You understand all this, don't you, Val? I have always relied on your understanding. Just as you – surely – relied on mine? We know now that it was not a happy day. My first love was already doomed. Hattie was suddenly conscious that she was tied to one man, which was . . . impossible . . . for someone like Hattie.'

He stared at her, wondering where she was going with all this; he felt again the spectre of Joe Adair. Not for the first time he wondered whether Joe was more powerful in death than life.

She took his hand as if reassuring him. 'Let's sit in the summer house and get away from the midges. Perhaps we should say . . . one or two things.' She led him, unresisting, to the steps of the summer house and settled him on the top one, then sat beside him. He felt numb. He saw suddenly that this had very little to do with Joe. She knew. She knew about Edmund. This was the end. She looked at him; she was smiling.

'Did you not hear what I said, darling? About being happy, secure, certain . . . in your love for me, in mine for you? Today – in contrast to Hattie's first wedding day – en-capsulates that. All of it, Val. Nell is back with us. She's not happy because of Joe Adair's son, Michael. We knew that, surely?' He nodded, swallowing convulsively. She put his hand to her face. 'But it's not history repeating itself. If that is what is making you look so anxious, stop. I was . . . power-less. As Joe was too. We could not help and support each other. Joe found his wife . . . Her name was Julie. And I found my husband. The girl and boy we managed between the four of us are so different, Val. They are not powerless. They can take hold of their destinies in a way we never could.'

With a conscious effort Val managed to speak. 'Allie. What are you trying to tell me?'

'Nell thought she might be Joe's child. She managed to ask me—' He made an exclamation of horror and she put a finger to his lips. 'It could have happened, Val. But it didn't. That's all. And when she found the courage – the resolution – to ask me about it, I told her that.'

'You told her that it could have happened and it didn't?'

'Yes. And she accepted that. And then she said – and this is what I want to tell you today, Val – she said, "I couldn't have borne not to have had Valentine Ryecroft as my father." In other words, darling, she could have borne – somehow or other – to have had Michael Adair as a brother. She would still have had me as a mother, whether she could have borne it or not. But to have had anyone else as a father . . . She had thought about it all through the summer term and had known at the end that *that* was what mattered.'

Happiness and relief poured through him like balm. They held each other and he knew that, against all odds, he had not lost his daughter or his wife. She did not know about Edmund. And . . . though Nell could so easily have been fathered by Joe Adair, she was not. She was his daughter. And this fragile creature was his wife. Almost accidentally these enormous gifts had been given to him. He had imagined he had engineered the whole thing. And he had not.

He said, 'I wrote to him, Allie. I asked Mo to come back. Made an excuse about the new line from Orchard first of all. Then just . . . asked him to come back.'

'And he refused?'

'He did not reply to my letter and he is not here. So yes, I suppose he refused.'

'Poor Michael,' she said sadly.

'What about Nell?'

'Of course. But she still has us. And he has no one. She could give him everything. And together they could walk towards the morning.'

'Is that a quote?'

'No, darling. I simply meant that after midnight you have to move forward to the next dawn. They could have done that.'

'Oh Allie. Oh my dearest Allie.'

She smiled. 'Come on. Let's go back into the house. Mum and Dad must be boiling up for a row by now. I expect you realize that Dad is even more disapproving of this marriage than he was of the last!'

Val laughed. Ted and Doffie Pettiford were living proof that opposites could sometimes be matched. From the open window of the sitting room came the sound of Edmund thumping out 'Let's All Go Down the Strand'. It would be 'The Lambeth Walk' next and Hattie would be there holding her skirt up and kicking her way through it just as she had in the war. The Pettifords were – were – indefatigable!

Doffie called, 'That's enough for me! I'm going to conjure up a pot of tea in the kitchen. Hester, give that baby to her father and come and give me a hand.'

Hester gave up Millie without regret; the baby was waking up and in any case smelled rather strange. Duggie took her gladly, proud to be addressed as father, and insisted on going upstairs to change her. 'The sooner I learn how to do it, the better,' he said to Hattie, who was not protesting anyway.

Hester found Mrs Marvel already pouring tea at the kitchen table and took the opportunity to tell her that she would be away from the following Monday for two weeks at least.

'There will be a great deal to do here,' she said regretfully. 'I expect you will find it difficult to fit me in next term.'

Mrs Marvel flushed uncomfortably. 'I intended to have a word with you, Miss Ryecroft. My sister could give you a couple of hours a week, if that would help?'

Hester tried to smile gratefully but the feeling of being deserted by yet another person was almost overpowering. She said something to Doffie about taking a turn in the garden and almost ran through the kitchen door. Val and

Alice were sitting on the steps of the summer house and she made for them, but then she saw that Val was holding Alice and looking very upset. Hester stopped in her tracks and put her hand to her mouth. Alice must know that Edmund was Val's son . . . That little idiot Sally Gold must have said something. Oh God, what would happen now? She turned hastily and almost ran into the shrubbery and Ted. Uncle Ted. She had so much wanted him to be her father . . . and then there had been Tibbolt and then Percy and then for a short time there had been Duggie, and now there was no one. She flung herself into Ted's arms in floods of tears.

Ted, startled but also flattered because Hester had not sought him out for comfort for some time, clasped her and said, 'What has happened? Has Doffie said something thoughtless? There, there. Nothing is as bad as it seems. Here. A nice clean hanky . . . there . . .' He continued to cluck and dry her face and smooth back that magnificent hair. It was exactly what she needed; to be treated like a little girl again. 'Now, that's better. Tell me what is wrong.'

She kept her forehead pressed to his shirt front. She adored the smell of starched shirts. 'Mrs Marvel is leaving me. Hattie has inveigled her here. And all she can offer me is her sister! For two hours a week!'

Ted was slightly disappointed. He had imagined Doffie had offered some unwanted advice about Richard Tibbolt, which would have given him an opportunity to tell Hester that Doffie often spoke out of turn and he had had to cope with it all his married life because she did not mean it. Not really. Ted had suppressed his annoyance about Duggie Marsden muscling in on his family, first of all by rescuing Doffie from the clutches of Reggie Ryecroft – and if anyone had to rescue Doffie it should have been her husband – and then, after making his intentions perfectly clear where Enid was concerned, suddenly switching allegiance to Hattie of all people! And Hattie should know better – producing a child at fifty-two and then marrying someone who was nothing whatsoever to do with either Pettifords or Westbrooks. It was all embarrassing anyway and rather distasteful. Hattie had always been oversexed, that had to be accepted, but that Duggie should suddenly display his desires so openly was downright disgusting. And that Doffie should back him up . . . He could no longer send her to Coventry as he had done in the past, but there was a slight satisfaction to be had in obliquely sympathizing with Hester now. Except that it appeared to be nothing at all to do with Doffie.

Hester continued to blub all over his clean shirt.

'No one stays with me, Uncle Ted. Have you noticed? Oh, there was Mother of course. If only she were here now.

'I don't need a cleaner, not really! I just need someone on my side. Mrs Marvel is the last straw, Uncle Ted. And it was an easy job for her – she lives just round the corner. But no, Hattie can just crook her finger and they all come running. Percy and Val and Duggie and heaven knows who else through the war!'

'Quite, quite.' It was one thing to be angry with Hattie himself, but he wasn't too happy to hear someone else's complaints about her.

'And though Percy left her in a sense, he left her something of himself, didn't he? Maybe if I'd been in that night, the night he died, he would have left Millie to *me*!'

'Oh, I don't think that would have done, Hester. Not really.'

'No, of course not! And I was glad and thankful that he died after he and Hattie . . . I mean it took all the responsibility off my shoulders, didn't it?' She looked up, her face drowning. 'Perhaps that's it, Uncle Ted. I can't take responsibility. Yes, that's it! I . . . cannot . . . take . . . responsibility!'

'Dear girl. Please don't upset yourself. You take responsibility for about three hundred girls nearly every day of your life.'

'But not for one person's happiness!' She stopped crying and looked past his head at the azure sky. 'It's true, Ted. I couldn't do it for Richard. He wanted to marry and settle down and I couldn't do it. And I let Alice down too . . . when we were children. I didn't want her to be happy with Joe Adair and I wouldn't make a stand against Father . . . And then there was Percy too. He wanted me so much and I wouldn't go to bed with him, Ted. I told myself it was loyalty to Hattie, but it wasn't. So maybe I wouldn't have gone to bed with him that night either and Millie could never ever have been mine!'

Ted felt he was losing his grip on the narrative. He said feebly, 'Look, old girl. Hattie isn't the evil woman a lot of people think. All right, she's a bit over the top when it comes to boyfriends . . .' Even to Ted the word boyfriends sounded odd when applied to Hattie. 'But all she has ever really cared about is having children. Don't you remember how she was after little Mitzie died? The men she cares about most are her sons. Duggie is the icing on the cake, but Edmund and Perry are the cake itself.'

Hester blinked and looked at him properly. She said, 'Is it like that for Tibbolt? His children mean more to him than anyone or anything?'

'Probably.' Ted felt inspiration surge through him. He said, 'So you see what it would mean to him if you were there to help him. Can you understand that, Hessie? Sharing that responsibility? Halving it?'

She was silent for a long time and he thought he must have said the wrong thing. Then she whispered, 'So I don't go out there begging him to come home? I go out there to see if I can help?'

'Something like that,' he agreed.

She gradually relaxed away from him and at last stood alone.

'I've messed up your shirt,' she said.

'I'm proud of that.' He smiled down at the damp patch.

'Uncle Ted . . . how do you *know* so much?'

He laughed. 'Did you know that your aunt Doffie threw a cup of scalding hot tea all over me once?'

She said resignedly, 'Yes. You told me . . . Oh, you know you told me! You're reminding me. Is that it?'

313

'Sometimes, Hessie dear, for someone who is both clever and beautiful, you are extremely *thick*!'

They walked back to the lawn in time to see Val and Alice disappearing into the kitchen, arms round each other tightly. Hester smiled and used Ted's handkerchief again. She would ask Mrs Marvel whether her sister could possibly manage an extra hour now and then. After all, she could shop for herself and do her own cooking. She wasn't entirely helpless.

Nell decided she liked Sally Gold and with her usual frankness she told her so.

'I thought at first I was jealous of you – perhaps I've always been a bit possessive of my cousins and you bowled them over with one look!' She pulled a face. 'It seems as if I must resign myself to being an old maid.'

Sally was dismayed. 'I know Edmund thinks he's in love with me and I will eventually give up being a lesbian and fall for him in a big way, but it's not like that, not really. He's sweet and kind and understanding and – and everything. But I love – I really love – your aunt. I expect that disgusts you – my parents absolutely hate me speaking about it and I have to say I do it more because it appals them so. But it's true, Nell. I shall stay an old maid so that I can look after her when she is old.' She stopped and pulled a face. 'Though I know why we are going to Provence. Of course I do. And I love her so much that I want her horrible professor to love her back and marry her or live with her again or whatever. But if it doesn't work then I'll be there.'

'You're mad,' Nell said flatly. 'Hester can be just awful. She and Hattie sort of took me under their wings when I was a kid and they used to squabble over me terribly. Drove me round the twist. Anyway, she'll never be able to return your feelings. If the Tibbolt thing doesn't work out she'll just go back to being in love with my father.' She laughed at Sally's expression. 'Yes, she was always in love with him – her own brother! That's the sort of family we are, Sally – get used to it!'

'You're really rotten,' Sally said admiringly. 'I thought I was pretty awful – I've made a specialist subject of being outrageous – but you take the biscuit!'

'Take no notice of me,' Nell said, suddenly serious. 'The Pettifords and the Ryecrofts are united in my ma and pa. It's what my mother dreamed of when she was young and she's made it happen. And whatever they've done in the past, they're all kind and generous. You could do a lot worse, Sally.'

Sally flipped at her netted hair and some of it escaped wildly. 'I know,' she said, just as seriously. 'Maybe . . . later . . . Edmund and me . . .'

'Only one request. Try not to hurt him. He's rather like my father. He seems to be so up-together. But he's not really.'

Sally said, as if sealing a bargain, 'I'll do my level best.'

From below came Duggie's voice summoning them for tea and scones.

Sally said, 'Thank you for telling me about your family. You've been very honest.'

'The truth and nothing but the truth,' Nell said, and laughed.

Sally was about to point out that she had missed out the middle part of the oath. But then she glanced at Nell, who was frowning as she looked out of the window, and she said nothing.

Nell said, 'Come on. Let's get some tea. I'm having hallucinations or something. Keep thinking I can see people who aren't there!'

Twenty-six

Provence was as Hester remembered it from twenty-seven years before. She had forgotten the haze that hung over the vineyards – Tibbolt had called it a grape haze – which seemed to make places, people and events slightly unreal. She understood only too well why she had succumbed immediately to Tibbolt's overtures; indeed, why Hermione had permitted them. She could understand, too, how easy it must have been for Toby and Eve to forget their basic relationship and drift into a romantic love.

'Nothing seems quite so – so immoral here,' she commented to the others as they stood beside the car for their first view of the farmhouse clinging to the slope of a valley.

Edmund nodded but still said, 'I thought the farmhands, locals, whatever, would have been . . . well, judgemental.'

Hester nodded too, perplexed. It was Sally who said, 'There would be no judgements on the English visitors. They were in a separate slot. The war had not long been over and they were the saviours. And then it must have been obvious the English were fairly crazy, so anything went, I suppose.'

Edmund agreed doubtfully. But Hester nodded vigorously. 'You've got it, Sally. We never integrated at all. Hermione was always painting the locals but she never got to know any of them. A really separatist regime, that's what they ran.'

'And the whole thing was accepted by this ghastly Hermione. So you had no one to turn to.' Sally looked at Hester. 'My God, Piecrust, it was practically rape!'

Edmund said, 'Careful, young Sally!' But Hester laughed.

'Actually, Sally, no. It was not rape. I think I might possibly have been a victim. But a more eager victim it would have been hard to find.'

'But you hated him afterwards!'

'Who told you that?'

'Alice. She said darling Miss Plant – your English teacher at school – met you at Bristol because you could not bear to be brought home by him.'

'Well, that was true, I suppose. By the way, she wasn't *my* darling Miss Plant, though I am eternally grateful to her for meeting me that day. Not many people had cars then and I was in no state to battle with the trains.'

'No . . .' Sally cleared her throat. 'Actually, Miss Plant was Alice's darling. That's why she can understand how I feel about you.'

'Oh *Sally*!'

Edmund said, 'I'm still here, by the way, in case you'd forgotten. Shall we get on? Where did you say the *pension* was, Hester?'

'Just north of the farmhouse. We stay on this road. I wonder whether we've done the right thing to come over without letting them know?'

'Yes. Definitely. We need their reaction.' Nephew and aunt exchanged glances; both of them were alarmed at how intimate Sally had become with Alice.

They had brought Edmund's car over on the ferry and driven south through France the next day. It had been necessary to wind all the windows right down because of the heat, and the breeze blowing through the car had made conversation impossible. Edmund thought gloomily that if Sally kept reminding Hester of her reason for being there, she would probably wreck the whole fortnight. He wondered about having a private word with Richard Tibbolt so that Hester would find some kind of welcome and he could take Sally off exploring the area. He felt tired and disorientated and began to wonder what they hoped to achieve by coming here anyway.

They chugged past the farmhouse. It was a two-storey dwelling but the roof swept low over it, almost to the ground. Gazing through the rear window they caught a glimpse of a verandah that appeared to jut from the back of the house; Hester commented that that hadn't been there before. Below it, shaded by trees, some water glinted suddenly. 'I tried to drown myself in that,' she said, her tone amused. There was a horrified silence then Sally said, 'I would like to kill him!'

And Edmund said, 'You're not serious?'

Hester wound up her window and sighed. 'I suppose I wasn't. Immediately I found myself out of my depth I swam. So no, I wasn't serious then and I am not feeling very serious about it now. It must have seemed the thing to do . . . I was reading Virginia Woolf at the time.'

Edmund laughed. Sally's silence was palpable. She needed to talk to Edmund about this love-hate thing between men and women, to point out to him that her love for Piecrust was not a bit like that; she wondered whether Hester would spend time at the farm and then she and Edmund might explore or something. There were some things she did not understand and she suddenly felt very young and inexperienced.

The *pension* was a rambling building fronted by a bar, with newly built rooms added at the back. The old pump had been retained and from somewhere near at hand came the sound of hens. Cypresses guarded the area like sentinels. There were tables and benches at the front and two elderly men were playing a board game at one of them. They did not look up when Edmund drew to a halt but when Hester got out of the car they jumped to their feet.

'Madame . . .' They almost bowed and then directed her and the car round to the back of the building and one of them went inside to alert the manager. Sally said delightedly to Edmund, 'Travel with royalty and you get treated like royalty!'

Hester came back to them. 'That was odd. It was as if they remembered me – surely that's not possible?'

'Of course not.' Edmund pushed the door wide for her. 'You have a presence, dear Aunt Hester. Regal . . . just as Sally said. Hop in quickly and watch your coronet, for Pete's sake! I need to get the car out of the sun before the radiator boils over.'

So they settled into the Pension Provençal as if they had indeed been there before. The rooms were thick-walled, deep embrasures to each window, furnished sparsely but adequately. The shared bathroom boasted a pedestal bath on a platform, a shower one end, a lavatory the other. The tiled floor sloped down to a drain in the middle of the room; the tiny window was without glass and screened by an arrangement of dried flowers. Outside and immediately behind the bar were the dining room and kitchen. Sally rushed around ecstatically.

'This is really France!' she carolled from the pump, sniffing whatever was cooking in the kitchen. 'We're really abroad! We're here! In France. Provence. Where the romantics wrote their poems! Oh Hester – I do love you!'

Unexpectedly Edmund frowned at her. 'Listen, young Sal. We're here for Hester – we know that. Let her now be free of all our mixed-up feelings. Don't put anything else on her. At all. Whatsoever. Understood?'

'Understood,' she said, just as unexpectedly subdued.

'So, we eat our dinner. We have a good night's sleep. Tomorrow we decide what we're going to do. Understood?'

Hester and Sally spoke together. 'Understood.'

Duggie Marsden knew that he had never been so happy. He was not an adventurous man, yet in the last year he had become the chairman of a private railway and had married a woman who was at once shocking, beautiful, generous and . . . experienced. He had been prepared to marry Enid and become her surrogate father but he had known from the outset, as he knelt by Hattie while she gave birth, that no man on earth was a father-figure to her. She had no idea who her father was anyway and her grandfather had stood in for him

319

admirably, so she had never missed him, never wanted a replacement. What she wanted was a man she could care for, much as she cared for Edmund and Perry. She did not ask him to give up his freedom, change his opinions, change himself in any way; she simply wanted him there. And she wanted to sleep with him.

Duggie admitted to himself that he had been nervous about the sexual side of this marriage. Hattie had experience; he had very little. But he had had complete faith in her and had put himself in her hands. She had said, 'It's like dancing, darling Duggie. But you must let me lead for a while. Just until I stop feeding Millie. A slow foxtrot, darling, for a few weeks. And then –' She laughed. 'The paso doble! The tango!' He laughed too. He had continued to laugh a great deal, which was unusual for Duggie Marsden.

Their honeymoon was idyllic. They 'pulled up the drawbridge', as Hattie said, and Leckhampton House became Eden for the first two weeks in September. They established a loose routine to suit Millie and discovered it suited them just as well. Duggie had a feeling that any routine Hattie devised would suit them all, but this one was delightful. While Hattie fed Millie, he cobbled together a breakfast tray and took it upstairs. He had to pause in the bedroom doorway, not only to get his breath but to marvel at the sight of Hattie still nursing the baby, her frilly nightdress framing a picture that was worthy of Leonardo himself. Most days Millie had dropped off to sleep by that time, but Hattie still held her, knowing what pleasure it gave to him. Then she would say, 'Hello, husband,' and he would say hoarsely, 'Hello, wife,' and then he would put the tray on the dressing table, take Millie from her and settle her back into her cot for a nap before bath time. Hattie would hold out her arms and he would carefully lie by her side and let her enfold him. They did not make love at night; Hattie was often bone-tired and asleep before he came out of the bathroom. But after the six o'clock feed she declared herself a new woman and wanted to start the new day in a new way. And amazingly, incredibly, she found a new way.

Always afterwards, he told her how much he loved her and that he could hardly believe this was happening to him. And she would snuggle into his shoulder, smiling, accepting this turn of events as she accepted everything. She could have said, 'A year ago I was married to another man who loved me – I know that – but who was also attracted to a younger and more beautiful woman than me. And now I am here with his child and with you.' But Hattie had never believed in facing facts and she did not do so now. When things like Edmund's conception, Percy's . . . dalliance, or Enid's terrible battering floated to the surface of her mind, she found something that immediately needed her attention. During her second honeymoon it was always breakfast.

'That tea will be getting cold! Oh darling boy, you know I can't bear orange juice.'

Without fail he said, 'I put the tea cosy on, darling, so that the tea wouldn't get cold. And please drink your juice. Just for me.'

And she did.

For the first time in his life Duggie was delighted he had money. He wanted to spend it on Hattie and Millie.

'What about this new plane, Hattie?' He looked up from the newspaper on their third morning when she brought Millie downstairs for her mid-morning cuddle. 'D'you fancy a trip in her? I'm not sure about the French half, mind. I mean, we know what happened with the Entente Cordiale so why should the Concorde be different? But I'm happy to give it a try if you would like it.'

'But why?' She was wide-eyed with surprise. 'We've got everything we want here. Why on earth should we go on a plane trip?'

He had known that was what she would say but he couldn't get enough of it. She told him for at least the third time that she had done all the travelling she had wanted to do during the war but if he was keen . . . ? He reassured her.

'I'll go and make the coffee in a minute,' he said comfortably.

'That would make everything perfect,' she said with a sigh.

At Lypiatt Bottom the contentment was not quite so over-whelming but after the cold war of the early summer it was still there. Nell had an extra two weeks' holiday because the new heating system at the school had run into trouble. She had already said her goodbyes to Edmund and Hester and though it was good to be so close to her parents again she could not help feeling she was delaying their return to the Pumpkin Line. Then Shirley phoned to say she and her Darren were sharing a flat in the middle of Birmingham and she would catch the seven forty-five to North Heath each morning and everything would be the same.

'How marvellous!' Nell spoke over a slightly sinking heart: there would be no more bicycle rides with Shirley into the Lickey Hills.

'It will be, Nell. Wait till you see him! He really is God's gift to women – not that I intend sharing him but—'

'I get the message. Lucky you.'

That afternoon her mother suggested they should all go down to the Pumpkin Coach and take a picnic. 'The last summer picnic of the year,' she said. 'This weather can't go on for ever.'

'Aren't you still a bit overcrowded down there with all the volunteers?' Nell demurred.

'Not too many in the week. And they're working beyond the coach.' Val grinned encouragingly. 'Come on. We could swim, it's quite warm enough.'

So they went.

Nell was surprised at how much had happened since she had been there last. It was just three months; a traumatic three months for her, during which she had come to terms with so much. She had hated her mother for taking away the man she had thought to be her father; hated her even more for taking away the man she had thought she loved. But long before Alice had talked to her properly, she had known in her heart that Valentine Ryecroft was her father – how could it be otherwise? And that meant Mo was still Michael Adair. She had shelved that thought because there were other, far more serious concerns about Michael Adair. And as time went on they would seem to be valid too; when he went to America wasn't that his final message to her and to the whole family?

And then there had been Hattie's incredible wedding. Twice during the wedding party she had thought she saw him. It hadn't been him, of course, any more than it had been him at the Lynx Hotel last Christmas. But until she had verified that, as she had done then, she could not entirely discount the possibility that he had come home.

That night, after the wedding, when her parents had gone to bed, she walked restlessly round the house, trying to recall the brief time last year when the attraction between them had surely been stronger than any hateful, vengeful plans he might have made. Even that very first time at the theatre, when their eyes had met and locked behind Uncle Edward's substantial back, even then he must have known and abandoned the idea that he could use her in some way to devastate her mother? But then there had been the quick and horrible groping in Aunt Hattie's garage ... the deliberate tricks he had played on Alice ... and then, so strangely, the cold shoulder he had turned to her when they had gone to look at the Pumpkin Coach. He must have known her intention in taking him there – he must have known the legend of the coach. All right, she should not then have let Perry seduce her ... and he hadn't even done that, they had simply come together ... But if Mo had been serious he would have come after Perry, knocked him down just as he had done in the summer house that time. And instead he had worked like a maniac on his presentation, landed a super job thousands of miles away and ... gone. Leaving a mess behind him that might well be his idea of revenge.

She groaned aloud, then stopped herself and crept through the kitchen and into the garden. The scents were heady, the tobacco plants still lingered, the roses and the early chrysanthemums . . . She could see the dahlias through the darkness, plates of blossom that nodded to her in the faint breeze. And Mrs Mearment's house was in complete darkness.

She said aloud, 'Why should he be here? You know very well he is in America. He is *not here* – get it into your skull, woman!' The 'sightings', as she now called them, were the kind of things her mother must experience . . . or rather, suffer from. The Pettiford Curse.

Yet, when her father suggested a picnic at the coach, she knew that there was still some stupid idea in her head: he would be there. It was his place as much as anyone's – more. But whether it would be the real him or an illusion conjured up by her poor fevered brain – a phantasmagoria – she did not know.

Hester made one stipulation: she would go alone to the farmhouse, unannounced and completely alone. Both Edmund and Sally tried to persuade her to accept their support. 'Hessie, there are a lot of snags – whether we go together or alone.' Edmund went so far as to take her hand. 'It could be really embarrassing . . . If Hermione is around we may not be at all welcome. And there are the twins too. And supposing Richard isn't there? He could have gone to Nice or Grasse or anywhere. My God, he might even have gone home!'

'That's not likely after all this time,' Hester said. 'He would have phoned anyway.' She smiled at the two of them anxious on her behalf. Even without Richard she no longer felt isolated and wondered how she could have imagined she was. Edmund and she knew they were related so the new bond was very strong; but Sally, supposedly 'in love' with her, was a different thing altogether. Hester sighed and wished that the girl's adoration would soon consolidate into a sensible and deep friendship.

It was Sally who surrendered first. 'All right then. Edmund and I won't sit at home and worry. We'll climb to the top of the valley and look down the other side.'

'It's another valley. The ridges run straight down to Nice. Why don't you go to Grasse and visit the parfumeries?'

'*Bonne idée!*' Sally said, emphasizing her Gloucestershire French. 'I could buy some perfume. Perhaps if we went bearing gifts . . . ?'

'Let's see how Hester gets on first of all,' Edmund temporized.

So the next day they split up. Edmund drove south, dropped Hester practically outside the farmhouse and then he and Sally went on in the general direction of the coast. Hester took the grass-choked steps down the side of the valley until she came into the lemon grove that gave the name Maison des Citrons to the old farmhouse.

Nothing seemed changed. From this level she could not see the new verandah that they had spotted from the road, nor the pool. The front of the house was like a child's drawing, a door in the middle, two windows on either side of it and a chimney stack sprouting from the roof. She could remember her disappointment when she had first seen it after the tedious journey from Calais; the Tibbolts had been thrilled. They had bought it for a song before the war and had been delighted to find it still intact afterwards. The pool, new then, had been excitedly discussed on the journey.

Hester avoided the front door; it was rarely opened in the old days. She went to the left-hand side of the house where a trellised gate opened with just as much difficulty – she remembered it had to be lifted free of the paving beneath it – and followed the path round to the back where a short flight of steps led to the verandah. Four chairs were ranged at intervals along its length and Toby Tibbolt was crouched before the middle one with a paintbrush and a tin of varnish. He did not immediately see her, which gave her time to study him as objectively as she knew how. After the last meeting she had imagined how the twins might be, ensconced with both parents in this idyllic place. She had pictured a pottery, carefully set up by Richard and inspired by the artistic Hermione; or a studio built on to the back of the house, or among the neglected vines. But not this. A very ordinary young man, no longer gaunt, long hair curling round his ears, very long fingers grasping a paintbrush, dressed in smudged jeans and what looked like one of his father's old shirts. What was more, occupied – deeply – in a very mundane task. While she was still staring, one of the doors opened and Eve backed out clutching a tray to her chest. 'Coffee up!' she carolled, put the tray on one of the other chairs, turned and saw Hester. At exactly the same time – had they always been synchronized? – Toby glanced up to smile at his sister and saw her too. The unnerving thing was, neither of them jumped or looked in the least surprised. They simply froze into their positions and returned her stare.

She said, much as she had said before at the squat in Bristol, 'May I come in?' And when neither of them spoke, she climbed the three steps to the verandah and walked towards them.

Still Toby did not move but Eve scrabbled the tray on to the floor and drew the chair forward.

'The others are wet,' she said. 'They take ages to dry. Toby is on the last one and then we'll have somewhere to sit again.'

'Thank you, Eve.' Strangely, Hester was definitely tired and almost fell into the chair. She remembered being exhausted after their last short meeting. She said, 'I'm here with my nephew and a friend. They went to Grasse. I wanted to . . . see the house again. And you of course.'

There were just two mugs on the tray. Surely if Hermione or Richard had been there, Eve would have made coffee for them? She added, 'All of you, that is.'

Eve glanced at Toby and he put his brush into a jar of what smelled like turps, wiped his hands on the sides of his jeans and sat back on the floor of the verandah. He said flatly, 'Ma couldn't take it any more. She gave up Solange to try to make things work here. She's gone back to her. Dad's in hospital in Nice.'

Hester felt her eyes dilate. 'Why?' she asked.

'Ma loves Sollie. She's been with her for a long time. Probably that's why we're queer. It's in the genes.' He smiled briefly. 'Yes, I know you're asking why Dad is in hospital. It's just that you need to know other things first . . . We don't think Mum is a criminal. We love her very much. And we saw Dad desperately trying to hold everything together until Evie and I sorted ourselves out. He seemed to think if Mum and he were together we would –' he wrinkled his nose and spoke with assumed distaste – 'we would "sort ourselves out". That's what he said. Poor old Dad.'

Eve said suddenly, 'I'll get another cup. Hang on.' She disappeared back into the house. Toby looked up at Hester and pressed his lips into a wry smile.

'Dad has very set ideas. And he's not very good at accepting anything that isn't what he sees as normal. How do you feel about that?'

'Astounded. We were together for a long time. And he knew my father was a madman. A sadist. A would-be killer at the end.'

'Yes. He can bend his own rules sometimes.'

'But . . . what has happened? I thought he was staying out here because everything had . . . sorted itself out . . . and he was happy.'

'No. The funny thing is he got Evie and me on to the domestic bits . . . We've painted the house. I know you didn't notice so don't pretend you did. We've done the inside as well. Most of this verandah thing was us too.'

Eve backed out through the door again and handed Hester a mug of coffee. She smiled. 'He thought it would be a kind of punishment. But we've loved it. We've really loved it. And Mum kept laughing at him. And then she said she'd had enough. And when he realized that Sollie had been waiting for her in Nice all this time, knowing that his attempt at happy families would collapse . . . well, that's when it happened.'

327

Hester took the mug and thanked the girl. She was also in jeans and a shirt. They both looked well. Eve said flatly, 'Dad snapped. He hit Mum. Mum screamed at him and took the kitchen knife and stabbed him.'

Hester felt her eyes stretch – her whole face stretch – in horror. She tried to speak and stammered so badly her questions were incomprehensible.

Toby spoke quickly. 'He's all right. Really. She got him in the shoulder. Left side so he can still write and things. But it will take time.' He glanced at Eve. 'It's the end, of course. It was before but . . . well, you know.'

Eve said eagerly, 'We wanted him to write to you but he said you'd feel bound to come and look after him and he really can manage . . . but . . . here you are!'

'Don't push it, Eve. She's here on holiday.' Toby looked back at Hester. 'Obviously Dad's not bringing charges. Sollie went to see him and he told her she was welcome to Mum. Sollie and Mum came home, told us he was OK, asked us if we were OK. We said yes. They took a lot of stuff plus the car and went.' He shrugged. 'We're almost thirty. We're clean now.' He grinned as if it were a joke. 'We're a – a unit. More than a couple, more than twins. A unit. And we're right into this nesting thing. It must be the stage we're at.'

Hester forced herself to sip the coffee slowly and breathe deeply. She could almost feel her brain spinning inside her head. She could not think of a thing to say.

Toby picked up his own mug and drained it dry. He said, 'Look. Mum's got a thing about women's rights. Everything Dad does, she sees as an aggressive act. The atmosphere was terrible. Dad snapped. She snapped. It's no good sitting there judging anyone or anything.'

Eve said, 'You understood things before. When you came to Bristol that time. We were impressed.'

Hester willed her mind to slow down. She held her mug in both hands and said, 'I do understand. Honestly. So long as he's going to be all right.' She summoned a small smile. 'How are you two? That's the important thing. Are you coping?'

Toby spread his hands. 'You can see. We love them both but we can't live with them. This . . . here and now . . . it's heaven. It's just . . . heaven.'

'You're still in love.'

He said again, 'You can see. Did you think it was a fad or something?'

'No. But . . . what will you do?'

'You mean, how shall we manage without handouts?'

'I didn't mean that. Your father will never cast you off without a penny.' She tried to smile and could not.

'That's what he says he is going to do. We can have the house so long as we do not sell it or mortgage it. But no allowance. We have to earn a living.'

'Can you do that?'

'Easily. We can sleep rough every summer and let it to the tourists.'

Eve said quickly, 'But we don't want to do that. We want to make a home. We quite liked the squat, you know. But it wasn't ours.'

Toby said slowly, 'We're going to try to farm the place. There are eight acres of land here. The vines are run down but they gave a small yield this year. There's an old chap further up the valley who might help us if we let him live in the barn.' He grinned. 'Sounds mad . . . The sixties have gone. We know that. But there were some good things to come out of them. Living close to the land was one of them.'

Hester lowered her eyes; she was very close to tears. This was the sort of dream she had had as a very small girl; Mother and Val and herself in a cottage in the country, away from everyone else.

Toby gave a tentative questioning cough and Eve said, 'She's thinking up all the snags. Just like Dad.'

Hester lifted her head and they saw the tears. 'I think it's marvellous. Of course there are snags. You might have to change course at some point. But that doesn't make it less marvellous.'

They stared at her. Eve said, 'It's a dream you had as a kid.'

Hester managed a smile. 'Actually, yes. But this is so . . . practical. You don't feel beholden to anyone – after all, this is your home and it doesn't sound as if your mother wants it any more. I don't know about your father . . . I don't know much about your father.' She drooped, then rallied immediately. 'You've got a means of livelihood in this place. You've worked on it already. You've found what you want to do. Not many of us are that lucky, you know.'

Eve said impulsively, 'Will you have some lunch with us? It's only *casse-croûte* – we cook something in the evenings.'

Hester thanked her and then immediately stood up. 'May I have a look round? I know a little bit about vines. I'd like to see them. I've got an easy term this autumn – lots of free periods. I could read up things, let you know . . . if you wouldn't mind. I mean, I don't want to interfere or anything, but I've got time and access to a jolly good library.' She needed desperately to be by herself.

They exchanged that communicative stare again and then nodded in unison. 'It would be marvellous. An objective view,' said Eve.

'Do you want company?' asked Toby.

'No. I would like to be by myself.'

They did not look offended; of course they must know about her previous visit, perhaps they even remembered it. She flushed as she went back down the verandah steps and took the path to the pool. How long ago, how overdramatic, how *stupid* it had been.

Nell swam in between her parents; Val on her left, Alice on her right. They swam quietly as if not wanting to disturb the glassy surface of the pool. They had driven to the Orchard engine shed and found Bert hard at it cleaning the *Devon Belle.*

'Taking years off me, this is,' he told them, climbing from the footplate with obvious difficulty. 'New lease of life. Reason for being here for a bit longer.'

'A lot longer please, Bert,' Val said. 'You're the only driver, you know.'

'It's a question of understanding zackly what is 'appening in 'er belly,' Bert pontificated. 'Same as with all of us. Belly all right, body all right.'

Nell grinned. 'And is *Belle*'s belly all right?' she asked.

'No need to be pert, young woman!' Bert gave her a look of disapprobation that came as a bit of a shock to Nell. Most of his generation had known her parents and approved of them and she expected that approval to stretch to her as well. As she watched her father going round the locomotive, it occurred to her that Bert had probably known Joe Adair as well as Valentine Ryecroft. She heard her father's unmistakable voice say something about 'the boy'. Then Bert's reply: 'Why would 'e keep in touch with me, Mr Ryecroft?' Then her father: 'I don't know, Bert. I don't know much when it comes to the crunch!'

Now, swimming so gently through the dark waters of Bracewell's Pool, she knew, with a small jump of panic, that she and Mo shared that 'not knowing' with her father. With her mother too. They shared this sense of being just slightly out of touch with something . . . something important. Something to do with their joint past . . . something so powerful that it almost excluded other relationships.

Her father, swimming beside her, cleared his throat. Alice and Nell turned their heads in the water to look at him. He said diffidently, 'I just want to say something. You know it already, but now and then . . . I love you. I don't ever want you to have doubts about that. Alice . . . you made a life for me. And Nell, you celebrate that life. You do know that, don't you?'

Her mother whispered, 'Yes. I know it. I feel exactly the same.' Her murmur was amplified by the water, hit the trees and came back to them as clearly as the chime of a bell.

Nell said, 'That's lovely. Both of you.' She shipped some water into her mouth and spat it out vigorously. 'You know I echo it with all my heart. But . . . why now – when we're swimming – why?'

Val waited for the echo to come back to them and then said, 'Because we never know when we are being given our last chance.'

She yelped with horror and the clearing, even the Pumpkin Coach behind them, shook with sound. And then she caught her father's eye and started to laugh and they all came together in a tight knot, hugged each other, sank below the surface, came up spluttering and began to swim back.

And it was then that Nell saw him, disappearing into the trees beyond the coach, a pickaxe over one shoulder. She expected the usual sense of unreality, of shock, even of anger, but none of those feelings even touched her. She felt relief. Because now she knew that he was here. Close. Somewhere.

That night, when Alice got up from saying her prayers at the window, she said to Val, 'You saw him too, didn't you?'

'Yes. And it wasn't Joe. It was Michael. He wasn't a ghost, I promise.'

She looked surprised. 'I knew that, darling. But why do you think he has come back?'

'I wrote to him, love. I wrote to him about the spur line. Asked his advice.'

'Bert knew he was around,' she said thoughtfully, getting into bed.

'Yes.'

'But he doesn't want us to know.' She looked at him. 'He doesn't want Nell to know.'

'No.' He sounded terribly sad.

'She's forgiven him, Val. We must try to speak to him. Tell him that.'

'I'm fairly certain it's not that way round, Allie. I rather think it's himself he can't forgive.'

She said, 'Perhaps it's not meant to be.' She looked at him. 'Like before.'

He smiled at her. 'Not really, my love. We were always meant to be. Don't you remember I asked you to marry me when you were only sixteen?'

'I said no,' she breathed.

'But you didn't mean it. Did you?'

He climbed in beside her and held her against his shoulder. She smiled and kissed his throat. 'I suppose . . . looking back . . . no.' She remembered Gran's words as if from another life. 'You are my last love,' she whispered.

Downstairs, Nell, always the last to bed these days, read through what she had written on her Basildon Bond from last Christmas.

> Dear Mo. I know you are there. You seem to be everywhere.
> If you still love me then meet me in the garden tomorrow
> night at ten thirty. If you are not in love with me any longer,
> then meet me in the garden tomorrow night at ten thirty. I
> love you. More than ever.
> Yours, Nell Ryecroft.

She put the sheet of paper into its matching envelope and sealed it, then went into the garden, climbed the fence and posted it through Mrs Mearment's letter box. It was pitch-black, starless, moonless, not a light on in Mrs Mearment's house. Nothing had changed, not really. Yet Nell felt her old confidence rising inside her. She smiled and went back to bed.

Duggie said, 'Not a bad honeymoon. I've nothing to compare it with, of course, but it seems fairly . . . perfect.'

The tray was on the dressing table, the teapot under its cosy, the orange juice waiting next to the toast rack.

Hattie said dreamily, 'It will be cold tea this morning, darling. I didn't know you could do . . . that.'

Duggie said, 'Neither did I.' He opened his eyes and focused on the face so close to his. It was still beautiful though in close-up the creamy skin was a myriad of tiny wrinkles and the hair – why did anyone think it was still gypsy-black when it was so coarsely threaded with grey? And why did women mind so much about lines and grey hair when both could combine into a beauty that was so much more interesting than the blandness of youth?

Duggie whispered, 'Shall I pour?'

And Hattie, who had always known the right thing to say, whispered back, 'Not yet. Let's savour this moment, my dearest husband.'

Duggie felt the tears in his throat and swallowed convulsively. He too closed his eyes and tried to imagine what his face would look like to Hattie if she studied it. His mind drifted happily along the lines of spring, summer, autumn and winter. Hattie was a wonderful autumn, still glowing with colour, whereas he was definitely winter. Millie was not even spring yet. Millie was . . . perhaps Millie was there representing poor Percy. Who, incidentally, had turned out to be very lucky Percy. Because of Hattie. Just as he was very lucky Duggie because of Hattie. And perhaps Millie was part of Percy's gift. To Duggie. His thoughts were becoming just a little muddled; he realized that when an image of the cupola he had seen from Northgate Street imposed itself on Percy's imagined face.

Next to him, almost in his ear, Hattie gave a gentle snore and Duggie, full of contentment, smiled and let himself drift into sleep.

Twenty-seven

When Mo did not appear the next night at ten thirty, Nell could not believe it. She waited for an hour then went back into the house; the weather was definitely autumnal and she could not get warm in bed. She got up again and went outside and prowled the garden and then climbed over the fence and circled Mrs Mearment's house too. Quarter past midnight chimed from Lypiatt Bottom's old church; naturally all Mrs Mearment's windows were dark, not even a chink of light anywhere. She stood, looking up at the bedroom where he'd slept before, and wept. Now, with that letter, even the tattered remnants of her pride had gone.

She went back inside and while the kettle was boiling she scribbled another note and ran over to Mrs Mearment's front door with it. It said simply, 'I think your revenge is complete now.' She did not sign it. She came back, made herself a cup of cocoa and a hot-water bottle and went back to bed.

A week later Hester, Edmund and Sally arrived home just in time for Millie's christening. They called at Lypiatt Bottom on their way into the city and gave a hasty sketch of their time in Provence. It sounded completely crazy to Nell; she looked at Sally's flushed and vibrant face, Hester very quiet and somehow complete and dear Edmund trying to be all things to both of them, and knew she could not tell any of them about Mo. In fact she could never tell anybody because it made him sound so dreadful and she could not have borne to hear him criticized.

After they had gone, Alice said doubtfully, 'Hester was awfully quiet. I didn't quite understand about Richard Tibbolt's injury – did Sally actually say a kitchen knife? There must have been some kind of accident. And of course poor Hester had to come home, with term starting next Tuesday.'

Val said reassuringly, 'But didn't you notice that with the typical Hester stillness went a confidence – a quiet confidence?'

Alice said, 'So you think they might get back together? When he comes out of hospital?'

'Possibly. It doesn't matter. She's got hold of some answers from somewhere. Laid the past to rest? I don't know.'

Nell said almost sadly, 'She certainly knows who she is, doesn't she? And I think – perhaps for the first time – she's happy with who she is.'

Val said, 'Is that what you want for yourself, Nell? It's difficult for Hester because of the kind of father we had. But I never forget the kind of mother we also had and then . . . my wife.' He smiled at the formality then was serious again. 'Don't tell me Hester's anxiety has come down to you, my darling girl? Does it worry you that your grandfather was . . .' he purposely did not use the word 'mad' but said instead, '. . . completely ga-ga?'

'Of course not. I used to show off about it at school.' Nell forced a grin. 'But in some ways I'm very like Hester. And I envy her that . . . what did you call it, Dad? Quiet confidence.'

'You're too young for quiet anything!' he joked. But he remembered Alice, younger than Nell now, almost careworn.

Millie's christening took place during the morning service at Leckhampton church. Already, at only two months old, she seemed able to observe the world around her and when the vicar, on behalf of all the congregation, welcomed her into their midst, she stared at them all over Nell's shoulder and, after a slight frown, smiled beatifically. There were a few laughs, and then the vicar began to clap and everyone joined in. It was Millie's first applause and it was quite obvious she enjoyed it. Afterwards, Hester said dotingly, 'She's going to be a performer, like her mother!'

The christening lunch was brief: Nell was returning to Birmingham the next day, Edmund and Sally were taking some of Sally's stuff to her room at St Hilda's; and even Mrs Marvel wanted to get away early so that she could inspect the work her sister had done at Hester's little house in the cathedral close.

'Mr and Mrs Marsden didn't want me for the past two weeks, Miss Ryecroft,' she explained to Hester. 'So I was able to show her the ropes the first week, then I let her do it on her own last week. I just want to check that your freezer is well stocked—'

'Mrs Marvel.' Hester smiled, realizing that not even her cleaning lady had really deserted her. 'I've been back home since Friday evening. Everything is fine. It's as if you never left me.' Her smile widened. 'Well, it sounds as if you haven't yet! Thank you so much for being concerned.'

Mrs Marvel flushed. 'I felt awful about it all,' she admitted. 'But to tell the truth, I never really felt needed at your house. You could have managed perfectly all right without me.' She shook her head as Hester began to protest. 'You know what I mean, Miss Ryecroft. I am certainly needed here!' They both laughed and Hester nodded.

'Thank you for everything anyway. And for fixing me up with . . . what shall I call her, Mrs Marvel?'

'Well, her maiden name was Margaret Mallow. She got married to a man who left her after three weeks. She calls herself Mallie. Could you manage that, Miss Ryecroft? It seems to cover everything somehow.'

Hester felt a prick of interest. She knew nothing of Mrs Marvel, had never been curious. Now she had someone whose history she knew immediately.

She said, 'Mallie. Yes, I can manage Mallie.'

Everyone went out on to the drive to wave goodbye to Sally and Edmund. Edmund leaned out of the car. 'This seems peculiar, Hessie. We've been like the three musketeers over the past few days. Are you going to be all right?'

'Of course. Teachers' meeting tomorrow. Back to the grind. For you too.'

'Yes. But it turned out to be a wonderful holiday. Thanks.'

Hester looked past him. 'For you too, Sally?'

'I can't believe it's over.' Sally had her drowned look. 'I don't go up for good for another week. Why can't I come to see you?'

'You need practice. We all do.'

Edmund lifted his hand to his mother, kissed the plump cheek of his sister as it was thrust through the car window, then glanced across at Nell standing next to Perry. 'Good luck with next term!' he called.

'Thanks, Ed.'

'Good luck yourself!' said Perry meaninglessly.

They were gone. Alice and Val took Hester and Mrs Marvel off. Perry was going to show Nell the work he had done on his 'flat'. At last the house was quiet again.

'It's only three o'clock!' Hattie discovered, amazed.

'It seemed an age, didn't it?'

'Yes. Yes it did,' she said, still surprised. 'Oh darling, I hope I'm not becoming a recluse! That wouldn't do at all! I want to show you and Millie off to the world.'

'Tell you what . . .' He took Millie to her pram and settled her among the spread nappies. 'Let's take a walk round the garden and plan our autumn.' They began a sedate tour, more or less a lap round the tennis court, made interesting – for Millie, Duggie maintained – by his running commentary.

'Through the dark wood,' he announced thrillingly as they entered the shrubbery. 'And past the prison compound,' inserted Hattie as they came close to the tall wire fence of the tennis court. They both giggled foolishly.

Duggie paused, rocking the pram gently. 'If Perry really has made a good job of the attics, we could have the rest done up, darling. You could choose papers, fabrics, furniture . . . What do you say?' Hattie flashed her eyes delightedly. 'And then at Christmas there are always carols. We could get a part-time nanny for Millie and go to the concerts at the cathedral . . . You could have coffee with the girls and I could go on with my investigative work on the city . . .'

'Duggie, it sounds wonderful. And it might stop me from becoming a recluse!'

Duggie pushed the pram on towards the summer house and the few apple trees behind it, euphemistically called the orchard. 'The field of magic apples,' he said to Millie as she reached up clutching hands.

'Not just the apples!' Hester almost sang. 'Everything, darling! Everything will be magical when you're with Mummy and Daddy!'

Suddenly Duggie was weeping. And then, as she clasped him to her, so was Hattie. Millie set up a wail that might well disturb the neighbourhood for miles. They both gathered her into themselves and began to laugh. And then it was the very first time they had heard Millie laugh. It was enough to make anyone weep all over again.

Perry flung open the attic door with a 'Terrrrumm!' and stood back for Nell to get a full view. He had painted everything either yellow or orange. The cupboards were picked out in both colours. The carpet was what he called burnt umber. Only the black cast-iron grate was different.

'Well, what do you think, coz?'

He was surprisingly nervous; he wanted her approval. She gave it unstintingly. 'Oh Perry! It's beautiful! Like a burst of sunshine! Won't it be marvellous in the winter when it's snowing and bleak and grey and here you will have your own little sunny room—'

'There's more than this!' He was elated. 'I knew that if I took this first room then the others would have to be mine because Duggie couldn't expect to walk through my room to anything he might feel he wants.' He opened another door. 'See? There's a tap here. So I'm going to get the plumbers up – there's a chap I knew at school – and I'll have one of those fitted kitchens. Then he can put the piping through to here . . .' He opened another door on to a tiny box room. 'And fix me up with a bathroom.'

She was entranced. 'It's wonderful. This room is huge – and these roof lights are just so – so – artist's-studio-type thingy! You could have a long refectory table under this one and a sort of built-in sideboard to separate cooking from eating, then you could have the most marvellous dinner parties.'

'You can share it, you know.'

She sighed. 'Unfortunately I can't, Perry. Not even when we're both forty and no one else wants us. Sorry, coz. I've led you up the garden!'

'Not really. I went off you ages ago. But what do you think?'

'About the attic? Wonderful. But you'll have to pay a proper rent to Duggie. Seriously. Otherwise it's not yours and you're just sponging again.'

'Try to be straight with me, Nell. This velvet glove thing is getting me down!'

'Sorry, sweetie. But someone has to talk to you properly and we started a long time ago, didn't we?' She grinned. 'Listen, where are you going to sleep? A convertible tucked under the sloping roof in the living room?'

He grinned back. 'Well. Ackcherly, sweet coz, on the other side of the landing there's this accommodation all over again. D'you think I dare pinch more?'

'Put it to Dug, Perry. Seriously now. He's crazily happy with your ma and he'll listen and I think when he sees what you've done here . . . In fact wait until the kitchen and bathroom are finished and then . . .'

'Yes. OK. I suppose you wouldn't put in a word for me?'

'Of course I will if you think it will help – though I honestly don't think you need it. But still . . . Oh, it's lovely, Perry. Well done! I wish I had come and grabbed a paintbrush now, I'd love to have had a hand in this.'

'Here's another bargain then. If we get Duggie to agree, you can help me with the other half. How's that?'

'I could swoon with delight!'

'Come and poke your head out of this skylight. I'll take the one next to it.' He opened up the two windows and they both wedged themselves through. 'What do you think of the view?'

She stared. Opposite was Gloucester's school of art, the museum, the library. Slightly to the left was the almost-new technical college. Behind both it was still possible to see the old Greyfriars. She turned, and there was the park diagonally cut in half by the pitch of the roof. Below her line of vision she knew was the old railway running to the docks and the war memorial. Everything was russet red with beech leaves and she remembered scuffing through them in crocodile formation as a schoolgirl, on her way to the swimming baths. She was suddenly lost in a welter of memory and gripped the edge of the skylight as if she could somehow be whirled away into nothingness by the force of the past.

Perry said quietly, 'Can't you tell me what it's all about, Nell?'

She jumped and turned to face him again and force a grin. 'Not really. It sounds so . . . trivial.'

'You told Edmund.'

'Did he tell you?'

'Of course not. You know he wouldn't.'

'There was something to tell then. Something to get in a state about. Or so I thought. Now it's . . . just being in love with the wrong person. That's all.' She smiled properly at him, then craned her neck until she could see the tower of the cathedral. 'This really is marvellous, Perry. Thank you for bringing me here. It sort of helps to see things in perspective.'

'Oh God. Another of Ed's adages – how come he's . . . who he is, and I'm who I bloody well am?'

She laughed. 'And I am so horribly . . . me!'

Perry squeezed an arm through his window and reached a hand across the tiles so that she was unable to turn away.

'You're not horrible, Nell. Not a bit. If that's all Ed gave you then – well, he's an idiot. Which I knew already of course.' He suddenly grabbed a handful of her hair. 'Tell me now what's bugging you before I pull your hair!'

She laughed again, this time protestingly. 'Honestly, Perry, nothing to tell you that you don't already know. I'm in love with Mo Adair. And he doesn't love me. And that's it.'

'What's he done? What's he said? Something has happened, I know.'

'Lots has happened. But he's said nothing and he's done nothing.'

He gave a slight experimental tug on her hair and she yelped. He opened his hand and withdrew his arm through the skylight.

'That's it?'

'Yes.'

Then, with a flash of intuition worthy of his great-grandmother, he said, 'Like when your grandfather used to send your grandmother to Coventry? So that it becomes an aggressive act, an insult?'

She widened her eyes, surprised. 'My God. Yes. Just like that.'

Perry opened his mouth then closed it. Then he said, 'Crass fool. Bloody idiot.' He sighed. 'Come on. I'd better take you home. I know it's Sunday but we'll go via Les Fabriques. I want you to see a sofa they've got in the window. It's brown. Sounds awful but I can't have too much orange and the brown will tone it down a bit.' He wriggled away from the sloping roof and held out his hand to help her. 'It's a big one. I could sleep on it while I'm doing up the rest of the place.'

She went to the door, turned and looked at the room again. 'But not with me,' she said sadly.

His tone echoed hers. 'Not with you. No.'

Edmund delivered Sally back to Painswick at ten o'clock, refusing to come in on two counts: first, her father's glasses, and second, he needed to see Hester. The second reason silenced her protests.

She sat in the dark car, quiet for ten seconds so that he began to worry about her, then said, 'Are you going to ask Hester what happened in the hospital?'

'Yes.'

'What if it was nothing?'

'There's nothing and then there's nothing.'

'Oh, *Edmund*!' She shook his arm.

He laughed. 'You're cold. Here, take my jacket.' He reached into the back and wrapped her in an enormous anorak. She did not throw it off impatiently but said, 'Listen, I'll be outside your office at five thirty and let you have it back.'

'Will you? Don't you think you should be getting the next load ready to take up to university?'

'I've got all day for that.'

'Not quite. Hester's meeting will finish by three o'clock and you will want to be lurking near the school in good time to walk her home.'

'Sometimes you're too clever for your own good. I'm not going to see her this week. It's an act of self-denial and self-discipline.' She opened the door, half got out of the car then leaned back to peck his cheek. 'I can't believe this old jalopy went all those miles.'

'Are you referring to me?'

'Of course.' She slammed the door then opened it again. 'Ed, if you really are related to Hester then obviously you share genes.'

'First assumption is hypothetical, Sal.'

'Yes. Anyway, by the time I come down I'll be twenty-one and you only go for teenagers.'

'Quite.'

'I hate that word . . . *quite.* But quite. So we've only really got two years. Not even that.'

He lunged across the car to grab her and kiss her but she slammed the door and was gone, laughing like a hyena. He watched her use her key and skip into the lighted hall. Then he started up the car. He was still laughing as he drove slowly into the close and parked outside Hester's house.

Hester had trailed dutifully round the house after Mrs Marvel and Mallie, tried not to notice when Mallie rolled exasperated eyes above her sister's head, listened when Mrs Marvel told her about the kind of dishes that could be either frozen or left on a low gas and had known that in the future there would be none of them. Mallie would clean and she might leave some ready meals in the freezer but she would not use the cooker herself. Hester discovered that she did not mind. The prospect of devising her own meals was not unpleasant.

Finally the two women left and Hester collapsed into a chair, exhausted. The last three days had been constantly busy and, though Edmund and Sally had been as supportive as they knew how, still she was unused to being in company – however sympathetic – for so long. She put her legs on the Victorian footstool once used by her mother, and stared through the window. There must be a special evensong; people were arriving at the west door in droves. Her eyes half closed; she remembered how Val had loved going to the cathedral 'after hours', as he put it, to listen to Mr Makin playing the organ . . . the time she had gone herself and found Alice showing Joe Adair round like a proud hostess . . . the games they had played in the whispering gallery and Alice's theory that it was a jolly good lesson in communication skills . . . so much . . . Too much. Her eyes closed properly and she was asleep.

It was dark when she woke to the sound of the knocker. For a moment it was impossible to orientate herself and she had to concentrate on where she was, and what time it was and who on earth would be calling so late.

Edmund was not particularly apologetic.

'I thought I said I would call in. To let you know what Sally's room is like and so on. No? Well, sorry. But I can't go home, Hessie, have a heart. You've got a perfectly good spare room—'

'Why can't you go home?'

'Well, think of them. Turtle doves and all that. Perry's not there so I'm the complete and unabridged gooseberry, for God's sake!'

'Millie's there.'

'Millie doesn't even know about gooseberries so she doesn't count. Aren't you going to let me in?'

'Of course. I'm sorry, Edmund. I was asleep and couldn't think what was happening.'

'Well, that's good because you'll be fresh. Come and make a pot of tea and have you got any bread? I could murder a jam sandwich.'

'My God. Mrs Marvel laid on that wonderful lunch and you can think of food?' But she was already filling the kettle, taking the bread out of its crock and pointing to the fridge. 'Luckily for you, she brought down some leftovers. The rest of that quiche and some salad.' He was right, she did feel fresh after the sleep and Edmund turning up like this ... After all, he was her nephew-proper now and he needed looking after and she should learn how to look after people. She felt a small surge of excitement.

He assembled a meal and tucked in; she poured tea, took a sip then left it to cool while she went upstairs to make up the bed in the spare room. She liked the spare room; it was at the back of the house and looked over the school and the broken archways that had been an abbey once. She fetched him a glass of water and piled books on the table, drew the curtains and switched on the bedside lamp. He was Val's son; her nephew. He shared their blood and their terrible relationship with their father and because he was so nice and ordinary and played the piano and was in love with the absurd and glorious Sally Gold he vindicated all that. You could surely outgrow your own genes?

She went back downstairs and discovered him poking in the fridge for 'something sickly'. She found him a slice of lemon meringue pie, poured more tea and sat down opposite him.

'Perry isn't actually sleeping at Dug's house, is he?' she asked.

'Yes. He tells me he's sleeping in Dug's bed. They more or less kicked him out of Leckhampton House.'

'So does that mean you want to stay longer than one night?'

'It's awfully kind of you to offer, Aunt Hess—' He pretended to shield his head from blows. 'Seriously, no. I'll go home tomorrow. But it's rather late now. Besides, I wanted to talk to you.'

'Ah. Ulterior motives.'

'I suppose so. But do you realize that you visited Richard Tibbolt three times and we don't know what happened, except that he is getting better nicely and you put his mind at rest about the children and you ran into Hermione in the hospital corridor and she called him a shit and said you were welcome to him.'

'Sounds about right. There's not a lot more news really. He could go home actually but he's a bit low. In fact, he's wallowing in self-pity and I understood very well because I'd been doing the same thing.'

'You might have felt sorry for yourself but Hester Ryecroft does not wallow.'

She smiled but said nothing.

He said, 'It's not worth putting that tiny piece of pie back in the fridge. Would you like it?'

'No, thank you. You'd better eat it.'

'It's one of Mrs Marvel's triumphs. I'm really sorry my ma pinched her, Hessie. What will you do next term?'

'Her sister will clean. And I'm going to cook for myself.' She smiled again. 'I'm really looking forward to it. You must come to dinner once a week and tell me how I'm doing.'

'That's a bargain. Listen, may I come twice a week and one of the times I'll cook dinner?'

'Oh Edmund. That would be lovely. Thank you.'

He looked at her. 'So does that mean Richard is not going to come and live with you?' he said.

'How could he, my dear? He's retired. He'd be here all day on his own. It's too small for him to spread his books around if he wanted to do research or take pupils . . . We decided against it.'

346

'Hester! Don't tell me we went over there for nothing?'

'Oh no – not a bit. Not a *bit*. We had to get rid of the after-midnight thing, Edmund. I think we've done that.'

'What are you talking about?'

'You remember, the Cinderella spell that we associate with the Pumpkin Coach. Everyone who stays too long at the Pumpkin Coach is . . . well, cursed.'

'What a load of rubbish!'

'Isn't it?' She spoke almost smugly. 'Even so, we took a hotel room in Nice for the day and made sure about it.'

'You mean a short dirty weekend?' He looked really shocked and she laughed.

'Not a weekend and not a bit dirty, darling. I ought to be offended with you but I'm not. Sally will help you through that sort of thing.'

'My God, you are so condescending!'

'Sorry, Edmund. I don't mean to be. You wanted to know what happened and why it happened and I've told you.' Almost idly she had been removing the pins from her hair and collecting them on the edge of the table. Suddenly it all fell about her shoulders and she raked it through with her fingers and then shook it back. She grinned at him. 'They all thought I'd been sent by providence to cheer him up. So I did.'

He drew his mouth down in pretended disapproval. 'And now . . . What happens to him now?'

'He's going back to the Lemon Grove – the twins have promised they will look after him. He knows one or two people who might help to get the vineyards tended properly. I have said I will read up on vines generally. I'm going there for half-term, then again at Christmas. We thought we might get a flat in Nice. There's an airport there. We can . . . manage . . . quite well.'

He stared at her. She wrapped her hairpins in a tissue, stood up and began to clear the table. Her hair seemed to double in size and fell around her face.

'So nothing was really decided.'

347

'Only the most important thing of all. That I love him and he loves me. We're both rather solitary people but gradually we might learn to live together. It's worth a try, don't you think?'

'It doesn't sound terribly romantic.'

'No? It seemed to us to be infinitely so.' She pushed one side of her hair behind her ear and looked at him. 'A series of honeymoons. That's how it seemed to us.'

He surrendered suddenly and stood up to hold out his arms. 'Oh Hester! I'm sorry – I wanted the two of you neatly married and tidied away somewhere. I'm really sorry to be a grouch.'

She went into his arms. She was overwhelmingly conscious that he was her family. He could never be acknowledged as such and that made the relationship even more precious. A secret nephew. It was as if Val had given her something of himself.

She lowered her head and pressed her forehead into his shoulder, wondering whether that was a deviant thought. And then she lifted her face and laughed up at him.

'I don't care!' she said. 'You're the son I'll never have. I love you, Edmund, and I want you to be happy for me! Can you be?'

He smiled at this beautiful creature who was his aunt.

'Oh yes. I am very happy for you. Dear Hester.' He put his hands behind her head and twisted her hair into a knot. 'The two sides of Piecrust! Richard is a lucky bloke!'

'No. I am the lucky one.' She planted a kiss on his cheek and stepped back, shaking her hair free again. 'Come on. I have a teachers' meeting tomorrow and you have work. Who does the cooking tomorrow night?'

'You'll be home before me.'

She said, 'All right. How about coq au vin?'

Twenty-eight

After Perry had taken Nell home, he could not get her obvious unhappiness out of his head and his helplessness turned into frustration and then anger. He was sure anger was the right emotion in the circumstances and he fed the flames with memories such as the incident in the summer house when the upstart Michael Adair had punched him for kissing Nell – his own cousin!

It was late afternoon of that Monday, Edmund's first day back at work since his mother's wedding. Smithers and Jameson occupied premises in Clarence Street opposite a dentist's surgery; Edmund had worked all day next to an open window because he felt stifled in the heart of the city. Unfortunately he was well within earshot of the dentist's drill. He was in no mood to conciliate his brother, who had been in the waiting room for almost half an hour and was visibly simmering.

'Where have you been?' Perry demanded, leaping to his feet. 'I went home thinking I'd find you there – Ma didn't even know where you were!'

Edmund glanced at the other occupant of the room and ushered his brother out and through the hall. Perry's latest acquisition, a bull-nosed Morris, waited at the kerb.

'You're not supposed to park down here! My God, you're lucky to get away with it.' Edmund opened the passenger door and crammed himself inside. Perry got in behind the wheel.

'You can park these vintage models anywhere – no one would dare to hand out a ticket.' Perry turned with difficulty and looked at his brother. 'What the hell are you playing at? Have you finally got into Sally's bed? It's disgusting the way you've hounded that poor girl.'

Edmund was too tired to enter into it. 'I'm with Aunt Hester,' he said. 'It was obvious Ma and Duggie wanted to be by themselves for a bit longer. What's the panic anyway?'

'No panic. Who said anything about panic? It's just that . . . oh hell. Let's go and get something to eat. I'm bloody well starving. I've been home, I've been to Aunt Alice's. I've been in that damned waiting room for hours – how you stick that place I do not know.'

They were chugging along Eastgate Street by this time. Edmund closed his eyes and said, 'I can't be long. Can you look for an off-licence? Hester's cooking tonight but I thought I'd get some decent wine.'

'Good God. Habits picked up in France, no doubt. How pretentious can you get.' Perry raised his voice to falsetto. '*Hester's cooking tonight!*' He snorted. 'How long have you been there? One night?'

'What's biting you, Perry? I'm tired, it's been a hell of a day, Sally wasn't happy with her room yesterday—'

'That's right, rub it in. Sally this and Sally that. All I ever hear from you is a cockcrow of triumph that you pipped me at the post!'

'Dammit, Perry! You know very well that Sally is not interested in either of us. She's a kid with a crush on Hester. And I haven't got a job that allows me to take time off to swan around in a vintage car so that everyone looks at me and thinks what a fellow I must be—'

'That's rich from someone just back from a foreign holiday!' Perry swerved round a line of parked cars and into Brunswick Road. Edmund opened his eyes on an incoming bus and closed them again quickly. There was a great deal of honking but that was all. They turned into the square and drew up outside Duggie's house.

Edmund said, 'I refuse to go on with this. It's ridiculous.

350

You're spoiling for something. Just tell me what the hell it is and let me get home.'

'So Hester's is home already, is it?'

'No.' Edmund looked bleakly through the windscreen. 'I don't think I've got a home now.'

Perry was stopped in his tracks, his anger immediately dissipated as it was so often. 'I know what you mean, brud. We've been turned out of the nest effectively, haven't we?'

'We are grown-up, Perry. Earning a crust – cake in your case—'

'Yes, but . . . it was all a bit sudden really, wasn't it?' Perry looked at the reflection of Edmund in the mirror and grinned wryly. Then he said, 'Come on, come and see what I'm doing upstairs. There's bags of room. I'll start on your side. It'll be great. A proper bachelor pad. I was beginning to feel lonely in it already and then – along comes you!'

Edmund found himself grinning back and following Perry up two very long flights of stairs to the attics. He was as impressed as Nell had been, more so when he saw the identical set of rooms on the other side of the landing.

'This will be your bedroom, I take it. And this . . . my God, brud! This is amazing. Like those enormous studios you hear about in New York!' Edmund strode around, opened a sky-light and looked out, then crouched and stared at Perry. 'Listen, old man, if you're serious – you're sure Duggie won't mind? We can pay him a decent enough rent between us and Mum will love having us around but not having us around, if you get me.'

Perry laughed. 'Of course I get you. God, this has made it for me. I half hoped Nell might move in but . . . Actually, Ed, Nell is why I wanted to see you. I'm worried about her.'

Edmund walked through into what would be Perry's kitchen. There were two ancient chairs and a table there. He sat down. He was bone weary.

'Yes. Well. She told me she had worked through it. And I think she has because I've been round there for meals since she was home and she seems absolutely fine.'

'You're always round there. You don't fancy Nell as well as Sally, do you?'

Edmund almost smiled but it was still too close, too painful. He wondered whether he could pass on this little gem to Hester. What a relief it would be to get back to Hester, who knew and understood.

'No. No, I don't *fancy* Nell. I've always loved her. And now, I really admire her. She was in a terrible state at the beginning of last term. And she worked her way through it.'

Perry flung himself back in his chair. 'Not good enough, Ed. I know it's the way you've always been. Softly, softly catchee monkey, all that stuff.'

'And you've been the opposite. You want instant solutions.' Edmund looked across the table with a wry smile. 'Sometimes there aren't any. Sometimes we have to live with our problems and get used to them.'

Perry hated that. He brought his fist down on the table. 'If you could have seen her last night, Ed—'

'I know what you mean.'

'I don't mean she broke down. She never let go for an instant. But she's still such a kid and she's just accepting loneliness. She thinks she's going to end up like Hester. A teacher first and a woman very much second.'

'Hester's not done too badly.'

'But Nell hasn't got that Ryecroft streak, has she?'

Edmund thought about it and shook his head slowly. 'No. She hasn't, has she?' He closed his eyes again. 'Nothing we can do, brud.'

'There's plenty I can do. And I'm going to do it too. Open your eyes and listen up!' He grinned at his own words delivered with an American twang. 'Seriously, Ed. I want to talk to our Mr Michael Adair.'

Edmund opened his eyes all right. 'You're going to the States? I know you've got the garage in your pocket, brud, but there's no way they will let you have that kind of time off work.'

'He's over here. I don't know where he's living but Nell has seen him. Down in the forest where it all seems to bloody well happen to the Pettifords – and that means us as well.'

'Yes. Of course. But . . . people in love often tend to imagine—'

'Val and Alice saw him too. They were swimming across the pool and—'

'They called out? All of them?'

'No. They let him go. He seemed to be working on the line.'

'What did Val say about it? And Alice?'

'They didn't talk about it at all.'

'So Nell does not know whether her parents saw him or not?'

'Dammit all, I'm not in a witness box, Ed! I'm telling you what Nell told me and she simply knew that they had all seen Mo. And I happen to believe her!'

'I didn't mean that I didn't *believe* her.' Edmund shook his head. 'And I didn't mean to cross-question you about it. The thing is, I have no reason to think Mo is in this country again – so soon after he took his American job. If he was, wouldn't it be to see Nell again? In which case—'

'Look. I don't know why the hell he is here but I know he is. And Nell says he's not at Mrs Mearment's, so where is he?'

'How should I know?'

'It's obvious. He's with Helena and Edward Maybury.' Perry's breathing sounded like the snorting of a dragon. 'But I've been there and nobody's in and there's no sign of his stuff—'

'You didn't go inside the house?'

'I bloody did! Searched the place from top to bottom. He's not there.'

'That's breaking and entering!'

'So it is.' Perry held out his hands, wrists together. 'So arrest me!'

Edmund sighed. 'Let's cut this out, Perry. What do you want me to do?'

'That's more like it.' Perry sat back in his chair. 'After this

353

oh-so-cosy meal with Aunt Hester, I want you to go up there and find out where he's hiding. Then let me know. I'll telephone Hester's about eleven o'clock – you should be back by then—'

'Hester goes to bed just after ten.'

'Bully for her.'

Edmund gave up. 'There'll be nothing to report, I'm telling you. But, all right. And then what will you do?'

'Go and see him. Sort it out.'

'Does that mean you're going to knock him senseless?'

'He bloodied my nose once, remember? He's due for repayment.'

'Oh, for God's sake, Perry!'

'No. Actually it will be for Nell's sake.' Perry's hand shot across the table and gripped Edmund by the shoulder quite painfully. 'Listen, brud. If you'd seen her being damned brave, being so bloody vulnerable – so hurt – so damaged—'

'All right, all right. I'll do it. It's just that I can tell you now, he won't be there and they won't know where he is.'

'Just try. That's all I ask.'

'All right. D'you want to come to Hester's for coq au vin?'

'Lord, yes. Will she mind?'

'I haven't got the faintest. Shall we try?'

'Lead the way, brud. Lead the way.'

Val drove Nell back to North Heath; she found it much harder to say goodbye to him than to Edmund. She was fine while they both humped books up the stairs and read the little note that said welcome back. But when it was time for Val to leave she clung to him and fought not to cry.

'Sorry, Daddy.' When was the last time she had called him daddy? 'It's as if I really had lost you and got you back again! And now I can't bear to let you go.'

He untwined her arms and held her where he could see her.

'Admit to me that even in your most unhappy times you never seriously thought that your mother would have passed you off as my daughter unless—'

'Yes! Because I know darned well that would be what *you* would want!'

He drew her to the mirror and turned her so that their faces were level, looking back at them.

'Can't you see? I know the obvious resemblance is the Pettiford one. But your hair is fairer, your eyes paler, and that nose . . .'

She sniffed. 'It's all right. I don't need blood tests or anything. I'm just so glad. So *glad*.'

He held her still. 'And what about Mo?' She stared back at him and then shrugged helplessly. He said, 'I'm sorry. So sorry, darling. He was there, wasn't he? At Bracewell's Pool.' She nodded, unable to trust her voice. Val held her close, his chin on top of her head. 'At some point he'll come to see me. About the new line from the engine shed. I'll try to find out . . . something.'

She forced her lips to move. 'To see you? He's come to see you?'

'I think so. I wrote to him for advice.'

She made a slight sound in her throat then turned and gripped his upper arms. 'That explains so much. Please, please, don't say anything, don't mention my name, anything. Please! I couldn't bear to see him now.' He did not ask her why. She said insistently, 'Promise me, Daddy. There's so much you don't know. It's too late now. It's over. Promise me you'll keep me out of it.'

He wrapped his long arms round her. 'If it's what you want, chick—'

'I do – really do!'

'Then I promise.'

All the way home he cursed himself for writing that letter. How was he going to face Michael Adair after that last frantic sentence? How could Mo ignore it? He had seen them swimming and had turned his back and walked away. He was breaking Nell's heart just as Joe Adair had broken Alice's. And Alice had had him to fall back on. Who was there for Nell? Certainly not Edmund. Perry? Val shook his head irritably.

And in her room, surrounded by her books and muddles galore, Nell sat and wept. He hadn't been drawn back to her at all; he had come at her father's request. She tried to imagine how sickening her provocative note must have seemed . . .

Hester was not happy to see Perry drawing up in his latest acquisition. And with Edmund too. She would have to invite him to dinner and she had catered for two normal appetites, while Perry was well known for his enormous portions. She fetched more potatoes from the larder and began to scrape them hurriedly. The trouble with Perry, he was much too much like his mother.

Three days later Bert Lewis followed Michael Adair along the fifty-odd yards of exposed track bed that led from the stabled Pumpkin Coach, followed the edge of the pool and then plunged into the part of the forest which Nature had well and truly reclaimed for herself. It was ten days since Michael Adair had started this particular line of exploration; ten days since he had run like a scared rabbit from the unexpected sight of the three Ryecrofts swimming in the pool.

The weather had changed since then. The pool no longer sparkled darkly; it was a solid black and a day of continuous rain had made the area into a quagmire. Nevertheless, the track bed had been raised with ballast many years ago and was still draining off excess water in most places. Mo, busy with pick and spade, still found time to marvel at the standard of engineering that had gone into it over a hundred years before. Bert took a different stance. 'They knew 'ow to do things in them days,' he remarked smugly.

'Thing is,' he said, standing with the sack of tools over his shoulder. 'Thing is, you know very well this yer track is gunna end afore it gets anywhere. That ole Sir Dickie whatever-'is-name-was—'

'Bracewell,' Mo supplied. He heaved the pickaxe and used it to angle out an enormous stone. Under the stone, scraped clean by it, shone another length of metal. 'Here we go again,' he added triumphantly. 'Another foot of steel! How far have we come in this past week?'

'Ten yards, I'd say. Not much further.'

'Your encouragement really keeps me going, Bert!' Mo grinned over his shoulder and Bert grinned back. Even if he'd had a son it couldn't have been as good as this.

'I'm only telling you what you knows yourself, boy. That Bracewell chap, 'e stabled his love nest where he did for a lot of reasons – the pool, the secrecy of it and . . . because it was on a branch line to a mine what even then was bloody well defunct! If you go on long enough you'll find a clearing and the state of the ground will tell you it were another open-cast job. And that's what the line was for in the first place. To serve that perticler mine. Nothing else.'

Mo stopped work and leaned on his pick handle. Sweat came from under his straight black fringe and ran down his face. Above the forest canopy it was still raining but not hard enough to penetrate the autumn foliage, and it was equatorially hot beneath the trees.

He waited till he had breath. 'What is important,' he said, 'is the direction the line takes. We'll go and make tea in a minute and I can show you the map again. If the line curves to the left . . . well, depending how far it goes . . . our ultimate ambition could be . . . I'm not sure. Kempley. Even Gorsley. I can take levels, see which routes—'

'Have you got any idea what a lot of strings 'ave been pulled so far to get lease-land? An' Mr Maybury 'ave always been able to argue that the railway were there before, already laid, even if it did 'ave to be unearthed! You're talking about a new line. Land to be bought or leased. People to see and persuade and be paid.'

'I am. It's a long-term thing. We've got to look ahead, Bert.'

'I know, my boy. That's for you and Mr Ryecroft to discuss, I reckon. He'll enjoy it, I can tell you. Likes nothing better than to get the maps out, start drawing and speckerlating.

But you can't get past the fack that 'e asked you to come and sort out the junction business. An' you 'aven't done so much as one solitary sum!'

Mo laughed. 'No. It's a waste of time, Bert. Much cheaper to build our own engine shed right next to the start of the actual Pumpkin Line. That will give us an area for waiting, buying tickets, refreshments and so on.'

'It's railway land, Mike.'

'Next to the illegal ground frame, I believe?' Mo grinned again. 'Listen, Bert. Whoever has pulled the strings for Edward Maybury will pull them harder still to get that ground frame removed. The ground frame means that we are using the main line to get to ours. Still unofficially, I believe. Without the points and the extra bit of track, there will be room enough for an engine shed. And no worries about using British Rail track any longer. They'll be delighted to pull those strings!'

Bert frowned, thinking about it. He said slowly at last, 'Aye. I reckon that's right. And we'd be independent then. Yes. That 'ud be a good thing for them as well as us.'

'And these landowners beyond our terminus . . . they might think it's a good thing to have a means of transport right through to the main line. And a tourist attraction to add to their . . .' He paused and raised his brows. 'Well, to their attractions – whatever they may be!'

Both men laughed. Then Mo shouldered his pickaxe and they trudged back towards the Pumpkin Coach, where Mo had been living since his arrival a fortnight before.

The rain was pocking the surface of the pool and the surrounding trees dripped monotonously on to the roof of the coach as they emerged into the clearing. They climbed the steps and sat just inside to remove their boots and jackets. Mo went through to the kitchen for a towel, rubbed his face and hair and flung it at Bert before lighting the calor gas stove and putting the kettle on. They both sat at the table that Bert had brought in on the *Belle* and Mo spread out his much-thumbed copy of the Severn and Wye map he and

Alice Pettiford had found over a year ago in the cellars at Hooper's Mansions. The two men bent over it with great enjoyment, tracing the old lines with grubby thumbnails. Mo encouraged Bert to tell him all the 'tall old tales' he could remember. It was a shock to hear that Nell's grandfather – Valentine Ryecroft's father, in fact – had been a director of Turner's Iron Products.

'They did some work for me on the *Belle*,' he put in.

'That's why.' Bert grinned. 'Sometimes it's quite useful to 'ave 'ad a madman around. Bit like a loose cannon rocketing all over the place. Best to be nice to the relatives . . . just in case, you know.'

'But he's dead!' Mo protested.

'Aye, but his son and his daughter are still around.' Bert shook his head as Mo started to protest. 'You know they're all right and I know they're all right. But they still might have some inside facts that Turner's don't want anyone else to know!' Bert made a crafty face and tapped his nose. 'If you can't be a saint like the Pettifords, then go right the other way!'

He laughed, but Mo, recalling Val's clear and far-seeing gaze, was still. He should have waved, called out, done *something* when he had seen them swimming all together. But the three of them . . . so together, so strong . . . He had run, hating himself again, wanting only to hide.

He said, 'I must see Val. Tell him what I suggest about the engine shed. And then get back to Michigan. I've lost my place here.'

Bert protested indignantly. 'You've made it yours! Not just yours – you've given it all back to Joe Adair. You can't go now, lad! You got to talk to that young Nell. It's the only way to put the past to rights. If you can't see that, then you're not the man I took you for and I shall get in that loco and get back to Markham an' – an' try to forget you existed! Now then!'

Mo half smiled. 'Sorry, Bert. I'm really so glad you took to my dad like you did. I wish you could have known him later – when I knew him. There's nothing to "put right", not really.

He was happy. He and my mother . . . they were so happy. I was bitter when they died together – selfishly so. Because if one had been left without the other . . . it would have been awful. So all my stupid, childish efforts to avenge Dad . . . He wouldn't even be mad with me. He'd be totally bewildered.' He looked down at the map. 'My God, Bert. What was I thinking of?'

Bert got up and made the tea. He said gruffly over his shoulder, 'Lots of folk get angry when they lose family. You were angry and you lashed out.' He set down two steaming mugs between them. 'That's why you got to patch it all up before you goes back. If you do go back.'

'I'm going back. And the more I think about it the less I need to see any of them. I can write to Val.' Mo picked up his tea. 'I'm better out of it, Bert. I just make them unhappy.'

Bert had a sudden and uncontrollable urge to take hold of the coarse black hair and bang the perfectly rounded head on the table. He reached out. And then the door flew open, and there was a cry of recognition and triumph. Perry Westbrook, soaking wet and almost completely covered in mud, stood there framed from the waist up. An avenging satyr.

It had taken Edmund two whole days to get around to trying to contact Helena. On the Monday evening he and Perry had told Aunt Hester all about the attics in Duggie's town house. She had waxed unexpectedly enthusiastic and fetched her sketch book, and it had been ten thirty before they'd had time to tell her about their ideas for running Mo Adair to ground. On the Tuesday she had gone off to school very early to talk to the new Lower Sixth and see them ensconced in their studies, and when she got home she told Perry that, as it was Edmund's turn to provide a meal, they would have to wait for him to come in and she would appreciate having sole use of the parlour so that she could revise her lesson plans. Perry had sat in the cathedral and thought unchristian thoughts about Michael Adair, and then had got talking to a very pretty girl from Canada who wanted to know all about Edward II and the way he had been murdered. 'I guess it wasn't really with a red-hot poker?' Her jeans were unfashionably pristine and her white shirt was wholesome. He wanted to rip it off and . . . 'Well, it was, actually. Or so they tell us. I'm sure that's right because my aunt always stands just there when she wants to talk to dead people and I think he would let her know if . . .' She laughed and asked him if he was a history professor.

'Good God, no. Why would you ask that?'

'Your hair is so wild, and you know so much.'

He was amazed how easy it was to fool some of the people some of the time. 'I deal in vintage cars. But everyone knows about poor Edward II. They try to imagine how painful it must have been and then they can never forget him.'

'I'm reading Philosophy at Vancouver. I must try to remember that.'

He said, 'Would you like some real English fish and chips? There's a restaurant just by Westgate Bridge – at the exact spot where the Romans crossed the river in AD something-or-other.'

'That would be just great!'

He let himself into the house again at ten fifteen to find all the lights off and a note on the kitchen table which read, 'Obviously Edmund is not coming home tonight so I am taking a cheese sandwich upstairs.'

His ill-humour returned with a rush and when he practically flounced back out to the car and met Edmund walking up the path, he exploded.

'Where the hell have you been? You were meant to do the supper! Hester's gone to bed in a strop. It can't have taken you all this time just to find out exactly what Helena and Edward know?'

'I haven't been there. Sorry, old man. Ma phoned. Needed stuff for Millie. Then I went up to Painswick to check on Sally and sort of . . . stayed.'

'Christ Almighty! You can't even do a little thing like – I'll go up myself. Tomorrow morning. There's no food in the house. I had fish and chips.'

'Oh, that's all right. I ate with Sally's folks. Her father is a bit of an oddball. He wears glasses but never looks through them—'

Perry brushed past him without another word. And after a bad night in his sleeping bag on the floor of the attic, he drove up to Leckhampton before work and discovered the Mayburys were still out. During the morning he telephoned three times. The third time the receiver was picked up by their gardener. They were in Weston-super-Mare, enjoying an autumn break. That evening Aunt Hester told him that Edmund had gone off somewhere. He'd telephoned her at school. He was taking Sally on an outing; a 'mystery outing'.

She said, 'I do hope something will come of those two. It's ideal if only Sally can see it. She needs a stable partner and Edmund is so very stable.'

'You just want her off your neck,' Perry came back sourly.

She was surprised. 'Is it that obvious? I thought she was cooling down considerably. Anyway, university will get her off my neck, as you so elegantly put it. Actually I'm concerned for her. She is so impulsive, so vulnerable.'

'Everyone is concerned for her. Nobody seems to give two hoots for Nell, who is, after all, family!'

'Nell will be all right, Perry. Try not to worry too much.'

'She'll end up like you, that's what worries me!'

Hester wondered whether to take umbrage. In the end she said nothing. She was not completely certain what the conversation was about.

However, much later that evening, when Perry was trying to get comfortable in his sleeping bag, Edmund arrived at Duggie's town house and panted up the stairs. He stood in the open doorway, clutching the jamb.

Perry said, 'I hope you've brought your own sleeping bag. I haven't got any blankets or anything. And you're not having Duggie's bed. I changed the sheets today.'

'I'm staying at Hester's. Remember?' Edmund held his

side. 'Thought I'd better come and report. When you phoned me at work I couldn't say much. Young Smithers standing over me like a miniature dragon. Hope I didn't put you off.'

'I'm used to it.'

'Suppose so. Anyway, I promised Sally I'd take her for a drive. So I did. I have. Been to Weston-super-Mare.'

Perry sat up; he was wearing vest and pants. He said, 'Gosh, Ed. I thought you were just mucking me about. Mucking Nell about. So you went to Weston. Did you find them?'

'They always stay at the same hotel. The Daubenay, Madeira Cove. They do a cracking dinner there. We had lobster. I wish you could have seen Sally dealing with it. She was a bit squeamish but once she'd tasted—'

'Get on with it, Ed! I don't need a menu.'

'Sorry.' Edmund hung his head, finally getting his breath back. He looked up and said calmly, 'They don't know anything about it.' There came a cry of disgust from the floor and he went on smoothly, 'But Edward said that if he was looking for a place to sleep and he didn't want to bother anyone, he'd go for the Pumpkin Coach.' He paused. They looked at each other. Edmund said, 'He's right, isn't he, brud? That's where Michael Adair will be. It's his home after all. I know he's sold it but . . .'

'Yeah. Yeah, that's it! Oh, bully for you, Ed! I'll go tomorrow. Get off work early afternoon and be there by four.' He grinned, not pleasantly. 'I'll give Mo bloody Checkers something to remember us by!'

'Remember what happened last time,' Edmund cautioned. 'He's not enormous but he's stronger than either of us.'

'I don't care. He can beat me to a pulp if that's how it goes. But I'm getting mine in first! OK?'

'I suppose so. OK.' Edmund went back down the stairs and into a windy autumn night. Rain was forecast for the next day; Edward Maybury had commented on it and suggested they should go home. Edmund got into his car and sat there yawning jaw-splittingly. He wondered whether he had done the right thing in giving Perry the go-ahead to commit violence. But he was so tired that he could barely think straight and there was a part of him that thought Mo needed a damned good hiding anyway. He drove back to the close and collapsed into bed, thankful that Hester had obviously had another of her early nights. He thought that the next morning, when he got to work and before Smithers arrived, he would telephone Val and put him in the picture. He would shift responsibility for one of the family at least.

Twenty-nine

Alice and Val collected Duggie and spent the whole of that Wednesday morning with the bank manager. Doffie and Ted would have joined them except that Doffie had developed a cold that she did not wish to share. 'Ted will come of course,' she said nasally over the telephone. 'He's quite good with figures. Remember that time he spent at Paddington.' Val had also spent a great deal of time in Paddington but developing what had been euphemistically called 'the larger picture'. Actually neither Val nor Ted was particularly good with 'figures'. But Duggie was, and most of the money they were dealing with had belonged to Duggie. After all, as Ted pointed out sarcastically, he was the chairman of the Pumpkin Line. Edward and Helena Maybury were having a short break in Weston-super-Mare, though probably, with the change in the weather, they would be home later that day.

All the retired members of the board received an honorarium only, but Val drew a salary and that worried him.

'We're not in a position to pay for staff yet,' he told Alice. 'I gave up work prematurely.'

Alice was up in arms. 'But you're the one who has done all the work. All right, Edward has spoken to his cohorts but you have pointed him in the right direction, you have found out what we need to do, you have been the one to talk to the old gavellers and you have organized all the voluntary help. Everyone else will go home for the winter. You will still be working. You and Bert between you do more than any of us.'

'I may try to get some consultancy work this winter.' They were sitting in the bank manager's office, which was very plush; he thought of their office, the Pumpkin Coach, and smiled slightly. 'I wish Mo Adair would turn up and tell me what to do about the parallel line.'

'There would still have to be some kind of points system,' Alice cautioned. 'And I've a feeling that Mo has come home to talk to Nell as well as to you.'

'Why the hell did he run off that day? We could all have sat on the grass and talked together like human beings instead of this hole-in-the-corner thing.'

'You know very well why he ran off,' Alice said reasonably. 'The three of us like that. Too much. He'll get in touch when he's ready. Meanwhile, he's obviously working down there.'

Duggie and Ted arrived together, bickering as usual. They both looked rather dishevelled: Ted because he was anxious about Doffie, Duggie because he had come almost straight from what Hattie called 'the breakfast bed'.

Duggie kissed Alice and said, 'Edmund was trying to get hold of you and Val this morning. Something to do with Perry going to see Michael Adair.'

Alice opened her eyes wide. 'We were just talking about him. Where is he? With the Mayburys?'

'They think he's probably staying in the Pumpkin Coach.' Duggie smiled peaceably. 'Hattie reckons that Perry is going down to beat him up! Typical Hattie, yes?'

Alice said, 'I'm not sure. Perry and Mo . . . there's some rivalry there.' She looked across at Val, who was explaining to Ted just why they had to have Duggie with them at all times.

'If he's going to jerk the purse strings—' Ted blustered.

'You know very well he would never do such a thing!' Val was unusually sharp. It irked him unbearably that in effect Duggie was paying him a salary.

Alice said, 'Val, I think we should go down to Leadon after this. Apparently Mo is staying in the Pumpkin Coach and Perry has gone down to – to – see him.'

Val noted her wide blue eyes and understood. He nodded. Ted, glad to change the subject, said, 'I'll come with you, old man. Two of them, two of us. Sounds fair.'

'I'll come too.' Duggie came to an instant decision; Hattie was hurt that both her boys were absent from the newly marital home.

Val exchanged looks with Alice. They had both imagined a very private meeting between Val and Mo. This was turning out to be another family party. Alice said to Val on their way to a restaurant for lunch, 'There's no putting it off, darling. At some point Perry has to return that punch of a year ago.'

That day Perry closed the showroom at three o'clock. That meant that any enquiries regarding the vintage cars that were his speciality would have to go through the garage, and the owner was clearly fed up about it.

'Another family crisis?' he asked with unveiled sarcasm. 'What is it this time? Mother having another baby – oh no, she's only just had her last, hasn't she, and she is still fifty-two, I assume? Is she getting a divorce perhaps?'

'Look here, Jenkins—' Perry began.

But John Jenkins had no real wish to quarrel with Perry Westbrook. Since Perry had joined them the profits had doubled. He had the charm of old Nick and contacts for buying the old crocks that seemed to be selling so well. Jenkins had seriously considered offering him a partnership in the hope that he would then put in more hours. It had been his wife who pointed out that Perry was never off the job. 'Even when he's out with his latest girl, he's spreading our reputation. I've watched people point him out as he goes past in one of the cars.'

So he said quickly to Perry, 'Sorry, sorry. No jokes about your respected – revered – mother. Or any of the girlfriends. Or your cousin. I forgot. Just momentarily of course.'

'If it was anyone else . . .' grumbled Perry.

'I know. Fist in face.'

Perry grinned. John Jenkins wasn't a bad sort of bloke . . . could be worse, much worse. It would be about four o'clock by the time he had walked along the newly minted line to the coach. A day like this, emptying rain like cats and dogs, he had no wish to come stumbling back in the dark – maybe with a few bruises too. He grinned as he followed the river past Newnham and Westbury; he could just about admit it to himself – he was spoiling for a fight! And after he'd knocked some sense into that Chinese idiot, they might end up in the Leadon Arms over a pint of cider.

He parked the car outside the waiting room and walked along to the ground frame, half hoping that the *Belle* would be there, steam up, ready to go, and Bert wiping her over with an oily rag. Of course, no such luck: the engine wasn't there. And the ground was like a bog. When he reached the area Nell always called the cathedral and crossed the line to where it seemed slightly dryer, his heel caught in a sleeper and he went head first into the mud. It broke his fall but he emerged liberally coated in the stuff. He stood there, face lifted to the rain that dripped off every leaf and twig, and cursed loud and long. By the time he reached the pool and began to skirt it he was in no mood to discuss the problem, or even to engage in immediate and angry argument on Nell's behalf. He simply wanted to hit Michael Adair and then fling him into Bracewell's Pool.

There was a light on in the coach; the windows were steamy with condensation so he must have some kind of heating in there. Perry suddenly realized how cold he was. Maybe he was ill; he was furiously hot inside and shivering with cold outside. Which made him angrier still.

He flung open the door with unnecessary force, slammed it back against the side of the coach and started up the steps. He was vaguely conscious of Bert Lewis, lifting a mug of steaming tea to his moustached mouth. All he really saw was the schoolboy face of Michael Adair, black eyes, black hair, snub English nose, determined mouth and chin. Determined to use people – not only Nell, but all of them.

Perry made a sound like the roar of a lion. He leaped up the last two steps, kicked the chair from under Mo, grabbed that black, coarse, Asian hair and pulled Mo round so that he was facing the open doorway, then he put his foot in the middle of the T-shirt and shoved hard. As Mo landed in the mud, Perry hurled himself on him, pulled him up and yelled at him, 'That's for me! Everything else is for Nell! Got it?'

Mo, taken completely by surprise, said helplessly, 'Nell? Where is she?'

'Who is she?' Perry was never quite certain afterwards whether he deliberately misheard the question. 'Who *is* she?' He stuck to his guns. 'She's the girl – who happens to be my cousin – the girl you seduced and then you ditched. The girl you humiliated – over and over again until she can't say your name without crying—' With each of these phrases Perry delivered a punch, and they got harder and harder until Mo fell beneath them, barely defending himself, completely bewildered.

There was a pause then because Perry had run out of breath and words. Mo squirmed round in the mud and got to his knees. He looked up at his tormentor. The anger he saw seemed to spark a reaction. He lifted one knee and planted his socked foot in the mud.

'You – you have the nerve – the bloody nerve – to talk of seduction? You *took* Nell – your cousin – you traded on her affection for you – you took her over! You didn't love her – she didn't love you – not really – it was disgusting, it was—' He stood up. Without any shoes he was lighter on his feet than Perry. He landed his first punch from below, straight on to the point of the Westbrook chin, and at the same time he shouted the single word, 'Incest!' He flung himself on to Perry and they both fell and rolled down the muddy bank to the edge of the pool. Bert, up and watching from the steps of the coach, described it later as mud-wrestling. It was impossible to see what was happening. Grunts, groans and the occasional yelp gave nothing away. Two only just recognizable human forms grappled together like primeval reptiles. Bert saw that in that state they could not really harm each other, and fairly soon they would be in the water, which would hamper them even more. He wondered whether to light up his pipe while he was watching and decided against it in case he missed something. He reached behind him for his tea and held it in both hands, rather enjoying the spectacle. He smiled to himself: usually in a fight like this both parties were losers. He had a curious feeling that, in this case, both men – well, boys to him of course – would emerge as victors.

And then he became conscious of something else. The coach. Something was happening to the coach. It was moving. Ever so slightly. He glanced to his left where the forest closed in again and saw that it was nearer than usual. That damned kid – Perry woteverisnamewas – had done all those bloody acrobatics on the steps and tilted it in some way. It had long since come off its bogey and was propped above the ground on piles of forest stone. Suddenly, even as he was working it all out, one of the stones shifted and the coach lurched sideways.

'Oy!' he shouted. The mud-wrestlers ignored him. His mug of tea slopped on to his knuckles. 'Oy!' he shouted again.

He realized that he was weighting the coach in the direction of the slide and moved backwards up the steps and into the kitchen. A supporting stone on the other side went and the whole of the long sleeping coach with its saloon and its bedroom slewed round and began inexorably to move towards Bracewell's Pool. Bert shouted in real alarm now as he was pushed towards the open door again. The coach was tilting . . . It was going to fall into the water and he was going with it and taking the mud-wrestlers with him. His voice went up an octave and he yelled at the top of his voice, 'Watch out! Watch out, lads!'

He was just in time. Mo saw the leviathan bearing down on them and on his knees, with Perry's hands still trying to reach his windpipe, he dragged the two of them clear. They fell helplessly into the water just as the coach hit it alongside them. For a moment the whole elderly construction floated and they watched in horror as the six windows caught the light and appeared to wink at them. Then there were awful gurglings and it began to sink.

'Christ! Bert!' Mo was in the water, his hands on the door handle the other side of the coach. 'Perry – quick!'

The door on that side had not been opened for some time; they struggled with the handle. The gurgling was fierce, and the coach was sliding further away from the bank into water that legend claimed was bottomless.

'For God's *sake*!' Mo was sobbing now. 'The handle won't move – Perry—'

Perry was still wearing his boots. He heaved himself up on to the door and stamped on the glass. Over and over again he stamped and got through just as Mo managed to turn the handle. Together they lifted the heavy door and it crashed open, water spouted up as if from a whale and with it came a shocked Bert, still holding his mug though now it was full of black water. They dragged him towards the bank. Incredibly, willing hands were there to pull them all ashore. Mo stared in disbelief, Perry with a kind of resignation. Alice and Val, Duggie and Ted.

'How did you get here?' Perry asked and was surprised – but delighted – when Duggie burst into tears and wrapped his arms round him.

They dragged each other up to the old locomotive. Bert seemed unaffected by his entrapment and immersion. 'Shot out like a cannon ball I were,' he announced several times. They all clustered round the *Belle*. The rain had worked its way through the forest canopy and began to wash them clean. They ignored it; with one accord they watched as the chocolate and cream livery of the Pumpkin Coach was swallowed by the water of the pool. And then the finale: inside the coach, the calor gas canister detached itself from the cooker and with the last small flame beneath the kettle the gas ignited.

The explosion could be heard in Gloucester – or so Bert said in the Leadon Arms that night.

'The old girl went up like a torch and took the waters with it. It were a sight to see, I'm telling you. A sight to see. The biggest water spout in the world, I wouldn't be surprised. If

371

she had to go, then she went with a vengeance. Yes, that coach has taken her secrets with her, you may be sure of that.'

Val had taken off his coat and wrapped it round Bert's shoulders; Alice was discovering handkerchiefs and scarves with which to mop the mud-wrestlers, who were slapping their arms round their bodies in an effort to get warm, spraying water and mud like a pair of dogs; Ted and Duggie were hanging on to their dry clothing and making sounds of distress as the coach was swallowed in its own explosion – and then there was the curious silence after the event. For five whole minutes, perhaps more, the water gradually settled, the rain pocked it again, the sound of dripping was heard everywhere and normality returned.

But the pool had not finished with them. Disturbed by the explosion, and maybe by the work of relaying the track, hauling stones and ballast so close to its shores, the pool gave something up. In its centre, its deepest point, appeared an object. A floating object that had not been there before.

At first they thought it must have come from the coach.

'Old clothes?' Val guessed. 'We kept work clothes in the sleeping area.'

'Too far from where the coach went down,' Ted replied.

'Mo's boots, I expect!' Perry guffawed. 'Good job you took them off – made you lighter than me. The coach would have hit us if you hadn't pushed us through the mud like you did.' He actually clapped a hand to Mo's shoulder. Mo looked surprised, then smiled suddenly. Something had happened besides the death of the coach. Something rather special. He was one of them now. One of the magic circle of Pettifords and Ryecrofts. He glanced at Val, who took his eyes away from the floating object long enough to grin back. Mo could not believe it; after all that had happened, all he had done . . . was it over?

He turned back to the pool and narrowed his eyes. He was the youngest there: surely he could identify whatever it was that was lapping gently and surely away from them?

He said uncertainly, 'I think . . . my God . . . it's a body! It can't be. There have been no reports . . . It can't be.'

Perry said, 'It is. That's hair floating behind it.'

'I'll go and look.' Val was already walking towards the pool. Everyone began to trail after him, Bert hugging his borrowed jacket round his shoulders, Perry and Mo sloshing along faster than anyone else. Then they slowed down.

'It is a body,' Perry called back. 'If you don't want to see it, don't come any further.'

Val said, 'We'll have to report this.'

It was Duggie who said, 'Not after so long.'

No one picked up on this and they struggled on; the bank rose higher on this side of the pool and they could look down on the body, which appeared to be perfectly preserved and was obviously female.

'It – it's black,' whispered Alice.

Val said, 'From the coal dust. It's been preserved by the coal.'

Mo felt hypnotized by the whole situation. He began to wonder whether he were really here with these people. 'For how long?' he asked.

Val shook his head. 'Who knows?'

Bert moved forward. 'I knows,' he said. 'So do you, Mr Ryecroft. And I reckon Mr Pettiford should know.'

Ted joined him at the very edge of the steep bank. He looked down. He felt his eyes fill and run over. He reached out an arm and encircled Alice.

'She disappeared the year you were born,' he said, almost choking. 'Forty-six years ago.'

Alice held his free hand tightly. 'Is it your sister, Dad? You can't know that. Even the coal wouldn't keep her for forty-six years . . . and why would she come to the surface now?'

'Well, that's it, isn't it? She was weighted down, Alice. Probably stone from one of the mines. And the old coach blowing up moved the stone . . . Oh God, Alice, she was always just a kid. Mucking about. Playing. She never grew up

– but she didn't deserve . . .' He broke off and Alice tried to hold him. Duggie came and patted him awkwardly. The others gazed down with new horror. And even as they watched, the body of Mitzie Pettiford rolled gently over and disappeared again.

They said nothing. After a while they walked back to the locomotive and somehow clambered on board. Val fired for Bert and as soon as there was enough steam they chugged in reverse back to Leadon Markham and the cars. Mo took Bert back to his cottage and the family huddled together again and tried to decide what to do.

It was Duggie who took charge.

'Mitzie has gone again, that's obvious. And I suppose everyone here knows who killed her. That means we don't say a word. We don't report it to the police and we tell no one – and I mean no one. It wouldn't take Hattie long to work out that in all probability the murderer was her own father and that he was Reggie Ryecroft. Sorry, Val, but it's got to be clear in our minds. The police would drag all this out and Hattie couldn't bear it. And there's Millie to consider.'

Val was silent, working it out . . . Edmund . . . it meant that he had fathered his own nephew. He stared at the man who had been such a close observer of this long-ago drama. He said hoarsely, 'I agree. Entirely. No one else must know.'

Ted said predictably, 'I'll have to tell Doffie. Oh God . . .'

Alice gave a watery smile. 'It'll be all right, Dad. Mum was so close to Gran in spite of all their squabbling. At the end, Gran loved Mum. She won't mind Mum knowing.'

They were silent again. Perry thought, they're talking about my grandfather . . . about Val's father . . .' And then he thought, if Ed knows he is related to a madman, he won't marry Sally Gold. He will expect the two of us to be celibate. Oh God . . . I can't tell Ed. It'll be no good reminding him how much worse it must have been for Val . . . he's such a *stickler* . . .

And Val said, 'Perry, I don't want Edmund to know about

this. You can take it – you are taking it – very well. But Edmund is different. Can you keep it from him?'

Perry nodded once. He no longer trusted himself to use his voice.

Duggie said, 'So we are all agreed? We'll have words with Bert and with Mo and then we'll forget today. Is that all right, Ted?'

'So long as I can tell Doff. I want to get home. I have to tell Doff.'

'Come on, Dad, we'll take you.' Alice opened the door of their car and eased him inside and Val got behind the wheel. It was left to Duggie to pick up Mo and take him to the Mayburys' house overlooking the Devil's Chimney.

'You'll be all right with Helena,' he said. 'Let her look after you. Tell her about the fight and the coach and the explosion. That will be quite enough to satisfy her.' He got out of the car and rang the doorbell. Then he said very calmly, 'And when she has finished making a fuss of you and you have talked to Val about the Pumpkin Line, then you can go to Birmingham and see Nell.'

Mo said nothing. He had wiped his face and hands clean of mud and swilled his socks under the tap at Bert's cottage. He had helped the old man into the tin bath in the kitchen, dried him tenderly afterwards and put him to bed. He was exhausted.

Duggie insisted. 'Is that all right, Mo? Will you go and see her?'

Mo said, surprised, 'Yes. I will. Today . . . I can go now. Can't I?'

'You could have gone at any time. And when I told you to go to Birmingham and see Nell, I meant that. You don't have to talk or try to explain. Just see her.'

Helena, who had seen them arrive, flung open the door with exclamations of horror followed by a cataract of questions.

Mo smiled at her and asked whether he could stay the night.

'Oh my dear boy! Of course you can stay as long as you like. But first a bath, then some clean clothes – have you brought your clothes?'

'They exploded,' he said simply and walked past her into the hall.

Thirty

The headlines in the Saturday edition of the *Citizen* were confusing enough to warrant a host of visitors on the Sunday. 'Gas Explosion in Bracewell's Pool' was followed by a description of the event as reported by 'Driver Bert Lewis of the light railway known as the Pumpkin Line'. Driver Bert Lewis spoke of an old sleeping coach that had been a love nest before the Great War and had seen many a scandal since then. He was quoted as saying, 'We always called it the Pumpkin Coach down here in the forest. It was put there for the first Cinderella and there's been many a Cinderella since then. And they've usually come to grief if they've stayed there too long. Now the coach has gone and we feel as if we can really get down to business. The clock has ticked right round and we've come back into real life. The Pumpkin Line is going to be good for everyone. It's a way of seeing parts of the forest that have been lost for a long time. And as a mineral line it will still have its uses. Come and see us now, then come and see us in two or three years' time. Keep an eye on the Pumpkin Line!'

Val said admiringly, 'None of us could have done better than this! Perhaps Bert ought to double as our public relations wallah!'

Alice said, 'I think he's right about the clock ticking us round to real life again too. I don't know how or why but it's going to be all right for Mo and Nell, isn't it, Val?'

'Well, if it isn't, Mo had better avoid Perry for the rest of his life!'

*

377

The day after the explosion, Helena took Mo into Cheltenham to kit him out again. He said, 'Actually, I've got heaps of money – they are paying me a ridiculous salary – but I didn't give myself time to get anything organized. I had this wonderful letter from Mr Ryecroft and I just phoned my manager to tell him there was trouble at home and he said to take as much time as I needed . . . and I came . . . and then I couldn't face Mr Ryecroft.' He smiled at Helena. 'I'm sorry to be so hopeless. Now that it's all over I find I can't plan anything properly.'

'Perhaps you've used up all your plotting capabilities!' Helena had heard half of the tale from Alice and had wondered what all the fuss was about. She recalled Joe Adair so fondly; he had never been a plotter, a manipulator. He had been open and honest and . . . oh so very vulnerable. Mo was terribly like him. She smiled back quickly before she broke down in tears at the thought of his father.

Helena was used to choosing clothes for Edward and she enjoyed it as much as choosing them for herself. Mo was quite happy to let her do everything; he managed to pick up a pair of Levi's and some T-shirts for work but new underwear and slightly more formal outfits were entirely Helena's choice. He came back home wearing conventional grey flannels, white shirt and tweed jacket. Edward pronounced him 'smart as paint' and added encouragingly that Nell would fall for him all over again when she saw him outside school tomorrow.

'Tomorrow is Sunday,' Helena said. 'So I think Mo had better borrow my car and go up quite early before Nell has time to do anything else.' She turned to Mo. 'Nell has a very good friend – another teacher – and they often take cycle rides out into the hills. If she's not at her digs, ask the landlady – very nice apparently – in which direction—'

Edward said, 'Why don't we telephone?'

Helena clapped her hands. 'Dear Edward, so practical. But it's to be a surprise, darling.' She turned back to Mo. 'If you start early enough of course she'll be in. And whatever she is

378

doing won't matter. Will it?' He shook his head. 'Get there in time for coffee, dear. Then it will give her something to do.' She beamed at Mo. 'There now. All nicely settled. It will be an enormous surprise for her. You'll be able to tell her about the explosion and then a nice cup of coffee . . . Be careful not to get it on that white shirt, dear. Coffee is notoriously difficult to wash out of things. And afterwards, when everything has been sorted out, perhaps you could go for a drive. Not if it's still raining, of course, but if the weather clears up—'

Edward said, 'Your aunt Helena will write all this down for you if you're likely to forget it, Michael!'

Mo was still in a state of confusion. He said, 'Aunt Helena?'

'I'm Aunt Helena to a great many people,' Helena said. 'It makes up for not having any children of my own, you know.'

Mo looked at her dumbly. She had talked about his father and evidently had thought a great deal of him. He swallowed and managed to say, 'I'd be honoured . . . Aunt Helena.'

Edward said solemnly, 'And that makes me Uncle Edward! And in that capacity may I enquire whether you came to any conclusions about getting rid of that blasted ground frame down at Leadon?'

At last Mo was on firm ground. He said, 'Oh yes. I haven't mentioned it yet to Val. Perhaps you could tell him and see what he thinks. Bert's for it too.'

'And it is . . . ?'

'Sorry. Yes. I'm not quite . . . you know. It is to erect our own engine shed where the ground frame is now. Get rid of the spur. Build a booking office. There's room for quite a lot. Maybe a refreshment room. Cloakroom.' He glanced at Edward's face. 'It would all be cheaper than laying a new track alongside the Leadon branch line. I've done a costing – Bert cast his eye over it and he's a canny one.'

Edward grinned. 'He is that. The whole idea sounds good to me. We won't have to toady around getting people to turn a blind eye . . . and that ground frame and spur will be off my conscience.'

Helena called them in to dinner – as Helena told Alice later, 'like a proper family'. And it was then that Edward expounded his recent idea for the Pumpkin Line.

'Getting shot of that old sleeping coach could be the best thing to happen since we started. We need something there, especially as it's our terminus at present. Something possibly with children in mind. The whole place has a kind of magic and we could use that to good purpose. A gingerbread house, for example. A Santa Claus grotto.'

'What are the chances of getting a Pullman coach one day?' Helena suggested. 'Each table could contain a character or two from a well-known book or poem. The passengers could choose which table they joined.'

'I like that!' Mo said. 'The Pullman would stay the same, but the characters could differ from season to season.'

Edward and Helena exchanged smiles. Mo was going to be all right.

Nell had a new class. After that first short week she was already getting the hang of them. A boy called Brian Larch was going to be trouble; he was terrorizing a tiny girl called Maria Garrow. Jennifer Peachey, tall, self-assured, was the bright one. Another girl, Sarah Bush, liked to change her name every day; she had started last Tuesday as Sally Bush, which was fair enough; by Friday she had been Margaretta Bush, Victoria Bush and Susannah French. Nell was wondering how she could use this sort of thing in a project. Shirley had suggested teaching Brian Larch to sing 'Thank heaven for little girls' and then name them all. 'At the rate Sarah Bush is going, that will keep him busy for some time to come,' she said.

'Oh Shirley, I have missed you,' Nell said, spluttering with laughter.

'Me too. This living together isn't all it's cracked up to be. I'm glad we tried it before tying any knots.'

They had a delightful conversation about relationships generally and then the afternoon bell went. 'Come to tea on

Sunday,' Shirley said hastily. 'I want you to meet him. Then you can give an entirely objective opinion on whether this thing is going to work. Or not.'

'Are you sure? OK.' Nell was grateful for the invitation. This first weekend was going to be pretty awful.

She managed Saturday very well as she had promised to visit Martin Trickett and see his new train set. Now that she no longer taught him the head had given gracious permission for her to accept the Tricketts' insistent invitations, and Nell had a wonderful afternoon playing with Martin's train and then telling the family about the Pumpkin Line.

'If ever you're in the area and you have time, do try to see it. My father would love to show you round.'

Martin was ecstatic.

So there was only Sunday to go and that was now filled with seeing Shirley. She spent Saturday evening on lesson plans and had an early night, woke at seven and decided to go to the early service at North Heath's ancient church. There were four other people there, who welcomed her effusively. She wondered whether brass-rubbing might work with her new infants.

As she walked back up the snicket, she stopped at the place where she could see her house through the acacia trees. She loved that particular view: the trees were dropping their leaves, it was still only just light . . . eight thirty. And halfway up the road was Aunt Helena's car.

Immediately, she feared the worst. She stood still at her vantage point, gripping a concrete fence post . . . If it were her mother then Val would have come. If her father, then Alice would be driving the family car. But Aunt Helena had driven up in her own car, which meant she was alone because Uncle Edward did not like being driven.

Nell closed her eyes and forced herself not to faint. She had never fainted in her life and assumed that the nausea and vertigo must precede loss of consciousness. She scraped her hand along the concrete until the pain was all she could think of, then she let go and ran to the corner and up the crescent of houses under the trees to the front door. Somehow she fitted the Yale key into the lock and let herself in. And there was her dear landlady filling the kitchen doorway, talking to someone in the kitchen.

'That will be her!' She glanced over her shoulder, smiling broadly. Surely that meant something positive? 'Ah. There you are, Miss Ryecroft. I said you wouldn't be many minutes. Church, was it? Oh my dear girl, what have you done? There's blood all down your coat!' She moved towards Nell but she was not quick enough. Mo slid past her sideways and was at Nell's side, picking up her hand, exclaiming, reaching into the pocket of his tweed jacket and pulling out a handkerchief the size of a tray cloth.

'Let me . . .' He wrapped her whole hand up. 'Have you had a fall?'

'No. Mo . . . my parents . . . are they all right?'

He looked up from his bandaging and saw the fear in her blue eyes. 'They're fine. I thought they would have telephoned. Sorry – sorry, Nell. Helena thought it would be a surprise. I've done the wrong thing again, haven't I?'

She shook her head dumbly and swallowed convulsively then choked out, 'It happened to you, didn't it? Why not me?'

He held on to her hands and said nothing. A bowl of water appeared at his elbow, a packet of plasters. He released her, took them and Nell led the way upstairs.

'It's nothing. Really. Honestly. I did it deliberately when I saw the car. You know how pain sometimes makes you focus?'

'Of course.' He was busy dabbing. She watched him; his bent head so darkly different, his hands square and capable.

She whispered, 'I'm sorry. About everything. That silly letter, all my histrionics . . . I think I understand better now. It must have been so awful for you. Both of them. Together.'

He glanced up. 'I was saying to Bert Lewis the other day . . . I'm thankful now that they were together. Because – frankly – they were inseparable. Like your parents.'

Her hand was plastered up to the wrist now. He held it and said, 'I'm sorry, Nell. So sorry.'

She dropped her eyes and stood very still. He said, 'Shall we drive up to the Lickeys? We could have breakfast somewhere and walk to the top. It's good to do that, Nell. Gives you a better perspective.'

Her smile was more natural this time. 'Edmund says that. Yes. Let's do that. There's a golf course up there somewhere and a hotel called the Lynx. We could go there if you like. What about my bloody coat? You look so . . . smart.'

'Helena took me into Cheltenham yesterday – kitted me out. My clothes were in the Pumpkin Coach and it blew up. Let me just sponge you off . . . there!'

'Mo! Stop being so maddening! The coach blew up? Were you in it? Was anyone hurt?'

'Answer to last question is no. But Bert was in it. We rescued him.' He stood back. 'Hardly shows. Come on. I'll tell you everything as we drive.'

They went back downstairs, called out that everything was fine and they were going for a drive. Nell had the strangest feeling of increasing lightness; it was as if she had been shedding weight ever since Mo had appeared and taken her hand. She settled herself into the familiar atmosphere of Helena's car; the scent of lavender enclosed her, and she put her head back, closed her eyes and felt tears ooze from beneath the lids.

'Are you crying?' he asked.

'Just getting rid of a bit of weight,' she replied. She turned her head and looked at him. 'Turn left at the top of the road and just keep going.'

'All right.' He smiled without returning her gaze. And then he began to tell her about the coach and Perry trying to kill him and how together they had got the door open and Bert had popped out like a cork from a bottle.

He said, 'There's a copy of last night's *Citizen* on the back seat if you're interested.'

She reached for it and made noises of shock, of amusement, of horror.

'I can't believe this! Why didn't Mum and Dad phone me?

My God – you could have been hurt – you could have been killed!'

'I suppose so. As a matter of fact we were all pretty shocked. But much later . . . driving up here actually . . . I saw the whole thing as a kind of catalyst.'

'A . . . what? Oh, I see. You shared something pretty devastating. And you and Perry . . . Oh my God, I'm glad they didn't phone. I would have gone mad.' They took the road signed to Barnt Green and he changed into first gear. She said, 'I can't believe you're just accepting it. It was yours . . . your father's . . . his mother's gift. Oh Mo, I'm so sorry. And that wretched Perry, catalyst or no catalyst, that was terrible. How dare he!'

He said, 'Because he couldn't bear the fact that I had been trying to hurt you, Nell. Look, d'you want me to stop while we thrash it out?'

'No – no. Anyway, what's to thrash out? It's gone.' She began to weep. 'That wonderful, magical Pumpkin Coach! It's gone.'

'Yes.' He sounded very calm about it. 'It's gone and taken the past with it, my love. All that strife and carrying-on. It's gone. We're free, Nell. You and me. Can't you see that?'

She was silent while the car continued to climb. Then she took a deep breath. 'Yes, I suppose I can see. Of course I can. For us. And maybe for my parents. And Hattie. But what about the Pumpkin Line? What happens now, Mo?'

'There are heaps of ideas. Aunt Helena thought if we could buy a Pullman coach we could—'

' "Aunt" Helena? And you keep saying "we". But you live in America now.'

'She suggested the aunt thing. And . . . even if I never saw it again, I would always be part of the Pumpkin Line, Nell. You know that.'

'Yes.'

'As for America, you know I have a two-year contract. Will you come and join me after Christmas, Nell? Please? We can talk about everything else for the rest of the day. But if I

384

could come home for Christmas and take you back with me
. . . Could you bear to leave your school?'

She almost gasped. He had jumped so many hurdles. She almost asked, why – what for? – but that would have been coy. She knew all that was implicit between them.

She said, 'You know I want to. More than anything. Will that do for now? I might have to work another term's notice . . . I just don't know. But . . . yes, I want to come with you. Be with you.'

He said, 'Thank God. I wasn't sure you could ever forgive me. And then, when it seemed as if you did, I was still in a state of hating myself, thinking I was a jinx on all your family, telling myself that we were never meant to be together.' He stopped speaking because her hand slid gently across his mouth. He mumbled through her fingers. 'The coach thing . . . fight with Perry . . .'

She said, 'D'you remember I had to teach you to make conversation? Forget all that I ever said. You are talking . . . you are telling me things.'

'Am I?' He looked round at her anxiously. 'What things?'

She laughed and hugged his arm. 'Oh . . . Michael Adair. I knew you loved me but when you kept running, not communicating, I began to think it was all a silly schoolgirl dream. Like Sally Gold and Aunt Hester.'

'Sally Gold?'

'I'll have to tell you later. We've got time at last.' She wound down her window and a chill breeze filled the car. She said, 'We've got the rest of our lives.'

After the *Citizen* article, Val and Alice planned a quiet Sunday morning and a visit to Alice's mother in the afternoon.

'I hope she felt better before Dad broke the news about . . . well, about everything really.'

'How did she sound on the telephone?' Val asked.

'A bit . . . exasperated really. You know how impatient Mum can be where Dad is concerned.'

'Did she know Mitzie very well?' Val prayed that Duggie

would keep it to himself. Hattie would have hysterics. And when she realized that Edmund was the son of a union between a brother and sister . . .

As if she could read his thoughts, Alice said, 'Stop worrying about Hattie, Val! You're as bad as Dad, he's always worried about her – even when she married Duggie! Hattie is a down-to-earth survivor! If she discovered her father was Lucifer himself she wouldn't give it a thought – except as a jolly good joke!'

Val said nothing. He knew all those things about Hattie; he also knew that Edmund was her favourite son. Yet Edmund was so level-headed, intelligent, sensitive.

He was relieved when they heard Edward's car coming down the lane and Helena swept ahead of him straight into the kitchen.

'Darlings!' she announced. 'It's all right. He's gone to see her – left at seven thirty this morning, can you imagine? And he promised he would find a phone box and ring us if anything went wrong. And it's eleven clock, he hasn't rung, so . . .' She seized the kettle and filled it. 'Let's have coffee and celebrate!'

Edward came in and closed the door behind him. 'Cold out there,' he commented. 'I suppose Helena has already told you?' He followed Alice into the living room, where a fire burned brightly. He rubbed his hands before it appreciatively. 'I remember Mo's father . . . one of our Christmas do's . . . in my office.' He smiled at Alice. 'It seems so right. Doesn't it, Alice?' She nodded, not trusting her voice. 'Let's hope they're not parted for long. It's been long enough already and I always feel that partings are . . . risky.'

She cleared her throat. 'It's not the same, Edward. Joe Adair and Alice Pettiford were not destined for each other, anyway. I'm certain of that.'

Edward smiled. 'Especially now! You two bowed out so that Nell and Mo could . . . exist! And be together.'

'Perhaps. I quite like that idea.' She smiled. 'What a good

job you married Helena, Edward! Mr Maybury could never have talked to Alice Pettiford as you are doing now.'

'Exactly. We were different people, Alice.'

Val ushered in Helena and the coffee tray and heard those last words. Somehow they comforted him.

He said, 'Listen to Helena's ideas for the future of the Pumpkin Line, Alice!'

And Helena said, obviously continuing a previous conversation, 'And then we'll pop in to see Bert Lewis and if he's all right we could be on duty this afternoon by the *Devon Belle*. Just in case people turn up and want a ride to the pool.'

Alice heaved a sigh of relief. 'That would be marvellous. We want to see how my mother is feeling. Check up on Dad.'

They sat around drinking their coffee, smiling, reminiscing.

'You must be here this evening for Nell's phone call,' Helena reminded them both as they were leaving.

'What makes you think she will phone us?' Val said, grinning at last.

Helena did not bother to reply.

The 'breakfast bed' lasted longer than usual because Millie slept blissfully on. Hattie drank her tea stone-cold and bent the toast into a marmalade sandwich.

'This is extra delicious,' she said, feeding Duggie the middle of the sandwich because his dentures weren't up to crusts any more. 'Which compensates for the tragic fact that I missed all the fun on Friday – I simply cannot get over it, Dug! I thought you were going to visit the bank and maybe lunch with Ted somewhere. And you steal this enormous march on me!'

'Darling, I'm glad you missed it.' Duggie chewed and swallowed with difficulty. 'I know it sounds hilarious now. But at the time it was pretty awful really. We all thought poor old Bert had had it. And when the whole damned coach blew up . . . well, if you'd had Millie – which you would have done – she would have been terrified!'

'You're right. I hadn't thought of that.' She dipped the

toast crusts into the cold tea and chewed. 'Tell me the bit about the fight again. You think the boys are now good friends?'

'I think Perry feels Nell's honour is satisfied. And I am pretty certain the whole thing cleared the decks for poor old Michael Adair.'

'Sounds like a song, doesn't it?' Hattie kept chewing. 'An Irish folk song. Except that Nell Ryecroft doesn't rhyme. What about Nell so fair, loved Michael Adair?'

'Pretty awful.'

'Yes.' Hattie sighed contentedly. 'It's all so romantic. And d'you know, I thought the other day, I bet you five pounds that my poor old ma was seduced by Reggie Ryecroft! I was working it out – Edmund got me in the mood, he's forever working things out – and I was born just before Reggie left the station house at Leadon Markham.' Duggie was completely silent and still. Hattie giggled. 'Just think if it happened like that, Val and I would be half related!'

'I hardly think it's likely,' Duggie said firmly. 'Do you? You're so dark and wild and Val is fair and . . . controlled.'

'Not always he's not.' She was still giggling and almost choking on the crusts. 'Darling, I've never told you this, in fact the only person who knows is Doffie. But I thought Percy couldn't father children and I wanted him to have a baby as much as I wanted one. So I chose – yes, chose – Valentine Ryecroft! And Edmund was born nine months later!' She sat up in bed. 'Sweetheart, isn't it just marvellous that I can tell you that? Doesn't it show the sheer depth of our love? Oh Duggie, I do love you. Very much.'

She kissed him and Duggie lay there, rigidly electrified. She said, 'D'you know, I can feel you tingling! Shall we . . . is Millie still asleep?'

He got out of bed and looked into the cot. 'Yes.' He came back and looked down at her. 'Hattie, you won't tell anyone else, will you? If you think about it, it can't be right because Edmund is perfectly normal, in fact a very clever chap.'

'Of course he is! He's got my – what's the word, Dug –

acumen? And he's got Val's intelligence.' She slid out of her nightdress. 'Cheer up, darling. I won't tell a soul if you won't!'

He lay down beside her and she wrapped her arms round him. Before he fully surrendered he whispered, 'You are a very remarkable woman, Hattie Marsden.'

'I know.' She began on his right earlobe. 'Doesn't Hattie Marsden sound absolutely marvellous?'

'It does,' he agreed.

Perry and Edmund spent all day working on the attics in Brunswick Square so that Edmund could move out of the house in the close as soon as possible. Perry was in such good spirits that Edmund was bound to comment on it.

'I understand that you feel somewhat cock-a-hoop about having a go at Michael Adair, but what about the poor old coach?'

'Poor old coach be damned. And it wasn't so much having a go at Nell's precious Mo, it was rescuing poor old Bert Lewis. Together! He couldn't shift that door till I'd broken the glass – released a vacuum, I suppose – then we got it open and Bert shot out like a—'

'I know, I know. You've told me so many times. It's the adrenalin flow from that, I suppose. Anyway, thank God about Mo. I wonder whether Aunt Helena will let him go up to Birmingham today and declare his undying love!'

'No need to be so sarky! If we hadn't got Bert out quick the three of us would have gone up in the explosion. That has created a bond, I'm telling you!'

'Ye-e-s. Nothing like a brush with death to create an undying bond.'

'For God's sake, Ed! Get on with scrubbing that floor and try not to be such a pain in the neck all the time. You think you're so bloody superior but . . .' Perry paused and then went on, 'you weren't there, were you? So there's just one experience I've got over you. And you don't like it!'

Edmund looked up, surprised. 'Sorry, brud, was I being

unbearable? I'm damned glad to have you back from that brush with death, actually.'

'Why? Because of the flat? Duggie would have let you have it anyway.'

'Don't be daft. I couldn't have lived here without you.' Edmund sat back on his haunches. 'The business on Friday, with the coach and everything, made me realize – I don't think I could manage without you. You're like Mum. You keep my feet on the ground.'

Perry looked amazed then, unexpectedly, embarrassed. 'Shut up, Ed. Just get on with it, will you?' A minute ago, for the first time in his life, he had been feeling superior to his older brother; now he didn't. Again. They worked for ten minutes in silence, then he said irritably, 'Anyway, the boot is on the other foot. I certainly couldn't manage without you.'

And infuriatingly, Ed looked across the scrubbed planks and after very brief consideration said, 'No, I don't think you could.'

That was when Perry threw his scrubbing brush at his brother and they rolled across the floor together laughing like hyenas.

Doffie had felt pretty bad before Ted told her about Mitzie; she felt worse afterwards.

'Gran didn't know he'd killed her,' she said bleakly. 'She knew he was Hattie's father. Gramps tried to make him take some responsibility but of course he wouldn't. I wonder when . . . how long . . .'

'D'you mean Gran told you this? You've known for years that Reggie had fathered our Hattie?'

'She said I mustn't tell anyone. And I haven't. And I never will.'

She wanted to tell him about Edmund but she could not. Ted had a habit of blowing his top quite suddenly and he might go down to Lypiatt Bottom and try to give Val a good hiding. And maybe Val himself did not know . . . Alice certainly did not. And must not.

Ted sat on the edge of the sofa where she was lying with a hot-water bottle and a very flushed face. He had imagined weeping on her shoulder and she was obviously in no state to offer a shoulder. But for some reason, he was not bothered about that. For some reason he wanted to weep about someone other than poor Mitzie.

'Oh Doff . . .' he said. 'I knew Gran loved you. The two of you would get so uppity with each other, but underneath . . . And you must have known too. At the end when she passed on this secret. You must realize . . . and love her a little too.'

Doffie looked at him, astonished. Then she held his head as best she could and kissed the white hair.

'Ted . . . you're such an idiot. Do you think she came to live with us just because of you? I knew that she could never admit to loving me but that was her way of telling me. She could have gone to Hattie but she chose me. That was some years before she told me about Mitzie and Reggie.'

He lifted his face; it was wet. 'And you . . . how did you feel?'

Doffie smiled. 'I loved your father best. You knew that. But when he went and your mother struggled through that terrible grief . . . I'd always loved her, Ted. I didn't know she loved me so I always reacted to her barbs. But then . . . oh Ted, you silly old fool. Go and make yourself a cup of tea. And can you refill this hot-water bottle? And make me an iced lemonade?'

'Of course I can. I'm Ted Pettiford.' He tried hard to smile. 'I can do anything.' He stood up and looked down at her. 'Doffie, let's stay together as long as we can. I love you. And if you want to throw another cup of tea all over me, then—'

'Ted!' she warned.

'Going, love.'

That Sunday evening, nearly mad with boredom, Sally drove her car illegally into Gloucester and went to the evensong concert at the cathedral. She had seen the headlines in the

391

Citizen the night before and had telephoned Alice to hear the unexpurgated version.

'And Hester wasn't there?' she asked.

'Hester was teaching. Edmund was at work. Hattie decided to have a rest. Don't worry, Sally. So much good has come out of it. How goes the enforced separation from Hester?'

'Not good. And I've sort of extended it to Edmund too. I'm trying to be a good daughter. It's terribly difficult.'

'Is it? It shouldn't be. Perhaps you're overdoing it a bit?'

So Sally drove into Gloucester and chose to go to the cathedral in the hope that Hester would be there. She wasn't. Neither was Edmund. After half an hour she left, found her car again and drove along the ring road towards the Bristol road. She knew what she would do with the rest of this unsatisfactory day; she would find where Edmund's great-grandmother had lived. The famous Gran Pettiford. She would find the cottage by the river and look at it and try to imagine the eccentric old woman who had lived there. Unfortunately, she could not remember the name of the village by the river. Passing the cemetery, she saw that the gates stood open and the next thing she knew she was at the office enquiring where the Pettiford grave was.

It took her a long time to find it even with directions; too many people had died and were buried here. She passed the brook that might be the beginning of the River Twyver; she passed the group of watering cans and the big wire rubbish bin, and discovered that the third stone past that was dedicated to Albert Symons. And then, next to that, was the white marble with the greyish letters proclaiming the last resting place of 'William Makepeace Pettiford, late of Leadon Markham, Dean Forest, aged 68. Also his beloved wife, Patience, aged 90 years. Together at last.' Sally stared at the stone and then the empty vase buried in white chippings. No one had been to put flowers on Gran's grave. Without a second thought Sally Gold walked across the path, wound her way between the leaning stones, took a bunch of chrysanthemums from a nearby grave and put them in

Gran's vase. She suddenly felt a sense of peace; for once she had done the right thing. She straightened slowly and went on looking at the inscriptions. She thought that she would go home now and make supper for her parents and ask them whether they would come with her to St Hilda's next week and help to sort out her room.

And then, as she moved away, there came a loud 'Oy!' from the cluster of watering cans. Coming down the path, holding a very full and dripping can, was a woman the size of a tank.

'Couldn't believe my eyes!' she roared. 'I've heard of people like you – looking so innocent as you rob the graves!'

Sally was immediately contrite; the woman drowned out her feeble explanation that she imagined the flowers had been enjoyed for at least a week – 'What did I just say? Put them there ten minutes ago, if that!' She roared at Sally as she turned away to leave and then she flung the contents of the can all over Sally's best suit, worn in case Hester should come into the cathedral.

The woman hustled her along the path and into her Morris Minor. Sally continued to apologize but it made no difference. They ended up at the central police station, where the officer behind the counter picked up his pen and began to write the date and time at the top of a form.

'I can only say I am sorry,' Sally repeated sullenly. 'Obviously I will pay for the flowers—'

'Address, please, miss,' said the officer on duty.

Sally gave it and wondered what her father would say about this.

'How did you get down to Gloucester? No buses on a Sunday.'

Sally thought quickly. No insurance on the car, no driving licence . . . 'I had a lift,' she said.

'And how are you getting home?'

'I have a friend who will take me. May I use your phone?'

She dialled Hester's number and was full of gratitude when Hester answered immediately.

'Could you possibly? I'm at the police station . . . nothing serious.' There came another roar from the woman. 'What I mean is I have committed an offence rather than a crime—' She covered the mouthpiece as the woman contradicted her. 'Yes . . . please. Oh thank you, Hester.'

She began to feel very much better. Fate intended her to see Hester after all. She had fought against it, but Gran Pettiford must have decided otherwise. She smiled kindly at the woman. 'It's all right, I won't claim for the dry cleaning of my suit.'

After an idyllic afternoon on the hills overlooking Birmingham, Nell and Mo moved into Aunt Helena's car and sat looking at the same view for another hour.

A ground mist was rising and eventually ran in ribbons, obscuring the distant lights. They had been silent for some time and Nell was wondering whether he had fallen asleep when he said into the top of her head, 'The thing is, you could teach in America. It would be quite a different experience. Might be interesting.'

She chuckled. 'You don't have to worry that I might get bored, darling. I shall sight-see like mad and cook you wonderful meals and at weekends we can find a hill – like this one – and get everything in perspective and talk like Americans—'

'Oh Nell. I do love you so. I want you to be happy and – and free! I won't limit you in any way. When we met first I was quite shocked by you – your hair was dyed bright red and you were wearing a petticoat and no bra—' She began to protest and he kissed her quiet. 'Listen. When I went back to that old signal box – d'you remember, I was sleeping there? – I thought you must be one of those free spirits I'd heard about—' She gasped with laughter. 'Seriously. And actually, you are. But not in that way. You are so open. I don't want to close any doors in your face. Ever. Don't let me.'

Later she said, 'I cannot believe this is happening. And it is. I can't wait for Christmas. Can you come home early because I've got a terrific idea for our Christmas entertainment. I want Brian Larch to be a camel's hump with two other boys . . . and carry one of the wise men to Bethlehem and . . .'

He laughed and kissed her. They both knew that, at last, they had broken all the spells and were free to fall in love.

It was very quiet by Bracewell's Pool. The rain had stopped but there were ragged clouds moving across the face of the moon and every now and then a little wind shook the trees free of their dampness and created a miniature shower. Mitzie Pettiford's body, released from the preserving coal dust and held now by tree roots, would soon disintegrate and become part of the forest itself. That would probably have pleased Mitzie very much; Gramps had once told her sadly that she was a child of Nature and she had tried to live up to that by sleeping under the trees most of the summer, not often alone. Feckless Mitzie Pettiford, people had called her. But she had united the Ryecrofts and the Pettifords, albeit at a terrible price, and from that union had come so much.

Such as Val and Alice's strong marriage. After all their troubles they had achieved enormous peace of mind, which they dated to the death of the Pumpkin Coach. They counted their blessings often. For Val the foremost was Alice's gradual return to full health. She blossomed that winter and he swore she had lost thirty years and was the schoolgirl he had first loved. She told him to get some new glasses and anyway he hadn't loved her then because he'd chased her up the dark stairs of his house and she had locked herself in the bathroom to escape him! Their greatest joy was seeing Mo and Nell together and so happy. 'Another union!' Alice announced joyfully. 'The Ryecrofts and the Pettifords. Then the Adairs and the Ryecrofts!' Val felt not a twinge of insecurity. He hugged her hard and told her she had always been stuck on Romeo and Juliet.

Everybody was happy. Even Hester, who had to collect her car from a nearby garage and drive round to the police station to rescue a supposedly contrite Sally. Incredulous, she had asked her what on earth she was thinking about, pinching flowers from another grave. The girl was utterly tired and fed up. She said, 'Oh Piecrust, please don't start. This is the first good thing to happen to me for ages. Surely you can see it was meant to be?'

'Did you do it on purpose?'

'Well, of course I did – no one twisted my arm! But it didn't seem so awful at the time. Not like real grave-robbing, for goodness' sake!' Sally decided to take the offensive. 'And no one had put flowers on the Pettiford grave for absolutely ages – that was obvious!'

'Good job too. When I think how Alice's gran used to sit by that stone, crying and crying and crying. Poor Alice was always with her. Six years old.'

'Oh, dear God!'

'Quite. Anyway, haven't you heard what has been happening on the Pumpkin Line? No? Well, listen up!'

Hester recounted Sally's reaction with some relish when she returned home and telephoned Richard Tibbolt.

He said, 'I'll come to you at half-term, Hessie. Is that all right? Will Edmund still be there?'

'No fear. He's pitching in with Perry. They've got the attics at Duggie's house in Brunswick Square.'

'Poor Duggie.'

'He is having the time of his life. Oh Tibbolt, are you well enough to leave the Lemon House? What about the twins?'

'They're dying for me to go. The sooner I move into the Nice place the better. Christmas?'

'Yes, please.'

She put down the phone, smiling still, For some reason she found herself thinking of Mitzie Pettiford. She and Alice used to talk about her a lot. Hester decided that she must see a great deal of young Mitzie . . . Millie. Millie Westbrook. For Mitzie's sake.